Praise for the

"The prose is fast-paced and exciting, making this a breathless page-turner."
—*New York Journal of Books* on *The Bookstore on the Beach*

"An abundance of heart and humor. *The Bookstore on the Beach* is an escapist treat with emotional heft."
—*Apple Books*, Best Book of the Month selection

"This heartwarming story of sisters who bond as adults is sure to please the many fans of Novak as well as those who enjoy books by Susan Mallery and Debbie Macomber."
—*Library Journal* on *One Perfect Summer*

"I adore everything Brenda Novak writes. Her books are compelling, emotional, tender stories about people I would love to know in real life."
—RaeAnne Thayne,
New York Times bestselling author

"Brenda Novak is always a joy to read."
—Debbie Macomber,
#1 *New York Times* bestselling author

"Brenda Novak doesn't just write fabulous stories, she writes keepers."
—Susan Mallery,
#1 *New York Times* bestselling author

Dear Reader,

This is such a landmark year! It's been twenty-five years since I published my very first novel, marking a career in publishing spanning a quarter of a century! And almost all my books have been published by Harlequin, so it's fitting that I would have the privilege of writing a special novel for their big 75th anniversary. When I was in high school, their stories brought me so many hours of delicious escapism, and they've continued to bring me joy throughout my life.

This book is also special because it completes my popular Whiskey Creek series. There's one Amos brother who's been waiting to have his story told—Grady—so I'm excited to finally bring him his happily-ever-after. Although this book also stands alone, if you'd like to read the rest of the series, it goes like this: *When Lightning Strikes*, *When Snow Falls*, *When Summer Comes*, *Home to Whiskey Creek*, *Taking Me Home for Christmas*, *Come Home to Me*, *The Heart of Christmas*, *This Heart of Mine*, *A Winter Wedding* and *Discovering You*.

Thank you for celebrating this special milestone with me and with my publisher!

Brenda Novak

TYING THE KNOT

NEW YORK TIMES BESTSELLING AUTHOR
BRENDA NOVAK

FREE STORY BY
MONA SHROFF

SPECIAL RELEASE

SPECIAL RELEASE

ISBN-13: 978-1-335-00771-1

Tying the Knot
First published in 2024. This edition published in 2024.
Copyright © 2024 by Brenda Novak, Inc.

Road Trip Rivalry
First published in 2024. This edition published in 2024.
Copyright © 2024 by Mona Shroff

Harlequin Enterprises ULC
22 Adelaide St. West, 41st Floor
Toronto, Ontario M5H 4E3, Canada
www.Harlequin.com

Printed in U.S.A.

CONTENTS

Author **Brenda Novak** is a *New York Times* and *USA TODAY* bestselling author with more than ten million books in print, translated into twenty different languages. She also runs Brenda Novak for the Cure, a charity to raise money for diabetes research (her youngest son has this disease). To date, she's raised $2.7 million. For more about Brenda, please visit brendanovak.com.

Books by Brenda Novak

Whiskey Creek

When Lightning Strikes
When Snow Falls
When Summer Comes
Home to Whiskey Creek
Taking Me Home for Christmas
Come Home to Me
The Heart of Christmas
This Heart of Mine
A Winter Wedding
Discovering You
Tying the Knot

Visit the Author Profile page
at Harlequin.com for more titles.

TYING THE KNOT

Brenda Novak

To Janet Costanzo Robel

I love your zest for life! Thanks for infusing my online book group on Facebook with your positive energy and for all you do to support me as a friend and a reader. The bookish community I look forward to interacting with every day wouldn't be the same without you.

Chapter One

"You want me to do *what*?" Grady Amos had been leaning toward the woman he'd just met—Winnie…something.
He couldn't remember her last name. But he liked her. She
was attractive in a polished, fashionable way, wearing a
long straight skirt and a sleeveless blouse—obviously de-
signer clothes that fit her trim figure to perfection—with
her blond hair pulled back in a sleek ponytail at her nape. A
woman in high heels who smelled like the perfume counter
at Macy's wasn't something he ran into very often in the
small Gold Country town in Northern California where he'd
been raised. Folks were pretty casual in Whiskey Creek.
So when he'd walked into Sexy Sadie's to relax after a long
day at work, she'd stood out—enough that he'd veered over
to the bar to claim the empty seat next to her.

But what she'd just said had him scooting back by a
foot at least.

"You'd make a great contestant on the dating show I'm producing," she repeated.

He made a face to show he wasn't excited by that idea. She'd said she was in town for two days visiting a friend on her way to Los Angeles. She was coming through after spending the weekend in Lake Tahoe at her parents' cabin. But she was obviously recruiting along the way. She was probably always recruiting. She seemed ambitious, the type to take her work very seriously.

"You're making a reality TV show?" he said. She'd told him she was a producer, but she hadn't gotten specific until she'd learned that he was unattached. When she'd started to probe to find out his status, he'd assumed she was asking because she was interested in him the same way he was interested in her, so that was part of his disappointment.

She looked a bit crestfallen herself. Most people probably showed a great deal more interest when she mentioned what she did for a living. "We're in our third season. You've never seen *Tying the Knot*?"

"I'm afraid not." He'd never been interested in reality TV...other than *Survivor*. He made an exception for that show because it was freaking amazing. And maybe *Naked and Afraid*. He considered the dating ones—*The Bachelor*, *The Bachelorette* and all the others—to be for women.

She adjusted the straw on the Moscow mule he'd bought her. "You should give it a try, see what you think."

He doubted it would be anything he'd enjoy, but he liked talking to her and was hoping to get her to go out with him even if it meant he had to drive six or seven hours to LA. "What's the show about, exactly?"

"It's a study of first impressions—whether human beings can choose a mate based on looks and instant chemistry, or if they need time to get to know each other in order to have a successful relationship."

"Oh, it's like that show my sister-in-law was talking about the other night." He cast about in his mind for the name. "What's it called? The one where they meet at their own wedding?"

"*Married at First Sight?* Not really," she said with a shake of her head. "On my show, you'd get to choose your bride."

He finished his beer and signaled for the bartender to bring him another. "How does it work?"

"Our contestants take a battery of personality tests. Then they're sent on three dates, each with a different woman—" she selected a peanut out of the bowl in front of them "—all of whom have been vetted and handpicked by psychologists as being compatible. And then they get to choose one of the three."

"To continue dating?"

"To marry."

Of course. He knew there'd be a catch. The show had to have a shocking premise. That was what gave it word of mouth, made it worth tuning in. "Sounds like whoever does this is asking for trouble."

Her eyes widened at his response. "Not really. If the marriage doesn't work out, they can always have it annulled," she said as if it was no big deal. "It's not that different from dating in the real world. There are connections and breakups. Some relationships work and others don't."

If it was that similar to real life, they wouldn't be making a show out of it. But he didn't say so. "The women don't get to choose?" He grinned. "Isn't that a little misogynistic?"

She arched her eyebrows. "The men chose in season one, the women chose in season two."

So it was the men's turn…

He rubbed the beard growth on his chin. He wanted to find a good woman with whom he could start a family.

He'd wanted that for a long time. And yet, here he was staring down his fortieth birthday and he hadn't yet found love.

He was beginning to worry he'd be single for the rest of his life, which was why, for a brief moment, a small part of him was tempted to try something this unconventional. At least it would put him in close proximity to Winnie, whom he considered the real prize. He didn't want to spend the rest of his life alone. But with all the posturing and deceit on those matchmaking sites, online dating was already out of his comfort zone. Why would he take an even bigger risk? "Meeting someone on the internet is about as wild as I get."

"You've tried that, then?"

"I have, here and there." He'd pulled down his profile probably four years ago, after one of the women he'd met began to stalk him, so it'd been some time.

She popped another peanut into her mouth. "And how has that worked out for you?"

He gave her a dirty look. "It hasn't, but there's no guarantee this would, either." There had to be a lot of heartache involved in something like this. Embarrassment, too, since so much of what happened would be made public. He wasn't one to seek the limelight, even if he could leave Whiskey Creek for as long as it would take to shoot the various episodes…which he couldn't. "Would my odds be any better going onto a reality TV show?" he challenged.

"Maybe. We have three couples from seasons one and two who are still married," she said proudly. "I plan to incorporate them—in a small way—in this year's show."

He straightened. "Three out of how many?"

"Eight."

Nearly 50 percent wasn't bad. "I'm shocked to hear the success ratio is that high."

"We do a lot of testing before we even get started," she

said with a measure of satisfaction. "We want people to be happy."

He began to peel the label on his locally brewed IPA. "How do you find your contestants?"

"People apply online. We've nearly finished casting this season. I just need one more guy. Actually, I need two guys. There's one person I'd like to replace." She grimaced. "I'm not totally sure about him."

"What do I have that he doesn't?" Grady asked.

"You're not vying for attention, not already applying for every other show on TV or looking for a way to break into showbiz. That alone will give you more sincerity, make you more convincing and appealing in general."

He'd suspected reality shows weren't actually "real." They were well-choreographed, and this proved it. But he supposed that was the only way they'd ever work, so he couldn't get too upset about it. Most people understood they weren't completely unscripted. "I doubt I'll be any good on TV. I've never been on before. And there has to be drama, or it'll be boring. You won't get much drama out of me."

"Trust me, the situation brings its own drama," she said with an appealing laugh. "I don't need you or any other contestant to be difficult. The odds are already stacked against us—against the survival of long-term relationships in general—and yet that's exactly what we're striving for. Our viewers are rooting for our contestants to fall in love."

"I think I'm too private of a person."

"You'd be well compensated."

"I have a job," he pointed out. She'd asked him what he did when he sat down, so she already knew that.

She took another sip of her drink. "You said you work at an auto body shop?"

Clearly, she wasn't dazzled by his vocation, but he made

a good living. Money wasn't one of his problems. "I don't just work there, I own it," he clarified. He wanted to impress her, or he would've added that he didn't own Amos Auto Body entirely on his own. He and his four brothers were partners, but they'd grown the business a great deal since they'd taken over from their father. They had three locations now—the original shop here in Whiskey Creek and two others, one run by his second oldest brother in Reno, Nevada, and the other by his younger brother, the baby of the family, in Silver Springs, California, which wasn't too far from Los Angeles.

"But this could make you a star," she said as if it was the ultimate enticement.

He didn't want to be a star. He just wanted to find a good woman. "There's no way I could take that much time away from my business even if I wanted to."

He assumed she'd let it go at that, but she didn't. "If you're the boss, don't you have employees who can take care of things while you're gone?"

Since Aaron and Mack had moved away, he, Dylan and Rod had taken on a couple of guys to fill their slots, plus one more to give them some breathing room. Dylan and Rod had families and couldn't work the kind of hours they'd put in before. But *he* was still there all day, every day. Although they split the money evenly, it made sense that he should carry more of the load since he didn't have quite so many demands on his time. "I have a few."

"Then do something unexpected, something wild." She lowered her voice. "It could change your life."

"We'll see." It was hard to turn down such a beautiful, earnest face. But he simply wasn't the type to go after something like this. She'd said that three of the couples who'd been on the show were still together, but that didn't mean they'd withstand the test of time. This was only the third season!

Maybe once they'd passed their tenth anniversary, he'd believe they had a fighting chance.

"Don't you want to get married?" she pressed.

He craved the committed and hectic but happy lives his brothers were living. But he doubted this was the way to get it. "I'd like to find someone," he admitted. "But it would need to be the right woman, and I can't imagine meeting my wife in such a way."

"Don't knock it 'til you've tried it," she said. "Best-case scenario, you find the woman of your dreams. Worst case, you come back here and do what you've always done."

When she put it that way, staying in Whiskey Creek didn't sound all that appealing. Just lonely.

But a reality TV show? No way. "I'll think about it."

She checked her phone, seemed startled by the time and slid off her stool. "I've got a conference call. But here's my card." She winked as he accepted it, and her smile hit him right in the gut. "Give me a call if you change your mind."

He slid the card in his pocket as she walked out. He wanted to give her a call, but it wasn't because he wished to be on her TV show.

Chapter Two

She was going to disappoint her mother. There was no way around that now.

Aja Kermani frowned at the latest text she'd received from Esther. A picture of another wedding dress. Last night, her mother had sent color schemes, suggesting black and ivory would be "lovely." And yesterday morning? Ideas for the cake. Esther didn't know that there would be no wedding. Aja had broken up with Arman four days ago, the night he proposed. She couldn't continue the relationship; it gave him false hope, led him to believe she felt something she didn't.

Bottom line, she wasn't interested in living the life her parents had carefully choreographed for her, didn't want to become an exact replica of them.

There was nothing wrong with them, of course. She loved them dearly, had tried to please them as far back as she could remember. She understood the sacrifices they'd made to immigrate to the United States, hoping to build a better life, and the opportunities that provided for her and her brother, and she was grateful.

But Aja wanted something more. Or something else, she thought, quickly correcting herself. As much as she kept trying to follow what her parents insisted would be the best course for her, she was no longer interested in forcing herself into a mold she clearly didn't fit. As time went by, the vague lack of fulfillment she'd battled through the years was turning into a deep dissatisfaction. She wanted to be free to dream her own dreams and then try to accomplish them, and the hunger to do so had been growing for years…since all the way back in middle school.

Do you like this? It's nearly $7,000, but I think you'd look stunning in it.

Aja read her mother's follow-up message twice. Her parents would be willing to spend seven thousand dollars *on a dress*?

That was a lot of money. But they had it. Her father was an ophthalmologist, and her mother an orthodontist—both professionals. They lived in a beautiful home in Newport Beach, an expensive part of Orange County, and spent a lot on vacations, cars and other things. It didn't surprise her *too* much that they'd go all out for her wedding.

So…what were they going to say when she told them that she couldn't bring herself to marry their best friends' son?

She sank into the soft leather chair behind her desk in the small office of her dental practice and sighed as she gazed at her diplomas, pictures of her family and various friends hanging on the walls. She'd been a dentist for eight years, had built a solid practice in a relatively short amount of time.

But it was getting more and more difficult to make herself come to work each day. It was her parents who'd really wanted her to become a dentist. She'd done it to please them, and because she didn't have a clear alternative—knew they'd be mortified if she told them what she really wanted to do—she'd fallen in line.

But how much longer could she continue slogging through each day? She was feeling cornered and claustrophobic, needed to break out of the same old routine.

She just didn't know how, or if she'd regret it later.

It was the fear of regret—and dashing her parents' hopes for something that wouldn't turn out to be successful—that had held her firmly in place. But then Arman had proposed, and she'd realized that marrying him would set the rest of her life in cement. The fear that'd swamped her in that moment had chilled her to the bone.

Knowing she couldn't continue to ignore her mother's texts, she gathered her resolve and called Esther.

"There you are!" her mother chirped. "Are you still at the office?"

Aja worked long hours. Too long. That was part of the problem. She didn't have much of a life outside of her practice. She'd had very little time to work on her pottery, hadn't been in the studio for months. And before she got her degree, it'd taken everything she had just to make it through dental school. Biology, anatomy and physiology had been such difficult subjects for her, especially because all she'd wanted to do was create. "I am."

"What do you think of that wedding dress I sent you? Isn't it absolutely stunning?"

Her mother had good taste; Aja had to give her that. "It is."

"So? Do you want to try it on? Tomorrow's Saturday. We could have lunch and spend the afternoon shopping."

Aja squeezed her eyes closed. *Here goes...* "I'm afraid not." She opened her mouth to continue, but Esther filled every break in any conversation and spoke before she could.

"If tomorrow won't work, we could go Sunday before dinner. Your father could grill, and I could arrange the sides in advance."

They had family dinner every Sunday. It was a tradition, and a weekly opportunity for her parents to make sure their children were still on track. "No, Mom. It—it's not the day that's the problem. I need to tell you something."

"What is it?" she asked, obviously surprised by the serious tone of Aja's voice.

"There isn't going to be a wedding."

Silence. Then her mother said, in a panic, "Arman told his parents that he was going to propose on Monday. Did I blow it? Jump the gun? Oh, my God! Has he not asked you yet? I'm *so* sorry! Now I know why you didn't call to tell us. He hasn't followed through quite yet."

Wincing, she cleared her throat. "Actually, he *did* ask, but I said no."

"Why would you do that?" her mother snapped.

Aja squeezed her forehead with one hand. "Because I'm not in love with him."

"Arman's a good boy. He'll make a wonderful husband and father."

"I'm sure that's true. He's a nice person. The problem is... I don't love him," she explained.

There was another long stretch of silence. Her mother had to be stunned. Her parents and Arman's parents had believed for years that they'd one day be celebrating the union of their children, thereby bringing the two families even closer. "So...*that's* why we haven't heard from the Kahns," she said as she processed what Aja had just told her. "They must be heartbroken for their son and—and angry with us."

"I hope not," Aja said. "It wasn't my intent to...hurt anyone or cause problems in your relationship with them."

"Your father and I believed... Well, we obviously thought marriage and a family was what you wanted."

"It *is* what I want, Mom. Just not with Arman."

"With who, then?" she asked, as if he was the only logical choice.

"I don't know! I haven't been free to find someone who excites me, who makes me feel...how I should feel before committing myself for the rest of my life."

"You're not interested in Ali, are you?" she asked suspiciously. "I know he's shown a great deal of interest in you. But Arman is a heart surgeon, Aja! Ali is...well, he's nice, but..."

But Ali was a dance instructor. His earning potential couldn't match Arman's. It wouldn't be nearly as advantageous of a match.

"I wouldn't recommend a man like him," her mother said.

Aja had circulated within the Persian community in Los Angeles her whole life. She wanted to expand beyond the people she already knew, but saying so would only upset her mother. Her father, too, when he heard. They'd wanted to come to America for safety and upward mobility but didn't really want their children to be *American*. They clung to the old world, the one they'd left.

But she'd been born here. To her, living in the United States meant embracing change—looking forward, not back. Almost everyone in America had originally come from somewhere else. It was the world's great melting pot, and yet her parents didn't want her to conform. "I don't plan on dating Ali, Mom. We're just friends." That was true and yet she admired him. He'd stood up to his own parents, was being who and what he most wanted to be.

"Who then?" her mother asked.

She remembered some of the young men she'd met at UCLA. There'd been several she'd found attractive, and yet she'd turned down those who'd asked her out. Some had even been in dental school with her, meaning they'd also be professionals, but they weren't Persian, which meant she'd have to cope with upset and disappointment—and possibly downright antagonism—at home. Since she'd already been struggling just to get through school, she hadn't dared take on that fight at the same time.

But now... She was thirty-four. She'd lived her parents' way long enough to know, deep in her soul, that it wasn't *her* way. As well-intentioned as they were, as much as they loved her and thought they were doing what was best for her, she had to insist on more freedom and autonomy—had to be able to, like Ali, forge her own path.

Better late than never, she thought. But... She frowned as her eyes once again circled her tiny cubicle of an office. Did that mean selling her practice? Or bringing in another dentist so she could have time to focus on her pottery?

Either was a risk. She didn't have the financial security of her parents, couldn't withstand a serious mistake...

Could she dare take action?

This was the question that always drove her back into the same old corral.

"I don't have anyone in mind," she told her mother. "I just...know it wouldn't be right to marry Arman."

Aja could feel her mother's disapproval coming through the phone; it washed over her like a tidal wave. "I think you might live to regret that," her mother said.

"I know."

"Arman is handsome and smart—"

"But I'm not in love with him," she said adamantly, breaking in. "I've now said that two other times."

"Love grows from respect, Aja. And that head-over-heels feeling isn't all it's cracked up to be. Arman adores you. He treats you like a queen."

"I'd be doing him a disservice," she insisted. "I like him too well to saddle him with an unhappy wife."

"Unhappy…" her mother echoed.

"Yes—unhappy. I'd be unhappy if I married him," she said, and that was probably what finally convinced Esther to back off.

"Okay," she said. "Only you know what's best for you."

Exactly. Those words felt like a soothing balm, and yet Aja knew her mother didn't truly believe them, or she'd be in an entirely different situation.

"I'd better call Behar and try to explain."

Aja liked Behar and Behram, Arman's parents. She liked his brother, too. They'd been part of almost every holiday, several vacations and lots of Sunday dinners. It was going to be difficult to face them, given they probably no longer liked her. "I'm sorry for disappointing them," she said. "I'm sorry for disappointing you, too."

"It's fine," her mother said stiffly. "I just… I hope you're not making a terrible mistake."

So did Aja. Life was fluid. There were no guarantees.

She said goodbye and disconnected, then looked at her watch. It was six thirty on a Friday night. Her receptionist and hygienist had left at three thirty. They had families to go home to and enjoy the weekend with. She had no plans. Except on Sunday, of course. But showing up at her parents' house for dinner this week would not be easy.

She was just finishing annotating various patient charts and calling to check on a couple of people she'd given root canals earlier in the week when she received a text from her brother.

Oh, no, you didn't.

She frowned. Her mother must've called him about Arman. She'd essentially kicked the beehive that was their world, their status quo, and sent her parents and all their friends buzzing.

Oh, yes, I did.

Are you going to stick by it?

She knew *he'd* want her to. Any barriers she busted through left a hole for him.

I have no choice. I simply can't marry Arman.

How'd he take the news?

Not well. I'm guessing he thinks I might change my mind because he hasn't told his parents. Otherwise, they would've contacted Mom and Dad.

Or he *did* tell them, and they're mad.

That's what Mom thinks.

Damn. I didn't know you were such a troublemaker.

I wish I had an older sibling to knock down barriers for me. ;)

News flash. You've conformed for thirty-four years. That's not knocking down barriers. But now you're giving me a little hope.

Very funny. Have you told Mom and Dad that you don't want to be a lawyer? That you'd rather be an actor?

Not yet. I haven't received any great opportunities that would force my hand. But I have another audition coming up.

What is it for this time?

A reality TV show called Tying the Knot.

Aja googled the show and read the premise. Are you kidding me? You could wind up married!
I could also be discovered, Darius replied.

You don't care about the risks?

Not really. It's something for my résumé, a potential start. And it pays a decent amount.

But what about Mom and Dad?

They don't watch reality TV. They'll never know.

You'd just bring your wife home to meet them when it's all over? What are the chances she'll be Persian?

Admittedly, not great. But if I love her, it'd be worth fighting that fight. And if I don't? I'll get an annulment, and they'll never be the wiser.

You're so reckless. [rolling eyes emoji]

We have only one life. I plan to live mine.

Aja wanted to live hers, too, but it wasn't that simple. If you make them too mad, they could cut you off, quit paying for school.

Then I'll drop out. Unlike you, I can't be bought. ;)

Tough talk for someone who only does what he wants in secret. ;)

That's called being smart. Why make waves if I don't have to?

Aja chuckled. When's the audition?

Tomorrow. Want to go with me? We could grab lunch after.

That would certainly be more fun than laundry and housecleaning. Why not go and offer him some moral support? Seeing how auditions like that worked could be interesting...

Sure. What time?

Ten. But I'll pick you up at nine. You know what traffic can be like in this city.

I'll be ready.

Setting down her phone, Aja took a deep breath. She'd refused the marriage proposal of her parents' best friends' son and longed to quit dentistry so she could have her own pottery studio. Darius had no interest in becoming a lawyer, even though he was in law school. He hoped to become an actor, which was even riskier than being an artist. Almost everyone in LA wanted to be an actor...

She bit her lip as she considered the dark clouds gathering on the horizon. Her parents were soon going to realize that they didn't have either one of their children under control.

Chapter Three

They arrived twenty minutes early—traffic had been light—and waited in the lobby of an office on the fifteenth floor of a high-rise in Burbank. The office didn't seem to be fully staffed, and the receptionist was dressed casually, giving Aja the impression Saturdays weren't normal workdays. She assumed they were putting in extra hours to finish casting the show. From what Darius had said in the car, they were supposed to start shooting soon.

The receptionist looked up when they checked in, then motioned them to the leather couch and chairs surrounding a very modern-looking coffee table. They were reading the magazines they'd found on that table when the producer walked out ten minutes later.

She shook Darius's hand before turning to Aja. "And who is this?"

Darius explained that she was his sister and had just come along for the ride, but the producer, who'd told them to call her Winnie—invited them both back to her office.

Aja tried to beg off. She didn't want to intrude. But Winnie insisted it wouldn't be a problem, so she sent her brother an apologetic glance, in case her presence was hurting his chances of getting on the show, and he gave her a little shrug as if to say there was nothing they could do about it now.

One whole wall of the producer's office overlooked the busy street below. Aja wanted to walk over to it and sip the coffee she'd purchased on the ground floor while letting the two of them talk, but Winnie pulled an extra chair up to her desk and motioned for them both to sit down.

Wishing she'd waited in the car, Aja clung to her coffee as she complied.

"So… I've had a look at the application you filled out online," Winnie said to Darius, lifting a piece of paper that was probably a printout of that application. "You definitely look interesting to me. You're attractive, well-educated with great earning potential. And you scored well on the personality test. The only problem is…you're a little young."

"I'm almost twenty-six," he said.

She made a face that suggested his age might be a sticking point. "Most of our contestants are over thirty. The psychologists who help us with the show feel we'll have a better chance of success with those who are slightly older. They have more experience with relationships, tend to know more about what they want and are more likely to be content when they settle down." She dropped his application back on her desk. "What makes you want to be on a show like *Tying the Knot*?"

"I'm an adventurous person and think this might be an interesting way to meet someone. I also enjoy psychology, so the experiment aspect appeals to me."

Aja silently applauded the fact that he said nothing about

becoming a star. But she could tell the beautiful, poised woman dressed in cream slacks and a matching blouse was no one's fool. Aja was willing to bet she saw right through him…

"You aren't currently in a relationship…" she said.

"No."

Her gaze shifted to Aja. "How old are you?"

Aja had just lifted her coffee to her mouth, so Darius answered for her. "Thirty-four."

"And…are you attached?" the producer asked.

Swallowing, Aja lowered her cup. "No, um, I'm not seeing anyone right now."

"What do you do for a living?"

Uncomfortable with the attention, she shifted in her seat. Wasn't this supposed to be Darius's interview? "I'm a dentist."

"Here in LA?"

She nodded. "I've been in practice for the past eight years."

"And you're not dating anyone?" she asked again, as if she couldn't quite believe it.

"I just broke up with my boyfriend. But… I'm not applying to be on the show." She gestured at her brother. "We're getting lunch afterward. I didn't mean to intrude on his audition…or interview," she corrected, since he wasn't actually running lines.

"You're not intruding," Winnie insisted. "I'm glad you're here. There's been some last-minute jockeying with the cast. Now, I need another female contestant, and I'm out of time to advertise. But you seem ideal. You're *very* attractive."

Aja was glad Winnie didn't mention the Disney princess Jasmine. So many of her patients asked if she worked for the park in her off hours. But then, Winnie probably knew better than to perpetuate racial stereotypes. "I appreciate the compliment. But—"

"If you'll come on the show, I'll take your brother, too," she said matter-of-factly, cutting off Aja.

Aja blinked. She could feel the heat of Darius's gaze—it seemed to be boring holes into her—as he willed her to accept. He believed this could be his big break. But she couldn't even imagine being part of a reality TV show. "Um, I'm not sure... I mean, I have patients I need to see."

"You could reschedule them," Darius said quickly. "You work too hard, could use some time off. You've told me that before. Why not grab hold of this? Challenge yourself in a different way?"

Hadn't she just been hankering for change? The idea of doing something daring appealed to her. She'd played it safe for so long. But she wasn't convinced this was her type of daring... "I'm just not...cut out for TV," she said with a laugh that sounded nervous even to her own ears.

Winnie cocked her head. "What makes you say that?"

"I've never aspired to be an actor, never even tried out for anything."

"I'm not looking for professional actors," she said. "Just solid contestants. Men and women who want to fall in love and would make good spouses, so that any couples who get together as a result of the show stand a good chance of lasting."

Aja had thought Darius was reckless for agreeing to find a mate in such a way. *She* couldn't do it, too! And yet... She could sense him silently pleading with her. "Darius would be perfect—"

Winnie interrupted her again, this time with a skeptical expression. "He's a little young."

Damn. That wasn't just a statement. It'd come off like

a decree. The woman was going to stick with her both-or-neither offer…

"Come on, Aja. Live a little," Darius murmured, and she couldn't bring herself to disappoint him. Why not throw away the rule book for a change? It'd be an adventure, an experience. Besides, she could be one of the contestants who got rejected after the first date. Then, she would've helped her brother without it even costing her much time away from her practice.

But just in case, she asked, "How long would it take to film the whole season?"

"A little over a month," Winnie told her. "But you'll be well-compensated. Even if you get kicked off the show, you make about three-fourths as much as those still on it for promotional support, in case we need you to come back for an episode here or there, or do a talk show or something. And we do our homework. The psychologists who work with our contestants are some of the best. They do an analysis on each person to establish an in-depth personality profile that takes into consideration their hopes and dreams."

"How long would I have to notify my patients and shift my schedule around?" Aja said.

"We start filming in three weeks," Winnie continued. "Before that, though, I'd need you to come back and meet the director, take some pictures and test video for promotional purposes, get a medical exam, which, just to warn you, includes some drug testing, and go through a pretty rigorous psychological exam."

"The psychological exam is different from the personality tests?" Darius asked.

"It is. This one's designed to weed out any fragile or dangerous people." She waved a hand as if to say it was just a formality. "I'm sure you'll both pass with flying colors, but I wanted to mention it so that you're prepared, and also to reassure you that the people you meet will have been put through the same safety precautions."

"Sounds like it'll be busy even before we start to film," Aja said.

Winnie tightened the ponytail at her nape. "There will be some appointments, for sure, but we can work around your schedule to give you the time you need."

"Will you do it?" Darius pressed.

Why not? This meant so much to him. Maybe it really would be his big opportunity. "Okay," she said.

"Yes!" Her brother pumped his fist and a smile spread over the producer's face. Winnie was obviously pleased to have gotten her way. Aja guessed she was rarely denied.

"Wonderful." The producer got to her feet. "Just give me a minute while I grab the contracts, and we can go over them together."

"So...you're really going to do this?" Mack asked skeptically. "This...producer woman is *that* gorgeous?"

Grady had driven six hours to Silver Springs, where he'd spent the night with his youngest brother and his wife, Natasha. He was now only two hours from LA and, after having breakfast with them and their three kids in their new home tucked back in the hills, he was just climbing into his truck to be able to make his lunch appointment with Winnie Bruckner. "She's *that* gorgeous."

Tasha stood next to Mack on the sidewalk, holding their youngest, a little girl who was about to turn one, in her arms while their oldest kicked a soccer ball in the front yard with his brother. "But you're going to be marrying someone else," she said, her forehead creasing in confusion.

"Winnie needs one more male contestant, and she's

out of time. Filming starts in a week. I'm just doing her a favor…and hoping to get to know her in the process."

"In the process of marrying someone else," Mack responded, going right back to the point his wife had made.

"It's just a show!" he said in exasperation. "The marriage can be annulled."

Mack grimaced as he stretched his neck. "Doing this… It…doesn't seem like you."

It *wasn't* like him. But he had an opportunity; he figured he might as well take it. All his brothers had wives and families. So did his friends. It felt as though he was being left behind. And it wasn't as if he'd reached out to Winnie. A week after he met her, she'd gone to the trouble of looking him up and calling him at the auto body shop, and what she'd said made a lot of sense. "If you do what you've always done, you'll get what you've always got," she'd said. "So why not take a chance?"

Agreeing to participate could be a big mistake, something he'd live to regret. He was well aware of that. But playing it safe wasn't getting him what he wanted. At least this way he'd be in almost daily contact with her. "I'll just pick a contestant I'm completely incompatible with—who will refuse to marry me, so no one gets hurt—and see how it goes with Winnie in the time I'm there."

"No doubt she'll be grateful that you've made the effort to take so much time off work and drive to LA to save her show," Tasha said. "But…it's weird to think she'll be trying to pair you up with someone else."

"And even if it goes great, and you wind up seeing her instead, what happens if word gets out that you're dating the producer?" Mack asked. "Won't that cause a big PR fiasco? One that could ruin the show?"

Grady got in and buckled his seat belt, leaving the door open so they could continue to talk. "I guess if things go that well, we'd just wait until the show's over before we start to date."

"But it films before it airs," Tasha said. "You might be waiting a while."

"It'll air right after, and we can always talk behind the scenes."

"Okay, but..." Tasha adjusted the bow in baby Hazel's hair. "Are you sure she's not taking advantage of your interest in her?"

He lifted his hands. "I'm not sure of anything. But you know what they say—nothing ventured, nothing gained. We'll see how it goes."

He took the baby and gave her a kiss before handing her back. "I'll stay in touch." He yelled goodbye to the boys, who yelled back, almost in unison, "'Bye, Uncle Grady!"

Mack and Natasha exchanged a worried look, but he'd already arranged for the time off and come this far. He wasn't turning back now.

He closed the door and started the engine. Before he could drive off, however, he heard his phone ding with a text.

It was from Winnie: You're still coming, right?

I'll be there, he wrote back and waved as he pulled away from the curb.

Chapter Four

In just a few days, Grady had signed the contract setting out the rules of the show, including a nondisclosure agreement, been photographed, filmed, given a physical, taken a drug test and had a psych evaluation. He knew the show was doing a background check on him, too. And that was all before they'd started the personality tests, which had taken the better part of the past two days.

But because he'd come at the last minute just to help Winnie out, she'd agreed to make an important exception for him. Instead of having the psychologists employed by the show select the three women he would meet, he'd convinced her to give him the profiles of the female contestants so he could choose himself. After all, Winnie had the final word and had admitted to making changes after receiving recommendations in the past. She'd said that sometimes she had to make certain decisions for the good of the show, so he didn't feel too guilty about pressing her to bend the rules. Especially because, when looking through those profiles, it'd been easy to find the woman who was going to help him escape this sticky situation—the one who'd all but guarantee he'd be free to date Winnie when the show was over.

Her name was Aja Kermani. She was well-educated—a dentist—and had been born and raised in the big city. He was an auto body repairman whose mother had committed suicide and father had gone to prison when he was a kid, so he'd been raised by his oldest brother and had only a high school diploma. She'd had two loving parents who'd given her the benefit of everything money could buy. He'd had very little growing up, including supervision, and he lived in a Gold Country town that was so small it'd probably bore her to tears. She liked art and theater. He preferred action movies. She liked to read. He fell asleep whenever he opened a book and would rather spend his time outdoors.

They had absolutely nothing in common.

He stared down at her picture. She was beautiful, with large brown eyes, smooth, light brown skin and thick dark hair. And her mouth…what a smile! But there was no way someone like her would ever want to marry to him.

He chuckled as he leafed through the rest of her profile. This was turning out even better than he'd thought. Apparently, her younger brother was a contestant, too. Grady had found a handwritten note in her file saying Aja had only agreed to come on the show so that her brother, Darius, could participate. Whoever wrote that note, probably Winnie, felt that having siblings on the show would be an interesting twist, and Grady had to agree. He was curious to see how it would play out. And he was glad this Aja woman didn't have her heart set on coming out of the experience with a long-term relationship. That meant he couldn't disappoint her.

It was all so perfect, especially because he was getting to see the woman he *really* wanted almost every day.

His phone signaled a text. "Speaking of the devil," he mumbled. It was Winnie.

Are you coming down?

The show was putting him and the other men up in a huge mansion in Hollywood. He supposed the women were in a similar situation, just somewhere else. Tonight was the big kickoff of the show, where they were going to film a meet-and-greet, first with the women and then with the men. They had to do it separately, since the two sexes couldn't meet until they had their "dates."

He checked his watch. I was told seven. Are we doing it earlier?

I'm not talking about filming. I need to get those files back before someone finds out I gave them to you.

I thought you were the boss. ;)

Very funny. I am the boss, but breaking the rules could damage the image of the show, especially if someone leaked it to the press.

A good scandal might actually help her. She could use the headlines to boost ratings. Her show hadn't taken off quite like she'd hoped—at least not yet. But he was glad she wasn't out to get that kind of attention, because this time it would involve him.

Understood. Just putting on my shoes. Where do you want to meet?

Everyone's getting ready, so it's quiet down here. Have you been to the pool house out back?

No, but he'd seen the pool from his window. I can certainly find it.

After he hustled through the corridors of the house, through the kitchen and out onto the deck, she was waiting for him with a satchel when he finally reached the pool.

"Do you want to go inside the pool house?" he asked.

"No. That might look even more odd," she replied. "No one's out here. Just give them to me."

He handed her the files, and she immediately stuffed them in her satchel.

"Did you find someone?" she asked.

"I did. Aja Kermani."

"The Persian woman? Why?"

He grinned. "Her personality test, of course."

She rolled her eyes. "Just so you know, that isn't one of the women our panel of psychologists recommended for you."

Somehow, that didn't surprise him. No doubt they'd seen exactly what he'd seen—there was no way they'd be compatible. "Who do they think I'll have a better chance with?"

"I'm not going to tell you, so at least it'll be a surprise when you meet the other two."

"I guess I can go along with that," he said with a shrug. "Just out of curiosity, can you tell me who they paired her with?"

"Omar Hussan."

"Because he has a similar ethnicity?"

She looked alarmed. "You've already met him? You were supposed to be kept separate from each other until tonight."

"Don't worry. The security guards are doing their job. I guessed from the name."

"Oh, of course," she said, visibly relaxing. "We're playing the odds here. For something like this, we have to. Two people often find it easier to get along when they share the same cultural heritage, religious beliefs, political beliefs and so on."

He gave her a funny look. "You've read her file, right? She's not Muslim."

"No, but he is. And I'm guessing she'll be more familiar with his religion than any of our other contestants. I certainly can't see her with you. You probably won't even be able to agree on the type of food you want to eat when you go out."

Grady wasn't worried about that. He could be flexible since it wouldn't really matter in the end. "I'm sure we can compromise. Thanks for letting me have the profiles."

"You're welcome." She glanced at the house and lowered her voice. "But we're even now, okay? You have to play by the rules from here on out. I can't be granting you any more favors."

"No problem."

She smiled up at him. "God, you're handsome. I just know you're going to be a favorite on the show." Her smile turned slightly devilish. "I hope you're ready for the attention and publicity."

He liked the first thing she'd said. He wasn't so thrilled about the second. "Did I forget to tell you I'm a private person?" he asked.

She glanced over her shoulder as she walked away, her heels clicking on the cement. "The psychologists have filled me in—I know all your dark secrets," she said with a wink.

* * *

Last night, after the meet-and-greet that would serve as the first part of episode one, the director—a man named Jim Kline—and Winnie had debated for almost fifteen minutes on whether to take Aja's cell phone away so that she couldn't communicate with her brother during the month they were filming. They didn't want the two of them passing information back and forth—what certain people were saying at the girls' house and what certain people were saying at the boys' house.

Fortunately, in the end, they'd let her keep it, but only because of the possibility that what she and Darius said to each other would create more drama.

Witnessing that conversation had made Aja more than a little uneasy. She knew she'd signed a contract that gave them a lot of power over her life—even down to what she could say about the show for five years after it aired—but she'd never really thought she'd be at risk of losing her cell phone. She was a dentist. Her office should be able to get hold of her if one of her patients had an emergency. Her receptionist and hygienist were still working, doing cleanings and the like. And she'd arranged to have a colleague handle the appointments she hadn't been able to reschedule as well as be on-call in case of an emergency. But she cared about her patients, wanted to know what was happening with them.

Besides, she and Darius had told their parents they were taking a month off to travel to Italy together, but Esther and Cyrus would still expect to hear from them on occasion.

"You look a little lost."

She turned away from the kitchen window, where she'd been staring out into the backyard since they got up from the breakfast table a few minutes earlier, to see that she'd been approached by one of the other eleven contestants—

Barbie LaFaver, who looked remarkably similar to her namesake, even down to the way she dressed. The rest of the women were standing around the room talking as they waited to film the final segment of the opening show, which would involve receiving the name of their potential groom.

"I didn't sleep well," Aja said, which was true. She'd tossed and turned for hours, wondering why she'd allowed her brother to get her involved in something like this.

Barbie lowered her voice. "Don't tell me you're having second thoughts..."

"Maybe a few," she admitted.

"I understand. I don't like that they're watching our cell phones so carefully. But filming won't last forever—only a month, right? This is a great opportunity. Even if we don't find love, the notoriety that comes with it can open so many doors that would remain closed to us otherwise."

Aja nodded. She'd heard that some reality TV stars were able to parlay their start into something that made a lot more money.

"Are you nervous about your date?" Barbie asked.

Aja was actually eager for it. If she was eliminated from the show, she wouldn't have to worry so much about how she was going to survive a whole month of being micromanaged—where other people limited her cell-phone use and denied her access to the internet, television, even books. She hadn't truly understood how demanding and confining it would be. But she was quickly learning that those running the show planned to test them in various ways; reality TV wasn't any good without an abundance of emotion and people were more likely to exhibit emotion if they were under a great deal of stress. "Maybe a little," she said.

Barbie gripped her hands tightly in front of her. "I'm *super* nervous."

"Since we aren't the ones choosing, I wish they'd let us watch the segment they filmed last night, introducing the men."

"I do, too, but they want it to be a 'cold meeting' on both sides so they can film our faces when we first see each other."

Before Aja could respond, the director came into the room with a film crew. "We're starting in five," he barked out.

They were about to hand out the envelopes. The men would get three names in theirs, of course; the women, this year, only one.

The people in charge of makeup scurried forward to blot the shine from their foreheads and slick back or tuck away any strands of hair that weren't fully cooperating, while the sound crew performed mic checks.

A few minutes later, when all was in place, the host, a man named Danny Schular, smiled and said, "Everyone ready?"

The director looked around and seemed comfortable with what he saw, so he lifted his hand to signal for silence. "Action!"

"As you know, this is the day when you get the envelope containing the name of the man who might soon be your husband," Danny said as the cameras rolled. "It won't mean much to you, since you haven't even seen a picture of those who are participating this season, but since we've just introduced them to our viewers, it'll mean something to them." He grinned for the cameras' sake. "So, tell me, are you eager to meet the man you could spend the rest of your life with? Or are you a little anxious you won't advance beyond the first date?"

Barbie spoke first. "I'm not super confident, but I can't wait to see how I do. I've never been lucky in love. To have a psychologist pick someone who is compatible with me? That sounds awesome."

Another one of the women, Vana Kozlowski, talked about how traumatized she was from past relationships, and how she was working on overcoming her fear of intimacy to be able to give the relationship she hoped would come from the show a fighting chance. Another woman, Sheila Golding, shared some of her not-so-pleasant experiences with online dating, including one relationship with a narcissist that had just about destroyed her.

Several of the others chimed in, too. Some of the footage would probably be cut during editing—only the best sound bites would air—and plenty of people responded, so Aja thought she was off the hook, until Danny looked at her.

"What about you?"

Aja froze for a second. She couldn't tell the truth—that she was longing to break out of the mold her parents had created for her despite the love and gratitude she felt for them. If they ever saw the show, it would break their hearts. So she said something about being so busy as a dentist that she hadn't had time to focus on her love life, and now that she was approaching thirty-five, she was feeling her biological clock ticking and decided the show might be able to help her find the man of her dreams.

She was happy about her response but surprised when she was the only one to get a follow-up question.

"How do you feel about your brother being matched with one of the women you've just met?" Danny asked, gesturing good-naturedly toward her fellow participants.

Several of the women straightened, others leaned forward to hear her response, but all seemed duly surprised. This was, of course, the first they'd heard of her having a sibling on the show, and she couldn't help wondering if they were pleased or put off by the idea.

She couldn't see her brother with any of them, but she couldn't say that. What if Darius married one? They'd soon be sisters-in-law. "He's my baby brother, only twenty-five. Of course, I feel protective of him. But he, too, has been very busy. He's in law school at UCLA and will be taking the bar soon, so, like me, he hasn't had a lot of time to date. If he could find someone special... I can't imagine that wouldn't be a good thing for him."

Danny leaned in close. "But which one of these women would you choose for him?" he asked.

She laughed as if she wasn't uncomfortable, even though she was. He was hoping she'd make either an ally or an enemy, get the intrigue started right away. "I haven't had the chance to see what they're really like."

"Well, you know this is a show about first impressions..." he persisted.

"*My brother's* first impression, not mine," she quipped and was relieved when he simply chuckled and let it go.

"Then we'd best get on with it and see who will be going out to dinner with him," he said as he handed out the envelopes he'd just taken from his jacket pocket. "As soon as you open your envelope, be sure to get together with the participants who have the same potential groom so the three of you can draw a number from the buckets we'll be passing around. That's how we will determine who'll go first, second and third when it comes to the dating sequence."

The cameras came forward to get close-ups as they opened the envelopes and pulled out the slips inside.

"Darius Kermani!" Barbie exclaimed, reading hers aloud. "That has to be your brother. Kermani's your last name, right?"

Aja's heart pounded as she nodded—she wasn't sure why. Probably because she was afraid Darius had also made a mistake coming on the show. Although she liked Barbie, she couldn't see how any self-respecting psychologist would pair her with Darius—she was nothing like the girls Aja had seen him date before—so she was losing confidence in a system that'd once sounded fairly logical.

"Neal Kirkpatrick," a woman named Liz called out. "I like his name," she added with a laugh.

Cindy—Aja couldn't remember her last name—held up her slip. "I've got Omar Hussan! So if you've got him, too, watch out. I'm bringing my A game, complete with six-inch stilettos on our first date."

Everyone started laughing and connecting with those who had the same potential groom, as instructed. Aja was the only one standing alone when the exclamations and random comments died down.

"Who do you have?" Danny asked as everyone looked at her.

She read her slip again before holding it up. "Grady Amos."

"Taylor and I have him, too," a woman named Genevieve said and motioned her over.

It was the first time Aja had really considered the competition aspect of the show. Until this moment, she'd simply told herself she didn't care if she was eliminated. But when she saw that Winnie and Jim—or the psychologists behind the scenes—had put her up against two of the most beautiful, confident women on the show, she had a feeling Grady was their prize catch.

Chapter Five

Aja had texted her brother to learn more about Grady, but Darius hadn't been much help. In typical Darius fashion, he summarized everything in one general statement. Seems like a cool dude.

Unsatisfied, she tried to draw out more detail. Do you think we'd be a good match?

Depends. Does it bother you that he's white?

Their parents would not be pleased, but Aja wanted to be blind to race, to entertain the possibility of growing close to any nice man she was attracted to. Not at all. What does he look like?

He's tall, fit. I guess most women would consider him handsome. I don't know. You'll have to judge for yourself.

She sighed. Again, that didn't tell her much. But at least she wouldn't have to wait long to see Grady for herself. She was first in the lineup for the dating portion of the show, which was starting in just a few hours.

She got another text from her brother: What about the women who've been chosen for me? Which one do you think I'll like best?

Now she could understand why he'd been so vague. She didn't know them very well, so she couldn't share much about their lives or personalities. And she thought one was prettier than the others but wasn't sure he'd agree. The last thing she wanted to do was criticize the woman he ended up marrying. Barbie's super friendly, she told him.

What does that mean? Pick her?

A text came in from the director. A driver will be there in thirty. Make sure you're downstairs.

I don't know, she wrote to her brother. I guess you'll have to judge for yourself, too. I have to get ready. I'm first.

Good luck.

She was determined not to get swept up in the competitive spirit that'd taken hold of the participants earlier— changing the sisterhood they'd all felt last night for making the show and being in the same challenging situation to adversaries for fear of being eliminated—and simply be who she really was. But taking something so unusual in stride was easier said than done. She grew more and more nervous as the time drew closer to her departure.

When her alarm went off five minutes before she was supposed to be downstairs, she took one last look in the mirror. They'd been directed to wear evening gowns, so she was dressed in a burnt orange mermaid-style dress that fell off the shoulders, and she was wearing her hair down, brushed until it was gleaming and curled. A professional had helped with her makeup, so she'd look good despite the bright lights necessary for filming, and had painted her nails to match her dress.

A ball of nervous energy sat in the pit of her stomach as she descended the stairs. The rest of the contestants were waiting in the entryway to see her off and looked up when they heard the rustle of her dress.

A gratifying murmur went through the crowd, and Barbie met her as she stepped onto the slate floor to tell her that the color of her dress was absolutely perfect for her. "And it contrasts so nicely with your gorgeous white teeth," she added.

There was a sweetness in Barbie, a sincerity, that was making Aja hope Darius *would* choose her. "Thank you," she murmured, and was immediately ushered outside and into a limousine with darkened windows.

Winnie and Jim had insisted Grady wear a suit, which meant he'd had to go buy one. The last time he'd gotten this dressed up was over two decades ago, for prom.

The support crew and gaffers had set up tables and cameras with the appropriate lighting on the veranda, in the dining room, in the kitchen and in a wine cellar, so they could film all four dates one right after the other, two hours apart. He was up first, which meant he had to have dinner with his date in the wine cellar, where they could control the lighting to make it look later, as if it was dark outside.

He was stationed at a candlelit table for two, set with linen, silverware and fine china, as well as a bottle of champagne on ice. He was no expert in the finer things of life, but everything looked classy to him. He liked the brick walls and floor, the wooden casks and wine racks to one side, the stylish lights that hung from the ceiling and the general ambience. It was a cool place to have dinner.

Hearing footsteps on the stairs, he scooted his chair back and looked up as the cameraman entered the room.

"She's here," he announced and got into position as someone else started to descend the stairs.

This would be his date. Grady didn't know which of the "choices" he'd meet first, but he'd seen all their pictures because he'd had the files. He just had to be careful not to let on that he knew more than he should about whomever showed up.

He reminded himself to show the proper amount of surprise, so it would look natural on camera, but didn't end up having to fake it. He'd seen pictures of Aja Kermani, but they simply didn't do her justice, not in that stunning dress.

He came to his feet. "Wow! Hello, I'm Grady Amos."

"Aja Kermani."

Her hand felt small and cold when he shook it, and she glanced away with a blush, suggesting she was shy or self-conscious.

He moved around the table to hold her chair while she sat down, but she stepped on her dress and pitched forward. Fortunately, he caught her before she could crash into the table and send everything flying, and then she *really* blushed.

"Sorry," she mumbled.

"Don't be nervous," he said with a grin.

She claimed she wasn't, but he could tell that she was. He understood. He'd never had a camera pointed in his face when he was trying to get to know someone, either. But he had an advantage over her. He wasn't taking the show seriously, so it was probably easier for him to ignore the unusual circumstances. He also wasn't competing against the other guys the way she was against two other women, so he didn't have anything to lose. He knew he was on the show for the duration...unless she refused to marry him, which was exactly what he hoped.

He popped the champagne and poured them each a glass. "So I guess we should start with the basics," he said. He needed to have her tell him the information he already knew—like the fact that she was a dentist—so he couldn't blow it by mentioning any of those details before she did. "Where are you from?"

"I was born and raised in Newport Beach."

"Is that where you'd like to settle?"

"I can't go too far from the area. I'm a dentist, and my practice is here in LA."

Bingo. He smiled. "Of course. It'd be difficult to rebuild a practice."

"What about you?" she asked.

"I'm from a small town in Northern California with only about two thousand people called Whiskey Creek."

"I've never heard of it." She took a sip of her champagne. "What do you do there?"

"Auto body work."

She cleared her throat. "You fix cars?"

"Not the engine. The body, after a collision."

To her credit, other than that slight pause while she cleared her throat, she didn't act as if a man with a blue-collar job was totally out of the realm of possibility for her. Given that she was so educated, he would've thought she'd be a little more put off. But the camera could have something to do with her tempered response. Maybe she didn't want to come off as arrogant or stuck-up...or do anything to make him choose someone else, which would mean she'd be eliminated from the show. "And do you like it?" she asked.

"I do."

She put down her glass. "Were you born in Whiskey Creek? Is that where you'd like to spend the rest of your life?"

"I really like it there, but…" He thought of Winnie, who would be watching this. She probably wouldn't be any more eager to leave the Los Angeles area than Aja. "Nothing's set in stone. I could always open a franchise here."

She sat back. "Oh, so you own the shop."

"In partnership with my brothers. We own three—one in Whiskey Creek, one in Reno and one just two hours from here in Silver Springs."

She put her napkin in her lap as someone entered with a crab cake appetizer. "How'd you get into that line of work?"

He settled his napkin in his lap, too, and leaned back as the plates were put in front of them. "My father started the business. But he went to prison when I was only twelve, so my oldest brother had to take over and try to provide for the rest of us. Otherwise, we would've been put into foster care and likely split up."

Her eyes widened. "Where was your mother?"

"I didn't have one at that time. She suffered from depression and overdosed on her meds not too long before my father went to prison. So it was just Dylan taking care of the rest of us."

Her fork hung in the air with her first bite. She glanced at the camera and quickly lowered it. "I'm so sorry. How many siblings do you have?"

"Four—all brothers. And Dylan had to finish raising us. Can you imagine?"

"I can't. That means your father must've been in prison for…a while."

"Almost twenty years." This information would come up with each date—and Winnie probably already knew about it because of his background check—so he figured he might as well state it up front, get it out of the way. Plus, with Aja, scaring her away was part of his strategy. "He wasn't usually violent, but he started drinking after my mother died and knifed a man in a bar for taunting him about her death."

Aja's jaw dropped. This was obviously completely foreign to anything she'd experienced. Grady almost started to laugh. He didn't find any part of his childhood funny, but he was shocking the hell out of her—that was the funny part. This was going down exactly as he'd expected. Winnie would have to be pleased with the drama.

"That must've been terrible," she murmured. "How old was… Dylan, did you say his name is?"

"Eighteen. He had to drop out before graduating and take over at the auto body shop."

She blinked several times. "Wow, that is young. He must be an amazing person."

"He is." Grady had nothing but love and respect for his oldest brother, who'd taken on a task few people could. Dylan hadn't been a perfect substitute father, but he'd done his damnedest, and he'd turned the business around, too.

She finally took a bite of her crab cake. "Where do you fall in the family?" she asked.

He cut into his food, too. "Right in the middle."

"So…you have two older brothers and two younger ones. Five boys wouldn't be easy for anyone to raise, let alone someone only eighteen."

"You got that right. We were such hooligans that we had quite a reputation. People in town called us the Fearsome Five," he said with a chuckle, "because we were always in some sort of trouble. Fortunately, we've cleaned up our act since then."

"I get the impression your father's out of...prison now. How's he doing?"

There was a lot he could say about JT but he figured he'd stick with the facts, which were bound to come out, anyway, because of being on this show. "Better," he said. "He's come a long way."

She took another drink of champagne, and he couldn't help noticing that her manners were impeccable. "Do you have a relationship with him?" she asked.

"I do. He works at the shop with me these days and comes to the house now and then."

"I'm happy to hear that."

He put more sauce on his crab cake. "There's a guy on the show with the same last name you have and looks a great deal like you. Could it be that he's your brother?"

Her chest lifted as she drew a breath, and her smile grew less strained. "Yes. He's my only sibling, younger by eight years."

"And what do your parents do?"

"My father's an ophthalmologist. My mother's an orthodontist."

"And your brother's in law school. You're a family of professionals."

"My parents really pushed us in school."

The same person who'd brought the appetizer returned with two plates filled with garlic-encrusted filet mignon, au gratin potatoes and asparagus spears.

"What made you decide you wanted to do a show like this?" he asked as the person waiting on their table cleared away what was left of the crab cakes.

"I, um, I had a couple of reasons, actually."

He started to cut into his steak, but when she paused, he looked up.

"I've been too busy to date in the traditional way and was...looking to introduce a bit of daring into my life, I guess."

He felt his eyebrows go up. "You've always played it safe?"

"I guess I have."

She was the classic "good girl." And he was the classic "bad boy." This reminded him of the movie *Grease*. "And? What do you think? Are you glad you did it?"

"So far?" She gave him a sweet smile. "I go back and forth."

Perfect answer, he thought. She couldn't be completely honest on camera, but he got the impression "no" was what she wanted to say—and that was reassuring, at least as far as he was concerned.

Chapter Six

Aja felt like crying. She'd done terribly on the date. Although Grady seemed like a nice person—and he certainly wasn't bad looking—she didn't think he'd be a good fit for her so she tried to console herself with that. But it was hard to fail at anything—she'd been taught failure wasn't an option—and was willing to bet, after tonight, he wouldn't hesitate to choose someone else. No doubt both of the poised women who were next in line would perform better than she had. Before signing up for this show, she should've given more weight to the fact that she was an introvert, and this setting would be extremely stressful for her. She would have if she hadn't been trying to make her brother happy.

Oh, well, I wasn't really expecting anything to come from it, anyway, she told herself as the limousine drove her back.

Still, she felt overly emotional, so maybe that wasn't

true. Maybe she just wasn't willing to admit that she actually found Grady quite attractive and *did* have her hopes up that this would be the start of something new and exciting—a breath of fresh air as she burst out of the box that'd confined her since she could remember. She'd broken up with someone she'd known her whole life and now missed—not in a romantic sense but as a friend—and couldn't even call him without him thinking there might be a chance at reconciliation. And she'd done it—and upset her parents and threatened their relationship with Behar and Behram, who were like an aunt and uncle to her—because she desperately craved *something else*.

She managed to hold in her emotions and smile for the other girls, who were waiting for her, eager to hear all about the experience, when she walked into the mansion. She told them Grady was charming and the food was delicious and the camera wasn't too intrusive, even though she'd been far too nervous to be able to taste the food and she'd been so self-conscious about the camera she'd tripped and nearly fallen...and not much had improved from there. She couldn't understand why they'd been paired in the first place. They didn't seem to have *anything* in common.

Genevieve and Taylor, the other two women who'd also been selected to meet Grady, watched her closely. She could feel the difference in the way they looked at her versus anyone else and got the feeling they were sizing her up, trying to determine just how high the bar had been set. They were also trying to pick up any nuggets of information that might prove helpful to them.

Everyone else congratulated her, complimented her dress and speculated on the men they'd meet.

She stayed in the living room with them long enough to make her response to the date seem convincing. She didn't want to tip off the assistant producer, or anyone else who worked for the show, that there was anything deeper going on, or the cameras would follow her to her room.

But as soon as she felt she could get away, she told them she had a headache and went up to change and go to bed. She needed a few minutes of privacy—something they didn't like to allow on the show because they were afraid the contestants would decompress and thereby avoid an argument or something else that might prove interesting to viewers—and had just changed out of her gown when she heard a knock.

Holding her breath for fear it would be someone with a camera, she tightened the belt on her robe and hurried to the door. "Who is it?"

"Barbie."

Aja let her breath go. She really wanted to be alone. But Barbie was better than Winnie or Jim or any other *Tying the Knot* personnel. She opened the door and forced a smile, hoping the dim lighting in the hallway would hide the evidence of her tears.

"Is something wrong?" Barbie asked.

Aja stepped back to let her in as she shook her head. "Just the stress. I have a headache."

Barbie closed the door behind her. "That's why I came," she whispered. "When I got here, they took away all my meds, even my antihistamines, so I'm guessing they did the same to you and everyone else. They expect us to ask for a doctor if we need anything, so I wanted to see if you needed some painkillers."

"Do you have some?" Aja asked in surprise. "I thought you just said they took away all your meds…" They probably would've taken hers, too, but she didn't have any.

Barbie grinned conspiratorially. "They did, but they missed a small pack of ibuprofen."

"And you're willing to give that to me when it's all you have? You're *too* nice."

"We have to stick together. It'll make this experience so much more enjoyable."

"Even though most of us will be going home soon? They'll be done filming the first dates by tomorrow night, you know. They're starting first thing in the morning and going all day."

She handed Aja a small envelope containing two pills. "Well, I'm hoping you and I will still be around."

"Me, too," she said and was amazed to find it was true. As difficult as it was, she wasn't the type of person who liked to lose and didn't want to return to her practice to find she was in the same exact position she'd been in before taking this leap.

"I'll let you get some sleep." Barbie started to leave but turned back at the last second. "Aja?"

"What?"

"Do you think your brother will like me?"

"I don't know anyone who wouldn't," Aja said and meant it.

Barbie must've heard the sincerity in her voice because she impulsively hugged Aja. "Thank you."

"What time is your date?" Aja asked.

"I go right after lunch tomorrow—at one."

"I'll come help you get ready."

Barbie's face brightened. "Really?"

"Why not?" Since her date was over, she wouldn't have much else to do. She'd just be waiting for the big reveal, which wouldn't happen until the day after. First, they had to film the guys ruminating over their choices and struggling to make the right decision.

"Thanks," Barbie said and left.

Aja put the pills in her purse in case Barbie needed them

later. Just having a friend stop by to show some concern had made her feel better.

She got in bed and texted Darius.

How was your date tonight?

Not that great. What about you?

I did terrible! It was so embarrassing.

What went wrong?

To start things off, I tripped on my dress and would've wiped out the whole table if my date hadn't caught me.

[crying laughing emoji]

Stop! It's not funny.

Okay. Seriously, that's not a big deal.

It is to me!

I'm sure a guy can overlook that. What did you think of Grady?

She pictured the tall, dark-haired man she'd met. He had piercing hazel eyes and a five-o'clock shadow that covered a strong jaw and chin. But it was his smile she liked best. His teeth weren't perfectly straight, but the way one front tooth lapped slightly over the other gave his smile a unique character. He's okay-looking, I guess.

Would you say you're compatible?

One date really isn't enough to be able to tell. To be honest, if I were to get into a serious relationship with him, I'd be a little worried about his childhood. Anything terrible that could happen did.

Anything? Like what?

You'll see. Suicide. Prison. Five boys trying to raise themselves. He must carry some very deep scars, and who knows how that informs the man he is today.

That's concerning.

Right?

I gotta go. They're calling a meeting about tomorrow.

Just one more thing. Keep an open mind when it comes to Barbie.

You've picked a favorite for me, after all?

I guess so. She's got a very kind heart.

[thumbs-up emoji]

An hour later, Aja was just feeling better, more optimistic, when she got a text from the director.

Can you come down? I'd like a word with you.

Winnie held her wineglass loosely in one hand as she studied him. "How'd it go? Do you think you chose the right one?"

Grady leaned back as he considered the question. It was late. Everyone at the mansion was asleep. At least, all the lights were out over there. He and Winnie were sitting at the small kitchen table in the guesthouse, where she was staying so she could be on-site to take care of any problems that cropped up in their off hours, as well as oversee all the filming. "I haven't met the other two women yet," he said. "That's tomorrow, right?"

She poured him some more wine. "But you already picked Aja from the profiles. I'm asking if you think you'll stick with her after having met her."

"I don't see why not. She seems ideal." He took a drink of his chardonnay. "Well, ideal in that she's all wrong for me," he added.

Winnie grimaced at his response. "We've never had a participant sabotage their own journey on the show. You'll be able to capitalize on this opportunity much better if you can be one of its success stories. It'll keep you on the show longer, you'll be asked to return in future seasons, you'll have more interest from the press. You might even get booked on other shows—"

"Except I'm not here for the money, the fame or any more of the same kind of work," he interrupted.

She must've known where he was going with that comment because she narrowed her eyes in mock anger. "What *are* you here for?"

He met her gaze. The question was sort of a challenge, but he wasn't afraid of it. "I'm here for you."

"For *me*," she said, pressing a hand to her chest.

"That comes as a surprise?" He chuckled. "I tried picking you up at a bar. Obviously, I like what I see."

"Okay, maybe I'm not entirely surprised…" she said.

Grady resisted a yawn. He was dead tired. It'd been a long day doing things he definitely wasn't accustomed to doing. "So…are you going to go out with me when this whole thing is over?"

She got up and went to the window. "Grady, this show means a lot to me. I really want you to give it your best shot."

He crossed his legs in front of him. "I'm giving it my best shot. Didn't you like the footage from my date?"

She hesitated, then admitted, grudgingly, "That footage was pretty good."

"Lots of dirty laundry there," he pointed out. "Perfect for prime time, but it came at my expense. I had to talk about my past. That isn't something I like to do." In previous years, he wouldn't have done it no matter what the incentive. It was the passage of time and having a much better life in the years since that made it possible.

Winnie looked slightly abashed. "I can see why. I'm sorry. But you were using it on purpose, trying to make yourself unappealing to Aja."

"There's that," he admitted, then got up and walked over to her. He liked that she'd invited him over to "check in on how things were going for him on the show," as her text said, but he wasn't going to try to take it any further than a conversation she could have with any of the participants. There wasn't any reason to create a scandal that could threaten her hopes for the series…and her career in general. He only wanted to get close enough that she'd look up at him again. "You never answered my question."

"What question?"

"You know what question. Are you going to go out with me after this is all over?"

Continuing to stare out the window, probably because it allowed her to avoid his gaze, she didn't answer.

"I hope I'm not doing this for nothing…" he added.

She finally shot him a grudging smile. "Yes, I'll go out with you when the show's over. You have this—this thing about you. Charisma, charm or whatever. It sort of grows on people."

She didn't sound happy to admit it, which made it even more of a victory. He gave her a broad smile. He'd been wanting to find someone for a long time.

Maybe he finally had.

But first, he had to get through the show.

Chapter Seven

Jim had demanded Darius's phone and had taken screenshots of the texts Aja had sent for possible inclusion in the dating episode, which meant Grady would see them. She hated the idea of that, hadn't written them with that in mind. She'd argued against it, but the show's director had insisted people would love the vulnerability she felt, as well as her candid reaction to the trauma Grady suffered as a child. He also liked the guidance she'd offered her younger brother, which revealed her budding friendship with a fellow contestant.

"The women in the audience will definitely be able to identify with your concerns," he'd said. "Grady's background is something a potential wife *should* consider. This will allow everyone some insight on your decision—whatever that will be if he chooses you as his bride—and make them root for you. Bottom line, it's engaging stuff."

She'd asked if she could take out a few lines—censor

it a bit to save her and Grady some embarrassment—but he'd refused. Those were the parts he found most valuable.

"This will make you popular among viewers, and that's never a bad thing," he'd said.

She was willing to bet he used that excuse with contestants whenever it served him. He didn't care about her. He didn't care about Grady, either. He cared about boosting the show's ratings.

"You didn't say anything *really* bad," Jim had insisted when she'd continued to argue.

At least that was true. But there were still things in that exchange that made her cringe when she imagined Grady reading them. She'd said he was "okay-looking," for one. And she'd basically said, with a background like his, he must be damaged goods.

Punching her pillow, she flopped onto her other side. She'd been tossing and turning ever since she'd gotten into bed. At this rate, it would be morning before she fell asleep, which meant she'd have even lower emotional reserves.

She knew one thing, though. If she stayed on the show, she'd be a lot more careful in the future, would never let Jim or Winnie or anyone else with *Tying the Knot* get one over on her ever again.

Grady's other two dates weren't very remarkable. He might've asked Genevieve out on his own, had he met her somewhere else, but he didn't feel strongly about her one way or the other, and he really wasn't attracted to Taylor. He couldn't say why. She was pretty enough and said all the right things. There was just no chemistry.

He was ready to be off camera as evening approached, but he knew they'd be filming the big "decision" tonight, where the men would meet to discuss the pros and cons of each woman they'd been matched with. They'd decide if they'd marry one, and if so, which one it would be.

He considered bowing out. This whole thing was beginning to seem too ridiculous. But he'd committed to it and couldn't hurt the show Winnie was trying so hard to make a success. So he figured he'd go ahead and leave it in the hands of Aja Kermani. Regardless of what she decided, at least he would've done his part. He couldn't imagine she'd ever agree to marry him, anyway.

He was in his room, getting changed for the final taping of the day, when he received a text from his brother Rod.

I haven't heard from you. Now that you're going to be famous, maybe you don't have time for those of us who are less important. But I wanted to see how you're doing. Have we lost you from auto body work for good?

His brothers constantly teased him, about anything. Actually, he did his share of the same sort of thing. This is an experience, but don't hire anyone to replace me. I'm not going anywhere.

Acting's not your thing?

Definitely not.

But are any of the women interesting to you?

There's one. With the way Jim, the director, was acting about cell phones—how carefully their behavior was being monitored—Grady wasn't about to get specific and tell his brother that the "one" wasn't even a contestant.

Are you going to marry her?

I announce my pick tomorrow. We'll see what she says, he wrote, switching back to Aja in his mind. But I'm fairly certain I can start packing my bags.

You don't think she'll say yes...

I think she'd be crazy to. [laughing emoji]

You don't seem too disappointed.

I'll be okay. Something might still come from the show later.

Mack told me about that. Nothing's changed there?

Nothing's changed.

Looking forward to watching the show.

Grady was not excited about having his friends and family watch, but he was reconciled to the fact that it was going to happen.

Someone knocked on his door.

"We're waiting for you downstairs," a voice called through the panel.

Surprised, he checked his watch. Sure enough, he was running late. "Be right there!"

Jim must've leaked the texts she'd sent her brother, because when Aja went to breakfast the morning of eliminations, everyone was talking about it.

"You don't think Grady's attractive?" Barbie whispered, seemingly shocked.

Aja nearly swallowed her tongue. She'd known those

texts would be revealed at some point, but she assumed it would be when the show aired, and by then they'd all be off living their separate lives again. "I... It's not that I think he's *un*attractive. He has a great smile when he actually smiles. It's just that his appeal is more...intangible."

"Genevieve and Taylor claim you must be blind, that he's totally hot."

Aja tried to defend her position. "He's got sex appeal, for sure. But there's also a certain wariness inside him that can be seen in his eyes. He's not exactly open. He's defensive, and it makes sense that he would be."

Barbie gave her a pitying, sheepish look. "I hope it makes sense to him, or..."

Or she'd be off the show. Barbie didn't say it, but Aja understood what this would likely mean. The director had sabotaged her. Maybe he thought she wasn't turning out to be interesting enough, after all.

"What happens happens." She was doing this for her brother, anyway, she reminded herself. If she had to go back to her regular life, with nothing changed, she'd try to figure out a saner path toward finding contentment.

Barbie squeezed her hand under the table. "Okay. I'm glad you won't be disappointed."

"It'll be fine," Aja said stoically.

"I wonder who your brother's going to choose..."

Aja squeezed her hand back. They'd spent most of yesterday together, were quickly becoming close. Barbie was the opposite of Grady—totally open and trusting—and Aja knew she really liked Darius. Aja didn't want to see someone like Barbie get hurt. "If he's as smart as I think he is, he'll choose you."

"He hasn't told you?" she asked uncertainly. "You'd say so if he did, right?"

"He hasn't told me. I won't text with him anymore. Not

after the show took screenshots of our last exchange," Aja said and looked up to see Genevieve watching her.

The other woman smiled like the Cheshire cat while eating her egg soufflé, and Taylor, who was sitting next to her, leaned in to whisper something. They knew they had an advantage over her now.

Winnie came into the room, trailed by Jim. "This is going to be a big day," the producer announced to the room at large. "It's always exciting to narrow the show down to our couples. But it's also hard to say goodbye to the people who will be leaving. I just wanted to thank you all for being part of the experience and to tell you that even if you're eliminated, we'll look for opportunities to bring you back on and include you when we can."

The women glanced at each other, no doubt wondering whom this would pertain to…and hoping it wouldn't be them.

"We've decided to shoot the reveal segment here," Winnie continued. "Since we'll be cutting the cast on the female side from twelve to four, we won't need this much space, so tomorrow we'll be moving to a different house. That way, we can capture people packing up and leaving and get their take on what going home feels like—if they believe they could've made a successful match with the man they met even though they weren't chosen, that sort of thing."

Aja was so certain she would be leaving that an hour later, when the men filed into the living room where the women were already waiting, and all the contestants were together for the first time, studying each other curiously, she sat in a chair in the back, behind the others, her bags packed in her room.

After the normal drama and preamble to pump up the suspense, Neal Kirkpatrick took the floor. He opened a ring case to show a gold band to the camera. Then he walked over to one of the women he'd met as if he was going to propose, moved on to another as if it was really her and finally got down on one knee to propose to the third.

"Will you marry me?" he asked Liz Cheyne.

The other two girls began to cry in disappointment as Liz beamed at him. "I will!" she exclaimed, and he got up to embrace her.

Omar Hussan went next. He opened his ring but didn't mess around with trying to mislead anyone. He walked directly to a woman named Mirabelle Lacey, who seemed shocked that he'd picked her, and a little uncertain, but ultimately agreed.

They had two of their couples...

Aja swallowed hard as Darius got up. He showed off his ring before dramatically moving toward one woman before changing direction and getting down on one knee in front of Barbie.

After a quick celebratory glance at Aja, Barbie threw her arms around him before he could even ask her to marry him.

Everyone laughed as the two of them fell over. Then the focus turned to Grady. Aja couldn't help wondering how he felt about the texts she'd sent Darius. She had little doubt he'd heard about them and wished she could completely disappear. But she had to gut it out until those who were eliminated were interviewed.

The other contestants kept craning their heads to look at her, even though everyone knew he was going to choose between Genevieve and Taylor.

Aja watched him walk over to Genevieve, saw the confident expectation on her face and assumed that was it. But all he did was tell her she was a beautiful woman who would, no doubt, make someone else a very happy man.

He gestured at Taylor and said the same was true for her. Then he wove through the chairs to reach Aja…and got down on one knee.

Grady thought he was in the perfect position. Three other couples had agreed to marriages. Providing they didn't get cold feet and back out in the next few days, Winnie could make a season even if he wasn't on it. And after what Aja had texted to her brother, he knew she didn't even find him attractive. But he tried to shrug it off because then he had an even greater chance she'd say no when he proposed.

He grinned as he opened the ring and showed it to her. It was nothing special—just a gold band provided by the show.

"Aja Kermani, I know you might not have enjoyed our date as much as I did, so I understand the risk I'm taking here. But I think I could make you happy…and prove that love isn't all about looks," he added jokingly, referring to the texts she'd sent her brother, which made everyone else laugh.

Her eyes widened and she covered her mouth with both hands, obviously shocked, maybe overwhelmed and probably embarrassed.

"If you could see it in your heart to marry me, I think we could prove that relationships can be successful when they're built on kindness, honesty and mutual respect instead of more superficial things. And maybe you can help me overcome the parts of me that aren't quite right because of the difficulties I encountered early in life."

Several of the women said, "Aw," letting him know they were sympathetic and liked what he'd said.

He was just trying to make a good episode, never dreamed that would sway her. He was positive she was going to say something conciliatory to cover for her texts, but ultimately refuse. He wasn't even worried when the woman her brother was going to marry jumped up, came over and kneeled down on her other side.

"Do it, Aja!" she encouraged. "If you don't, you'll never know what could've been."

"Let loose and take a chance for once," Darius added from where he stood.

And the next thing Grady knew, everything he'd planned, orchestrated and expected went right out the window. Aja looked from her brother to her soon-to-be sister-in-law, then back again, licked her lips nervously and said, "Okay, I'll do it!"

Chapter Eight

She'd turned down Arman but accepted the proposal of a stranger? What'd gotten into her?

Aja felt numb as they went through the motions of taking pictures for promotional purposes, holding hands with her "fiancé," showing her ring and filming short segments to tease the upcoming wedding episode.

The rest of the evening felt like a dream. But in those moments when reality intruded, a sense of panic would well up and she almost bailed out.

Maybe she would have, except it seemed too late—as though she'd already gotten on the ride and was committed to its climbs and falls and crazy corkscrews until it came to a stop on its own. And she was too much of a "good girl" to cause problems.

"What made you do it?" Darius murmured when, exhausted, she hugged him before heading to bed.

"I have no idea," she muttered. She knew if she said

much more, the mics they were forced to wear would alert Jim or someone else on the production team that there might be an opportunity to get some good "reaction" footage.

She didn't have a very good answer, anyway. She couldn't make Grady be the only groom who was refused. That was one thing. She'd also been excited for Barbie and Darius, and wanted to continue the journey with them instead of being kicked off and having to wait until they finished filming in a month to learn how things went.

And after how superior Genevieve and Taylor had acted, maybe it was also a little gratifying that she was the one who'd gotten the ring.

Of course, if marrying Grady turned out to be a bad thing, *they* would be the lucky ones. But when her brother said, "Let loose and take a chance," she'd simply closed her eyes and, metaphorically speaking, made the leap.

As she went over the evening in her mind after she was in bed that night, she was stunned by her own behavior. And she felt bad for their parents, who would be mortified when they eventually learned what had happened. She and Darius, their only two children, were marrying people they wouldn't approve of—not to mention they were doing it without including them in the *aroosi*, or wedding.

"Oh, my God," she muttered.

On the other hand, they were both adults and should be able to do what they wanted with their lives. And it was just a TV show. It couldn't *really* mean anything. It would probably be a memory they laughed at in later years, an experience worth having but nothing permanent.

She must've eventually fallen asleep because the next time she opened her eyes, sunlight was flooding the room, and she panicked, thinking she'd overslept. Grabbing her phone, she saw that she'd actually awakened just before her alarm and slumped back on the pillows in relief.

Today, they'd be filming the wedding-dress segment. Winnie had told them it was the most popular episode of each season. "Everyone loves to see the brides, with all their jitters and uncertainty, getting beautiful for the wedding," she'd told them. Then she'd pulled Aja aside to say she'd like to incorporate some Persian traditions into the ceremonies for her and Darius.

Aja wondered what Grady would think of that, especially burning *esfand* or incense to ward off the "evil eye" that might cause them harm, and the consent ritual, in which he would say "I do" immediately, but she wouldn't answer until she'd been asked three times. In Persian weddings, the crowd played a part in this ritual by yelling things like *"aroos rafteh gol behshineh!"* which translated to "the bride has gone to pick flowers!" It was all to symbolize the groom's journey of earning his wife's love, but it would probably seem strange to someone who'd never experienced it.

Her alarm went off. She silenced it, then dragged herself out of bed. Then she peeled off her clothes to get in the shower but paused in front of the mirror. What about the intimacy aspect of the wedding? Was she really going to have sex with Grady Amos on their wedding night?

At the rate they were filming, that would be in two days!

She might be able to go through with the wedding, she told herself, but she wasn't sure she could go through with *that*.

Grady hadn't slept much. He was getting the distinct impression that he'd let his attraction to Winnie lead him down a very dangerous path. The question was whether to go ahead and follow it to its conclusion, or pull out of the show and run for home.

Winnie had texted him last night after the proposals, as surprised as he was that Aja had agreed to marry him. He'd hoped she would be more disappointed, maybe encourage him to cancel the engagement and leave LA, for the time being.

But she hadn't. He'd gotten the impression she was kind of excited by this turn of events because it did such great things for the series. Now the siblings would remain on the show all season, and he knew that was a dynamic Winnie was eager to explore. Those texts Aja had sent Darius juxtaposed to her acceptance of his ring would certainly create a buzz, and she needed that buzz to make the show successful. Winnie had said everyone would be watching to learn why Aja had agreed and to see if they could overcome the gulf between them.

He'd pushed back, said the season would probably be interesting enough without him and Aja on the show. But Winnie had insisted he shouldn't be too rash. Let it run its course, she'd said. Who knows? Maybe you and Aja are meant to be. But if that's not the case, and you end up breaking up, then, when this is all over...

She hadn't finished that sentence. But he knew what went there. Then they'd be free to date and find out if they were "meant to be."

He wasn't convinced he was being wise not to take more control of his own destiny. Winnie cared so much about what she was trying to create, that she had ulterior motives. But so far, the control he'd tried to take hadn't worked out too well for him. Besides, according to the contract he'd signed, there'd be significant financial penalties for quitting early, and even if that wasn't the case, he'd committed himself. He hated going back on his word. Maybe he was old-fashioned, but to him it just wasn't honorable.

Darius, Neal and Omar were already at breakfast by the time he walked into the kitchen. Neal and Omar came off like the type of men who were often featured on *The Bachelor*—men who were hoping to get a start in Hollywood, make some good money and/or become America's current heartthrob. Aja's brother seemed less stereotypical—like a nice kid who was just eager to live the American dream. At twenty-five, he could be forgiven for getting involved in something like this.

But Grady was nearly forty. He should've known better…

He dished up a bowl of oatmeal from the food that'd been prepared for them and sat down at one end of the table, away from the others. He was hoping they'd leave him to his thoughts. The show schedule was so tight there wasn't a lot of downtime, and since his brothers had all married, he was used to living alone. He craved a few more minutes to himself.

But Darius broke the silence almost immediately. "You sleep okay?"

Omar and Neal glanced up but continued eating.

Grady'd had a hell of a night, but he couldn't say that to the brother of the woman he was engaged to marry. "Pretty good. You?"

"Tossed and turned a bit. This show is…stressful. Makes you second-guess everything. I mean… I can't believe what we're doing. But in case you're worried, I just wanted to let you know what you're getting into with Aja."

Now Darius had his full attention. "What am I getting into?" he asked.

"She's the nicest person you'll ever meet," he said as if it was simply a fact, then got up to take his dishes to the sink.

The nicest person he'd ever meet…and yet, so far, his heart and mind had been completely closed against her.

Putting down his spoon, Grady sat back while the others finished and then got to their feet. "In case you haven't heard, we leave in twenty minutes to be fitted for our tuxedos," Omar said, then turned right back and followed the others out.

Grady nodded, but his mind was a million miles away. Why was he so sure he and Aja could never be happy together? She was smart, pretty, accomplished. He couldn't even blame her for sending those texts about him. A lot of people would've felt the same way.

Besides, she'd thought she was speaking privately to her brother, in an emotionally safe space. She had the right to be totally honest.

Someone from the cooking staff came to clear away the food and the rest of the dishes, and he slid his chair back while the woman took his half-empty bowl.

He was in this thing now; he might as well make the most of it.

The next few days were incredibly busy—so busy Aja didn't have time for regrets or second thoughts. It helped that the wedding-dress segment was so enjoyable. They were taken to a small bridal boutique in Bel Air that had racks of stunning dresses, and a professional stylist helped them find a gown that was unique—so they'd each have their own "look"—and flattering.

Aja selected an ecru satin dress that reminded her of the A-line cocktail dresses from the '50s. She loved the classic simplicity of it—there was no lace, no sequins or patterns of any kind—and she thought it went perfectly with a waterfall veil in the same shade. She knew she'd found the right ensemble when the stylist gaped at her as she walked out of the dressing room. Aja was especially flattered when Winnie did a double take and said, "Wow!"

They spent the rest of the day at the spa having their hair trimmed and nails done and, of course, filmed part of it. But the fun ended when Mirabelle Lacey couldn't be found the morning of the weddings. Liz was the first to know. Like Aja and Barbie, Mirabelle and Liz had become close friends. She'd gone to Mirabelle's room as soon as she got up only to find it empty, her clothes and toiletries gone. Liz had started to freak out, which brought the rest of them to the landing of their new place, where they'd moved after the elimination round, to see what was wrong. The security guard of their house had told them she'd quit in the middle of the night. That meant they were down a couple, which was 25 percent of the show.

Not long afterward, Winnie called an emergency meeting in the living room to remind them that they were fortunate to have the opportunity to be on the show, that there'd been a lot of applicants and yet they'd been chosen, that the show could open up a world of other opportunities and when they'd accepted, they'd made a commitment. She'd clearly been upset, and probably worried, too. Maybe she was afraid that Liz would follow Mirabelle's lead.

"Can you believe she just…panicked?" Barbie said to Aja after the meeting as they walked upstairs to her room.

"I can't," Aja said. "Or…maybe I can." She thought it was more remarkable that the rest of them were going through with it…

Barbie shot her a worried glance. "You're not going to back out, are you? You heard Winnie. If we lose any more people, we might not be able to finish the season."

Aja had gotten into this for the sake of her brother. She wasn't going to ruin it for him—or Barbie—now. She wouldn't ruin it for Winnie, either, because she *had* made a commitment. Besides, if she did bail out, she'd have to pay for her wedding gown on top of the other penalties, and it'd been very expensive. "I'm going through with it," she said. "But we don't know how the men are feeling. There could be other surprises."

They hadn't been allowed to see or communicate with their grooms since the proposals, so she had no idea what Grady was feeling, whether he was getting cold feet or not.

"They'll show up," Barbie said. "I feel bad for Omar. He really wanted to do it."

"He might be able to come back next season. And the show should be okay. They can fill in a bit with the couples who are still together from previous seasons. Everyone will want to know how they're doing."

Fortunately, the shock of Mirabelle leaving—and the distraction it caused—didn't give Aja a lot of time to get nervous. Mirabelle was supposed to have been the one getting married first. Now that she was gone, they were moving the weddings up so they wouldn't have to film late, and Aja needed to get ready.

She was fully dressed in her gown, veil and a simple strand of pearls, and was waiting for the limousine that would take her to the wedding venue, before she started to feel shaky.

"You look gorgeous!" Barbie gushed.

Fortunately, Barbie hadn't left her side, even though she should probably be getting ready herself. "You think so?"

She smiled warmly. "There's no question."

Aja grabbed Barbie's arm. "Do you think we're doing the right thing?" She'd asked that question a million times, but she had to ask again.

"Something wonderful will come from this," her friend insisted.

A knock sounded at the door, and Barbie went to answer it. Aja heard her speaking to the security guard. "Is it time?" she asked.

"It's time," Barbie confirmed.

They'd been told they could invite their immediate family to the wedding, but Aja couldn't tell her parents what she was doing, which meant she couldn't tell anyone else, either. And her brother was on the show, so he and Barbie couldn't attend; they had to get ready for their own wedding, which was right after hers.

She wondered if anyone would come from Grady's side. She knew it would mean driving seven hours, so maybe not.

"Don't be nervous," Barbie added and gave her a quick hug before she could leave the room.

Aja tried to say she wasn't nervous, but she couldn't even bring the words to her lips. Her heart was pounding so loud she was certain it would give her away, regardless. "Thanks," she said and lifted her skirt to descend the stairs.

Chapter Nine

Grady's brothers had left their wives at home with the kids, but all four of them were sitting in the front row. Dylan was scowling. He obviously didn't think Grady knew what he was doing. Aaron, the second oldest, was grinning, because he loved that Dylan was disapproving of someone else for a change—since they were closest in age, there'd always been more conflict between them—and Rod and Mack, the two youngest, in that order, just looked nervous for him.

Winnie came into the venue and approached him just before the ceremony was to start to say that Aja had nixed a couple of Persian customs she'd been planning to include. Apparently, his bride didn't want her parents to see the episode on TV later and be upset by it. Winnie also wanted to let him know that she was going to surprise Aja by having Darius be available to not only attend the ceremony, but also to walk her down the aisle and give her away.

"Smart move," he muttered. He could see exactly how

that would play out on TV. Winnie was definitely good at her job.

"You look a little stressed," she told him sheepishly, likely because he would've backed out if he wasn't afraid of ruining her show and she knew it.

"I'm terrified," he admitted, keeping his eye on the closed doors at the back for when his bride would appear.

"It's going to be fine," Winnie assured him. "Aja's lovely, and I know this seems super serious—it has to be for the cameras—but you'll just be getting to know each other. That's no big deal. Think of it like…being roommates for a while."

Really? Maybe he was old-fashioned, too traditional, but to him, marriage was not a commitment he could easily walk away from. Maybe he'd tried to tell himself that in the beginning, when he truly believed it never would have gotten this far.

But there was also a small voice in the back of his head saying chances were good he never would've married had he not done something drastic like this. As much as he'd hoped to find someone, whenever he started getting serious with a woman he was dating, he'd dredge up an excuse not to move forward. The problem hadn't been finding someone. The problem had been the fortress he'd built around his heart. He didn't want to risk losing someone he loved that much, not after losing his mother—didn't want to be destroyed the way his father had been destroyed.

So maybe this—because it allowed him some emotional distance—would be just the thing for someone as damaged as he was.

The music started, and he shot his brothers a nervous glance. Dylan looked as though he was on the verge of getting up to put a stop to the whole thing, but Aaron reached out to keep him in his seat. Dylan was so protective of them all; he always had been, or he wouldn't have done what he'd done at eighteen. But this was Grady's choice. This time, Aaron had the right of it.

Grady cleared his throat. He seemed to be having trouble breathing. He adjusted the bow tie on his black tux, but it didn't make any difference. Then he started to sweat, despite the air-conditioning blasting into the room. He probably would've passed out if they'd made him wait any longer—but, fortunately, the doors at the back of the room were opened with a grand flourish.

The most beautiful woman he'd ever seen stood there looking at him, her eyes riveted on him as if she was looking for some kind of reassurance, without which she'd bolt.

He smiled, willing her to come forward, and was surprised when she responded so readily. Her lips also curved into a smile, and she allowed Darius to lead her down the aisle.

In his peripheral vision, Grady saw his brothers twist around to get their first look at his bride. He couldn't take his eyes off Aja long enough to even glance in their direction but they had to be astonished by her beauty, at least. He felt like it was his steady gaze that centered her and kept her coming toward him.

When she and her brother reached the front, and Darius put Aja's hand in his, Grady felt a strange sense of protectiveness. Her hands were soft, delicate and freezing cold. As his fingers closed around them, he looked down into her eyes…and suddenly felt breathless all over again, but for a much better reason.

This had to be one of the strangest weddings on the planet, he thought. And yet, despite all the reasons it shouldn't have felt right, it seemed like a pretty good start.

When she'd met Grady, Aja hadn't thought he was *overly* attractive. He'd seemed nice—she'd had no specific complaints about his behavior or his appearance. But today he was different. There was a much warmer gleam in his eyes. And his smile seemed far more genuine. It felt almost as if he was seeing her—*really* seeing her—for the first time.

The officiant started the ceremony. He didn't do it strictly in the traditional sense. He spoke about how love could grow out of respect and offered advice on how to build a strong union by putting each other first. He probably said some other valuable things before starting the actual vows, but she wasn't really listening. For a change, she wasn't self-conscious about the filming. Although there were people shifting and moving all around them, and the venue looked like a movie set, what with the lights and cameras just outside their very small circle, she was focused on other things. The warmth and inherent strength of Grady's hands as they held hers, keeping her steady. The quizzical yet hopeful expression on his face. The way his mouth quirked slightly to the side, as if he was oddly happy and tempted to grin, when he said, "I do."

When she was asked if she promised to honor, cherish and sustain Grady, she paused only a moment before she said, "I do."

"Now…you may kiss the bride," the officiant proclaimed.

Somewhere in the back of her mind, Aja knew those who'd be watching the show would be waiting for this moment when two people who barely knew each other would kiss as man and wife. The fear that'd mysteriously left her when Grady caught her eye at the door suddenly returned, reminding her of what a giant step this was, especially with a stranger.

But he didn't do anything that made her want to pull away. Didn't embarrass her, either. She caught a twinkle in his eye before he bent his head and gave her a soft, chaste kiss on the lips.

Relieved that he'd handled it so perfectly, she smiled up at him afterward and got the impression he knew she'd been more terrified in that moment than any other, because he chuckled as he squeezed her hands and said, "Thanks for taking a chance on me."

The show had arranged for each of the couples to have a different type of honeymoon, which would appear to be longer for the sake of the show but would really only last three days. Aja was told Winnie had come up with the varied settings to give each couple a unique environment to interact with.

Fortunately, there were plenty of options in or around LA, which made it more affordable than sending each couple to a faraway destination. Darius and Barbie were going to a penthouse suite at a luxurious downtown hotel. Liz and Neal were traveling to Palm Springs. And Aja and Grady were off to a small beach house right on the ocean near San Diego.

The other couples were expected to leave on their honeymoons right after their wedding, but Aja was allowed to witness Darius and Barbie's vows first. And Winnie told Grady they could also go out to dinner with his brothers while his family was in town, so as soon as their ceremony was over, they hurried to change out of their wedding clothes so they could be ready for both events.

The participants of the show weren't supposed to have much contact with the outside world during filming, and so far, they'd been severely limited. But Aja got the impression Winnie was trying new things to see how both the cast and the audience would react, and given Grady's unusual background, she was betting people would be intrigued by the dynamic of having all five Amos brothers in LA. Although Winnie didn't say it, Aja was willing to bet she also guessed viewers would be interested in seeing how the brothers got on with his new bride and was a bit nervous as they entered Cecconi's, an Italian restaurant in West Hollywood that had fabulous reviews.

"I hope you know what you're getting into," Mack said, giving Aja a playful nudge as they were seated. "This guy might be strong as an ox, but he's also stubborn as a jackass."

"Don't scare her away already," Grady joked with a mock scowl as the others laughed.

Aja grinned. She liked the men. Dylan was a little more morose than the others, but she knew it probably didn't have anything to do with her personally. No doubt he was concerned about his brother making such a "reckless" decision. She could only imagine how her parents would have reacted if they'd been invited to the wedding.

"Marriage isn't easy," Dylan stated unequivocally. "Even when you know and love the person you're marrying." He peered over his menu at Grady, drilling him with a pointed look.

"I know it's not easy," Grady said. "But we're having dinner right now, Dyl. Maybe you can save the lecture until I get home."

Dylan's eyebrows snapped together. Aja could tell he didn't like being shut down, but Grady was right. Why not celebrate while they were happy? It wasn't as if they could change their minds now. That ship had already sailed. Besides, this was being filmed.

Dylan shot a disgruntled glance at the cameraman, who was, fortunately, using an iPhone so they wouldn't make a huge spectacle in the restaurant, and lifted his menu higher, hiding his face.

Grady rolled his eyes at Aja as if to say "don't worry about him," and squeezed her hand under the table.

Aja was wearing a pair of beige wool slacks with a sleeveless sweater of the same color and a brown leather jacket, and she'd left her hair down, just as it had been at the wedding. Grady was wearing chinos and a button-down shirt, like his brothers. The Amos boys weren't exactly on the cutting edge of fashion, but they each were such tall, good-looking men it didn't matter. Grady seemed to be growing more and more handsome to her by the minute. And because he was around his family he seemed much less guarded...and more trusting and fun.

"Dylan, I understand your concerns," she said. "It's a very odd situation, which is why no one from my family was at the wedding. My parents would definitely not approve."

Dylan dropped his menu so she could see his face. "So why did you do it?"

Because of the camera, she couldn't talk as freely as she wanted, but she said, "I was missing something in my life. I guess this was my way of—" she shrugged "—trying to fill that void."

He looked skeptical. "And you think Grady might be the answer?"

"I know the odds aren't in our favor. But the fear of getting caught in the life I was living and not being able to change it if I waited any longer was what drove me here."

He seemed to grow more thoughtful. "You're a dentist, right? Did you grow up wanting to be a dentist?"

She sat back as a waitress passed out glasses of water. "No. It was my parents who really wanted me to be a doctor or a dentist," she said.

"Your parents..." He put his menu on the table. "What would *you* rather be?"

"I've always wanted to open my own ceramics studio. But—" she drew a deep breath "—the odds of financial success with something like that are...very low."

"That doesn't mean you shouldn't do it," Rod pointed out. "My wife also does ceramics. She loves to create."

"She's probably much better than I am. I haven't had

the time to develop my skills," she responded. "It wasn't easy to get into, or through, dental school. Then, of course, I needed to develop a practice and once you start down a certain path, it can be difficult to turn around, especially if you're not even sure you should."

"So do you just let that other dream fade away?" Rod asked.

Turning her attention his way, she smiled. "Maybe?"

Aaron spoke up. "What about your brother? Why do you think *he* wanted to do the show? For the same reasons?"

She couldn't say he was hoping to break into show business on camera, so she said, "I think he'd also prefer a different path."

"So…what types of things do you and Grady have in common?" Dylan asked.

Aja was at a complete loss. "I'm not sure, to be honest. But the psychologists who work for the show did extensive personality testing, so maybe it's the way we view the world more than our individual circumstances, which are, obviously, very different."

Dylan's gaze cut back to Grady. "Damn, she's smart," he said, as if he was impressed in spite of himself and started laughing. "I can't see where the compatibility is coming from—you have completely different backgrounds, completely different cultural experiences, completely different *lives*. But she's as sweet and beautiful as she is smart, so maybe you got lucky, kid."

They all laughed with Dylan, then Aja leaned over to Grady. "Why do *you* think we were paired together?" she asked.

Looking uncomfortable for the first time since he'd changed out of his tux, Grady cleared his throat. "Like you say, the psychologists who work for the show must've seen something deeper, something that isn't obvious at this stage of our relationship," he said. Then he looked away.

Chapter Ten

Grady had been having a great time at dinner—until Aja brought up the psychologists. He'd never dreamed she might've been relying on the personality tests they'd been given to help her find a mate. And he'd gone around those tests, paired her with himself even though the psychologists weren't going to. How could he explain that to her?

Regardless, now was not the time. The marriage was too new, and they had a cameraman in the back seat who'd been assigned to chronicle their honeymoon.

He swallowed a sigh as he navigated to the address where they would spend three days alone together—well, they'd be alone some of the time. They'd been instructed to take a certain amount of selfie footage, which wouldn't be too hard. But they'd also have someone else coming to film periodically. The cameraman who was with them now was supposed to take an Uber home after he documented their reaction to the beach house and to spending their first night together, and Grady couldn't wait for that moment—for the opportunity to be "off the show" for a bit.

"I'm glad we got the beach house and not one of the other options, aren't you?" Aja asked.

They hadn't seen it yet, but it sounded the most appealing to him, too. "I am."

Her lips curved into a faint smile. "Maybe that was one thing the psychologists knew we'd have in common."

Shit. Just when he was getting excited about the possibility of having a relationship with Aja—just when he was beginning to wonder if, maybe, by some weird miracle, this relationship would be just the thing for both of them—he had to face the fact that he'd gotten her to marry him under false pretenses.

He glanced over, trying to read her mood, and saw her cover a yawn with one hand. She was probably exhausted. She'd been quiet since they left the restaurant, but he was fairly certain she'd liked his brothers. She'd loosened up, and talked and laughed more than he'd expected. He could tell his brothers liked her, too—even Dylan.

The beach house was more private than he'd imagined. They had trouble finding it even with GPS. Then they had to leave the car parked on a paved road and carry their luggage down a dirt path at the foot of a cliff, where they finally found the cottage on the beach. He wondered who'd built it, and who owned it now. It looked like an artist's retreat, especially once he let them in and turned on the light. There were paintings, sculptures, photography and mixed media everywhere.

He remembered Aja saying she hoped to open her own ceramics studio one day and decided Winnie, or whoever had picked this particular honeymoon location for them, had nailed it.

"This is spectacular!" Aja gushed as she walked around

and inspected the house. "It's so private and intimate—the perfect place for a honeymoon."

"I can't believe how close we are to the ocean," Grady said. "You can hear the surf."

The cameraman trailed them to the bedroom and leaned in to take a shot. There was only one bed in the whole house. A small kitchen and living-room area that featured a piano and a wall of framed sheet music took up most of the rest of the living space. Other than that, there was only the big bathroom off the bedroom. But the best part of the whole place was the covered deck that looked out toward the sea and had a telescope, as well as a small sofa and chair with pillows and a throw.

"So…what do you think?" Aja asked him.

He thought it was going to be damn uncomfortable to sleep anywhere other than the bed and yet he knew Aja wouldn't be ready for that. The sofa on the porch was the only viable option, but it was more like a love seat, so he wouldn't have room to straighten his legs. It wasn't as if he could sleep on the floor, either. "I like it," he said.

"We can go for a walk on the beach first thing in the morning. Maybe get into the water if it's warm enough. Then we could find a tennis court and play some tennis."

She liked tennis? He didn't remember reading that in her file… "You play?"

"I do. I love it. What about you?"

"I enjoy almost any sport." He felt a measure of relief. Maybe they had a commonality or two, after all. Tennis was something they could build on, wasn't it?

At that point, the conversation faltered. It was late, they were tired, and no one knew what to say or do about the sleeping arrangements. He wasn't even sure there was extra bedding so that he'd have a blanket if he slept on the deck—just that one light throw he'd seen, which was mostly for decorating purposes—and it could get chilly by the ocean, even in Southern California.

He brought her overnight case into the bedroom. The Prada label suggested it'd cost a pretty penny, which once again reminded him of their many differences. She'd been born with a silver spoon in her mouth and had two parents who still doted on her; he'd had no parents for much of his childhood, had known nothing but poverty and hard work, and his father was still more of a liability than an asset.

"Would you like to take a bath or a shower?" he asked.

She looked up in surprise, and he realized she'd thought that maybe he meant *with him* and lifted his hands. "Sorry. I know you don't know me well enough for that. I was just…letting you go first."

The tension in her body eased. "Oh. Thank you."

"As a matter of fact, on second thought, I don't even need to take a shower tonight. So, assuming you won't mind if I steal one of the pillows from the bed, I'm just going to crash on the deck."

She seemed unsure of what to say. "I saw champagne on the coffee table…"

He lifted his eyebrows. "Would you like a glass?"

"If you're not too tired to stay up for a few more minutes."

It was their wedding night. He didn't want to disappoint her; he'd simply suggested going to bed so she wouldn't feel any pressure to act in a way that felt unnatural to her. "I'm happy to stay up a little longer. I'll go pour it."

"Okay, I'll be out in a minute."

"Take your time," he said.

When the door closed, Greg—the cameraman—lowered his voice. "That's promising."

"She's probably just going to the bathroom," Grady responded.

Greg gave him a suggestive look. "Might be a little more than that…"

Grady shook his head. "Sorry to disappoint you, but that isn't happening tonight."

"How do you know?" he challenged.

"Because it's too soon. And because I wouldn't want her to do something she might regret later. So… I'm not hitting her up."

Greg dropped into a chair. "Seriously?"

"Seriously." Grady stepped closer to him so he wouldn't have to talk very loudly. "So…is there any way you'd give us the next few minutes alone?"

He frowned. "I'm guessing Winnie would want me to stay and try to get a bit more footage so viewers can at least see you drifting in that direction."

"We've done all the drifting we're going to do, bro. There's nothing more to capture. I promise."

With a sigh, he came to his feet. "Fine. If you're that determined, you'll just wait until I leave, anyway."

"Exactly." Grady reached into his wallet and handed the guy a hundred-dollar bill. "But thank you for not making it harder than it had to be."

"To…" he prompted.

"Get rid of you," he said and showed him out.

He and Aja were alone. At last. There were no cameras rolling. The biggest decisions had already been made. Now they had three days to relax, unwind and see if they could be happy together…or if they'd just made the biggest mistake of their lives.

Closing his eyes, he drew a deep breath before cracking open the champagne. He'd just walked to the French doors leading out to the deck when he heard the bedroom door open behind him and turned to see his new wife.

She was wearing a silky, black, sliplike dress that fell

to midthigh with no shoes. He didn't think it was lingerie exactly. Or maybe it was. It wasn't transparent or suggestive, but, God, was it sexy.

She had such good taste, he decided. What she had on didn't invite him into her bed tonight. It wasn't that kind of nightgown. But it offered him hope for later, which was exciting enough…

He tried to think of Winnie but couldn't even conjure a good picture of her in his head.

He allowed his gaze to run down Aja's body, and when he finally lifted his eyes, she blushed and glanced away. "I hope that's a good sign," she said with a little laugh.

"You hope what's a good sign?" he asked.

"The way you just looked at me."

"If you're wondering if I want you, I do," he said and handed her a glass.

Her mouth dropped open.

"But tonight's too soon," he added with a wink. "Shall we toast?"

He saw her throat work as she swallowed. "Um…sure."

"I'll go first." He lifted his glass. "To the most beautiful bride I've ever seen."

Her eyes widened as he clinked his glass against hers. "Do you mean it?"

"I wouldn't say it if I didn't mean it," he replied.

"That's nice." She glanced around. "And you couldn't have said it for the sake of the show because there are no cameras. How'd you get Greg to leave?"

He smiled. "I simply suggested it. Well, maybe I strongly suggested it," he added.

She laughed with him. "Good job. And now for my toast… Here's to unusual beginnings—and the hope that this one will lead to something better than we even imagined."

"I'll drink to that," he said.

They each took a sip of champagne. "You're not really going to sleep on the deck, are you?" she asked. "Because I'd feel too guilty taking the only bed. That sofa would be *so* uncomfortable for you."

He gestured around the room. "They haven't given me a lot of options."

"You can sleep on your half of the bed."

"If you'd feel comfortable having me that close…"

"Of course. If I didn't feel I could trust you, I wouldn't have married you."

"Great."

He held out his free hand to take hers. "Let's go sit out on the deck for a few minutes."

Her smile suggested she was pleasantly surprised as she accepted his hand and let him lead her out.

When they relaxed on the sofa, he slipped his arm around her to help ward off the chill wind that was coming in off the ocean while they looked out at the white-crested waves and the glimmer of moonlight on water.

"It's so beautiful here," she said as she put her glass on the table.

He nodded in agreement. Then they fell into a companionable silence. After several minutes, he was about to suggest they go inside and get some sleep when he realized she'd already dozed off.

Chuckling to himself, he set his own glass down then shifted carefully and stood.

"Is it time for bed?" she mumbled, trying to rouse herself.

"It is. But don't worry, I've got you," he replied and lifted her in his arms to carry her inside.

Chapter Eleven

When Aja woke up, she found that she'd gravitated to the warmth in the bed, which just so happened to be Grady's body. She was smashed up against him, but he didn't seem to mind. She could hear his steady breathing, knew he was still asleep. Good. She wanted to have a few moments to herself to think about how it felt to be in the same bed as this man, who was mostly a stranger. Did she regret what she'd done?

That was the big question. Memories of last night filtered through her brain, and she found that she liked Grady. She'd enjoyed his brothers—loved the dry humor between them and the way they mercilessly teased each other. Seeing him in that setting had shown her a lot about her husband. He was funny, wry at times, part of a close family whose bonds had been forged in fire. And he was respectful of her. She didn't think the men she'd met last night would've behaved the way they did if Grady wasn't what he appeared to be, and that gave her some reassurance.

She was also impressed by the way he'd acted about the issue of intimacy. He'd been interested. She could tell by the way he'd looked at her when she came out in the slip-dress she'd purchased for their wedding night. He'd freely admitted it, which had been gratifying. But he hadn't pressed her, hadn't demanded she do anything she was uncomfortable with. That suggested he cared about their union and whether they had a future together.

So…could he be serious about her as a mate? And, if so, was she going to like being his wife?

"You awake?" he mumbled.

She immediately slid away from him so he wouldn't think she was ready for a greater physical connection. "I am. I'm sorry that I—I crowded you last night."

A crooked smile slanted his lips. "Believe me, I didn't mind."

She chuckled as she righted the slip that'd become twisted around her body. "What's our filming schedule today?"

"Greg will be back at nine for breakfast, but it's only seven. Why don't we take that walk on the beach you mentioned last night?"

"That sounds good." She got out of bed and went into the bathroom. She didn't bother with makeup. She just brushed her teeth and pulled her thick hair into a messy bun before putting on some yoga pants and a tank top with flip-flops. She didn't dawdle. She was afraid Greg would show up before they were ready for him and didn't want to miss the chance to go out and see the beauty of an early morning on the beach with her new husband.

"Your turn," she said when she emerged. "I'll put on some coffee."

"Coffee is your first thought? See? We have a lot in

common," he joked, and she grinned as she let him have the bathroom.

He came out a few minutes later in a pair of shorts, an Amos Auto Body T-shirt and flip-flops. "That's your business, right?" she said, indicating the emblem on his shirt.

He nodded.

"Great logo."

"Thanks."

"How do you take your coffee?"

"Black."

"That's easy." She poured it for him and handed him a mug that read The Adventure Begins...

"You found this mug in the cupboard?" he asked. "Because it couldn't be more apropos."

She winked. "I thought you might like it." She'd chosen one for herself that said Life is Better at the Beach.

"I feel like we should have a dog to walk," he said. "Considering all the animal lovers who probably watch the series, I'm surprised the show hasn't provided one."

She laughed but was surprised she'd failed to ask him about pets. They'd had their minds on so many other things... "Do you have a dog at home?"

"Not right now. Had to put my German shepherd down last year and haven't been able to bring myself to get another one. Apollo won't be easy to replace. He went everywhere with me, hung out at the body shop all day while I worked. I even trained him to fetch certain things I needed. He was the smartest dog."

"I'm sorry."

"It's sad they don't live as long as we do. What about you?" he asked as he opened the door to the deck. There was a stairway on one side that went down to the beach. "Do you have a pet?"

"My parents have a corkie I get to see when I go home.

But I haven't gotten a pet of my own quite yet. I'm gone too much, and I don't feel it's appropriate to bring a dog to a dental office."

A gentle breeze ruffled their clothes and hair as they reached the beach. "I can see where that might be a problem."

She sipped her coffee. "It's beautiful out."

His chest lifted as he breathed deeply. "It is. I don't get to see the beach very often."

"What's it like where you live?"

He took her hand as they started to walk, and it made her feel warm and secure and oddly happy, especially because it felt natural—not strained in any way. "Whiskey Creek sprung up during the gold rush in the foothills of the Sierra Nevada mountains," he replied. "It's small and doesn't seem to grow much each year, but it's drawing more and more tourists, thanks to all the wineries that are coming into the region. And it's not far from Sacramento, so if I want something only the big city can provide, I can get it easily enough."

She looked down at the sand as they walked. "How small is small? You told me there are only two thousand people, but it's hard for me to conceptualize that number. Do you have a movie theater? A major grocery store? How many stoplights?"

"No theater. No major grocery store—not a chain, anyway. Just a few antique stores, a bed-and-breakfast, some gift shops, several restaurants, a couple of bars that I've probably visited way too many times over the years, a mansion where they perform weddings, a bike shop, a corner grocer, that sort of thing. Only two stoplights."

"What's your favorite thing to do there?"

"Raise hell, I guess," he replied. "Lord knows I've done enough of it over the years."

"That's ominous." She gave him a dubious look. "What kind of hell?"

"Nothing serious. I'm just messing around."

She stopped, kicked off her flip-flops and picked them up. She wanted to feel the give of the wet sand beneath her feet. "Have you ever been in trouble with the law?"

"Couple of times. For fighting. But that was years ago when we had to fight just to survive. We were going through so much we weren't willing to put up with abuse from anyone, and that probably made us a bit too defensive—although there were plenty of people who tried to get up in our business." He picked up a small seashell and tossed it back into the sea. "And we were probably a little wild to begin with. Does that scare you?"

She liked the endearing expression on his face when he asked that question. She could tell he was just playing with her. "Maybe it would if I hadn't met your brothers. They seem to have turned out all right."

"They've calmed down a lot. Getting married and having kids does that to a man."

"Kids..." she said and stopped walking so she could stand and look out to sea.

He stopped, too. "Are you interested in having a family?"

"I'd like to have children." She glanced over at him. "What about you?"

"Same."

"How many?"

He shrugged. "I don't have a set amount."

"More than one?"

"If that's what...you want," he said awkwardly. She got the impression he'd been about to say "if that's what my wife wants," and then realized she *was* his wife.

She laughed. "It's going to take some time to get used

to the idea of…of being married to each other, let alone having kids together."

"I hope it doesn't take *too* long," he said jokingly. "I'm not getting any younger."

"You turn forty this year?"

"Yep. I'll soon be an old man."

She waded into the water, letting the surf foam up around her ankles before turning back to face him. "I'm not getting any younger, either, which means we shouldn't wait too long."

Their eyes met briefly before they both looked away.

"Do you think Whiskey Creek would be a good place to raise a family?" she asked.

"If I had my choice, it'd be there."

"You love it that much."

"I do."

"But…"

He shaded his eyes. "It's not only up to me, right?"

She tried to imagine leaving LA—her parents and her brother. That would be hard. And what about her practice? She supposed she could sell it and start over in Whiskey Creek. But that would also be hard. She wondered why the show hadn't paired her with someone in Los Angeles. There were millions of people in Southern California, most of whom were trying to get on TV or in a movie. They should've had more than enough to choose from.

And yet…maybe it wouldn't have been the same with anyone else; maybe she wouldn't have made it this far. "Have you ever been engaged?" she asked.

"I've gotten close to an engagement but never actually popped the question…before you."

"Why do you think that's the case?"

"The way I lost my mother, I guess. I don't want to love anyone quite that much."

"And *this* particular marriage didn't require love."

He didn't respond to her comment. They stood in silence for a few minutes, letting what had been said settle into their minds. Then he asked, "What about you? Have you ever been engaged?"

"No. But… I just broke off a long-term relationship that was definitely heading in that direction."

"Where did you meet him? Online?"

"I've known him most my life. His parents and my parents are best friends."

"Oh, damn. I can't imagine that went over very well."

"It didn't. I feel bad for putting my parents in the position they're in, but I couldn't go through with it. I didn't want to follow the script my parents have laid out for me, become just like them, if that makes sense."

"They're not happy?"

"Happy enough, I guess. But… I want something different, something of my own choosing."

"Because they've chosen everything else for you."

"Something like that."

"Is that why you came on the show? Was it some…big rebellion?"

"I came on because Darius really wanted to do it, and they wouldn't take him without me. But defiance might've played a small role. Maybe desperation, too. I felt the clock was ticking and yet… I couldn't find what I was looking for."

Grady picked up a seashell, rubbed the sand from it and presented it to her. "What're they going to say when they learn about me?"

She studied the grooves of the shell and the touch of pink on the underside. "They won't be happy."

"And your brother has done the same thing…"

"Yeah," she said with a wince.

"Oh, boy."

She gave him a sheepish look. "I hope you'll be patient with them. They—they mean well. They just...think we'll mess up our lives if they let us make our own choices."

She came out of the waves and put her flip-flops back on. "It's just one more challenge we'll have to deal with..." Then she offered him her hand, and he surprised her by smiling as he took it.

"We'll figure it out," he said.

"Will we?" She peered closely at him. "How badly do you want this to work?"

He studied her for several seconds. "More by the minute," he said, and she couldn't help grinning at his response. She thought he might kiss her. They hadn't really kissed yet and she was beginning to wonder what it might be like to feel his lips against hers in a kiss that contained more passion than restraint, more desire than politeness... and was surprised to find it left her slightly breathless.

"What is it?" he asked.

She lowered her gaze for fear he'd be able to read what she was thinking and feeling if she didn't. "Nothing. We'd better get back. Greg will be there looking for us."

Greg was obviously eager to see how they were getting along after spending the night together. When Grady let him in, he grinned meaningfully and looked from one to the other as if they might betray the fact that last night had involved more than just sleeping.

When they merely exchanged a glance, it must not have told him much, so he went to the deck, most likely looking for a pillow or blanket on the sofa. When he didn't find either of those things, he returned with a frown but began to film before actually asking.

"So...where'd you sleep last night?" He often prompted

them by asking questions to start a conversation, but some or all of his part would be cut during editing, leaving the two of them talking about the subject he'd introduced.

"I slept in the only bed there is but nothing happened," Grady said.

"Then how'd it go?" he asked Aja.

Grady loved the innocent yet sexy smile she shot him. She had a way of being warm and friendly *and* just slightly out of reach, creating a challenge he was hoping to conquer. "It was fine, comfortable. I liked having him there."

"No civil unrest the first night?" Greg asked, as if he was teasing them, and he sort of was. It was his job to get some good footage, and the sooner he had what he needed, the sooner he'd leave. He wasn't supposed to stay all day, so Grady tried to open up a bit more, which wasn't easy because "open" didn't come naturally to him. "It's been peaceful, relaxing."

Fortunately, Aja chimed in almost immediately. "I thought maybe it would be too awkward getting into bed with a virtual stranger," she said. "I mean… I know this type of thing happens on a regular basis in the lives of some people. One-night stands are a thing. But they've never been part of *my* life, so I admit I was nervous. I want my mate to be sexually attracted to me, but I also want to know who he is before we… Before we take the physical aspect of our relationship that far."

"Bottom line, we're still just getting to know each other," Grady said. "This morning we got up and went for a walk on the beach, and it was nice to have the time to talk without anyone to overhear."

"What'd you talk about?" Greg asked.

"Our romantic histories, our families and some other stuff," Grady replied.

Greg came forward to get a close-up. "Aja's parents won't approve, right?"

"No," Grady said. "And it'll be a difficult thing when they find out—for them because of the shock and disappointment, and for me if they reject me."

"And since Darius is also on the show," Aja added. "It'll make things doubly difficult for them...and probably for us, too."

Greg shifted to change his shot again. "Do you have exes who might cause problems in the future?"

"I just broke up with my boyfriend before coming on the show," Aja said.

"Why'd you break up?"

"He asked me to marry him, but I found it necessary to say no, and I didn't feel it would be wise to stay together after that. He definitely won't understand why I would then go and do something like this. But...marrying him wasn't right. I knew that much."

Greg turned to Grady. "And have you heard anything from your brothers? What did they think of your new bride?"

"I think they loved her."

"Even the one who raised you and sat there glowering through the wedding? His name is Dylan, right?"

"Dyl's definitely not pleased with me marrying someone I don't really know, but I think Aja won him over."

Aja took the seashell they'd found on the beach from the pocket of her yoga pants and showed Greg and the camera. "Grady found this while we were out walking on the beach this morning and gave it to me. I consider it a symbol of hope—that we can find happiness together. Maybe we'll even return here in ten, twenty or thirty years to celebrate our anniversary."

"I would love to see that happen." Greg handed it back to her. "Have you given any thought to where you'll live?"

"I'm surprised the psychologists would pair two people who both have jobs that aren't friendly to relocation," Aja said. "But they must've seen something in our personality tests that made them feel we'd be perfect for each other despite that obstacle," she added quickly, which made Grady squirm.

"It'll definitely require one of you to make a sacrifice," Greg concurred.

"I guess I could sell my practice and start over in Whiskey Creek…" she mused.

"Or I'll have to open a franchise of Amos Auto Body in LA," Grady said. "But we don't want to get ahead of ourselves. Before we make any decisions, I think we should spend some time in Whiskey Creek to see how Aja likes it. Then we should spend some time here to see how I like it and decide from there."

"Sounds logical to me," Greg said. "What're your plans for the day?"

Aja talked about going to breakfast and playing tennis. Grady added he'd like to take Aja out on a sunset catamaran cruise. Then, seemingly satisfied, Greg lowered the camera. "Great job, guys."

"Do you know how my brother is doing?" Aja asked.

"Not yet," Greg told her. "JJ's over there filming them now."

"Are you worried about him?" Grady asked.

"A little," she admitted. "Not only is he younger than I am, he's more reckless by nature. But Barbie seems like a nice person. I really like her, so that provides me with a little peace of mind."

"Can you bring her some word when you come back this evening?" Grady asked Greg as he showed him to the door.

"Sure." Greg stepped onto the front stoop. "I'll text JJ now."

"Thanks." Grady was about to close the door when Greg caught his attention by pressing a finger to his lips to signal silence before handing him a small, sealed envelope.

Grady blinked in surprise. Why would the cameraman pass him something he wasn't also giving to Aja? He arched his eyebrows—silently asking that question—and Greg whispered, "Winnie told me to give it to you and not let Aja see me do it."

Perplexed, Grady slipped the envelope into the pocket of his shorts and nodded. But he felt apprehensive. He didn't want Aja to find out about his previous interest in Winnie, didn't want it to hurt her in some way, and couldn't help being a little nervous about what might be in the letter.

Chapter Twelve

Aja heard from Darius that afternoon while she and Grady were getting ready to go on their sailboat tour. They'd spent the day playing tennis and had so much fun they'd stayed at the court for hours, then stopped for ice cream on the way home. Then she'd showered and put on her swimsuit under a pair of cutoffs and a white tank, and now she was waiting for Grady to shower.

So? How's it going? her brother began.

Finally, you text me!

What do you mean? Did I miss a text from you?

No. She'd been hesitant to send anything after what'd happened with their last conversation. But there was far less chance of the same thing occurring again. Right now, they had more autonomy.

Grady asked a cameraman to check on you.

That's why I'm reaching out. I guess you've been worried about me.

Just wanted to be sure you're happy.

I'm fine. Everything's pretty new with Barbie, so I don't know what will happen in the future, but she seems like a nice person.

A nice person? That sounded rather apathetic. Aja was beginning to worry about things she hadn't really considered when she let her brother talk her into being on the show. What if he wasn't truly open to loving Barbie? What if he'd only married her because it was best for the career he coveted?

What'd you two do today?

She wanted to go to Disneyland.

Barbie had grown up in Nebraska and had come to Los Angeles to attend film school; she desperately wanted to work in the movie industry.

Did you have fun?

It wasn't what I would've picked. There's not much to do without kids, IMO. But you and I have been there almost every year since we were little, so it was probably a different experience for her.

Aja hesitated but was concerned enough about her new friend to say a bit more. Are you serious about Barbie? You're not just doing this for the show, are you?

Jury's still out. What about you?

She'd never been in it for the sake of the show. But she couldn't say that her future was any more certain.

You and I were wrong to do this, Darius. We could break someone's heart.

Or we could get our own hearts broken, right? We all knew the risks when we signed on. I'm not going to feel obligated to make a decision that isn't right for me.

She frowned as she read his response. He had a point. They'd all made the dangerous decision to get involved in this experiment.

So I risked my heart for *you* to get into showbiz?

I don't think you really believed you'd fall in love, did you? Even with as long as you dated Arman, you didn't want to marry him.

And he'd been perfect for her in every way. From the outside. There just hadn't been any...magic.

Don't tell me it's different with Grady.

She didn't know. There were so many reasons they shouldn't "work." And yet... She was enjoying him, certainly wasn't ready to call it quits. That said something, didn't it?

I don't know yet. One day at a time, right?

That's the way to approach it.

Grady came out of the bedroom. "All set?"

I've got to go, she texted her brother. Be sure to delete this conversation.

What conversation?

Rolling her eyes, she shook her head. *Very funny.*

"What is it?" Grady asked as she got up.

"I just heard from my brother."

"And?"

"He and Barbie seem to be getting along okay for now."

"I wonder how many couples will survive their first year."

"So do I," she said. And would she and Grady, or Darius and Barbie, be one of them?

It was getting late when they got back from the sailboat tour. Greg was with them, filming the second night of their honeymoon—and obviously trying to get something that would suggest they'd sleep together tonight—when Grady excused himself to go to the bathroom. He needed a break. Being on the show was wearing on him. He hated how awkward and difficult it was to get to know Aja while navigating the show's demands.

As he came back through the bedroom, he listened to Greg quizzing Aja about their day.

"Do you feel you two are getting to know each other?… Which part of the honeymoon have you enjoyed most so far?… Are you looking forward to tonight?"

As she did her best to answer those questions, Grady tried to psych himself up enough to go back out there. But that was when he remembered the note Greg had handed him earlier. Since Aja had been waiting for him at the time, he hadn't read it. He'd stuck it in his suitcase because he didn't want it falling out of his pocket while they were playing tennis. Then, in their hurry to make the sailboat tour, he'd forgotten about it.

He glanced at his watch. If he made it quick, he could read it without seeming to be gone too long. After retrieving the note, he went back into the bathroom, and closed and locked the door.

The card had a fancy *W* on the front. Inside would've been blank had she not written there.

Dear Grady,
I don't dare send anything to your phone in case Aja is with you when it comes in. But I wanted to let you know that I'm grateful for all you've done to help me with the show. I know this isn't something you'd typically get involved in, which makes me appreciate it all the more.

I loved meeting your brothers, by the way. They're tall, strong and handsome—just like you. All five of you seem to have overcome a challenging past, and I find that absolutely inspiring.

I mostly just wanted to encourage you. The show won't last forever. Then…who knows what will happen? I desperately want *Tying the Knot* to be a success. But I've never been attracted to one of my "grooms" before, and that leaves me torn when it comes to you.

We'll see what fate has in store for us, I guess…
XO Winnie
P.S. If you ever need to talk, and you can get away alone, here's where you can find my house.

He stared at the Hollywood address she'd given him. Did she think he might show up at her place one night while he was married to Aja?

He got the impression she wouldn't mind, that she was giving him the option for a reason. At the very least, this note was an attempt to let him know she was more interested than she might've made it sound before. Maybe she was having second thoughts about encouraging him to go ahead with the wedding...

He'd been so infatuated with her—infatuated enough to do something that was *completely* unlike him. And now? He wasn't sure why he'd wanted her quite so badly. Because when he closed his eyes and imagined the woman he couldn't wait to make love to, it was Aja—with her sweet, beguiling smile—that appeared in his mind. He could barely remember the details of Winnie's face.

He tore up her note and flushed the pieces down the toilet. Then he forced himself to join his wife and Greg in the living room. "You about ready to leave?" he asked jokingly to the cameraman, "because there's no room here for you to sleep, and I'm exhausted."

"I was just wrapping things up for the night. What do you two have planned for tomorrow?"

"More tennis," Grady said. "She beat me too many times today, and I'm too competitive to let that stand."

"And then we might body-surf and lie on the beach," Aja added. "Since we've both had very little time off in the past few years—well, since we can remember—we're planning to make the most of the downtime."

Except they'd still be working...for the show. Grady wished he could have just one day alone with Aja...

"Sounds fun. I'll get out of here." Greg stood but he was still filming, which became clear when he pointed the camera right at Grady's face. "How attracted are you to your wife?" he asked point-blank.

"I'm *very* attracted," he replied. "She's gorgeous."

"Which means…you might take things a step further tonight?"

He shook his head. "Not until she's ready."

He lowered the camera. "The crew has been placing bets," he informed them as he started to pack up. "They think you two will be last to consummate the marriage."

"Why's that?" Grady asked.

"Because Neal and Liz already have," he said with a laugh. "That just leaves you two and Darius and Barbie, and with them, it's Darius who's holding out."

Grady saw a worried expression pass over Aja's face. "You might be right," he said. "We're giving it time."

"Are there also bets on whose marriage will last the longest?" Aja asked.

Greg glanced over at her. "Of course."

"And?" she prompted.

He winced. "On that one…you're not last—you're first."

She stood, too. "Why?"

"Because no one can see what you have in common. How are you going to overcome having such different pasts? The anger you're going to get from her parents when they find out? And who's going to give in and move to a different place to be with the other? No one sees that happening, least of all Winnie."

"Winnie?" Grady repeated.

"Yeah. She told me she doesn't see where you two stand much of a chance, but she admires you both for trying to make it work."

Grady didn't say so, but he was beginning to believe if they stayed on the show, they *wouldn't* be able to make it work. They had enough challenges to overcome; they didn't need the unnatural intrusion of the public and the cameras—and all the stress that created—making things more difficult.

He walked Greg to the door and thanked him. The guy was only doing his job. But in the silence that followed the cameraman's departure, Grady turned to Aja and said, "How would you feel about quitting the show?"

"So…you really want to break our contracts?" Aja sat across the coffee table from her new husband. When she'd realized he was serious about leaving *Tying the Knot*, she'd asked for a few minutes to change into her nightgown and pour them each a glass of wine before they discussed it.

"I do," he said, as if he was growing more convinced of it by the moment.

She felt her eyes widen. "Since when?"

He spread his hands. "Since today, I guess."

"Then you obviously didn't come on the show for the opportunities it could provide…"

He raked his fingers through his hair. "No. Did you? Because if that's the case, I'll stay."

She could tell he meant it, which showed he wasn't only thinking of himself. She'd been looking for warning signs, traits and characteristics, not to like in Grady. If there was something wrong with him, she wanted to find out early so she could get out of the marriage before the show even aired. "I have no plans of—of going on TV for anything else. In case you haven't been able to tell, I'm an introvert."

"I've been able to tell," he said with a wry chuckle, "which is part of the reason I'm even suggesting this. If I thought it was what you really wanted, I wouldn't ask you to leave."

She tucked her legs underneath her and pulled a throw blanket over her lap. "I appreciate that, but the way our contracts read, quitting will cost us some money. And not a small amount."

"I'll pay the fine for both of us. It'd be worth it to me."

That such a loss wasn't a concern for him suggested he had plenty of money. His business had to be successful. "You want out that badly?" She took a sip of wine. "Can I ask why you've suddenly changed your mind?"

"Because I have this terrible feeling that…"

When he didn't finish, she leaned forward. "That…"

"That staying on the show will ruin anything we could have," he finally said.

She sat up straight. He was doing it for the sake of their marriage? Early on, she'd gotten the impression he didn't truly believe the show would result in a long-term relationship.

He was turning out to be so different than what she'd anticipated—better, which both excited her and left her feeling vulnerable at the same time. What if she truly fell in love with him? What if she wanted their marriage to continue, but *he* decided he wanted out? "Can you give me a little more?" she asked. "What makes you think so?"

"The constant intrusions," he responded with a gesture that suggested irritation. "The unnaturalness of all the stuff we have to do. The public scrutiny we'll endure once the show airs."

"Won't we still have to face that? They'll use the parts we've already filmed…"

"It won't be as bad if we quit early. The focus will be on the couples who stay, not the ones who wash out."

"Even if we're still together?"

"If we can make it as a couple—if we're happy enough to want to stick together—that'd be a good thing, right? I'd like to give us the chance to get to that point and feel our odds are better outside the show than in it."

"I see. But how will they get by without us? I don't want to ruin it for my brother and Barbie."

"We've gone far enough, what with the wedding and

sharing part of our honeymoon. That footage should get them fairly deep into the season. We could even offer to send them more footage—selfie footage—from Whiskey Creek if they need it. At least then it'll be on *our* terms. We won't have a schedule to follow, or a cameraman showing up to say provocative things, hoping to film an argument or get us to discuss our sex lives, or the problems we have with various family members."

There was a lot to that statement, but one thing stood out above the rest. "You want to go to Whiskey Creek?"

"Why not?" he replied. "You've already arranged to have the next few weeks off work, right? I'd like you to see my hometown—to determine whether you could be happy there. Leaving LA also puts some distance between us and the production team. If we're seven hours away, they'd be much less likely to show up with a camera at our doorstep or talk us into doing more than we want to do at this point. And maybe…if they leave us alone for a few days, we might even be willing to come back for more filming later. I'm just…done with being a puppet. I want to feel like a normal human being again."

So did she. But once she decided to marry Grady, she'd assumed they'd finish the season.

"You want to stay in," he said, guessing when she hesitated.

"I don't," she admitted. "I've never been that excited about it. I just… I want to be sure we're not letting the others down."

"Our leaving won't hurt anyone. You came on the show for Darius, but they aren't going to kick him off now. They need him too badly."

"True, but we've come this far. Are you sure you don't want to see it through?"

"I would if I thought…" He huffed out a sigh. "I just want to take you home," he said.

His words made her happy, but if she went with him, she'd be giving him a certain amount of control over her life, and she didn't know him very well. Would she ultimately regret making such a decision?

Tough to say. But even if they stayed on the show, she'd have to figure out, at some point, whether she wanted their marriage to continue. Leaving would probably help her make that decision a lot sooner.

"Okay," she said.

He seemed surprised by her response…and eager to clarify. "Okay…what?"

"We'll quit the show and go to Whiskey Creek."

Chapter Thirteen

Winnie looked stricken. "What do you mean you're quitting? You told me... We agreed..."

Grady stood at the window of her office with his hands shoved into his pockets as she searched for the right words to convey her outrage. After his discussion with Aja last night, he'd gotten up early and texted Winnie to request a meeting before filming started, so the sun was barely peeking over the row of high-rises that made a canyon of the street far below. "I know what we agreed. But staying on the show will put too much stress on my marriage."

"You've got to be kidding me. Your marriage isn't real," she said. "I mean...technically it is, but it's more of an—an experiment for others to watch. You barely know Aja. You picked her instead of the women our psychologists felt were better suited to you. And now you want to protect that relationship by leaving the show?"

He turned to face her. "I knew this would be disappointing to you. But you were the one who encouraged me to proceed, who told me to give it my best. You said if it works out, great. If it doesn't, then…" He glanced away. "Well, we both know what we thought would happen then. But I've since realized that none of that is fair to Aja. I can't give our marriage my best effort if I'm thinking about you the whole time. That is inherently dishonest. And it gives me an escape hatch she doesn't have, a reason to bail out if she does the slightest thing wrong."

A muscle moved in her cheek. "Great time to grow a conscience," she growled.

"I didn't think coming on the show was a matter of conscience, didn't see where I was doing anything wrong. But it certainly feels like I'm doing something wrong now, which is why I'm trying to fix it."

"What about the cost of canceling?" she demanded. "It'll be expen—"

"Whatever it is, I'll cover it," he interrupted. It would be worth it to be able to ease his conscience.

"And you don't care about me or the show? How we'll get through the rest of the season?"

"Of course I care. Aja and I will provide you with the footage you need. It'll just happen a little differently, on our terms instead of yours. But who knows? That might go over even better with the audience. And it'll be free."

She shook her head. "I've never had a cast member do this."

"We both know I'm not your typical cast member. You understood what was motivating me going in. But the good news is that Aja and I don't want to let anyone down, so we're willing to help you in whatever ways we can."

"Staying would help me," she pointed out.

"Other than that," he clarified.

Tears filled her eyes, which made him squirm. He didn't

know if she was crying because them leaving would hurt the show, and therefore its chances of success, or if she was truly interested in him. "I don't know what to say," she said.

He cleared his throat. "I feel terrible. I'm sorry."

Suddenly all business, she sniffed, blinked away her tears and stood. "It's fine. No problem. Since you're leaving early, we won't pay you for the time you've been on the show, but we won't charge you the penalty, either, as long as you give us enough access and video footage to finish the season."

He spread his hands. "I've already agreed to do that."

"You also agreed to other things and are now going back on your word," she pointed out curtly.

"And you know why!" he argued. "I screwed up in the beginning by—by doing what I did. I feel this is the only way to fix that—to give Aja the serious and honest attempt she deserves."

"But the marriage isn't going to work, anyway!" she said, obviously exasperated. "You're ruining my show—and any chance you and I might've had at a relationship when it's over—for nothing!"

"How do you know my marriage won't work?" he asked.

"What are the odds?" she demanded, coming right back at him. "You didn't even follow the show's protocols!"

"Exactly why I'm taking matters into my own hands. I'm trying to make up for that!"

Lifting her chin, she glared at him. "You've decided, then. I can't change your mind?"

He thought of Aja, how she'd cuddled up to him in bed last night. He'd wanted to slip his hand under that silky nightgown she was wearing, touch her, kiss her...

He'd held off, but it hadn't been easy. He'd lain awake long after she fell asleep, thinking about her and how crazy it was that they were actually married. There shouldn't be anything special between them—they barely knew each other and had nothing in common—and yet there was a small flame. If he didn't protect it and fan it, help it to grow, it would go out. In his mind, *that* would be the real tragedy.

"I'm afraid so," he said. "But I'll try to make it up to you."

"I'm not sure that's possible." She consulted her watch. "But I'll deal with it. Now, if that's all, I have to rush off or I'm going to be late. I'm meeting the crew to give them their instructions for the day."

He watched her cross the room as if she'd walk out and leave him there by himself. "So… Aja and I can pack up and leave?"

"If you're quitting, I guess that's up to you." She turned to face him as she reached the door. "But we've paid for the beach house through tomorrow. The least you could do is try to enjoy it and let us finish filming your 'honeymoon.'"

With a sigh, he scratched the back of his neck. "Fine. We'll do that much."

The next two days were some of the most enjoyable Aja could remember. In the past, she'd always had school or work on her mind—something she needed to get done. But she'd checked in with her office twice. All was surprisingly quiet. And she hadn't even heard from her parents. According to some pictures she'd seen posted on Arman's Instagram account, they'd gone to Palm Springs with Arman and his parents. They were all probably mad at her—and maybe even strategizing on how to get her back into a relationship with him—but she was trying not to think about that. At least for the moment they were giving her some space, so she didn't have to talk to them and insist she was having a great time on her trip to Europe with Darius. She felt guilty about lying in the first place, knew how angry they were going to be when they learned the truth.

"You got everything?"

She looked up from where she'd been packing the rest of her clothes in the suitcase on the bed when Grady came back into the cottage after taking their first load out to the car provided to them by the show for their honeymoon. "Just about," she replied and finished stuffing her makeup bag into one side of the suitcase before zipping it closed.

"I'll get that for you," he said as she started to grab the handle.

As she stood back so he could reach it, she couldn't help smiling at him. They hadn't even kissed since the wedding—had spent nothing but chaste nights together in their honeymoon bed—but she was beginning to wish he'd do something to change that. Or maybe *she* would. Grady smelled *so* good to her. And having his warm body in her bed at the end of each day was something she was beginning to look forward to. She'd slept with Arman on and off for years, of course, depending on what they each had going, and yet…it'd never felt quite so exciting.

Grady's gaze briefly lowered to her mouth, making her feel as though he was having similar thoughts. But then he grinned. "Should we go get something to eat? Celebrate the fact that we're about to reclaim our freedom?"

"Sure. I'd love to get a slice of quiche or something. What are you in the mood for?"

"I'm easy to please. If it's food, I'll eat it. Why don't you choose the restaurant?"

"There are so many I'd like to show you in LA…"

"That's one benefit of a big city, I guess." He gave her a

worried look. "You won't have that many to choose from in Whiskey Creek…"

She laughed. "I don't live for eating out. I actually like to cook. I just haven't had the opportunity here."

"I didn't realize that," he said.

Resting a hand on her hip, she cocked one leg while she gave him a saucy look. "There's a lot you don't know about me."

His gaze moved down over her. "I'm looking forward to learning more."

"You're sure taking your sweet time," she said.

His eyebrows shot up. "I've been trying to wait until you're comfortable. But now you're asking for trouble."

She stepped back and put up her hands. "Okay. Maybe I went too far."

"That's what I thought," he said with an exaggerated wink and headed out with the suitcase.

She chuckled as she followed behind him. "Do your brothers know we're coming?"

"No," he said, looking back at her. "I thought it would be fun to surprise them."

Whiskey Creek looked as though it hailed from a different era. Wooden boardwalks lined the main drag that snaked through the small cluster of buildings constituting downtown. She liked seeing all the reminders of the town's past, including the small park with its gold-panning statue and the darling Victorian B&B they passed, not to mention the beautiful old mansion that was now used to host weddings.

"Where does this road go?" she asked as the buildings quickly gave way to raw land.

"There's another Gold Country town, not too different from this one, about fifteen miles away," Grady told her.

They'd turned in the car the show had rented for them and were now in his truck.

"Are there a lot of such towns?"

"Quite a few, sprinkled throughout the foothills." He lowered the volume of the music they'd been listening to. The drive had been long—seven hours—and yet they'd talked the whole time about myriad subjects, including how Winnie had reacted to them quitting, what they'd try to do to make it up to her, his brothers and their wives and children…and his father, who was someone else she'd meet. "Does this place seem too…claustrophobic for you?" he asked, watching her closely. "Too rural?"

She studied the buildings as they passed them again going the opposite direction, until he stopped at one of the lights and turned right. A lot seemed to hang on her answer, but she wanted to be honest. "I'm not sure. It's definitely a cute town… Where's your business?"

"That's where I'm taking you now."

She knew he was hungry. They'd talked about where they'd grab dinner when they arrived. But he seemed so excited to show her around; that was taking precedent at the moment.

Two blocks off Sutter Street, where there weren't many businesses at all—just a few houses in among the dirt roads, trees and shrubs—he turned into Amos Auto Body.

"Here we are," he said. "Would you like to see the inside or wait until another time?"

She could tell he was eager to show her, so she said she'd love to see it all now, and he hopped out. "You don't lack for work," she said as she looked over at a large, fenced yard filled with vehicles that needed repair.

"Fortunately, that's true. We have a pretty good reputation in these parts. People come from all around," he said, then walked her inside and through numerous paint stalls and repair bays in the back part of the building .

"What're your hours?" she asked as they came out.

"Eight to five every day except Sunday."

She stopped walking. "You work six days a week?"

"Until now, I haven't had a reason not to. My brothers all have wives and children, so more demands on their time."

"Meaning you've been picking up the slack."

He shrugged. "Keeps the business running smoothly. But now that I have... Well, if we have kids..." He didn't seem to know how to finish either of those statements. "I'll be reasonable with my hours moving forward," he said instead. "What's your schedule like?"

"Typically, I work Tuesday through Saturday. I'd rather work Monday through Friday, but that can make it hard for some of my patients to get their teeth fixed. At some point I hope to go down to every other Saturday, at least."

"That'd be nice."

He showed her the store, with its counter area, vending machines and vinyl chairs in the small lobby. Then he locked up and they returned to the front yard. "Do you want to continue to work even after you have kids?" he asked.

"As a dentist?" she clarified. "If I need to."

"What if you *don't* need to?"

"If I have the luxury of going either way, I'd—"

"Have a ceramics studio," he said, finishing her thought.

"Exactly."

He opened the truck door for her. "What about your education? You'd let all that go if you could?"

She grimaced in uncertainty. "It probably wouldn't be wise. It required so much work and effort. But it wasn't what I wanted to do in the first place. And we're just dreaming here, anyway, so...yeah, I guess I would."

Cocking his head, he studied her as he raised a finger to trace her jawline. "Most of my brothers' wives don't work. As far as I'm concerned, you'd have your choice," he said and closed her door.

Aja wasn't looking for anyone else to take care of her. But Grady's self-assured manner—his confidence that he could carry the load—was almost as appealing as his generosity.

She smiled as he climbed into the driver's side and as soon as he started the car, she took his hand.

"What?" he said as she watched him.

"I really like you," she replied, and although it wasn't the most romantic place he could've picked for their first kiss, when he leaned over to press his lips to hers, it was so natural she sighed and kissed him back.

Chapter Fourteen

Grady hadn't planned on kissing Aja in that moment. He'd wanted to wait for the right time and the right place. But it'd happened spontaneously, probably because he'd been thinking so much about it.

She parted her lips, allowing his tongue access to hers, and a tidal wave of desire slammed into him. The memories of her lying next to him in bed the past few nights flooded his brain, making him want her even more. He craved the feel of her breasts in his palms, his mouth on her neck, or anywhere else on her body, and her legs wrapped around his hips as he moved inside her.

This was nothing like what he'd expected—he was falling for his wife.

Suddenly, a pair of headlights hit them. Surprised, since it was well after closing time, he pulled back and watched a man get out of a truck and approach them.

"Shit. It's my dad," he muttered and lowered his window.

JT scowled as he reached the driver's side and craned his neck to see around Grady. "That's her?"

Grady ignored the question. It wasn't a very polite way to greet Aja—his dad was a little rough around the edges. "What are you doing here?"

"Thought maybe I forgot to lock up. Came back to check."

"*You* closed for the day?"

"Dylan had kids' stuff. And don't act so shocked. I'm the one who started this business, damn it. I used to close all the time, back when I was still wiping your snotty nose."

That was before he'd lost all of Grady's trust. But JT was doing much better these days. Once he'd finally been pushed into rehab and had been convinced to make changes.

"Door was locked when we arrived."

"Just wanted to be sure."

"I appreciate that."

His father tried to look around him again. "Aren't you going to introduce me to my new daughter-in-law?"

Grady leaned back so that Aja and JT could see each other. "Dad, this is Aja Kermani. Aja, this is JT, my dad."

"Nice to meet you," she said.

He scowled. "What is she? Middle Eastern?"

"She's sitting right here, Dad. Don't talk about her in the third person," Grady said, but Aja spoke at the same time.

"I'm Persian," she told him. "My parents immigrated from Iran, but I was born here."

"No one mentioned anything about that," he said.

"Because it doesn't matter," Grady told him.

JT spread his hands. "I was just surprised, okay? And isn't her name Aja *Amos* now?"

He and Aja hadn't even talked about whether she'd take his name, eventually. That seemed like a discussion for later, after the experiment was over and they decided if they were going to stay together. "That remains to be seen."

"So why aren't you in LA? I thought you'd be filming the entire month," his father said.

"We decided we didn't really like being on camera."

"You quit?"

"Not entirely. We just…negotiated better terms."

"What does that mean?"

"It means we're going to be here for a few days, at least." Grady attempted to change the subject. "Where's Anya?" His father had always had an explosive relationship with his on-and-off-again romantic partner, so he was afraid they'd had yet another argument when he didn't see her with him.

"She works at the bookstore, remember?"

"I didn't think the bookstore was open this late."

"It's the owner's birthday. They're throwing a party for her after hours."

So she hadn't moved out while Grady was gone. That was a good thing, because his father was coming to depend on her.

"That's nice." Grady turned to explain whom he was talking about to Aja. He hadn't even mentioned that his father was with someone. As a general rule, he avoided talking about JT whenever possible. "Anya's my father's ex-wife, but they're back together." He didn't add "for now," even though, in the past, Anya and JT had split up too many times to count. But now that they were both clean and sober, Grady was beginning to believe they might actually make it. And for the first time in his life, he was starting to like Anya.

"Why don't you two follow me over to the house?" JT asked. "Anya should be home soon, and she'd love to meet Aja. She's crazy about *Tying the Knot*. She's watched both the other seasons and can't wait until it airs with you two on it."

"We'll come by sometime this week," Grady said. "We haven't had dinner yet, and Aja hasn't seen the house. Give us a chance to get settled in. Then we'll make the rounds."

JT wasn't happy with this response. Grady had known he wouldn't be. He needed a lot of time and attention. Grady was usually okay with trying to make sure he got what he needed, but he wanted to be alone with Aja tonight. "We're still on our honeymoon," he explained.

"Oh, right. Dylan told me you went through with the wedding. That, in itself, is unbelievable, especially for you."

Afraid that JT was going to wander into uncomfortable territory, Grady lifted a hand. "Dad, that's enough."

JT leaned in to make sure he had Aja's full attention... but, fortunately, changed the subject. "You married a good man," he said. "My boys make excellent husbands." He hesitated briefly, then added, "I used to be an excellent husband myself once."

"Which is where we got it from." JT hadn't been "excellent" for long, but Grady was saying what he could, hoping this conversation wasn't about to unravel.

Seemingly gratified, his father addressed Aja again. "Dylan said you're a dentist in LA."

She smiled. "I am."

"How are you two going to handle the fact that you own businesses in two different parts of the state?"

"We haven't decided," Grady responded quickly to save her the trouble of coming up with an answer.

A skeptical expression claimed JT's face. "I don't see how you're going to make that work."

Grady cleared his throat. "You don't need to worry about it. Aja and I will figure things out between us."

"I can't help but worry," he said. "We need you around here."

Grady and his brothers had needed a father, too, when they were kids. But JT had let them down. "Aja and I are going to go eat, Dad. I'll talk to you later."

JT nodded and backed away, but only because Grady put the truck in Reverse, signaling that he was about to drive off.

"Is he going to be okay?" Aja whispered as they pulled away.

Grady waved through the open window before putting it up, but he couldn't help glancing in the rearview mirror to make sure his father was getting back into his vehicle. "Yeah," he said. "He'll be fine."

Aja didn't seem convinced. She twisted around to look through the back window. "Maybe we should invite him to come to dinner with us, after all. He seems sort of at loose ends. Might be a vulnerable moment."

Grady stepped on the brake. "You wouldn't mind?"

"Not at all," she said.

This wasn't what he'd hoped for with regard to their first night in Whiskey Creek, but the offer she'd made was certainly kind. "It's our honeymoon, and your first night in town, and—"

"Grady…" She reached over to take his hand. "Your father is more important. And maybe once he gets to know me, he won't be so disappointed that I'm Persian," she added with a laugh.

He grimaced. "I'm sorry about that. Honest to God, I don't think he cares about your ethnicity. He just loves to rock the boat, and he might do more of that type of thing at dinner. That's what I'm afraid of."

"If he does, it's okay. He can be himself. I'm more resilient than that."

Finally convinced, Grady got out, walked to his father's vehicle and waited for JT to lower the window. "We're going to that new Italian place—Amalfi's—if you'd like to join us."

"Really?" he said. "You want *me* to come?"

"We do."

"Okay. Sounds good."

Grady jogged back to his own truck and climbed in.

"Is he coming?" Aja asked.

He shot her a grin. "Of course," he said and took her hand and kissed her knuckles. "Thank you for quitting the show with me, for being willing to leave LA with me—" he studied the soft, smooth skin of her face and her wide, dark eyes "—and for being the type of person who cares about others."

"Well… I certainly understand about difficult parents." She shot him a rueful expression. "Just wait until you meet mine."

Aja couldn't help wondering how she'd found herself in a small town she'd never even heard of, married to a man she'd barely met. Had she lost her mind?

Maybe. For the first time in her life, she was acting impulsively instead of carefully measuring what she wanted against what her parents wanted for her. She felt like she was living, *truly* living for a change, so it was hard to regret the decisions that'd brought her to this place.

At dinner with Grady and his father, she realized JT was every bit as unpredictable as Grady had told her he could be. Some of the things he said obviously embarrassed Grady. But she wished her new husband would relax. She understood that he couldn't control his father. Learning more about the man she'd married and his lifestyle did make her wonder if she'd be happy in Whiskey Creek, however. She'd never imagined leaving Los Angeles. But the challenges of starting an Amos Auto Body franchise in LA could make Whiskey Creek their only option…if they stayed together.

Grady texted Dylan and Rod, the only brothers who were local, to ask them to come over to the restaurant to say hello and grab some dessert. That meant they weren't alone with JT for very long. The influx of people and laughter made it feel sort of like an impromptu party, because this time the brothers brought their wives and children. Even JT's significant other showed up eventually, when she was finished with the birthday party at the bookstore.

The restaurant was closing by the time they said their goodbyes. She and Grady were the only ones in the parking lot when he opened the passenger door to his truck for her. "That was quite the initiation," he said. "Are you ready to divorce me yet?"

Although he chuckled, she didn't laugh. His hopeful grin suggested he wanted to be reassured Aja was committed to their marriage, and she found that quite endearing. He'd been through so much in his life. As he'd said, he was probably afraid to love, which was why he'd married someone he *didn't* love. That way, in his mind, he could have a wife and children and not get hurt.

But he wasn't as impervious as he thought. He was lonely, or he wouldn't have come on the show. His defenses were wearing thin; she could feel his desire for love warring with his fear of actually loving. "Of course not, but I was a little overwhelmed," she admitted. "I can only imagine what it's like when Aaron and Mack and their families are here, too."

"The noise is deafening," he said with the same wry grin.

"You might have to remind me of some of the children's

names. You have more family than I do—more immediate family, anyway."

"You don't have anything to worry about," he said. "I'll remind you as many times as you need."

Their eyes met and held, and his gaze lowered to her mouth. He was going to kiss her. Just the thought sent off a riot of butterflies in her stomach. When she'd first met Grady, she'd been worried about whether she'd be willing to sleep with him. She'd only ever had sex with Arman. But she wasn't concerned about that anymore. It felt as though they'd be *very* compatible in that way. And the fact that he hadn't even tried to make love to her yet—other than that brief interlude in the truck earlier, when he'd kissed her and it might've gone further had they not been interrupted—was driving her mad. If he was holding back on purpose, just to make her want that kind of contact, it was certainly working.

Catching her breath, she let her eyes close in anticipation. But when nothing happened, she opened them again and read fear and doubt in his expression. He was afraid to let down his guard, to allow her past the fortifications he'd built around his heart.

"You must be tired after such a long day," he said, stepping back. "I'd better get you home."

Chapter Fifteen

That Grady had backed away bothered Aja. She'd thought they'd been making progress. But instead of becoming more openhearted as he got to know her, he seemed to be building a wall between them.

They made chitchat as he drove a few blocks, then turned down a country lane that followed a creek. He lived in a two-story home that was too big for one person, but he explained that he'd grown up there.

While Grady showed her the house, Aja asked about his brothers and how they'd met their wives. They all had interesting stories and she liked hearing him talk about Dylan, Aaron, Rod and Mack.

"You definitely didn't have a conventional childhood," she said. "But at least you had plenty of love."

"And protection," he added with a ghost of a smile. "For a while there, it was us against the world."

They'd walked through the house and were in the kitchen when Aja said, "You sure keep the place clean."

He gave her a sheepish look. "That's not me. I have a housekeeper who comes every Friday."

"Must be nice," she said with a laugh.

"It's clean, but this place is getting old and outdated. I need to remodel. I just don't know where to start."

The house had everything most men would think it needed—a big-screen TV, plenty of recliners, a wet bar and a garage full of tools. But he was right about it needing to be updated. He could tear out the carpets and put in hardwood floors, maybe knock out a few walls to enlarge the kitchen and make a great room. The appliances looked fairly new, but she noticed that he needed to replace all the blinds and tear off a lot of wallpaper, too.

He headed toward a sliding glass door at the back of the family room. "I've already done the backyard, though," he said. "Come see."

They stepped onto an expansive deck with a huge barbecue area and a firepit a few stairs below the deck on the adjacent patio. He had expensive-looking lawn furniture, and a great view, since the back lawn sloped down to the creek.

"Did you pay to have all this done?" she asked.

"No, I did it myself," he replied. "Took me the better part of a year, but I was only able to do it in my off hours."

The smell of freshly cut grass rose to her nostrils. "Who takes care of the lawn?"

"I do, but my dad said he'd do it while I was gone. He must've mowed this morning."

"It's gorgeous out here, perfect for parties," she told him. "You didn't tell me you were *this* handy."

"Most people could do this," he said.

She knew *that* wasn't true. "My father can't even change the oil in his car let alone build a backyard like this," she said. "But he's an incredible ophthalmologist."

He rested his hands on his hips as he surveyed his own work. "I enjoyed the process, and I'll be happy to do whatever you want on the inside. I just haven't gotten that far, don't really have an eye for what's best in there, so I'd be happy to take some direction from you if…if you want to get involved."

If things worked out was what he was really saying. They always had the possibility of failure hanging over their heads, weren't quite as committed as a normal married couple would be. "That would be a fun project," she admitted.

"Oh, and there's this." He beckoned her to the side of the house.

She followed him to a freestanding shedlike building that had a padlock on the door. After he opened it, she could see that it contained a couple of motorcycles, some mountain bikes, several golf bags, a lawn mower and other yard tools. "We could clear this out and get a kiln, turn this place into a pottery studio for you."

She stepped back in surprise. "*Really?* But then…what will you do with all this stuff?"

"I can always build another shed," he said. "We got five acres here."

She turned in a circle, trying to assess how it might feel to have this place as a studio.

"I'd dress it up for you, of course—add air-conditioning, some windows, shelving and whatever else you need," he added.

"Thank you. That's so nice." Having a place to create the way she'd always dreamed certainly made Whiskey Creek more appealing. She couldn't have anything like this at her condo. If she wanted to do pottery in LA, she'd have to pay for studio time or rent her own space somewhere off-site, and that didn't make a lot of sense when she was at her dental practice most of the time.

"If you decide to stay, I want you to be happy here," he said.

She turned to face him. "Does that mean you're no longer considering Los Angeles?"

"Opening another franchise would take time, maybe three years, so it wouldn't be right away."

"You're saying you'd expect me to shut down my dental practice if we stay together?"

"I prefer to think of it as offering to let you live your dream instead," he said with a crooked grin.

"You realize, if I were to sell my practice, I probably wouldn't have an income for quite some time."

"I understand."

"And you wouldn't mind?" she asked.

He seemed taken aback by the question. "Why would I mind? If this marriage becomes a *real* marriage, what I have would be yours, too. I have some savings, and the business is doing well. We could make it."

But what if they tried to stay together and their marriage failed despite that? She'd have given up her practice, and he would've spent a fortune helping her get started in the art world.

That he'd be willing to take such a risk after marrying her the way that he had said so much about the type of person he was—how far he'd go for someone he loved.

Touched by his generosity, she wanted to kiss him again, feel his arms go around her and hold her close. But he didn't reach for her; he stepped out of the shed and held the door so she could follow him.

Aja had suggested they sleep in the same bed and Grady had agreed, but that had probably been a mistake.

As she lay next to him that night, he wanted her so badly he couldn't sleep. But he was terrified to trust her enough to act on that desire. What if he fell in love with her and she let him down?

He continued to battle his growing desire. He needed to wait until he could be certain she wanted to be with him. What if there was a side of her he hadn't yet seen? Or what if she decided she'd made a mistake marrying him and wanted to back out?

There was a lot riding on their marriage. More than felt safe. She didn't seem excited to leave LA behind, and it would take a lot of time and effort for him to get into a position where he could safely move there. Would that be all it would take to make her leave him?

And what about her parents? They had to have considerable influence over her, or she wouldn't have found it so difficult to follow her own path before now.

That she'd allowed them so much control wasn't exactly a harbinger of hope that she'd defy them if they disapproved of him. But, possibly because of how she valued family, she seemed to be more tolerant of his father than he would've expected from just any woman. Although JT had said some things that'd made him squirm tonight, on the whole Grady had had a great time at dinner. For once, he wasn't the only one without a partner. At last, *he* had a wife and the chance to have a family.

Aja sighed in her sleep and cuddled closer. He could feel her soft breasts pressed against his arm and was so tempted to lift his hand to touch her. The scent of her shampoo rose to his nostrils and he closed his eyes to breathe it in, remembering the feel of her lips against his and the way she'd met his tongue with her own.

Nearly groaning in frustration, he rolled over to face the

other direction. Surely, this unorthodox marriage wouldn't last; he needed to be prepared for when it ended.

Movement in the bed woke Aja. Grady seemed miserable, couldn't seem to get comfortable. She felt him shift one way, then the other and then onto his back, and when she squinted in the dark to see if she could make out whether his eyes were closed, she found him staring up at the ceiling.

She had no idea what time it was, but she knew it was late and got the impression he'd been tossing and turning for hours. He'd been so eager to come home, so excited to show her his business and his house and the shed he was willing to make into a pottery studio for her. And it'd all gone well—even dinner with his family. So why wasn't he able to sleep?

They'd shared a bed at the beach house, too, so she knew he hadn't been quite *this* restless since they married...

She almost asked him what was wrong. But she was afraid he'd misinterpret the question, feel he was disturbing her and needed to sleep somewhere else. That wasn't what she was hoping to achieve at all. She just wanted him to let down his guard. She couldn't really get to know him if he wouldn't, and she was so hopeful what she felt for him would continue to grow. That was why she'd quit the show and come to Whiskey Creek with him.

When he lifted his head to look at the alarm clock on the nightstand, she decided it was time to do something drastic. Without a word, she shimmied out of her nightgown, tossed it on the floor and slid over to pull Grady into her arms.

Grady was wearing pajama bottoms but no shirt. Summer nights in Whiskey Creek were too warm otherwise.

So when Aja's bare chest came into contact with his, he nearly gasped. He'd been trying so hard not to even think of her sexually. But, of course, that had been impossible. He could no longer resist, was going to make love to her whether he regretted it or not.

Her hands delved into his hair as he began to kiss her, and she moaned as if that kind of contact was exactly what she'd been craving.

From that moment on, he could scarcely breathe. Pulling her more snugly against him, he slid his hands up her bare back, welcoming the incredible satisfaction of simply holding her naked body against him.

"God, you feel good," he muttered.

She didn't respond. She just kissed him again—this time holding his face in both hands while she did it—and the slow indulgent way she used her tongue, as if she was savoring every second, made the kiss more enjoyable than any he'd ever had.

Taking his time, he reveled in having such intimate access to her mouth and all the rest of her, but eventually rolled her onto her back and began kissing his way down her throat to her breasts. He liked curves—*loved* curves—and she had plenty of them, along with what seemed like miles of the softest skin he'd ever touched.

She moaned as his mouth reached her breasts, and he began to use one hand to explore the rest of her. When she arched her back, he knew he'd found something she liked.

Lifting his head, he grinned down at her. "Apparently, this is a good spot."

"It's a *great* spot," she admitted breathlessly, and he managed a chuckle, but all mirth fell away quickly because he was so intent on further discoveries.

He loved the smell of her, he realized, as he continued to kiss his way down her body. Not only the scent of the products she used, but also the scent of her skin and that musky, more intimate smell that was so individual to her. Everything about her appealed to him. He pictured her in her wedding dress as she came down the aisle toward him. That was the first moment he'd realized how truly beautiful she was.

She began to tremble as he kissed her thighs. He couldn't wait to peel off his pajama bottoms and bury himself inside her. But if he wanted to draw this out and make it last, he had to manage a little restraint, at least for now.

She tried to bring his head up…possibly to kiss him again. Or maybe being completely open to him made her feel too vulnerable.

"Let me taste you," he said, resisting, and when he reached the same spot he'd first located with his fingers, he felt her body jerk in reaction.

"That's…incredible," she said, her voice whisper-thin. Then, as her muscles grew taut and her breathing more ragged, he slid his hands under her so he could hold her lower body at just the right angle…until she shuddered and cried out.

Chapter Sixteen

She was making love to her *husband*. She thought it might be awkward being so intimate with a man she didn't know well. But it wasn't. All she could feel was Grady inside her, his fingers threaded through hers as he pinned her hands to the pillow above her head and stared down into her eyes. The way he was looking at her was probably the most erotic thing she'd ever experienced.

He moved slowly at first, as though he didn't want to miss one tiny nuance of having joined their bodies, but he couldn't seem to hold back for very long. Only a few moments later, his eyelids slid closed, and he began to move faster. Although he was using a condom, Aja had the somewhat curious thought that she wanted to get pregnant. Before tonight, she'd been so focused on her career that the idea of having a baby meant only calamity—at least when it came to reaching her goals. But a baby was becoming more and more appealing and important to her.

Closing her own eyes, she told herself to shut off her mind for once and simply feel. Even if her marriage didn't last, she had tonight, and she was going to make the most of it.

Grady went to the bathroom, then came back and dropped into bed. All the tension and anxiety that'd been building up inside him the past couple of weeks was suddenly gone, replaced with exhaustion.

When Aja scooted closer to him, he shifted so she could rest her head on his shoulder.

"That was the best," he told her.

"I think so, too." He could hear the smile in her voice as she curled more comfortably into him. "How soon would you want children if—if we decide to stay together?" she asked.

He felt it'd be irresponsible to have kids before they knew each other better. But he'd longed to start a family for a while now, so other than that, he was ready.

"Whenever you'd want to give them to me," he mumbled, and if she said something else, he didn't hear it because he sank into a deep, dreamless sleep almost instantaneously.

Grady was gone when Aja woke up. She stretched and yawned, then smiled as she remembered last night. Another gamble had paid off. She'd enjoyed every second of making love with Grady. And he'd seemed to enjoy it, too. But she had to wonder if her luck would hold…

Pulling the blankets higher, she listened for her husband.

When she didn't hear anything, she got up, dressed in yoga shorts and a tank top, and went to the bathroom to brush her teeth and put her hair up. Then she ambled downstairs and into the kitchen, where she found a pot of hot coffee with a sticky note.

Good morning, beautiful. Had to take care of a few things at the auto body shop but want to take you to breakfast. Call me when you're ready to go.

She checked the clock—8:08 a.m., which was an hour and a half later than she usually got up—and poured herself a cup of coffee. Could she get used to living in this town? she asked herself. Could she make this house her home?

She wandered onto the deck, where she saw two deer at the creek—they had to be used to seeing humans because they didn't run when she came out. She admired them as she sat at the patio table. It was beautiful in Whiskey Creek; she had to admit that.

She thought of how her parents would react to her moving away. They wouldn't like it. She'd be leaving the tight Persian community she'd been part of since she was born. But she wasn't sure that would be entirely bad. Whiskey Creek had a lot to recommend it, too.

Reminded of her family, she took her phone from her pocket and texted her brother.

How's it going? Aja began. Is it true love or what?

She didn't get an answer right away. She'd finished her coffee and gone back inside, was just rinsing her mug in the sink, when she heard the alert.

Barbie's a nice person. But probably won't last.

Aja bit her lip as she read that. Why not?

Just not right for me.

Does Barbie know that?

I can't imagine she doesn't.

Have you talked about it?

A little. We're happy to stay together so we can remain on the show. It could give us both the kinds of opportunities we're looking for. But other than that...

That makes me sad.

There's nothing to be sad about. She likes you a lot, too. We can all be friends. What about you? Are you falling for Grady?

That was a good question. She smiled as memories of last night floated through her mind. There's definitely something there.

Seriously? That's the last thing I expected my conservative, cautious older sister to say.

I know. It's scaring me, too. To be honest, I don't know whether to trust it.

So are you glad you quit the show?

It's been nice to be out from under those demands. But we'll take some video to send Winnie today.

How do you like Grady's hometown? Would you be willing to live there?

She frowned as she gazed out the window at the expansive front yard. The properties along the creek were large, which meant she didn't have any close neighbors. Jury's out, she wrote. But then she thought of the shed Grady had said he'd make into a pottery studio.

There was an entirely different life waiting for her here.

So which one would make her the happiest?

Grady was still at the shop when Winnie's text came in. Can you talk?

They didn't have anything more to discuss, not that Aja couldn't hear, but he got the impression Winnie was implying she wanted to talk to him without involving his wife. He wanted to write back "About what?" But he was afraid such a blunt response would come off as rude, so he called her instead.

"There you are," she said.

The sulky note in her voice confused him. "What's that supposed to mean?"

"I didn't hear from you all day yesterday."

He straightened. "We were driving, Winnie. Then I was introducing Aja to my father and showing her my house and business. Were we supposed to check in?"

"I just thought…" There was a pause, then she said, "I just thought you might have some video for me."

"Not yet. But I promise we'll get you something today."

"Like what?"

"Shots of us at breakfast after our first night in my house. That should be good, right?"

"That'll be great, but…how are things progressing?"

He wasn't sure what she meant. "If you're asking whether we're getting to know each other, we are."

"And you're enjoying each other?"

"I'd say so."

"What about sex?"

This was awkward because he knew she had a personal interest in the question. He wanted to tell her it was none of her business, but because of the show, it sort of was. Everyone would want to know if they'd consummated their marriage. "That part's good, too."

"Greg told me you hadn't slept together before you left here."

He swallowed a sigh as he looked out the window of his shop to see another customer pull in. "It happened last night, okay?"

"And?"

"And I don't know what else to say." He felt like he was somehow betraying Aja just by telling Winnie this much, and yet...surely Aja knew the show would be peppering them with such personal questions.

"You're falling in love."

It was a statement, not a question. "I don't know," he said.

"That's how it feels to me."

"I'm just trying to give Aja an honest effort. She's a beautiful woman, a great person. She deserves it."

"I wish I'd never paired you together," she said angrily and disconnected.

Grady stared down at his phone. Apparently, she'd been so confident his marriage wouldn't succeed, she hadn't worried about it. She'd thought she could use it for the show and he'd still be around after, and didn't like that things now seemed to be going in a different direction.

So...what might she do about it? He didn't want her to tell Aja the *real* reason he'd come on the show and gone through with the wedding. As if she knew he was thinking about her, his phone buzzed with a text from Aja. I'm ready.

I'll be there in five.

Then he sent a message to Winnie. I'm sorry. You know I didn't expect this.

You could stop it, she wrote back.

Actually, he didn't think he could. That was what made it so beautiful.

It was also what made it so scary.

Chapter Seventeen

Grady was excited to see Aja. He'd thought about their lovemaking the entire time he was helping his father and brothers get the shop open and going for the day. He could tell that with him gone they were beginning to fall behind. But he was only willing to do so much today, certainly wasn't going to spend more than a couple of hours at the shop when he was still on his honeymoon.

Aja must've been watching for him, because she came out as soon as he pulled into the drive. He admired her long black hair gleaming in the sunlight and the pretty white sundress that contrasted so nicely with her smooth skin.

When she reached the truck, he leaned over to open her door. "Morning."

She gave him a bright smile as she climbed in, and he realized that smile was what he loved most about her. It had to be the sweetest smile he'd ever seen. "Morning," she said. "How are things at the shop?"

"Busy. But that's better than not being busy." He reversed down the drive and swung out to return to town. "I hope you didn't mind that I ran over there for a bit while you were still sleeping. I didn't want to wake you."

"No problem. I know you have responsibilities."

"I appreciate it. What about you? Dental practice okay in your absence?"

"I just checked in with my assistant. Things there seem to be going surprisingly well. No real emergencies—nothing the on-call dentist hasn't been able to handle."

"Have you heard from Winnie?" He didn't want the producer to remain in contact with Aja. Knowing Winnie would rather see them break up, he didn't like the idea of the two of them talking.

"No. You?"

"She contacted me this morning, looking for more footage. I told her we'd take some at breakfast."

Aja wrinkled her nose. "Now that we've left the show, I'm so done with that. But we said we would, so, of course, we will."

"Yeah, we'll finish what we started, but I'm not excited about it, either."

Once they arrived at the restaurant, a kitschy place that'd been around forever called Just Like Mom's, he took Aja's hand as they walked in...and almost immediately spotted Heidi Fullmer, a woman he'd dated on and off over the past several years. She was sitting in a booth having breakfast with her sister.

He smiled and nodded because she looked up, but when the hostess tried to seat them on the same side of the room, he asked if they could sit over by the window.

She looked startled that he wouldn't just accept the table she'd offered him, and he could see why. He came here all the time and had never expressed a preference. "I just sat a party in that section," she complained. "It's Joanie's turn to get a table."

"Come on, Isabelle," he said. "I'm sure someone else will walk in soon. It's always busy in here."

She acquiesced with an irked "Fine," and led them farther from Heidi.

Once they were seated, had been given their menus and she'd walked away, Aja lifted her eyebrows. "What was wrong with the other table?"

"I just like sitting by the window."

Fortunately, she let it go at that, but while they ordered coffee, omelets and biscuits with gravy, Heidi and her sister finished their meal and got up.

Grady hoped they'd just go, but he didn't get that lucky. Her sister waited by the door as Heidi walked over.

"Hey." Although she spoke to him, she was eyeing Aja.

"Hey," he responded. "How are you?"

"Good. You told me you were going to California on vacation for a month. What are you doing back so soon?"

Why couldn't he have chosen a different restaurant? "Cut it short," he replied simply.

"Why? Didn't you like it there?"

"I liked it fine. I needed to take care of a couple things here."

"I hope everything's okay with your father and brothers…"

"I meant with the business." Feeling Aja's curiosity, he added, "We might go back in few days."

"We…" Heidi repeated and studied Aja that much more closely. "I don't believe I've ever had the pleasure of meeting your friend…"

"Aja, this is Heidi Fullmer. Heidi, this is Aja Kermani, a dentist from LA."

"My pleasure," Aja said.

"Did you two…meet online or something?"

Grady answered before Aja could. He wanted to retain control of this conversation. "We met in LA."

She finally held his gaze. "And you brought her home with you…"

He could tell Heidi was upset that he was with another woman, and he felt bad about that. But he'd never made her any promises.

"I see. That's great, just great," Heidi said sarcastically and turned to Aja. "I feel like I should warn you. You might think you've found a great guy and your relationship is really going somewhere, but I can promise it's not. He'll never marry you."

Aja blinked several times. Then she said, rather uncertainly, "But…he already has."

Heidi's jaw dropped and her eyes rounded as she turned to him. "You son of a bitch!" she cried before breaking into tears and rushing out of the restaurant with her sister trailing behind.

The silence after her departure felt deafening. "Sorry," he said. "I had no idea she'd be here."

"Does she have some claim on you?" Aja asked hesitantly.

"We've dated quite a bit over the years but have never been exclusive. It's always been difficult for me to make a commitment."

Lines appeared in her normally smooth forehead. "And yet you married me…"

"I didn't know you," he said. "Somehow, that made it feel like less of a commitment, I guess." It sort of was, he thought—on her part, too. Surely, she had to recognize that.

"And now?" she asked.

He spread out his hands. "I'm hoping this works. I'm planning on it, or I wouldn't have brought you here."

She looked out the window, where they could see Heidi being consoled by her sister at the car.

Afraid what'd just happened might make her have second thoughts about him or want to return to LA, Grady reached across the table for her hand. "Nothing's changed, Aja," he said.

She nibbled at her bottom lip as she met his gaze. "That's just it," she responded. "A lot has changed for me."

They spent the day kayaking at Lake Tabeaud, which was only twenty minutes from Whiskey Creek. Aja had never been kayaking before, but Grady seemed to have toys for every occasion…or he could borrow what he needed from one of his brothers.

Because breakfast at the restaurant hadn't gone as well as they'd hoped, they did some filming while kayaking and eating a picnic lunch on the big blanket Grady had brought. He wanted her to see the natural beauty of Northern California. But Southern California was equally beautiful, and the weather there wasn't quite as cold in the winter, or hot in the summer.

Still, Aja could see the appeal of this place—the unique history, the open spaces and opportunity to move around freely, without all the crammed freeways and lines at restaurants, and other places in LA—especially when she viewed it through his eyes. This was where he'd grown up. It was home to him.

After their encounter with that other woman this morning, she was just afraid she hadn't taken Grady's limitations seriously enough. She seemed to have broken down his walls a bit last night. It'd felt like they'd made a strong emotional as well as physical connection. But would he only put those walls back up?

"You've been quiet since breakfast," he said as they drank wine from plastic champagne flutes after eating broccoli salad and pastrami sandwiches.

"It's peaceful here," she said.

He peered more closely at her. "So…you're just relaxed? You're not worried or upset?"

Finished with her wine, she put the plastic flute back in the basket. "I guess I'm…thinking."

"About…"

"Your brothers. Your town. Your business."

He plucked a blade of grass, then leaned back on his hands as he began to chew on it. "What kind of conclusions are you drawing?"

"I'm impressed that your brothers seem to be so in love with their wives."

"When we fall, we fall hard, I guess."

She could see why. Once they made up their minds, they made up their minds. But would he be able to get beyond the past the way his brothers had? He had so much to offer. Why was it taking him so much longer? "What are you most afraid of?" she asked.

He removed the grass from his mouth and tossed it away. "Psychology is complicated, right? But I think a psychologist would say I'm afraid of trusting the wrong person, that I don't want to lose someone I love."

"But what have you gained if you never love in the first place?"

"Nothing," he said. "Which is why I'm trying to overcome it."

"And I see the effort. But if you couldn't overcome it for someone you dated for so long, what makes you think you can overcome it for me?"

He dropped his head as he considered the question. "You and Heidi are completely different kinds of people, for one," he said. "What holds true for her won't necessarily hold true for you."

Her phone buzzed with a text. She was going to ignore it. This conversation was important. But a call came in immediately after, so she knew someone had to get through.

"I'm sorry, but there must be an emergency at work," she said. "I have to check."

She dug out her cell. But it wasn't her office that'd been trying to reach her; it was her brother. Her heart leaped into her throat as she read his text.

Grady could obviously tell something was wrong. He leaned forward. "What is it?"

She pressed a hand to her chest. "My brother's been trying to reach me."

"Because…"

"My parents have been in a terrible accident."

Grady had tried to insist he'd drive her home or fly to Los Angeles with her, but Aja knew, at this point, it would only make the situation more difficult to have him there. Her parents didn't even know she was married. She needed to get back to LA as soon as possible so she could be there for them. The accident had occurred while they were on their way home from Palm Springs and had been so bad that her mother was in intensive care. Aja had packed her bags as soon as they could get back to Whiskey Creek and purchased a ticket on the first flight out of Sacramento— which was the last flight of the day to LA.

The drive to the airport took a little over an hour, and other than "Let me get that for you" and "Do you want a snack to take on the plane?" Grady didn't say much. She didn't talk a lot, either. She felt guilty for being somewhere else when her parents needed her, especially because she was doing something they would never approve of.

"Are you going to be okay?" Once they reached the airport, Grady had pulled to the curb and gotten her luggage from the back of the truck. He was standing next to it, a worried expression on his face, his hands shoved into the pockets of his jeans as she rummaged through her purse for her ID.

"I'll call you when—when I can," she said in place of a more direct answer and took her suitcase without even hugging him goodbye. The news of her mother—the possibility that Esther might not make it—had jolted her out of the dream she'd been living in lately and brought her back to the world she'd always known.

After checking her bags with an outdoor gate agent, she grabbed her carry-on and hurried toward the sliding doors of the airport. She told herself not to look back at Grady. She'd have to decide what she'd do about him, and her future, later.

But she only made it as far as the ticket counters on her way to the escalator before she turned around and saw, through the glass doors, that he was still there, staring after her.

Regretting the fact that she hadn't even hugged him, she waved, but he didn't wave back. He just dropped his head before lifting it to respond to the security officer who approached him a second later. Then he walked around his truck, climbed in the driver's side and drove away.

Chapter Eighteen

Grady made it home by midnight. He told himself he shouldn't feel so bereft. Nothing earth-shattering had changed. Aja had been in Whiskey Creek for only twenty-four hours.

And yet the house felt strangely empty without her. He kept picturing her with that carry-on she'd wheeled away from him so fast. He felt terrible that she might lose her mother, knew how hurt and upset she'd been…and he couldn't blame her. But he was afraid she wouldn't come back.

He shouldn't have begun to think their relationship could last. He'd been beating himself up over it the entire way home. Even if her mother recovered—and he prayed she would—it would take time for her to get back on her feet, likely so long Aja would slip back into her old life and give up on what they could've had. She was already worried about whether she could rely on him from an emotional standpoint. Since he'd never had a close, long-term relationship, he was worried about that, too.

Even if she didn't want a divorce, after this she'd be more likely to decide to keep her dental practice in Los Angeles. She couldn't displease her parents after what'd just happened to them.

It wasn't easy to fall asleep that night. All he could do was smell Aja's perfume on the sheets and remember the feel of her naked body in his arms.

Aja stood beside her mother's bed. After Darius had picked her up at the airport and taken her to the hospital, they'd both spent the night in Esther's room in a pair of uncomfortable vinyl chairs. He told her a drunk driver had run their parents off the road, and because it'd been raining at the time, they'd hydroplaned and plowed into a tree going sixty miles an hour, essentially wrapping the car around the tree on the passenger side.

It was a miracle they were both still alive. Their father had whiplash, several cuts and bruises, a lost tooth, and a broken arm, but his doctor said he would be able to come home in a day or two. At this point, they were only keeping him for observation.

Their mother had suffered the worst of the impact. Esther's face and arms were burned from the hot gas in the airbags that'd deployed, but those airbags were probably what'd saved her life. Although she had no injuries from the neck down, she had a subdural hematoma and a subarachnoid bleed, and she'd fractured both eye sockets. Now, she was in a medically induced coma as they attempted to stop her brain from swelling.

"I'm going to get coffee. You want any?" Darius asked, covering a yawn as he got up and headed to the door.

"No, I can't drink coffee on an empty stomach," she replied.

"I can grab you a breakfast sandwich."

"That'd be great. Thanks."

Barbie wasn't with Darius. Like her, he knew better than to bring his spouse to the hospital. They couldn't even tell their parents about Barbie and Grady—not now. They needed to get through this emergency first. Since Darius was planning to split up with Barbie, he'd probably never have to tell them. They didn't watch much TV, certainly no reality TV, so unless one of their friends saw the show when it aired, or an advertisement for it came up somewhere, there was a possibility they'd never find out about Barbie. Even if they did, Darius could say he was merely acting, trying to get a start in showbiz. But…what would *she* say?

She had no idea. As she held her mother's limp hand, she felt guilty for doing something Esther would consider so "reckless," and yet she couldn't bring herself to regret it entirely. Neither could she forget the expression on Grady's face as he watched her leave. He obviously didn't believe she'd be coming back. And she couldn't promise otherwise. She had no idea what was going to happen, just that she was lucky she already had some time off work because her parents were going to need her a great deal in the coming weeks.

A male nurse poked his head in. "Still here, I see. You've got to be exhausted."

"I'm okay. Just hoping she can hear me when I talk to her or feel me holding her hand."

"I doubt it. She's completely out. So if you need to go home and get some rest, now would be a good time."

She considered it but shook her head. "I can't leave. Not right now."

"I understand," he said and gave her a kind smile before moving on.

Darius returned a few minutes later. "You haven't even changed positions since I left. At least come over and sit down while you eat."

Reluctantly, Aja let go of her mother's hand and circled the bed. "You went to Starbucks instead of the cafeteria?"

"It was just down the street." He handed her an English muffin with egg, Gouda and bacon.

"Good choice," she said as she took a bite.

He winked. "We've been to Starbucks together often enough for me to know what you like."

She chewed and swallowed but could barely taste the food. She was too tired and worried. "I feel so bad, Darius," she said, lowering her voice even though the nurse had assured her their mother couldn't hear anything.

He took a drink of his coffee, which looked to be the only thing he'd ordered for himself. "About the show?"

"About marrying someone without including Mom and Dad. Now how are we going to tell them?"

He put his cup on the side table and leaned forward. "Listen to me, Aja. If you and Grady work out, you have nothing to apologize for. That's the best thing that could happen. And if you don't? You won't even have to tell them you were really married. You can say you went on the show to support me, and it was all an act. They don't know any different when it comes to reality TV, and as long as everything goes back to the way it was, I doubt they'll care."

Somehow, he'd always been more immune to their parents' demands. He did a lot of what was expected of him—hence law school—but he cheated more than she did. He told them what they wanted to hear, then he did exactly what he wanted to do. He framed it as living his best life without "upsetting" them. She was too honest for that.

She tried to be everything they wanted, even if what she wanted was something else.

"It's just bad timing to be doing something that will upset them so much," she said. "That's all."

"Not if you handle it right," he reiterated. "What did Grady say when you left? Does he expect you to come back?"

"I didn't promise anything."

He grimaced, as if it shouldn't be that hard to decide. "I can't see you selling your practice and moving to some small town in NorCal, can you?"

"Probably not," she allowed…and yet there was something charming about Whiskey Creek, something innocent and untainted. She liked that warm, fuzzy Hallmark movie feeling…

"So will he move out here?"

"It would be harder for him."

"Hard for an auto mechanic? There's got to be a thousand places he could work in LA."

"He's not just an auto mechanic, Darius. He's a business owner, and he's done quite well for himself."

"How do you know? Did he go over his finances with you?"

She thought of the moment when they were standing at the door to the shed, and he'd said he'd turn it into a pottery studio for her. "No, but I've seen his property and his business. He grew up the hard way, and it made him strong, resilient and confident. He doesn't owe his success to anyone else."

"Neither do we," her brother said. "I mean… Mom and Dad have given us a lot, but we got the education."

"He didn't even have a mom and dad. He was raised by his older brother."

A grin split his face. "Sounds as though you really admire him."

Grady was so different from her, but that was part of the appeal. He was more independent, more rugged and more self-sufficient than any man she'd dated so far. Even when they didn't have anything to say, she found it comforting just to be in his presence.

It was his quiet strength that set him apart. But if she stayed with him—and moved to Whiskey Creek—she'd be changing *everything* about her life.

Again, she wondered why the psychologists on the show had paired them together. What was it about their personalities that made them compatible? If she knew the answer to that question, maybe she'd have more reason to believe and hang on.

So this time, instead of just wondering, she decided she'd ask.

Grady couldn't believe he was back at the shop as if nothing had changed in his life. It was so anticlimactic, so…deflating. He loved his business—loved working with his brothers, too—but seeing Rod or Dylan walk in with a kid on their shoulders or with a cell phone pressed to one ear while they talked to their wives made him feel even more isolated and alone than when Mack had married and moved away, and he'd become the only single Amos brother.

He figured he'd continue to work the longest hours and do more to take care of their derelict father. No one else had the time. But he'd been excited to think he might have more to look forward to—like the birth of his own child.

"What is it?" Dylan asked during a momentary lull when it was just the two of them behind the counter. For the first time since they'd opened a few hours ago, they didn't have people coming and going, dropping off or picking up cars, and the phone wasn't ringing off the hook.

Grady hadn't told him what'd happened to Aja's mother or that she'd left. He didn't trust himself to talk about it without betraying too much emotion. He focused on straightening up the front counter so he wouldn't have to meet his older brother's gaze. "What's…what?"

"Something's wrong."

"Nothing's wrong," he insisted.

Dylan stepped closer. "Then why are you here? Did you have a fight with Aja?"

"No. Aja's not really the type to fight. She's strong because she has a good self-image and she's accomplished a lot. But she's sweet and calm at the same time. If I said something harsh, I think she'd just start crying, which would make me immediately back off."

"That's real strength," he said. "Being strong enough to show vulnerability without feeling it makes you weak. So what's happening?"

"Her parents were in a terrible car accident last night," he said. "I had to take her to the airport."

"And you didn't say anything until now? You made me pull it out of you?"

Because he was too upset. He didn't want Dylan or anyone else to know how deeply it would hurt him if his marriage imploded right when he was beginning to believe in it. "I… It's been busy around here."

He had a feeling Dylan could see right through him but made a calculated decision to let it go at that. "Are they going to be okay?" he asked instead of calling Grady on that bullshit answer.

"I don't know. It's too soon to tell."

He rested his hands on his hips. "Why didn't you go with her? She could probably use the support."

"Because it would be easier for her without me," he said and explained why.

Dylan leaned against the counter as he listened. Then he said, "I knew they wouldn't exactly welcome you into the family."

Someone pulled into the parking lot; they had only a few seconds before another customer came into the store. "And that hasn't changed."

"Once they see how you treat their daughter, how happy you make her, they'll come around," he insisted.

Bill Thorne pushed the door open, effectively ending the conversation. Dylan gave Grady a nod, as if to add an exclamation point to what he'd said, and Grady tossed his brother a smile for the encouragement.

But he wasn't optimistic Aja would give him the chance. He'd already tried to text her—twice—this morning. He'd called, too. He wanted to make sure she'd made it back safely and ask about her mother.

Unfortunately, he hadn't gotten a response.

Chapter Nineteen

Even with her mother in a coma, Grady filtered through Aja's mind constantly, especially because she knew he'd been trying to reach her. She planned to call him back, but she was waiting to get her legs underneath her again—didn't want to say anything that might cause more instability. Her parents' accident had leveled her. She was still trying to come to terms with it, was waiting to see how things would go so she could decide what she should do in her personal life.

It was almost noon when Darius insisted she go home, shower and get some rest. He said he'd sit with their mother and call her if anything changed, and only her trust in those assurances had released her from the responsibility she felt to stay at the hospital. She was exhausted, mentally and physically, and needed to do exactly as he said—take a long, hot shower and fall into the comfort of her own bed for a couple of hours. Then she'd go visit her father and

update him on Esther, if there was an update, before re-
lieving Darius, so he could get home in time for his next
filming segment with Barbie for *Tying the Knot*.

While she was in an Uber to her condo, she called Winnie to let her know what'd happened. Darius had been planning to break the news of their parents' accident once he
had more of an idea of how it would impact his schedule in
the coming weeks, but she'd asked him to let her handle it.

Fortunately, Winnie picked up immediately. "Winnie,
it's Aja…from the show," she said as soon as she heard the
other woman say hello.

The subsequent pause gave Aja the impression Winnie
was surprised to hear from her, and that sort of made sense
since they'd been communicating through Grady since the
wedding. "What can I do for you?" she asked. "Were you
and Grady able to get some footage for me yesterday? Because I haven't received anything yet."

"After what happened last night, Grady probably forgot
to send it. I'll remind him."

"What happened last night?" she asked.

"I'm afraid my folks were in a car accident and are both
in the hospital. Although my father will be okay, the situation is less certain with my mother. I had to fly home at
a moment's notice, so I'm back in LA."

"That's terrible!" she said. "I'm so sorry. But… Grady
didn't come with you?"

"No. Considering the circumstances—the fact that my
parents don't even know I'm married—I thought it would
be better to take care of this on my own."

"I see."

Surprisingly, Winnie didn't sound too disappointed.

"I apologize for having to change everything once
again, because this will definitely impact our ability to
do what we said we'd do when we left, but—"

"That's not a problem," she interrupted. "You just take care of what you need to. Your parents' well-being comes first, of course."

Grateful that the producer was being so accommodating and understanding, Aja felt some of the tension leave her body. "Thank you. I was worried that this might trigger the penalty and—"

Winnie cut in again. "No, of course not. Don't even think about that."

"But...what will happen with the show? How will you get by without us?"

"We'll use the footage we've already taken to maximum advantage. And we'll fill in with the couples from previous shows who are still together." Her tone suddenly changed. "Unless... I mean... Is your brother quitting the show, too?"

The idea of *that* definitely alarmed her. Aja could hear it in her voice. "No. I talked to him only an hour or so ago and told him I'd stand in for Mom and Dad as much as possible so that he and Barbie can continue filming."

"That's a relief. We can adjust their schedule here and there, if necessary."

"Great. I'll let him know. He's at the hospital right now, but he'll be able to film this evening."

"Great. So...you don't think Grady will join you even on weekends?"

Aja hadn't let herself consider that option, or any options. She'd just felt she needed to be free to focus and do what she needed to do. But now that such an easy solution had been suggested, she knew it would sound odd that she couldn't make something like that work. "He could, I guess. We'll probably try to arrange that at some point. And if he does come, maybe we *could* get some more filming done."

"No, that'll make things too difficult. You're going through enough. Don't worry about it. There will be no penalties if you'd rather just focus on your family."

She sounded so sincere, and that came as a relief. "I appreciate it, Winnie."

"No problem. Be sure to check in now and then to let me know how your folks are doing. Darius can keep me in the loop, too, of course, since I'll be seeing more of him. And if you decide you'd like to be on the show again in the future, we'd love to have you back. We've never had a contestant return for another try. And you're such a great catch. Any guy should be excited to have you as a partner, and I know the audience would love to see the return of a former contestant."

She'd said that as if she expected Aja to be single. But in Aja's mind, that had yet to be decided. She was just taking a break to find herself again…and figure out how to navigate the next few days and weeks. "I haven't given up on the marriage," she clarified. "We're still…going to try."

"Oh! I didn't realize that. I assumed if things were going well he'd be staying at your place or something, trying to support you through this."

"I had to drop everything and catch a plane, and…" Her words fell off. She supposed he *could* join her, and her parents wouldn't have to know about it, at least not until they were well again. But having him around while she was at the hospital all the time and couldn't be forthcoming with her parents would be so difficult—make her feel torn in two.

"And deal with a tragic event," Winnie said, finishing for her. "You don't have to explain yourself to me. I'll make do with the material we've got already, okay? You don't have to bring Grady out here."

Aja almost said "okay" and hung up. But she couldn't

figure out why Winnie didn't care more about whether they stayed together. When they were starting out, she'd seemed so invested in the success of each couple.

Maybe it was just that she'd already given up on her and Grady since they left LA and started to dictate the parameters of their own participation.

Still, Aja had one more question for Winnie, who was saying she had to run.

"I hate to keep you," she began. "But before you go, can you tell me why I was paired with Grady? What was it the show's professionals saw in us that suggested we might be well-suited for each other? I mean... I can't help but wonder. We don't even live in the same area."

There was such a long silence that Aja thought Winnie had hung up.

"Winnie?"

The producer cleared her throat. "Yes, I'm right here."

"I was wondering if the psychologists indicated why they thought Grady and I would be good for each other," she reiterated in case Winnie had missed her question the first time.

"I'm afraid they didn't leave any notes, Aja."

"So...how does it work? They just match brides with grooms and don't give you any supporting documentation?"

Aja heard Winnie sigh, then the other woman said, "If you're beating yourself up because you think you should be able to make this marriage work, and yet you can't, you should stop that right away. Because the psychologists didn't pair you with Grady, I did."

Aja gripped her phone that much tighter. "What do you mean? We took those personality tests for a reason, right?"

"Yes, but you weren't even interested in coming on the

show. You did it for Darius. So I didn't think you really cared who I paired you with."

"But you offered the psych evals as reassurance, never told me—"

"The psych evals are just so we don't let anyone dangerous on the show. We have to do our homework. The personality tests are used for pairing. But check your contract. It's all perfectly legal. The psychologists merely make suggestions based on the personality tests. As the producer, I have the ultimate say."

"So you ignored their advice and overrode their opinion, sabotaged my chances of success on the show? *Why?* Why would you ever do that?"

"I wasn't sabotaging your chances on the show. The way everything played out, I just...didn't have a better option. But I wanted to tell you now so that you didn't continue to try to make something work that—that isn't, especially while you're dealing with your parents' car crash. Otherwise, I wouldn't have mentioned it."

"You would've continued to keep that secret to yourself, in other words."

"It wasn't a secret. It was just...one of the decisions I had to make for the good of the show."

"And Darius? Did you do the same with him and Barbie?"

"No, I went with everyone's recommendation there."

"And the other couples?"

"I used their recommendations for the other couples, too."

"So it was just Grady and me."

The Uber driver had come to a stop in front of Aja's condominium complex. "Hello? Can you hear me?" he said. "We've arrived."

If he'd said it before, she'd missed it. She'd been too focused on her conversation to even realize where she was.

Numbly, she forced herself to get out of his car. But then she stood on the street looking up at the place she called home until another vehicle came and honked for her to get out of the way.

"Aja? Are you still there? What's going on?" Winnie asked, and Aja finally tuned in to the conversation again.

"Nothing, but I won't be doing anything more for the show," she said and disconnected. She felt duped, betrayed, and she had no doubt Grady would feel the same. Maybe this would make him decide to give up on their marriage, but she felt it was only fair that he know the truth, too.

After dragging her luggage into the elevator and up to her second-story condo, she turned on the air-conditioning as soon as she walked through the door to help dispel the summer heat and rid the place of the musty odor that often came with living so close to the beach.

But she didn't get in the shower and then drop into bed as she'd planned. Although her eyes felt like sandpaper, she knew she wouldn't be able to sleep.

Grady's morning had been a busy one, and when his newest tech ruined an expensive paint job, it grew frustrating, as well. But the moment he saw Aja's call come in, he told Dylan, who was working the front counter, to put out the bell and take over for him in back. Still, by the time he'd stepped outside he'd missed her call, so he called right back.

"Hello?"

Grateful to finally have the opportunity to talk to her, he breathed a sigh of relief when she answered. "Hey. How are you?"

"Not so good," she replied.

"What's going on? Don't tell me your mother is even worse than we thought."

"I don't know about that yet. The doctors won't say much. They managed to stop the bleeding and the swelling of her brain, but...there could be some long-term damage. We just have to wait and see."

"I'm sorry this happened, Aja. What about your father?"

"He's banged up, but it's nothing that won't heal."

"That's good, at least. Have you had anything to eat today? Been able to get any rest?"

"I've had a little food, no rest. But I saw your missed calls and wanted to get back to you. And I have something to tell you that's probably going to upset you."

Afraid of what she was about to say, he lifted his ball cap, then put it on again. Was this where she asked for an annulment? Told him it was over between them?

Because that wasn't what he wanted at all. The more he thought about her and the past week—their wedding, their honeymoon at the beach, talking for hours in the car on the drive to Whiskey Creek, dinner with his father, making love in his bed—the more he was coming to believe that, against all odds, she might actually be the perfect woman for him. And even if she wasn't "perfect" for him, he wanted to be with her, overcome whatever problems came up. "What is it?"

"We weren't paired together by psychologists, Grady. That was all bullshit."

He'd never heard her swear before, which showed him how upset she was. "What do you mean?"

"Winnie paired us together. That's why we have nothing in common and don't even live in the same part of the state."

His heart began to pound. "Who told you that?"

"She did. Can you believe it? And it's right there in the

contract we signed—that she has ultimate say. We just never paid attention to it because we didn't see any reason for her not follow the psychologists' advice—not after giving us all those tests—and we didn't truly believe we'd meet someone we'd want to spend the rest of our lives with."

Grady felt sick. "How'd that even come up?"

"I called to tell her about my parents. I wanted to make sure she wasn't going to charge the penalty—especially for you—when we have no control over the fact that we can't finish what we agreed to do for the show."

"What'd she say?" he asked, scrambling to come up to speed with what was going on.

"She said we don't need to worry, that she won't charge us. But then I asked her why the psychologists paired us together even though we didn't seem to have anything in common, and she said they didn't pair us, that she did."

Shit. He squeezed his forehead. "Why would she tell you that?" he asked, but he was talking to himself more than her.

"She said she didn't want me to feel I'm failing at something I believe I should be able to succeed at while I'm going through this with my parents."

"So she was looking out for you?" he said dryly. "She wanted to let you know that our marriage didn't have much of a chance to begin with so you wouldn't worry about sticking with it?"

"Something like that, I guess." She sounded slightly confused, and he couldn't blame her. "But she could've told us from the start that she'd decided to override the psychologists' advice. Instead, she led us to believe we had that going for us."

He didn't know what to do. He couldn't react with outrage, couldn't pretend he didn't know. That would be a lie. And he cared too much about Aja to destroy her trust in him.

But this was such a terrible time to have to confront this issue. He'd hoped they'd be able to get further into their relationship before he had to address the truth of how they'd come to be together.

Unfortunately, Winnie had forced his hand. She hadn't told Aja the full story, but she'd told her enough to put him in a terrible position. And he knew why she'd done it. She didn't want their marriage to last. He could tell how much it was bothering her during their last phone conversation. Having him unavailable and no longer interested made her want him that much more. Or she'd really believed his marriage wouldn't be successful, that it was just a matter of time before he'd be able to date her and was willing to wait…until she realized it might not go the way she'd expected.

Bottom line, she wanted to see their marriage fail.

"Grady? Don't you have anything to say about that?" Aja prompted when he didn't respond.

He rubbed his forehead for a second, bemoaning the fact that he seemed to have only one choice. Then he drew a deep breath and said, "I feel terrible because this is hitting at the worst possible moment, but there's more to it than you know."

Her voice went deadly serious. "What are you talking about?"

"I *promise* I was going to tell you at some point. But thanks to Winnie, I guess that moment is now."

Chapter Twenty

Too tired to fight the tears that welled up, Aja pulled her pillow in close to her body. The conversation she'd had with Grady had been a difficult one. She could tell he felt bad about how everything had played out, and she believed him when he said he would've told her the truth eventually…because he could've lied and *not* told her earlier.

But by the time they'd hung up, she was pretty disillusioned.

The real reason he'd come on the show was for Winnie? He'd just been putting in his time with her? He'd admitted he'd chosen her because he thought she was the *least* likely woman to be compatible with him…

With a sniff to stop her nose from running, she turned onto her other side and punched her pillow to get it right. That he hadn't been completely honest until today bothered her, of course, but it was the idea that he and Winnie had had this secret thing going on all along that upset her the most. She felt *so* stupid for joining the cast of the show and allowing them to use her as a pawn in their little game.

But as angry as she was tempted to be—with both of them—she had no one to blame but herself. When she signed on as a contestant, she'd known she was opening herself up to only God knew what. Otherwise, she would've been honest with her parents about what she was planning to do, and they would've told her that she was a fool for taking a leave of absence at her office to meet a man who would most certainly be "unsuitable" for her. They would've strongly advised her *not* to marry a complete stranger, especially one who had nothing in common with her.

Even Darius would say she'd taken it all too seriously. Look at him and Barbie! They were getting along just fine—were friends, he'd told her while they were at her mother's bedside—and working together to navigate the show so they could use it as the launchpad they'd intended it to be for their acting careers.

But somewhere along the line, Aja had screwed up and begun to let her emotions get involved. Now she was married to a man who lived seven hours away, in a town of only two thousand people, and she didn't know whether to have the marriage annulled and go on with her life as it was, forgive Grady and try to manage a long-distance relationship until they knew each other better, or throw caution to the wind and move to Whiskey Creek. If she did that, and the marriage ultimately ended in divorce, she would've ruined her dental practice for nothing. She might even have kids by then and be facing custody issues.

She sighed as she pictured her poor mother connected to all the tubes and machines in the intensive care unit. Esther and Cyrus would probably never forgive her for deviating from the careful plan they felt would bring their family the most happiness. She couldn't even tell them what she'd done; not while they were in such a fragile state.

"What a mess," she muttered to herself.

Her phone signaled a text. She'd left her notifications on in case Darius or someone else from the hospital needed to reach her, so as soon as she heard the sound, she shoved into a sitting position and reached over to the nightstand.

But it wasn't Darius; it was Arman. She hadn't heard from him since she refused to marry him, but she'd told him she wanted to remain friends. He probably just wanted to check on her parents, anyway, so she didn't feel it would be kind to ignore his call.

Drawing a deep breath in an effort to keep the tears out of her voice, she answered. "Hello?"

"Aja, my parents and I just heard from your father. We had no idea he and Esther had an accident after they left us in Palm Springs and feel absolutely terrible."

"I appreciate that," she said. "It's very nice of you to call."

"I'm worried about you. Is there—is there anything I can do?"

"Nothing. It's all up to the doctors now. They're working hard, trying to minimize the damage to my mother's brain. My father probably already told you that he'll recover."

"He did. But he's *so* worried about your mother."

"We all are."

"Would you mind if we came by the hospital?"

How could she say no? The two families were very close. "Of course not."

"What time would be best?"

She was *so* exhausted she couldn't face dealing with him or his parents tonight when she returned to the hospital to relieve Darius. "How about tomorrow morning?"

she asked and held her breath, hoping he'd accept the slight delay and not press for something more immediate.

"Sure."

She exhaled. "Thanks."

He lowered his voice. "I want you to know I'm here for you, if you need me."

His kindness caused tears to well up again. Should she have accepted his marriage proposal? It seemed as though she'd veered widely off course the night she refused. "I appreciate that."

"But…you don't want me around?"

She was married to someone else now! She gripped her forehead. *What* had she done? "It's not that. It's—it's just a very difficult time, but I'll manage."

"Don't you miss me? Let me help you through this."

"Arman, I can't deal with anything emotional right now. I'm in a difficult enough situation as it is."

"I thought it might make things easier. But…okay. I'll see you in the morning," he said and let her hang up.

She sat there for several minutes after that conversation, thinking about him. He knew her so well, knew her family. Her parents loved him; his parents loved her. Esther and Cyrus were probably right—he would've made a good husband. So…was she being spoiled by refusing to go that way? Selfish? Asking for too much?

She closed her eyes as she slouched back down in the bed. Maybe what she'd done would turn out to be an even bigger regret than she'd imagined.

Although Grady had tried to call three times, Winnie didn't pick up until that evening. He had a feeling she knew—or had guessed—the reason for his call. She had no business revealing what she'd revealed to Aja. She should've left that to him, which made him wonder if it wasn't a subtle form of revenge.

"You told her?" he demanded as soon as she finally answered.

There was a long pause. Then she said, "Calm down, Grady."

"I haven't even raised my voice."

"But there's a steely note in it. I can tell you're not happy."

"I'm *not* happy," he admitted, "and for good reason. Why'd you take it upon yourself to tell Aja that *you* paired us together?"

"Because I didn't want her beating herself up, thinking she had to make the marriage work because it was… supposed to, especially while her mother's fighting for her life in the ICU."

"Did Aja tell you she was struggling with our marriage? Or was she just letting you know she couldn't finish filming for the show?"

After another long pause, she said, "Either way, I felt I had to be more honest with her."

He got up and began to pace on the deck. "And what about me? You couldn't have talked to me about it first?"

"Grady, if she gives up on the marriage that easily, she wouldn't have stuck it out for the long haul, anyway, especially now, with her parents in the hospital. They are *heavily* involved in her life, which is completely foreign to you and me. They don't even know about you. What do you think is going to happen when she tells them?"

"Her mother might still survive and be fine, and if she does, we could've dealt with everything else after. I didn't need you getting involved, trying to sabotage the marriage you helped facilitate."

"That's just it! It was *because* I helped facilitate it—because I put her in the position she's in—that I felt guilty about not being more up front."

"That can't be true," he said with a scoffing laugh. "If it was guilt that motivated you, you would've told her the real truth. *You* didn't pair us. *I* did. You allowed me to do that, remember?"

"I couldn't go that far, and you know why," she said. "It would be terrible for the show if that ever got out, so I came as close to the truth as I dared."

"In other words, you told her what served your purposes," he clarified.

"So what? Do you want me to admit that I'd rather you be free? Of course I would!" she said, finally moving past the bogus excuses. "You know I'm attracted to you, and I thought you were attracted to me. But you're so caught up in trying to force this marriage to work that you're going to make us both miss out on what we could've had!"

He stood at the railing of his back porch and stared out at the creek. Was she right? Was he missing the main attraction? Winnie was gorgeous and smart and engaging. He couldn't argue with any of that. But so was Aja. And she had a wholesomeness to her that appealed to him more than anything else he'd ever encountered…

"Grady?"

"I'm still here," he grumbled.

"Aren't you eager to see what *we* could have?" she asked.

He tested that question on himself, but the answer was…no. Not anymore. Since Aja had come into his life, she'd changed everything. "I'm sorry, Winnie. I'm not trying to force my marriage to work because I don't want to fail. And it isn't just because I want to be fair to Aja. It's because…" He struggled for the words to finish that sentence and couldn't seem to grasp the right ones, but only because he couldn't believe what kept coming to the tip of his tongue.

"Because..." she prompted.

"I think it's because I've fallen in love with her," he said incredulously.

This met with dead silence. "You've only known her a couple of weeks, Grady."

"I realize that," he said. "But... I think she's got me. I never saw it coming, so I must not have put up my normal defenses and—"

"Oh, my God!" she moaned. "You actually mean it."

He did. As shocking as that was. The man who'd been unable to open his heart had finally lost it to a sweet, sincere, beautiful Persian woman he'd met only because he'd done something most people would call completely idiotic.

He thought Winnie might insist he didn't know Aja well enough, that he had to be wrong, but she didn't. She didn't say another word. There was no click or anything, either, but the phone went dead.

The night had been long and hard. Morning seemed to take forever. Aja had tried to get out of the hospital before Arman and his parents arrived. But Darius had called to put her off an hour, said he had to do a quick segment for the show before he could come relieve her, and the Kahns arrived first thing, right at eight.

Aja felt self-conscious when Behar and Behram walked in and saw her curled up in the vinyl chair where she'd been sleeping. Dropping the thin hospital-issue blanket she'd been using, she got up to greet them, still stiff and sore and with eyes swollen from all the crying she'd done last night. They'd never seen her so unkempt, but it was difficult to care too much about her appearance when she had so many other, more pressing concerns.

She wasn't sure what to expect from them. They'd known her since she was just a baby and had always been warm. But she'd recently refused to marry their beloved son. Maybe it was her imagination, but she thought they were decidedly cool toward her, despite their concern for her mother.

"Good morning," Behram said, sounding much more formal than usual. Behar merely dipped her head. But then, Arman walked in, and his big brown eyes showed much more sympathy.

"Have you been here all night?" he asked.

She nodded and tried to fix the hair that was falling from the messy knot on top of her head. "Darius has been…busy. Stuff he has to do for school," she quickly added so they wouldn't ask what he was doing or be tempted to judge him.

He came over to hug her, and the familiarity of his embrace, and the scent of his cologne, proved so enticing she couldn't help melting into his chest. "You must be exhausted," he murmured above her head.

Once again, tears pricked the backs of her eyes, but she blinked them away. "I'm tired," she admitted.

Behar moved to her mother's side and took her hand. "Have you heard anything?" she asked, her face pinched with concern. "What are the doctors saying?"

"They don't know what to say," Aja replied. "Not yet. They plan to bring her out of the coma sometime today. I guess we'll know more when she wakes."

Behar frowned. "This must be so frightening for you."

Extricating herself from Arman's embrace, she continued to try to fix her hair. "It's been terrible, upsetting."

"Of course," Behar said. "Why don't you let us sit with her now while you go home and get some rest?"

Aja longed for her bed. The hour nap she'd ended up

getting last night just wasn't enough. But she couldn't leave. "I don't dare. I don't know when the doctors will be bringing my mother out of her coma, and I definitely want to be here for that."

"Of course you do," Behram said.

"Check with them," Behar directed. "If they aren't planning to do it until this afternoon, you'll have plenty of time."

She was too out of sorts to even think straight, felt overwhelmed by the simple task of tracking down that information. "I don't know where any of the medical personnel I need are at the moment. They come in periodically and then they disappear."

"There's a nurse's station outside," Behram said. "Ask there."

"I'll do it," Arman volunteered. Then his gaze met Aja's. "Go ahead and sit down. Can I get you something to eat while I'm gone?"

It would be so easy to lean on him, she realized. He could step back into her life, and they could pick up right where they left off. Then she'd have the love and support she needed to get through the coming weeks, and there'd be no upset to her parents, no upset to her parents' best friends, no need to sell her practice and move, no question as to what she was ultimately getting in a mate.

Should she just let go of Grady and choose the safe and ordinary path? Right her wrong before it was too late?

She happened to glance down and catch a glimpse of her wedding band. She'd been so caught up in everything that was going on she hadn't even remembered she was wearing it, let alone considered removing it.

Terrified that Arman or his parents would notice it, she slipped her hand behind her and stretched her back to make it look like a natural movement. "That'd be great—

anything would taste good. I'll pay you via Venmo, so get something for yourself, too. And while you're gone, I'll talk to the nurses myself and try to tie down when the doctor will be back."

"Okay, but you don't have to pay me," he said and left.

Aja edged around the bed and gestured toward the seat she'd just vacated. "Behram, feel free to sit down. I'll let you know what I find out before I leave—if I'm able to leave."

Behar was still at her mother's side and didn't seem to hear her. "Can you believe this happened?" she said to her husband. "If we'd left when they did…who knows? We might've been following closely behind and…"

Then they could've been involved in the accident, too.

"She's going to be fine, Behar," Behram insisted. "Have faith."

Aja escaped the room, moving far more quickly than she'd been capable of moving just a few minutes ago, and found the nurse's station, where—after they'd made several calls over nearly twenty minutes—she learned that her mother's doctor was planning to bring Esther out of the coma around four.

Before returning to the room, Aja moved her wedding ring to a different finger, even though it barely fit, because she couldn't take it off entirely without the threat of losing it. She was wearing yoga pants and a stretchy top with no pockets.

"Sounds like I can head home for a few hours," she told the Kahns. "The doctor won't be here until later this afternoon."

Behar hadn't moved; Behram had taken the chair she'd been using before they arrived. "We'll stay until you get back."

"You don't have to. Darius is coming." Aja checked the

time on her phone. "Allowing for the drive, he'll be here in another forty-five minutes or so."

"We'll stay," Behar repeated as if it was more of a decree, and it was then Aja understood she probably wouldn't get rid of them today.

She approached her mother's bed from the other side and peered down into Esther's empty, slack face. Surely, this nightmare wouldn't last. Surely, her mother would recover. She was the strongest woman Aja had ever known.

Silence settled upon them. Only the wheeze and rattle of the ventilator and other machines filled the void as Aja waited for Arman to get back. She felt awkward and wanted to leave, didn't care enough about eating to wait, but she couldn't ask him to get her food and then be gone when he returned.

At last, he walked into the room and handed her a sack. "Sorry it took so long. There was quite a bit of traffic. But I got you the *halim* you love, with some flatbread, of course."

Halim was a stewlike dish made of meat, barley and dal with a delicious blend of spices—something Grady had probably never even tried, let alone something he'd ever bring her. "Thank you," she said. "That's…very nice."

"Do you want to stay here to eat it?" he asked. "I can request a rolling table—"

"No," she interrupted. "It'll be easier at home. But… thanks again."

"Arman's a good man," Behar said sullenly. "Any woman would be lucky to have him."

"Mom!" Arman snapped, and she shot him a look that suggested it was only right she say something before going back to her vigil.

"I know he's a good man," Aja said. The question was… was he the right man for her—or was Grady?

Chapter Twenty-One

"You've been moping around all day," Dylan said. "What's going on?"

JT answered before Grady could, even though the question hadn't been directed at him. "He's butt-hurt. Fallen in love with that beautiful Persian woman he married, and now he thinks he's lost her."

Dylan leaned the bumper he'd been carrying out to the paint bays against the wall and walked over to the counter, where Grady had been working since he came in this morning. "Things haven't gotten any better? I've been hoping she was just supporting her parents and the situation would improve."

Grady didn't want to admit that wasn't the case, that he'd screwed up what was probably his best chance at happiness. He felt he shouldn't have gotten carried away thinking he might've *finally* found the right woman. That was stupid. He'd never been lucky in love. "She *is* supporting her parents, but—"

Dylan cocked his head when Grady didn't finish. "Are we still talking about the fact that her parents won't accept you? Is she backing away from the marriage because she knows they won't approve?"

"That's part of it. Aja doesn't even want to tell them about me—not now. And that's understandable, given her mother's in a freaking coma."

"A *medically induced* coma," Dylan clarified. "There's a difference. They're trying to save her, and they might pull it off. So don't give up hope too soon."

Grady shoved the invoice he'd just marked *paid* into the appropriate basket. "It's not only the family thing. It's… Never mind. It's a long story—that's what it is."

Dylan didn't budge. Neither did JT. They both stood there looking at him expectantly, and since they had a strange lull in business, no one else was there to interrupt.

"We'll take the time," Dylan said when Grady didn't succumb to his meaningful stare.

"I made a mistake, okay?" Grady said in exasperation. "And I feel terrible, so the last thing I want to do is talk about it."

"What'd you do?" JT demanded.

But Dylan didn't bother with that. He caught Grady's eye and said simply, "Then ask her to forgive you."

Grady blew out a long sigh. "I can't imagine she will, not at this stage of our relationship. I'm sure I've scared her off."

"She went on a TV show looking for love," Dylan pointed out. "I can't imagine she'll give up *too* easily."

Grady gave him a look that said, "Nice try."

"She went on the show for her brother. *He* wanted to be a cast member, and the producer wouldn't take him without her."

"Oh! That sucks," JT said as if he now understood why all was lost.

JT's response irritated Grady. But that was often the case with his father. Fortunately, Dylan was the man who'd raised him and didn't have the same effect. Grady respected and loved Dylan more than anyone in the world.

"All I know is that if you want her, you need to fight for her, so you won't kick yourself later," Dylan said.

"And how do I do that?" Grady asked. "She's not even returning my messages."

Dylan walked back to the fender and lifted it over one shoulder. "You know where LA is, don't you?"

"You want me to drive to Los Angeles and interrupt everything that's going on? I don't want to bug her—"

"She came to Whiskey Creek because she wanted your marriage to work, right?" he interrupted. "She had to break her contract with the show in order to do it, give up whatever they were paying her. She cares about you, was hoping for a future with you, or she wouldn't have done that."

"But with the accident, I feel like my hands are tied."

"You can be supportive without going too far," Dylan said. "Just don't be demanding. All you have to do is show her you care."

That was the hardest thing in the world for him. When it came to love, he'd never been capable of taking much risk.

Dylan stepped toward the back door as he added, "But the window you have to save your marriage might be closing, so I'd leave right away. If you go now, you can be there by…what? Ten or eleven? And if she won't see you that late, maybe you can take her to breakfast—or bring her breakfast at the hospital—first thing in the morning."

Grady considered what showing up unannounced might be like. "That's…bold," he said.

"Sometimes you need to be bold," Dylan responded. "At least then you'll know that you did everything you could."

Aja slept deeply for six hours, until her alarm went off, bringing her to a foggy awareness. She had little doubt she could use even more sleep, but she felt somewhat refreshed after she showered, threw on a pair of jeans and a long-sleeved T-shirt, since it was always cold at the hospital, and rushed to reach her mother's room before the doctor showed up.

Darius had sent her a message while she was getting ready, saying the Kahns were still there and didn't seem to be planning to leave any time soon, so she knew she was about to have another awkward encounter with her ex and his family. Unfortunately, it would happen at a vulnerable moment. But she was so worried about her mother, nothing else mattered. The doctor had no idea if Esther would even be able to speak, let alone function in other regards, and the thought of her waking up and not even recognizing them was terrifying.

When she arrived, the room was as crowded as she'd expected. Her father was sitting in a wheelchair, and Darius was there along with a nurse, her mother's main doctor and the anesthesiologist. Thankfully, the Kahns were gone, after all.

"There you are!" Darius said with obvious relief.

She hurried to her father's side and dropped a kiss on his cheek. "What's wrong? Is everything okay?"

"I hope so." Her father looked pale and sounded uncertain, which was so unlike him. He'd always been large and in charge.

"Everything's fine," the doctor assured her. "My schedule changed a bit, so I juggled things around and arrived earlier than planned, that's all. But this process takes time.

Dr. Nguyen will slowly lower the propofol keeping your mother's brain quiet so that she can wake up gradually, at which point we'll change the mode on the ventilator to allow her to breathe on her own."

"You've already started that process?"

He nodded, but he was clearly focused on monitoring her mother's heart and brain activity. "Just a few minutes ago."

Aja sidled closer to her brother. "Where are the Kahns?" she whispered.

"The doctor asked them to leave, said there were too many people in here," he replied.

"Thank goodness."

He brought her forward, next to their father, who'd been wheeled to the edge of the bed, and left his arm around her shoulders. She knew then that as cavalier as he sometimes acted, he was as frightened as she was.

"How long will it take?" she asked the doctor.

"Depends," he said. "Some people take longer than others. Maybe thirty minutes or so?"

She felt as though they were in the way. "Should we step back?"

"No, we'll manage," he said. "We want her family to be the first thing she sees. This process can create a lot of confusion and anxiety. Having her loved ones close will reassure her."

Aja felt her brother's grip tighten on her shoulder. "Okay," she said.

"She'll be fine," their father said, but tears were gathering in his eyes. He was part of the medical community. He understood the risks and the odds.

Scarcely able to breathe, Aja gripped the hand he lifted for her, and they waited—grouped together and hanging on to each other—for what seemed like an eternity. Each minute, each second that ticked away created more fear. Would Esther wake up at all?

"Come on, *eshghe man*," her father muttered, his words a chanted prayer he'd probably been saying under his breath that'd finally become audible.

That was when her mother's eyelids fluttered open.

Aja gasped and her father dropped her hand to grab Esther's. "We're here with you, and you're going to be all right," he told her. "*Dooset daram.* Just relax. Don't fight those who are helping you and all will be well."

The distress in her eyes eased, and although she groaned when the doctor adjusted the ventilator to allow her to breathe on her own, she didn't try to grab at anything or resist.

She was awake! She'd come back to them! And she seemed to recognize Cyrus, at least. Otherwise, why would his words have calmed her so quickly?

That was all *very* hopeful. Now they just had to wait and see if things got better—or worse—from here.

Grady had no idea what to expect. He hated to drop into the middle of a family emergency, especially one this serious. But it also felt weird to be in Whiskey Creek while his wife was in LA.

He'd decided he wouldn't be intrusive. He'd get a motel and stay out of the way—simply let Aja know he was close and available to support her if she needed him. Then *she* could decide whether she wanted to see him.

Just in case it was a mistake and Aja absolutely *didn't* want to see him, he'd sent a message to Darius to let him know he was coming. He'd hesitated to bother her brother, so he hadn't requested any type of response. He'd just felt as though someone should know he was coming.

He arrived at midnight and stopped at a moderately

priced motel along the freeway not too far from the mansion where they'd filmed the show. His phone lit up while he was dragging his suitcase into the room. He assumed it was Dylan, making sure he'd arrived safely. His oldest brother had called him twice to make sure he wasn't getting sleepy behind the wheel.

But once he dropped onto the bed and checked his phone, he saw that the text had come from Darius.

They took mom out of her coma today. No one can say if there's been any lasting damage to her brain. The doctors are trying to ease her back into functionality, so we haven't tried to communicate with her too much. We'll know more tomorrow. Barbie and I are staying at my place for now. It's not as nice as hers, but it's closer to the hospital. You're welcome to sleep on the couch. Just know that my apartment is on campus, so very small.

There was so much Grady wanted to say that it would be difficult to put it all in a text, so he decided to take the chance of calling Darius and was relieved when he picked up. "Sorry to disturb you, especially this late," he said. "But I wanted to let you know that I'm set for the night. I've already got a room."

"No problem. I just got home from the hospital. Barbie says she'd love to see you. But I wasn't joking when I said my place was small."

"I'm fine," Grady insisted. "But it's nice of you to offer."

"Why wouldn't I? You're my brother-in-law," he said with a laugh.

That was the thing. Was he *really*? Would his relationship with Aja—and Darius—last? Because of the way he'd come to be married, Grady didn't know if he could count on it being real. He felt like he was trying to turn a dream into something tangible he could rely on, and that wasn't an easy task. "How's your sister?" he asked.

"This is hitting her hard, as you probably know."

"She hasn't said much to me recently. I think she's withdrawn completely."

"Because of the guilt. She feels bad having such a tragedy happen right when she was doing something that would upset Mom and Dad. She also feels bad for lying to them. She's always been too honest for her own good," he added as an obvious joke.

Grady chuckled. But it wasn't just the family dynamic that stood between them, and Grady knew it. Aja had good reason to be disappointed in him. He didn't see where he could've told her about Winnie and the psychologists before he did, however. Thanks to Winnie, he'd told her too soon as it was…and Aja's reaction proved it.

"I keep telling her that Mom and Dad are *both* going to be okay," Darius said. "Today couldn't have gone any better. Mom came out of her coma right away and began to breathe on her own, so they've removed the respirator. She even ate a little soup tonight. Now they're just trying to keep her comfortable and stable until she feels strong enough to interact. That's when we'll know if—if she's truly herself."

"Not knowing must be hard."

"It is. But I'm feeling better now than I have since the accident—I can tell you that much."

"Do you think it was a mistake for me to come to Los Angeles, Darius?" Grady asked. "Does Aja consider our marriage over? I don't want to make this any harder on her."

As the silence stretched, Grady imagined he was thinking it over. But if it required that much thought…

He braced for the worst.

"Depends," Darius finally said.

"On what?"

"Are you doing it for the show—so that you look atten-
tive and don't come off like an asshole? Or do you really
care about her?"

"I can promise you it's not for the show."

"Which means…"

As difficult as it was for him to talk about his feelings,
if he wanted Aja, he had to dig deeper, allow himself to
be vulnerable. "She's *all* I care about."

There was another pause, this one much shorter, and
Grady knew his sincerity had come through when Darius
said, "I'm happy to hear that. I'm going to send you the
address to her condo—along with the code for the gate so
you can get to her door. My dad felt well enough to stay
with my mom tonight. He wanted to have some time alone
with her. So Aja is on her way home right now. It might be
the perfect time to talk to her."

Grady breathed a huge sigh of relief. Maybe, just maybe,
he had another chance. "I appreciate it."

Aja had just pulled on the tank top she planned to sleep
in when she heard a knock at the front door. It was likely
her neighbor, DeeAnn, checking on her; she'd told her
about the accident earlier. With a yawn, she pulled on her
robe, belted it at the waist and padded out through the
living room in her slippers to peer through the peephole.

Then she froze. It wasn't her eighty-year-old neighbor.
It was Grady, and he was holding a huge bouquet of purple
and white hydrangeas.

She stepped back while trying to decide what to do. He
didn't fit into her life. They lived in two different parts
of the state, and she couldn't leave LA—not now that her
parents needed her. She wasn't going to do anything more
for the show, either. She felt like she'd gotten burned by it,
was done with Winnie. She just hadn't told him that she'd

come to these conclusions yet. It wasn't a conversation she was looking forward to having. She cried whenever she started rehearsing it in her mind, which was odd. She hadn't shed nearly as many tears over Arman.

But Grady had come all the way from Whiskey Creek. She couldn't leave him standing at her door. She wasn't even sure how he'd gotten through the security gate.

Steeling herself, she withdrew the bolt. "Hi," she said.

He studied her for a moment. "I'm sorry to surprise you. But...you haven't been responding to my texts."

"I apologize for that. It's been—"

He lifted a hand. "I know. I'm not criticizing or—or trying to put pressure on you. I just... I bought these flowers for you before I left Whiskey Creek and needed to get them into some water."

She couldn't help chuckling. "So you drove them seven hours?"

He grinned. "I did. And if you were in San Diego or anywhere else, I would've driven them farther. I've been dying to see you, Aja. I'm sorry. Truly sorry. I didn't intend for what happened to happen. Everything just got away from me. Because I was skeptical that the show could truly find me a wife I'd love. I was still trying to manage that on my own."

Politeness dictated she step back and let him in. It was rude to keep him standing on her stoop. But she wasn't ready. If she invited him in, it would be almost impossible for her to ask him to leave, because she was far too excited to see him. Then all the decisions she'd made recently would be upended, and she'd be faced with the same difficult questions she'd been asking herself all along—what she would do with her practice, her condo and her parents if they stayed together. "And now?"

"I'm glad I took matters into my own hands, because *they* never would've paired me with you."

She took the flowers and stared down at them. "That's very nice of you to say, Grady, but I don't see how we could ever make it."

"We can make it if we want to," he insisted. "I'm nearly forty, Aja. It's taken me a long time to fall in love. So I know how special this is. I don't want to lose you."

"You're saying you *love* me?"

"I must! You're all I can think about, all I want."

"But your business and my business—"

"I'll move here, help you take care of your parents and work for another auto body shop until I can get my own again."

Aja felt her jaw drop. "You'd do that?"

"If that's what it takes."

She gave him a wry smile. "Winnie's going to hate that she missed getting this on the show."

"Forget Winnie," he said. "Just tell me you feel the same way about me—that you'll fight for what we could have, in spite of the obstacles between us."

All the turmoil inside her suddenly eased, and her path forward seemed clear. Maybe Grady wasn't anyone her parents would've picked for her. Maybe they didn't have a lot in common. They'd have to figure out where to live and who would do what for work. But those were practical problems. As he'd said, they *could* overcome them if they wanted to badly enough.

"Aja?" he prompted, tilting his head to catch her eye.

She stood on her tiptoes as she threw her arms around him. She nearly dropped half the flowers she was holding in the process, but she didn't care. *This* was what felt right. It was the *only* thing that felt right. So they'd just have to deal with everything else. "I'm willing to fight for our marriage, too," she said.

Epilogue

Esther was getting stronger all the time, and there didn't seem to be any lasting brain damage. Although she was still fragile and would remain in the hospital for probably another week, she had no trouble with her speech or memory or motor skills. The doctors marveled at her recovery. And except for the cast on his arm, her father was back to his old self.

Aja nibbled at her bottom lip as she waited for her mother to finish eating lunch. Her father was in the room, too, reading the news on his phone. Darius was off somewhere, filming for the show. Since he and Barbie weren't going to stay together, he didn't plan on ever telling their parents about the marriage, and Aja certainly wasn't going to out him.

She did, however, need to tell them about Grady. He'd been staying with her in the condo for eight days so far, but had just recently started commuting to Silver Springs to help at the Amos Auto Body shop his youngest brother was running.

That seemed to be working out in the short term, but after her mother healed and they could make all the arrangements, they planned to move to Whiskey Creek, after all. Although Grady insisted he'd be the one to relocate if she wanted him to, she'd decided, since her parents were going to be fine, she'd go ahead and sell her dental practice and open a new one in Grady's hometown. She wanted to be able to contribute to their living—although he'd told her on numerous occasions that she didn't have to work if she didn't want to.

Maybe if she got pregnant, she'd focus on raising their children and building a pottery business instead.

It was nice to have options.

"What is it with you?" her father asked, jerking her out of her reverie.

She glanced up to see him studying her quizzically. "What do you mean?"

"You've always got a dreamy smile on your face these days."

Her mother put down her fork and peered at her. "Don't tell me you and Arman are back together…"

"I'm afraid not." The Kahns had been to the hospital several times, and she and Arman had been friendly to each other, but there'd been nothing to indicate they'd ever get back together. This was just another of her mother's many attempts to get her to yield to their wishes.

But that wasn't going to happen. And her father had unwittingly given her the perfect opening to bring up what she'd been waiting to talk to them about. "I've met someone else," she announced.

They both blinked in surprise. *"Who?"* they said in unison.

"His name's Grady Amos."

"Where'd you meet him?" her father asked.

She figured the less said, the better. "Here in LA."

Her mother shoved the rolling cart containing the remains of her lunch to one side. "At your practice? Is he a patient?"

"No, at an acting gig I participated in for Darius's sake."

Her mother stiffened. "Darius is acting now?"

"He's been doing a little of it lately." She had to admit certain things, just in case they learned about the show later. But she could keep it relatively vague—felt that was the smarter way to go.

"Why hasn't he mentioned it?" her father asked.

"Because of everything the two of you have been going through. He didn't want to worry you by making you feel as though he's been taking too much time away from studying for the bar."

Her father set his phone on the counter. "Who is this man you're seeing? And what kind of a name is *Grady*?"

"It's an American one," she replied and got up to show them a picture of him. She still wasn't wearing her wedding ring; she didn't plan to tell them she was married. She'd break that news later, maybe months later, once they'd adjusted to having Grady in her life.

Her mother frowned at his picture. "You're dating this man?"

"I am. And he's the most wonderful person on the planet. You're going to love him."

Her parents didn't look as though they believed it; she wasn't sure she did, either, because she wasn't convinced they'd ever be able to admit they were wrong about Arman. But their approval no longer mattered so much to her. She was finally happy. Better than happy—content in a deep-down, fulfilled sort of way. She'd managed to find what she was missing.

"What does he do for a living?" her mother asked skeptically.

"He owns his own business—an auto body shop." She didn't mention where. That they'd be moving was also something she was saving until they got to know Grady.

The whine of the bed motor sounded as her mother pushed the button that would raise the back up even higher. "You were with Arman until just recently. Is this why you broke up? How long have you been seeing him?"

"Grady isn't the reason I broke things off with Arman," she admitted. "I didn't meet him until right after. But we're already starting to get serious. I think he's the one."

Her parents gaped at her. "When were you going to tell us?" her mother asked.

She smiled as she walked to the bed and rested her hands on the railing. "When I was ready," she said.

Her mother's gaze grew stern. No doubt she thought Aja was being impertinent. "What's that supposed to mean?"

"It means who I date—and marry—should be *my* choice, right?" Aja spoke gently but firmly—firmly enough that her parents looked at each other as if to say "What's going on with our daughter?"

"I hope you know what you're doing," her mother grumbled. She often resorted to instilling fear as another form of manipulation.

Aja kept her smile firmly in place. "It feels like I do, but there are no guarantees. Even if I married Arman, there'd be no guarantees. And as much as I love and respect you both, I need the freedom to make my own decisions."

"We've never stopped you from doing that!" her mother snapped.

Aja could've argued that point, but she didn't bother.

They weren't going to see things from her perspective, not today. That would take time, if it *ever* happened. She now understood that if the way they interacted with her was ever going to change, she had to be the one to make it happen.

A nurse came into the room, drawing her parents' attention, so she slipped out to text Grady.

I told them.

She got a text right back.

What'd they say?

It wasn't what they said, it was what I said. And I feel good about it.

* * * * *

A Q&A with Brenda Novak

What or who inspired you to write?
I never dreamed I'd be a writer until I caught my daycare
provider drugging my children with cough syrup to get
them to sleep all day while I worked as a loan officer. Then
I quit my job to stay home with them myself but needed
some way to help make a living. I was reading a good book
at the time   Jude Deveraux's *Knight in Shining Armor*—
and remember wondering as I finished it if I could ever
write a book. Because that was something I could do from
home without leaving my kids, I started the next day and
have never looked back.

What is your daily writing routine?
I treat my writing like a regular job. I work Monday to
Friday all day and quit at suppertime when my husband
gets home—and I sit in a home office and handle social
media and other promotional efforts as well as writing.

Who are your favorite authors?
I love Diana Gabaldon, Susan Elizabeth Phillips, Kristin Hannah, Janet Evanovich, Jean M. Auel, Ken Follett, Elin Hilderbrand and so many more!

Where do your story ideas come from?
Everywhere! My brain is constantly sifting through everything I see, hear and read, looking for inspiration.

Do you have a favorite travel destination?
I love to travel and see new things, but the most incredible vacation I've ever taken was to Egypt. The antiquities held me enthralled. It was during Ramadan, and I enjoyed floating down the Nile while listening to the prayers that were being sung in the towns we passed at various times during the day.

What is your most treasured possession?
I'd have to say I have three equal favorites—my iPhone, my Tesla and my computer.

What is your favorite movie?
The Last of the Mohicans. Just hearing the soundtrack is enough to inspire and excite me. J

When did you read your first Harlequin romance? Do you remember its title?
I used to read Harlequin romances in high school. I don't remember the first title, but I remember how much I loved them. I still have a girlfriend from that time who teases me about always having one in my possession and introducing her to them too.

How did you meet your current love?
When I was in college, my roommate brought him home. He smiled at me when we were introduced, and I lost my heart in that very second.

What characteristic do you most value in your friends?
Reliability (and if I can add a second one, consistency).

Will you share your favorite reader response?
I love the emails that talk about how my work has helped carry someone through a very difficult time.

Other than author, what job would you like to have?
I would love to be a theoretical physicist. I love anything about the universe and go to sleep every night to a documentary on the subject. I guess I figure I'll finally understand quantum mechanics if I just listen to enough people explain it—but I'm not there yet. LOL

Mona Shroff has always been obsessed with everything romantic, so it's fitting that she writes romantic stories by night, even though she's an optometrist by day. If she's not writing, she's likely to be making melt-in-your-mouth chocolate truffles, reading, or raising a glass of her favorite gin and tonic with friends and family. She's blessed with an amazing daughter and a loving son, who have both left the nest! Mona lives in Maryland with her romance-loving husband and their rescue dog, Nala.

ROAD TRIP RIVALRY

Mona Shroff

To Jyothi and Kosha for making me laugh at my
own drama. No, no one is sick and
I am not having an affair.

Chapter One

Poorvi Gupta pushed her glasses up her nose as she ran her gaze over the crowded gate area, looking for a place to charge her laptop. Her flight to Dublin was running about an hour behind, and patience was wearing thin around her.

Toddlers were fussing. A mother with a small baby was wearing a hole in the carpet as she paced back and forth trying to keep her baby asleep. Teens sat on the floor hogging the outlets to scroll social media, their legs outstretched. A middleaged, brown-skinned man was informing an airline representative that his elderly mother would be on the flight alone.

Poorvi's stomach was in knots, but mostly about presenting her paper at the Irish College of Ophthalmologists conference in Dublin. It wasn't her first presentation abroad, but the International Conferences were always a bit more complex than a presentation locally at university like Hopkins.

She still needed to make some adjustments to her presentation, but doing so required an outlet to keep her fading laptop charged long enough to run the slideshow. As she searched, she noticed a man looking her way. She continued to look for an outlet, but her glance at him revealed a tall figure with medium-dark skin, a perfect nose and a chiseled jaw sporting a balanced amount of scruff—not so much that it was a beard, not so little that it appeared as though he had neglected to shave. He was dressed in nice-fitting jeans, a long-sleeved T-shirt and a ball cap. The way her heart pounded in her chest, as well as the fact that she broke out in a sweat, confirmed it.

He was hot, hot, hot.

Which meant she needed to steer clear of him. It wasn't that she was awkward around handsome men, it was that she was *ridiculously* awkward around handsome men and had no desire to sweat profusely and trip over her words in what would certainly be an embarrassing attempt at conversation with a guy who she'd probably end up sitting next to for the duration of the six-hour flight to Dublin.

Never mind all that, she needed to be convincing in her presentation of the possible detrimental side effects of the latest refractive surgical procedure, C-MORE. As it was right now, C-MORE should be discontinued until the side effects were addressed.

At least in her professional opinion.

Her new boss, Dr. Bobby Wright, had made it abundantly clear that he had wanted to see the presentation prior to the conference. He wanted to make sure she struck the proper balance between recommending further study, while not pushing too hard for the temporary discontinuation of the procedure. He was afraid that all the clinicians would come down on him for taking away their paycheck.

Whatever. Bobby's priority was the lab. Her priority

was the patients. And as the lead investigator, her recommendation carried the most weight.

Success had been drilled into her since she was a child. The reality was that she really loved ophthalmology and doing research gave her great satisfaction. Not to mention the added bonus of not having to talk to anyone for long periods of time.

Someone across the aisle stood up and unplugged their phone. Finally! Poorvi made a beeline for the outlet, while reaching into her bag for her charger. She passed the middle-aged man who had been talking to the airline representative and did a double take as she heard him speaking to an old woman in Gujarati. Her parents had made sure that she was fluent in the language. But she didn't hear it all the time. The old woman was wearing a sari, much like her grandmother had up until her recent passing. No matter how hard she had tried to convince her to wear pants, or maybe even a salwar, her grandmother remained true to her sari.

That second of hesitation cost her. She failed to navigate the maze of extended teenage legs and children's paraphernalia, and tripped over a tossed sneaker, nearly falling headfirst onto the ground. She didn't fall, though the flailing of arms and legs was considerably less than graceful. She managed, however ungracefully, to reach the outlet just as another charger was plugged into the open socket.

"I need that outlet," she blurted out. Laptop charger in hand, Poorvi brushed flyway strands of hair from her face. She looked up to see Hot Guy standing there. Great. She immediately flushed, sweat breaking out all over her. "You took my outlet."

"The outlet was open, wasn't it now?" His voice was butter smooth and tinged with that Irish accent. He drew his gaze over her. In a different situation, Poorvi would have melted into ghee. But she *needed* that outlet.

"I was running for it," she declared, pushing her glasses up her nose again as she tilted her neck back to really see him. Damn. He was taller up close.

"You weren't quite there," he explained.

"You saw me running for it," she spat at him. Handsome or not, this man had no manners. "And I nearly fell."

"I saw no such thing," he insisted.

"You just said I wasn't there yet, so you clearly saw me running for it and you took it anyway," she fired up. She really needed to charge her computer before they boarded so she could work on that presentation.

Hot Guy sighed and leaned toward her. He even smelled amazing. Like soap and leather. "Listen, my phone is dead and my brother is fixing to call any minute—"

"Well, I have to work on a presentation. Catch up with your brother on your own time," she snapped, inhaling deeply. Damn but he smelled great.

He furrowed his brow over beautiful dark brown eyes. The irises were so dark, they blended with the pupils. It only made him more handsome. "I'll not be giving up this outlet until my call is through." He spoke kindly, but there was no doubt that he was not budging.

She opened her mouth to protest, but his phone rang, and he answered it, turning away from her.

She glared at the back of his head for a second, his audacity infuriating. She decided he really wasn't all that handsome after all. Not only did she not get her outlet, she was sweating.

"I'm fixing to get on the plane, Bhai, I—" Kavan Shashane never should have answered the phone. But if he didn't, Naveen would just keep calling and texting. He spotted the beautiful, but irritating, woman stalking off in his peripheral vision, presumably to continue her search for an open outlet in the crowded gate area. If she'd hung about, he'd have been happy to let her have the outlet after his phone call.

He watched her push her blue-framed glasses up the bridge of her nose as she continued her search. Her dark hair was tied into a thick side braid, though some pieces had come free when she'd tripped. Clearly, she hadn't even seen him reach for her in case she had fallen over that sneaker. But there you had it—he tried to be kind, and no one noticed. Story of his life now, wasn't it? She was comfortably dressed in dark jeans with just the tiniest of intentional cuts and a white button-down, tucked in just so. He was distracted enough by her that he missed the beginning of what his brother was telling him.

"Say it again, Bhai. I'm not hearin' you," Kavan said, still looking at the woman.

"Just listen. You're on your way back from the States, anyway. I got you registered at the ICO conference in Dublin later this week. I need you to go on to the meeting, find this P. K. Gupta and be sure to convince him not to present that paper." He paused. "And I scheduled a photo shoot for you. We are needing to update."

"Bhai, this is ridiculous. If there are issues with that procedure, we should investigate it, there are other procedures—" Kavan paced back and forth while drinking his cooling coffee. Forgetting that he was attached to a cord, he took an extra step and was yanked backward, spilling his coffee.

"Crap."

"What did you do now? Spill coffee?" Naveen sighed into the phone. "Seriously, Kavan."

"It's fine, Bhai." Kavan said. The coffee had only spilled

a few drops on his sneakers, and a few more on his T-shirt, so no harm done.

"Fine. Then, stop thinking, you'll strain something. This procedure is becoming our highest earner. We need it, yeah? That paper will lead to research, and research takes time. And during that time, patients will be hesitating to try the procedure. They'll want to wait for the research. And the reality is that all current studies support the use of the procedure."

"Bhai. Have you even looked at the newest research? It really does suggest that—"

"Honestly, Kavan. I've been taking care of things in the clinic for years. Trust me. You should be doing this procedure as well. You're literally the only one in the clinic who isn't doing it, because you're waiting for more studies. And you know as well as I do, that there are *always* new studies coming out. They aren't always relevant. That's what I need you to convince this P.K. Gutpa of. That the relevant studies of our time contradict his research, so there's no need to present it." He paused. "I don't have to look at the research when I have a nerdy brother to do that for me."

"Exactly." Kavan let the dig slide. He'd been called worse than nerdy. Besides, that was hardly an insult these days, was it? "There's a reason I don't do C-MORE," Kavan said.

"It's the same reason you still live with Mom. You have no guts. Honestly, little bhai, if it wasn't for me, you wouldn't even have finished high school, let alone university and medical college."

Kavan inhaled. Naveen wasn't wrong.

"If we—I—stop doing C-MORE, what do you think happens to our bottom line, Kavan?"

Kavan stayed silent. He didn't have to speak. Naveen would do all the talking.

"It goes away," Naveen said. "We lose money—not a good thing. Just go and do what I ask, like a good lad, eh?"

Kavan closed his eyes and inhaled. Naveen had run everything since their father died. He'd learned long ago that it was easier to give in.

At least to some degree in this case. P. K. Gupta's data looked interesting. It certainly implied that a temporary hold was to be considered. What he needed to do was actually talk to this P. K. Gupta, see their results and discuss the best options for the patients. This was what conferences were for, weren't they? "I can talk to them." Kavan agreed. He'd never win the argument with Naveen if he didn't have proper facts.

"That's a good lad, then." Naveen assumed Kavan would do as he was told, like he always did. Fine. He'd deal with Naveen later, if need be.

"Yeah. Bhai, sure." Still aggravated with his brother, he ended the call and grabbed his charger, all thoughts of the beautiful woman gone.

Chapter Two

Poorvi found an open outlet at the adjacent gate. She opened her computer and pushed up her glasses again. She didn't actually need them; she'd had refractive surgery (the older, more studied procedure—a perk of being in the business), but she liked the feeling that there was something between her and the world, so she had multiple pairs of glasses. It was her one nod to fashion, making sure her eyeglass frames matched her clothes. So blue for blue jeans today. She'd even bought a few new pairs to go with her outfits for this conference. That wasn't for a few more days, but her little sister, Niki, had wanted her to go early and maybe do a bit of sightseeing. Poorvi had no interest in seeing anything while this presentation hung over her head. So while she had agreed to come early, she was going to use the time to fully prepare for her presentation at the ICO Conference.

She worked until she heard the announcement for board-ing. She got on the plane and noted that Hot Guy was seated across the aisle from her. And that he must have spilled coffee on himself. Whatever. He was inconsiderate and she had little time for another self-centered man. Her boss, Dr. Bobby Wright, fell into that category, and she had no choice but to deal with him. Her ex, Brooks Handel, was another. But she no longer had to deal with him, as he had ghosted her months ago.

She had just opened her laptop again when a small commotion broke out in the aisle just behind her. A passenger and the flight attendant were having trouble communicating. Mostly because the passenger was speaking Gujarati, which the flight attendant did not understand.

Taking a closer look, she realized it was the older woman she had seen at the gate. She was dressed in a light-colored sari, was neither thin nor heavy. Her gray bun was pulled tight at the nape of her neck, much the same style Poorvi's grandmother had worn. Her arms were free of bangles, and her forehead had no chandlo.

Poorvi grinned as she noticed what could only have been a slight eyeroll on the part of the older woman, as she tried—yet again—to communicate in Gujarati to the flight attendant. Her own grandmother had shared similar frustrations from time to time.

People were still filtering onto the flight. Poorvi stood, and turned back to the older woman. "Ba," Poorvi immediately refered to the woman as grandmother as opposed to auntie. She missed her own grandmother enough that seeing a woman who seemed close to her grandmother's age, the endearment just tumbled from her mouth. "Tell me what the problem is," Poorvi asked in Gujarati, just as another, much deeper, smoother voice did the same. She glanced behind her and sure enough, Superhot Guy was talking to the older woman in Gujarati.

Huh.

He rasied an eyebrow when she spoke. Poorvi rolled her eyes. "I got this," she told him.

"You sure?"

"Yes." She was the fixer in every area of her life. Of course she was going to help. She turned back to the older woman and again asked her in Gujarati how she could help.

The passenger explained that she was afraid to sit in the middle seat and preferred the aisle.

"She can have my seat." Hot Guy addressed the flight attendant. He pointed to somewhere behind Ba. "The aisle seat back there." He dropped his phone as he gestured, his computer slipped and a few papers fell from his bag.

Poorvi stared for a moment. Was this guy for real? "Not necessary, she can have mine. It's right here." Poorvi was unclear as to why she was fighting him, especially when he was doing something so selfless, but she was. She started gathering her things when the older woman spoke again.

"I want to sit near both of them," she said, looking at the flight attendant and pointing at them. "They both speak Gujarati."

Poorvi translated. The flight attendant pressed his lips together, but Poorvi stared him down. *Let the woman sit where she's comfortable.*

The flight attendant nodded and started the chess game that was involved in moving seats around to accommodate Ba. Some people were willing, others not so much.

"I really don't see why I have to move to accommodate anyone." One particularly stubborn man set his jaw.

Hot Guy glanced at Poorvi before addressing the man. "You don't have to, now do you? Completely understandable."

What was he doing? They needed that man to move. Poorvi was about to step in, but Hot Guy continued.

"You don't have to, but you could anyway, yeah? And

then you'd be the hero here, because then that woman would be able to fly to our great city of Dublin and boast about the kindness of the Irish bloke on the plane." Hot Guy smiled softly and gave a shrug as he glanced at Poorvi.

His eyes told her this was a shot in the dark and he had no way of knowing if the young man would be convinced.

She couldn't help her small smile back at him, but she should have hidden it, because as soon as she smiled, Hot Guy smiled back as if they now shared a bond.

The man glared at Hot Guy. "Nice, so if I don't move now, I look like the arsehole." He grumbled, irritated. He huffed as he gathered his things and made to move.

"Thank you," Poorvi said.

"Whatever." The man harrumphed as the flight attendant ushered him to his new seat and offered him a complimentary drink.

However it happened, Poorvi was now in a window seat, Ba was next to her in the aisle, and Hot Guy was just across the aisle from her.

"Do you know each other?" Ba asked. Poorvi had automatically started thinking of her as a grandmother.

They shook their heads.

Ba eyed Poorvi, her eyes narrowed. "You are married?"

Poorvi smirked and shook her head. "No."

A small crooked smile appeared on Ba's face, and she turned to her other side.

Oh no... Poorvi knew where this was going.

"And you." Ba pierced Hot Guy with her grandmother powered eyes. "You are married?"

Hot Guy chuckled and shook his head. "No, Ba. I am not married."

Ba's grin widened as she turned back to Poorvi. "You are a doctor?"

Poorvi sighed. "Yes, but—"

"But nothing." Ba held up a hand to Poorvi as she turned to Hot Guy. She opened her mouth, presumably to ask the same question, but Hot Guy's attention was on the flight attendant who was giving instructions.

"So," the flight attendant was saying, "Mrs. Patel's daughter, Devi, will meet her at the airport in Dublin, but if you all could help her through baggage claim and all that, it would be lovely."

Poorvi nodded and Hot Guy said, "Of course." He needed to stop using his velvety deep voice and fabulous Irish accent. Or was it British? It seemed to change. Why did she care?

The flight attendant flushed and did a double take at him. "Don't I know you?" she asked.

"Um… I'm thinking not," Hot Guy said quickly, pulling the cap down further on his head. "Thanks. We'll be sure she gets to her daughter."

We? Poorvi nodded. "Ba? I will take you to your daughter after we land, okay? Do you need anything?" Even though her parents spoke Gujarati with her and her sister, Poorvi likely had an accent. "I'm happy to make sure she gets to her daughter." Poorvi made eye contact with Hot Guy.

"Very good." Ba bobbed her head at Poorvi. "What is your name, beti?"

"Poorvi." She gave her name with a smile and returned to her laptop. She heard Ba ask Hot Guy his name.

"I'm Kavan." She heard him say, then his hand was hanging in her peripheral vision.

She looked up to see him offering his hand in introduction. He was Irish. And Indian. Oh Lord help her. She sighed and shook his hand. "Poorvi."

Ba grinned openly turning her head from one to the

other. "You would make a beautiful couple." She bobbed her head. "Atcha. Okay."

Poorvi flushed, but she rolled her eyes and returned her attention to her computer. A glance at Hot Guy showed him still looking at her.

"Sorry about the outlet. My brother and I are in business together, and we have a big meeting coming up—"

His excuses hardly made up for his rudeness earlier. She shrugged. "Whatever."

"I'm trying to apologize here," Kavan said.

"That's rich, considering you got what you wanted," Poorvi retorted. "And I got stuck standing in a corner, balancing a computer on my knee."

He furrowed his brow obviously irritated with her. "Never mind." He sat back and returned to his phone.

"He's very handsome, no?" Ba whispered loudly to her in Gujarati.

Poorvi flushed. Kavan, of course, could hear—and understand every word. "Hmph," she said, shrugging.

Ba's eye widened. "Open your eyes, beti," she continued. "And he wears expensive T-shirt and jeans. Too bad about those dirty sneakers." She rubbed her forefinger and thumb together, then gave Poorvi a hard look. "And you don't seem to be getting younger."

"Ba!" Poorvi glared at the older woman as if she really were her grandmother. She certainly acted like her real grandmothers. "I'm not interested in getting married. I have my work."

Ba harumphed. "Work is not going to give you love." But she seemed to give up on Poorvi, instead turning her attention to Kavan. "She's beautiful, isn't she?"

Poorvi groaned internally. She did a side-eye glance at Kavan. He was flushed.

"Quite. But she's also rude, isn't she?" he answered.

"Excuse me?" Poorvi fired up, and turned her attention to him.

"You heard it. I tried to apologize, and you blew it off." His gorgeous dark eyes flashed at her from across Ba.

Ba turned her head to each of them as they argued. Like she was watching tennis.

"I'm not rude because I didn't accept your apology. That's my choice," she hissed at him.

"A choice to be rude." He went back to his phone.

"It was rude to take that outlet," she shot back. Seriously? Who was this guy?

"I was there first." He glanced up at her from his phone, and she genuinely expected him to stick his tongue out at her. "Wasn't I?"

She opened her mouth to continue her retaliation. And then she shut it. Who cared what this stranger thought of her? Though she noted that her irritation had overcome her tendency to fluster around attractive men. At least that was something, she wasn't sweating. Anymore.

"What are you both saying?" Ba shook her head, speaking in Gujarati, and then sized up Kavan as well. "You are not getting younger. Give your mother some peace. Get married." She turned to Poorvi and nodded at her to include her in her chiding. "My daughter was like you both. Then she got married and had children, and now she is very happy. Also my son." She gave them both the side-eye and then waved a dismissive hand. "It's your life," she said and put her head back and closed her eyes with the superiority of someone who knows she is right but is surrounded by idiots.

They both stared at her, stunned, then looked at each other. Poorvi was beginning to wonder what she'd gotten herself into, agreeing to look after Mrs. Patel—and she wondered, just slightly, if Kavan was thinking the same thing.

Well, it didn't matter. Helping Ba was the right thing to do. It was how she'd been raised, and clearly Kavan had *some* manners if he'd been brought up to help an elderly woman on a long flight.

Still, Poorvi was not about to let some random grandmother mess with her head. She had stood up to both of her real grandmothers and her mother and was still happily single. Well, single.

Chapter Three

Kavan had work to do. It wasn't easy to concentrate with gorgeous yet irritating Poorvi just two seats over. She had given no indication that she was interested in him, or that she even found him attractive. Which was...odd. Not that he was full of himself, but growing up, he'd always been known as the "good-looking brother." To the point that Naveen exploited his looks by having him do ads for their office.

He wasn't conceited about it; it was a fact, and had been since he was a child. Everyone had fawned over him, how cute he was, and then as he got older, how handsome he was. Quite frankly, he found it off-putting at times. Particularly the way his brother tried to pull him off as being not much more than a "pretty boy" and downplaying his academic strengths, by referring to him as nerdy and awkward.

The fact was that Kavan had done better than his brother at every level of schooling. He had faltered only after their father died, when he was fifteen and Naveen was eighteen. It was true, Naveen had been the one to kick him in the pants to get him back on track, but Kavan had done the work. Something Naveen never seemed to remember and basically ignored.

Even the few girlfriends he'd had seemed to care less about him than how he looked. As a result, he hadn't really ever had a long-term relationship. They'd always been more than happy to have him escort them to a party, their arms draped possessively in his. They had no trouble sharing his bed either. But when it came to any kind of real connection, those women simply hadn't seemed interested, so the "relationships" such that they were, always ended.

He wanted more than a beautiful woman on his arm. And he wanted to be more than that handsome guy on hers. He was looking for true connection, someone he could be himself with, someone who was his *person*.

Kavan was working on a paper. Or rather data for a paper. His brother and two other surgeons in the office had been doing the C-MORE refractive procedure for a few years. In fact, they did more of that procedure than any other practice in the country. Kavan was compiling the data of side effects over time. He had included everything from age and gender to refractive error to tissue health. He had started because patients were coming back with side effects that were not necessarily going away with time, as they did with other refractive procedures.

Naveen had given him an impossible task. If Dr. Gupta was coming all the way to Dublin to present this paper, he must at least have compelling enough data to warrant further study. He did need to meet with this P. K. Gupta, but maybe not for the reasons that Naveen wanted him to.

He refocused his attention on his data. The distraction here—he glanced over at Poorvi, who had pushed the glasses on top of her head—was not simply how attractive he found her. It was more about the fact that he was almost instantly attracted *to* her, despite the fact that she seemed to instantly loathe him. She appeared engrossed in her work, so he did not try to engage her. Besides, Ba was asleep next to her.

The fact that he had to do a photo shoot wasn't helping, either. Naveen had realized long ago that Kavan's looks somehow made people trust him, so Kavan became the literal face of their little practice, which was fast becoming a large clinic. Kavan's face was everywhere in Dublin and in the surrounding area. Hence the ball cap. It was irritating and embarrassing, but Kavan did whatever Naveen asked him to. After all, he owed Naveen everything.

Naveen had taken over the family after their father passed. Their mother was grieving, and she was a tough lady, but the first year was hard on her. It had been during that first year, relatively unsupervised and grieving, that Kavan had gotten into the wrong crowd of people. The boys he hung out with ditched school, smoked everything and by the time Naveen caught on, Kavan had started experimenting with drugs. Naveen then had made sure that Kavan found better mates, had no access to drugs, got to school, did his homework and ate.

And he never let Kavan forget it.

He glanced up. The bathrooms were free. Normally he avoided the airplane loo because it was a small and cramped space, but he'd been chugging coffee for hours before boarding. And—he glanced at his phone—there were still three hours left before landing.

He inhaled and stood. Small, confined places just were not his thing. He wasn't Batman; he did not have a childhood trauma to blame this on. But his heart raced and his palms started sweating any time he had to go into a small space. Like now.

He entered the small vestibule, controlled his breathing as he had been taught and did his business, all the while telling himself he was fine. He went to unlock the door and pull it open it to the wider space of the plane, and the door wouldn't open.

No!

He tried again. His heart thudded in his ears. He locked and unlocked the door, but still the door wouldn't open. He broke out in a sweat, it was getting hard to breathe. He was starting to feel lightheaded. No! No! No! He jiggled the handle to no avail.

He knocked on the door. "Some help, please. I seem to be stuck." He could feel the panic entering his voice. Someone pulled the door open. He had been trying to open it the wrong direction. Of course he had. His heart rate calmed and he looked up to see who his savior was.

Poorvi was standing there with eyebrows raised at him. "You okay?" she asked, her voice gentle for the first time since he had laid eyes in her.

"Fine," he mumbled, mortified that of all the people on the plane, the beautiful Poorvi had caught him stuck in the bathroom having a panic attack. Her kindness only made him more embarrassed. He brushed past her without another word.

"You're welcome," she muttered under her breath.

Still embarrassed, he headed for his seat, planning to hide in his computer for the remainder of the journey.

Chapter Four

Poorvi just made it back to her seat when the jostling started. She glanced at Kavan as he stood to let her back to her seat, a slight flush still in his cheeks. She wasn't sure why he appeared to be so flustered, a lot of people have trouble with those doors. He avoided her gaze, which was not consistent with his behaviour so far, either. But what did she know? She'd exchanged a handful of words with him, most of them were unpleasant.

At least they had been on her part.

Whatever. She needed to go over her slides and make sure her numbers were up to date for her presentation.

Again.

A lot was riding on this event.

And Ba kept on chatting. She had slept the first half, but now she was going on about her daughter and how they will celebrate Holi with a huge feast and a huge variety of powdered colors to play with.

At first, Poorvi fought it, but finally, she gave in. She and her parents had never really celebrated Holi.

"Oh. You must celebrate," Ba said, her eyes lighting up. "Everyone knows it is the festival of spring and color. But it is also the festival of love. Holi celebrates divine love, but—" she raised her eyebrows and bobbed her head toward Kavan "—anything can happen, eh?"

Poorvi pressed her mouth shut and shook her head. "Nope. Ba. Not in a million years."

Ba grinned at her and gave her an exaggerated frown and shrugged. "Okay. What do I know?"

"I have other priorities," Poorvi insisted.

"Okay." Ba nodded. Ba closed her eyes and rested her head back against the seat.

Poorvi reached for the last dregs of her cooled coffee just as the plane jerked, spilling the last sip on her white blouse. That was going to stain. A collective gasp from the other passengers, followed by concerned murmuring. What the— The plane jerked again and continued to bump and rumble.

Poorvi gasped as her heart rate accelerated. Ba took her hand. "Beti. All is fine," she said. "This happens."

Poorvi knew about turbulence. She just did not like it. Nausea started to set in. *Please don't throw up. Please don't throw up.*

"This is your captain speaking. We have hit some severe storms and will have to make an alternative landing. Dublin is not an option at this point, so we will be making an emergency landing in Cork." Her voice was calm and competent.

Poorvi relaxed for a moment, until the captain's words registered with her. Cork? "Where the hell is Cork?" She turned to Ba, but it was Kavan who answered.

"Cork is south and west. About a two-to three-hour drive to Dublin," he said. He leaned over. "Are you okay?"

She nodded, forced a smile. "Of course." But she held Ba's hand as if she were her child while Ba chanted her prayers softly. It was soothing.

Kavan glanced at her, pointing at the stain on her blouse. "Is that coffee? I know how to get that stain out."

Poorvi stared at him. The plane was rocking around and he was talking about coffee stains? She turned away from him.

The flight attendants made one last pass of the cabin and then seated themselves. The oxygen masks popped down in the roll of turbulence, and they were instructed to use them. Ba was chanting her prayers, still calm. Poorvi was feeling much better, and she reached over to help Ba with her mask and bumped hands with Kavan doing the same thing. He had actually stood up and was fixing Ba's mask now. A ping of electricity should not flow through her just because she touched a handsome stranger's hand, but it did all the same. Kavan caught her eye as if he'd felt the same thing. Not likely.

She had no idea what her face revealed, but Kavan's next words were soft and kind. "I'm okay getting Ba settled. You go on and tend to yourself."

She nodded and managed to get her own mask on, just as the flight attendant approached Kavan, his lips pressed together in reprimand. "Sir. Please sit down."

Kavan met her gaze and raised his eyebrows as he sat down, mocking the reprimand he'd just gotten. Like they were friends.

He was mistaken.

They were thrown around in their seats as the plane tilted and bumped in the heavy storm. Every so often, a baby would cry, but other than that, the plane was silent. Poorvi was jostled when the landing gear hit the runway. She was then yanked by what felt and sounded like a screeching stop. The plane finally came to a halt and there was a second of silence as everyone realized they had landed safely.

Poorvi joined the other passengers as they broke into relieved applause. She caught Kavan looking over at them and flushed, before they both looked away. She and Ba got to work gathering their things.

Poorvi and Ba made a stop at the restroom before heading to baggage claim.

"Hey. Pretty scary flight, yeah?" Kavan drew up next to them.

"Um, yeah." She looked at him. "You okay?"

"Me? Yeah—especially now that we're on the ground. How about you?"

"I'm fine," she said, clipped. "Just not a fan of turbulence." She flushed and turned away.

"Are you okay?" he asked.

"Yes. Why wouldn't I be okay?" She stared at him.

"Well it just seemed… I mean you looked a bit…pale…"

"I'm fine." She stared at him. "Anything else?"

"Um well, yeah. See, I grew up in Ireland." He raised his eyebrows in what could only be pride. "So I'd be happy to help…with Ba, yeah?"

The last thing she needed was to be on a road trip with this man. No good could come of it, really. "Oh, that's okay. I was heading to Dublin for a conference anyway," said Poorvi. "So I'm happy to take Ba along with me, if she chooses to come."

"You call her Ba, too?" He grinned at her.

"Not really a long shot. She's certainly acting like my grandmother," Poorvi quipped, pressing her lips together. "Trying to get us married." She rolled her eyes.

Damn. Why'd she have to go and mention the woman's matchmaking?

"You sure you don't want the company?"

"Absolutely positive," she answered, pushing up her glasses.

Kavan sighed, disappointment on his face—or at least what she could see under his ball cap.

"Very well then." He reached into his backpack and handed her a bleach stick. He pointed to the coffee stain on her white blouse. "Just soak that in cool water, apply this and wash. Should be good as new. Good luck. Have a nice stay in Ireland, yeah?" He waved, walking backward and bumping into a woman. The woman's face turned angry, but as soon as he turned to face her to apologize, she broke out into a huge smile and waved off his clumsiness.

Who was this man who gave out bleach sticks at the airport? Poorvi did an internal eye roll. "Have a nice life," she said as he left.

Chapter Five

Poorvi splashed water on her face in the bathroom. She was still shaking from the plane ride. The turbulence was terrifying. Poorvi inhaled to calm her nerves. It hadn't helped to have Kavan breathing down her neck. Though it did seem as though he was genuinely concerned. But she could never admit to him that she had been afraid. If she'd learned anything in the last year, it was how to not show weakness.

She shook her head as if to clear the nice thoughts of him. The last thing she needed was a distraction in the form of an outrageously handsome and sweet Indian-Irish man.

People were everywhere. It seemed theirs was not the only flight that had been detoured to Cork due to bad weather. She needed to be at that conference in Dublin by Friday. According to Google, Dublin was just a few hours' drive from Cork. Today was only Wednesday, so no problem.

They made their way to baggage claim, which at first

glance reminded her of any one of the apocalyptic movies she had seen. Further investigation revealed it was simply organized chaos, which was only mildly better. Announcements about flight delays, where to find baggage and other things crackled and popped from speakers in various places. Airport representatives had taken to the floor to guide people. Their voices mingled with the announcements, assuring that nothing could be heard. Machines whirred and clanked loudly as the baggage belts started and stopped. People milled about in all directions, looking for bags, family members or the car rental desk. Various languages mingled in the air.

The belt number for their luggage was changed twice, forcing them to run from one end of the baggage claim area to the other. Ba kept close to her in the chaos. People crowded around, nearly ten deep, in the area where the bags were spit out. She never understood that. The bag was going to come around anyway. She went to where the crowd was thin and grabbed her bag from there. A large red hard-shell bag with duct tape on the corner came around and Ba made a break for it. Poorvi followed and got Ba's bag off the belt, but not without a small struggle. Lucky both their bags had wheels, as there weren't any carts available.

"If you had let him, Kavan would have helped with the luggage," Ba said. Was there some kind of grandmother class they all went to? Why did they all say the exact same things?

"We're fine, Ba," she said. "Let's call your daughter. Can she come get you?"

Ba called as they made their way to car rental. She stood apart from Poorvi and had a conversation that Poorvi could not hear. "No, she cannot come," Ba reported as she joined Poorvi in the never-ending car rental line. "Her husband is out of town until Holi and her children are too small to leave alone."

Poorvi sighed and groaned internally. Of course she would help this woman, but it would be easier if she could just be on her way. "I'll drive you." There was no way she was going to leave an old woman who didn't speak the language alone at an airport with no way to get to her family.

The rental lines were worse than the bag claim lines, if that was even possible. This day was trying her patience.

"What do your parents do?" Ba asked as they waited in the infinite line.

"They are both cardiologists," Poorvi replied.

Ba smiled and bobbed her head. "Both parents are doctors. How lovely."

Poorvi shook her head. Both parents being doctors had really left no other options for her. Luckily, she hadn't really wanted any other option. She had always been fascinated by the eye, so it was a natural choice to go into ophthalmology. They weren't sure what to make of her decision to do an MD-PhD as opposed to patient care, but research had always been her passion. Her favorite classes were always those that had a lab. She'd even played "lab" as a child. The other children thought playing lab was no fun, so she used her stuffed animals as the "staff" and examined everything from grass to lint.

There were times when she missed those days. At least her teddy bear and stuffed elephant didn't accuse her of having slept with the boss. No, correction, the boss's boss.

"How about siblings?" Ba asked.

"I have a sister, Niki." Poorvi smiled. "She is not a doctor. She's an event planner." Niki was a year younger than her, and they had an apartment together in Baltimore. "She's like my best friend." Poorvi gushed a little over

Niki. "Also, she can cook. Which helps because we live together and I do not cook."

"Henh?" Ba was impressed.

A free spirit and always the life of the party, Niki was currently working as an event planner for nonprofit organizations. She also had the biggest heart of anybody Poorvi knew.

"How about you? What kind of doctor are you?" Ba asked.

"Oh I'm an—"

"Next!" the agent at the car rental called them.

"Oh. It's our turn." Poorvi went to the desk. "Hello," Poorvi said to the attendant in her most patient voice.

"All I have left is manual," the agent said by way of greeting. Her hair was frazzled, her name tag—Shannon—was skewed. Shannon had not counted on turbulence either. "It's a small SUV."

"No problem. I'll take it." Poorvi had learned to drive a stick shift from her masi. Her mother hadn't really seen the need to learn the skill, but her mother's sister had insisted, saying it was a life skill.

Thank you, Kosha Masi.

"Really?" Shannon was surprised and seemed to relax. She had been ready to argue with Poorvi.

"Yes." They just needed a car. And a look at these lines indicated that getting a car—any car—might be harder than it should be.

"Perfect." The agent typed away, and in a few moments, Poorvi had the location of the car. She, Ba and their luggage slogged their way to the garage to locate the car. The garage was cold and damp; she was grateful for her winter coat.

She found the spot, A23, and approached, only to find a man sitting in the car. What the...?

She picked up her pace and went to the car window. She

banged on it, and then stepped back as Hot Guy—Kavan—turned to look at her. He caught her in that gaze of his and broke out into a smile as she looked at her phone, quickly scanning the confirmation email from the rental company.

Yep, this was definitely the right spot.

"Um…what are you doing here? This is my car!" she demanded, stepping aside so he could open the door.

He opened the door and unfolded himself from the vehicle, but not without bumping his head a bit—side effect of being so tall in a small car. Despite the incident, he had a slight grin on his face. She stepped back out of his space. He was really tall.

"Actually, this would be *my* car." He was calm and undisturbed by her demand, much the way he had been undisturbed by her need for the outlet.

She waved her phone in front of him and pointed to the number painted behind the parking spot. "I have A23."

He oh-so-calmly reached into the car and pulled out his phone, wincing as he bumped his elbow. "A23. My spot."

He turned his phone toward her. Sure enough, he indeed had been assigned A23. And he was already in the car. "Well, I suppose that according to your elementary school rules, you were here *first*, so…whatever." She shook her head and shivered. Ba waited patiently. She looked around in case the company had a kiosk in the garage to see what else they might have.

"A car is not the same as an outlet." He looked at her with those eyes and a small smile and she started to sweat inside her winter coat. "We can share. We're all going to Dublin."

She paused and narrowed her eyes at him. "What's the catch?"

He pursed his lips and did not quite meet her eyes. "You have to drive the whole time."

She looked at the car and then at Kavan, then back into the car. She saw the gearshift. "Oh, I get it. You don't know how to drive stick."

He said nothing, just stared at her.

"What were you going to do?" she asked, amused.

"I was going to figure it out." Irritation laced his words and Poorvi took some satisfaction in making him admit something he did not want to. "I need to get to Dublin, don't I?"

Poorvi chuckled.

"But now you're here. It's mutually beneficial. I have a car that I can't drive, yeah? You can drive it, but don't have a car. And we're going to the same city."

She really did not have a choice. This was her best chance to get to Dublin as soon as possible. She sighed. "Okay."

He came over and grabbed Ba's bag. "I'll handle this. You both get in, yeah?" He quickly reached for their bags. She really tried not to notice his muscles as he lifted the bags, but come on, how was she *not* supposed to notice beautiful brown-skinned muscles flexing like that? "I know these roads fairly well, so I'll be navigating."

Poorvi took off her winter coat and tossed it in the back seat. She sat down in the driver's seat. Whoa. This was weird. Shifter in her left hand. She pressed the pedals. They were the same.

"You'll be driving on the left," Kavan said as he clicked his seat belt and turned to the back. "All buckled up, Ba?"

Poorvi caught Ba's expression in the rearview. The older woman was positively beaming. She bobbed her head side-to-side, a large grin on her face. She seemed very excited.

"We need your daughter Devi's address," Poorvi said into the rearview.

"We go first to Blarney Castle," she stated in Gujarati.

Poorvi turned to find Kavan staring at her. "This is

the first I've heard of this." She held up her hands in surrender. Kavan narrowed his eyes at her. "I'm not lying. I need to get to Dublin as soon as possible. I am not here to travel." And she didn't want to be stuck with this man any longer than she had to be. A small—very tiny—but signifcant part of her was starting to *like* him. And she just couldn't have that.

"Ba. We need to get to Dublin. We both have to work," Kavan explained, a hint of desperation in his voice.

He didn't want to dawdle anymore than she did. Which was perfect, but made her a bit sad. She did not want to investigate the reasons for that.

"Ba," Poorvi added. "Devi is waiting for you."

"No. She isn't." Ba pressed her lips together and avoided Poorvi's eyes.

"Of course she is. Your son said—"

At the mention of her son, Ba tsked and waved a dismissive hand. "I told my daughter I will be there on Friday." She grinned, proud of herself.

"Ba—" Kavan started, the desperation in his voice obvious now.

"We really need to just get to Devi—" Poorvi said.

"I will see Ireland." She nearly smirked at them. She had the power and she knew it. "You both will show me. Blarney Castle is only twenty minutes away."

Chapter Six

Kavan just stared at the older woman. What was happening? As lovely as it may be touring his country with this beautiful and pleasantly irksome woman, he didn't have time to show Ba or anyone all of Ireland.

Once he found P. K. Gupta, he needed time to go over the data.

He glanced at Poorvi. The expression on her face made it clear that she hadn't had any idea that this was Ba's plan.

"I have never kissed the Blarney Stone. It won't take long." Ba said to them.

"Give me your daughter's number, please." Poorvi had her phone ready. She sounded clinical and authoritative. He certainly might have handed over whatever she had asked for.

"No." Ba clamped her mouth shut.

"Ba. She's probably going out of her mind," Kavan added.

Ba narrowed her eyes at them. "No, she isn't. I called her."

"What did you tell her?" Poorvi asked.

"I told her that I was with a tour group seeing Ireland. I would see her Friday," Ba said.

"You did what?" Poorvi spun around in her seat.

"I want to see Ireland," Ba repeated.

Poorvi stared at Kavan in disbelief. And, he realized, maybe a bit of panic, too. "But *we* need to be in Dublin in two days."

"Then we will see what we can in two days," Ba said triumphantly.

Kavan looked at Poorvi. She made eye contact with him and his heart rate increased. "Let's just drive to Dublin." Maybe after he settled this issue with P. K. Gupta he coud figure out what he was feeling about Poorvi.

"And do what?" Poorvi's already large eyes bugged out. "Drive around and see who claims her? She hasn't given us the address."

"Ba," Kavan started in his most charming voice. He had been known to charm an auntie or grandmother in his day to get permission to stay out late or ride a motorcycle. "I'm sure Devi is missing you very much, and your grand-children must be excited to see you. Both of your children would want you to be safe, don't you think?"

Ba narrowed her eyes at him. "I may be old, but I am not stupid enough to fall for your act." She set her jaw. "I am seeing Ireland." She mumbled something to herself that Kavan did not quite catch, but she was clearly agitated.

"Nicely done." Poorvi rolled her eyes. "Now she's angry."

"When is your conference?" Ba asked.

"Friday," Poorvi answered at the same time as him. They made eye contact again. He gave a side smile. He could get used to this.

Ba grinned. "Perfect. We will all arrive on Friday. You drop me at my daughter's and then go to your conferences."

Naveen was going to kill him if he didn't get to P. K. Gupta before he presented his paper. "Thursday," he spat out quickly. "I meant I have to be there on Thursday."

Ba shook her head at him. "Friday. It's an auspicious day anyway."

"Is it?" Poorvi asked.

Ba's face lit up. "It's Holi! My daughter always has the most amazing Holi party. That's why I came."

"So you should get there early and enjoy the preparations," Kavan tried again.

Ba waved a hand. "They can manage until I get there. And you can both come to the party." She clapped her hands together and her face lit up. "It will be fabulous. It's the festival of color and spring, but it also celebrates love." She looked meaningfully at Kavan. "The moon will be full that night. Anything can happen."

Kavan flushed and avoided looking at Poorvi. Ba pulled out a well-worn travel guidebook with a few dog-eared pages in it and handed it to Kavan. He opened it to find that Ba had made a checklist. Blarney Stone. Cliffs of Moher. Aran Islands (all three). Dublin. He showed it to Poorvi.

She widened her eyes and glanced at him. Her look said it all. She needed to get to Dublin, but she didn't want to hurt Ba. This itinerary was not part of her plan. She had other priorities. His thoughts exactly.

She opened her hands to him in a silent gesture of surrender, whispering to him, "What are we going to do? We have no choice."

He pressed his lips together and caught her eye yet again. She was right. In that moment they were on the same side. They had made a connection. Unwanted tour of Ireland and Naveen's assignment notwithstanding, that connection felt like a beacon of light.

Chapter Seven

Taking a road trip with a spunky grandmother and a highly irritating, though admittedly attractive, man was not how Poorvi had imagined seeing Ireland. She'd had a plan and she very much liked sticking to her plans. But she wasn't about to abandon an old woman. Something about Ba and her insistence on playing tourist was deeper than it seemed, though Poorvi could not place why. Kavan's desperation to reach Dublin mimicked hers, but she had the feeling he was going for more than just a conference.

Not that it was any of her business. Or that she cared.

Poorvi had her own conference that started on Friday, which put knots in her stomach just thinking about it. She wasn't presenting until Saturday, but Bobby wanted her there by Friday to go over exactly what she was going to say. Honestly, she had half a mind to blow him off and just get there on Saturday.

She pushed aside the feeling that this connected her to

Kavan in any way. They were two separate people with separate lives who happened to be sharing a car. Trying to get an old woman home. While taking in the sites in Ireland.

"Do you know where we're going?" she asked.

"That, I do," he said without looking up from his phone. "The question is, can you put up your part of the deal?" He cocked a smile at her.

Irritating man.

She narrowed her eyes at him. "Of course," she stated with much more confidence than she felt.

Poorvi spent an extra moment familiarizing herself with the car. Once she figured out where everything was, there was nothing left but to drive. She put the car in gear and gave it some gas. They eased out of the spot and into the lane. There. That wasn't so bad.

Hot Annoyance was still tapping away on his phone. Whatever. How hard could it be to drive on the—

"AHHH!" Her passengers screamed and she slammed the brakes just inches in front of a set of headlights. Her heart hammered in her chest. She had narrowly avoided a head-on collision.

"What part of drive on the left do you not understand?" Kavan barked at her.

"You're supposed to be navigating, not pretending to be a teenager with their phone!" she barked right back at him, her eyes wide and jaw set. So to drive on the left, one had to actually drive on the left.

He narrowed his eyes at her. "The left lane…is. On. The. Left."

She turned her gaze forward. The other car had gone. She moved the vehicle into the left lane.

"Now turn left here," Kavan said in a quiet rumble, his phone still in his hand. Notification dings were coming through rapidly. Then his phone rang. "We're leaving the garage, and it drops right into the highway, yeah?"

She was too occupied by driving to care who was calling him, but clearly someone was trying to reach him. He ignored his phone and continued to direct her. She nodded that she understood.

Her instinct was to shut him up. But there was none of the expected superiority and cockiness in his voice. She turned left. *Shift, check the lane, hit the gas.*

"Turn right here," he mumbled. She checked traffic both ways before making the turn and driving slowly out of the airport. It was dark, despite the morning hour, and rain was coming down in buckets.

"Now. You're going to merge, but everything here is opposite of the States, yeah?" Kavan's phone was still dinging, but he seemed unconcerned by it.

Probably because she currently held all their lives in her hands as she attempted to drive in what could only be described as an upside-down way.

"So the far left is the exit or slow lane, while the right lane is the 'fast' lane," Kavan explained.

Again, she bit back her glib response; her instinct had been to go to the other side of the road. She nodded without glancing at him, intent on the quickly approaching highway. She turned the wipers faster, gave her signal, checked her mirrors and the side of the road she was on, shifted and accelerated.

The car stalled.

What the? She could drive a stick with her eyes closed. She glanced at the shifter. She had moved it in the wrong direction.

She waited for Kavan's bark. But instead, he spoke gently. "You're still getting used to the gearshift." Kavan was checking traffic around them. "You're clear. Go ahead."

Poorvi started again and this time made it to the highway. It was difficult to see, but she decided they could just take their time. No rush. She could do this. She shifted and sped up, staying to the left.

Kavan continued to give soft direction, which helped Poorvi keep her mind on shifting and staying left.

Every time she switched lanes or took an exit successfully, Ba let out a call to thank God. "Hai Ram!"

She glanced at Kavan and caught a small smile on his face as Ba praised God for the umpteenth time. "Ba," he said. "She's fine. You go on and take a nap."

Ba was not having it. She shook her head and held her prayer beads in her hands with white knuckles. Poorvi rolled her eyes but couldn't help the smile that fell across her face.

They drove in relative silence for a small stretch; the only sound was Ba's soft praying and Kavan's "stay left" chant. Which, while annoying, was helping her remember to stay left.

"Relax. You got it now." He sounded excited for her.

"I'm relaxed," she retorted.

"Uh-huh." Kavan raised an eyebrow as his gaze shifted to her white knuckles clutching the wheel. She loosened her grip a bit.

"You'll go straight for a few kilometers, then take the exit for Blarney Castle." He put his head back and closed his eyes.

"What?" Poorvi panicked. "You can't sleep! You have to navigate!"

"Ha." Kavan put his head up. "So you do need me."

She glanced at him. "The same as you need me, Mr. I-can't-drive-a-manual."

"Ahh! Look at the road!" Ba screamed from the back seat.

Poorvi turned back in time to see that she was just fine. "Ba! I'm fine."

"Hmph. Just checking."

Poorvi shook her head as she tried to calm her heart rate. Although, between Ba screaming in the back and Kavan speaking softly in that amazing voice of his, that was hardly likely to happen.

Chapter Eight

"She's something, eh?" Kavan said softly while Ba continued chanting her prayers.

"She got us to take her to the Blarney Stone," Poorvi answered. It took her a minute, but she realized that she wasn't snapping at him anymore. Huh. "She reminds me a bit of my grandmother." She couldn't keep her voice from cracking, so she inhaled and paused. "We, uh…lost her last year."

"I'm sorry."

Poorvi shrugged as if it were okay. "She had a long life. She died peacefully in her sleep. *My* Ba lived on the same block as us, and we went there every day after school while our parents were at work." Her grandmother was tough and sassy.

"You're smiling at something." Kavan said.

"Am I?" Probably. Thinking of her grandmother always made her smile. "She was kind of sassy." She tilted her head toward Ba. "Like Ba here."

"Ah. So that's where you got it from." Kavan let out a warm chuckle.

"Well, yes." She continued looking at the road. "My mom always says I am most like her mother, which was why I drove her crazy."

"What about your siblings?"

"A sister. Niki belongs to my mom." She spared the gearshift her tight grip for a second to cross her fingers. "They're like that."

"Do you get along with your sister?"

"What's with all the questions?" She frowned at him. He had gotten her to talk about her family. To what end? This was too close for her own comfort.

"Just making conversation."

"Well, we don't have to do that." She changed the tone of her voice so there would not be any doubt as to the sincerety of her words. "We're just two people who are stuck taking an older woman on a tour of Ireland. We don't have to get to know each other. We can just coexist," she said. She didn't have the time or space to get friendly—on any level—with anyone right now. She side-eyed him. "We're not going to 'bond.'"

He stared at her a moment, something akin to confusion on his face. Without a word, he abruptly turned in his seat and started chatting with Ba. "Tell me about your daughter and her family."

Poorvi should have been relieved that he acquiesced so quickly to her request, but she could not shake the feeling that she had somehow hurt him. Maybe if she explained why she didn't want to share that might make it better. But she wasn't ready to share all that.

Ba, however, was more than happy to talk about her family. "My daughter is my eldest, Devi. She married Yash, a wonderful man. And they have my grandchildren. Dharm is eight, and his sister, Mira, is five." Her son in the States was married but no children.

"So why Blarney Castle, Ba?" Kavan asked, seemingly entranced with what Ba's answer might be. But instead, Ba looked out the window, refusing to answer. She must have her reasons.

Wow. Not a good day for Kavan. Poorvi glanced at him quickly.

"Well, I'm excited. I've never been here either." Kavan filled the silence. "The castle was built over six hundred years ago. The famous stone has many stories on how it came to be in the castle, but however it got there, its powers are undeniable." Kavan smiled at them. He continued to talk, basically about the castle and the stone.

"Your exit is in one kilometer," Kavan pointed out gently. "On the left."

Poorvi followed his directions and turned up the winding road. "Oh! We're here. Blarney Stone!" Considering she'd had no desire to come to the castle, her excitement surprised her. The castle sat among green grass, with trees on the periphery.

"It's about twenty-seven meters—uh, ninety feet high." Kavan told her as they all exited the car.

Poorvi simply stood there for a moment and took in the majesty of this castle.

"And technically this is Blarney Castle, but yes, the stone is up there." He pointed toward the top of the castle. The rain had stopped and the sky was still gray, but the sun must have risen because it was definitely lighter out.

The air held some moisture and a chill, a typical March day in Ireland, according to Kavan, their unofficial tour guide.

"It is gorgeous, yeah? I've never seen anything so beautiful." Kavan had paused to look up at the castle.

It was beautiful. Even in the gray of the day, the green was brilliant. The rectangular stone structure stood high and strong among the greenery.

Ba walked past them, her considerable purse on her elbow. With respectable speed, no less. The woman who had needed to sit next to them was no longer here. In her place was a spry lady with an agenda to see the castle.

"Wait up, Ba," Kavan called. "There are lots of stairs."

She waved him off. He and Poorvi finally caught up with Ba when she paused to take in the beauty.

"How do you know there are lots of stairs if you haven't been here before?" Poorvi asked.

"Well, I could tell you." He smirked at her. "But then we might actually 'bond,' and I know how you feel about that." He fell into step with Ba as they approached the narrow stone stairs. Poorvi was behind them. The stairs (125 of them, according to Kavan), located at what seemed to be a side entrance, twisted up in a spiral to the top of the castle.

If the view from below was majestic, the view from up here was simply breathtaking. Poorvi tore her gaze from the endless greenery and followed Kavan and Ba to the line of people waiting to kiss the Blarney Stone.

"Ba. They say if you kiss the stone, you become more…" Kavan paused and turned to her as the Gujarati word for eloquent eluded him. "What's Gujarati for eloquent?"

"Vathordyu," Poorvi said.

"That means talkative." He corrected her.

"True, but the straight translation of 'eloquent' is chatadara. Which really means more like 'declamatory.'" She shrugged. "Talkative is more like 'gift of gab,' which you clearly have."

"And which you do not." His bluntness seemed out of character, but what did she know, she just met him a few hours ago.

She side-eyed him. "As long as we understand each other." She shrugged. "Though your Gujarati is pretty good."

"My dad used to make us speak Gujarati at home all the time."

"Used to?"

"Well, he had to stop when he died, didn't he?"

"Oh." She snapped her head to him, shocked he'd been so flippant about that. But the look on his face defied his words and his tone. He still hurt from that loss. It was obvious. "I'm... I'm really sorry."

He shrugged. "I was a teenager. And after he died, we just sort of deferred to English."

"Gujarati reminded you of him." She sighed.

"Yes. Exactly." He furrowed his brow, surprised. "I tried to practice Gujarati, since it reminded me of him. But my brother and my mom..." He shook his head.

She nodded, understanding. "Too hard."

He stared at her as if that had not occurred to him. "Or it was Naveen not wanting to do anything he wasn't the best at, and Mom going along with him, as usual." There was more than a hint of bitterness in his voice, and Poorvi found she was curious to know why. She opened her mouth then closed it. No. She didn't have time for all that in her life.

"Well Kavan does not need to kiss the stone, then," Ba said with a smirk.

Poorvi burst into laughter.

"But you do," Ba told her.

"I communicate just fine, Ba," Poorvi countered.

Ba raised her eyebrows and widened her eyes. "No, beti, you don't."

Kavan laughed out loud while Poorvi shook her head at both of them. Ba joyfully took her turn when it came.

Two volunteers stood by what appeared to be a large

whole between the floor and the wall. There were iron rails to grip on either side.

Ba lay down on her back as instructed and gripped the iron bars. The two volunteers held onto her as they gently lowered her head to where the stone was embedded in the castle wall, so she could kiss it. They then gently pulled her up and she stood. The whole process took maybe sixty seconds.

Poorvi took her turn (they'd come all this way) lying down on her back, allowing the two volunteers to lower her down into the small opening that led to the stone. She kissed it and they pulled her up.

Kavan's heart pounded in his chest and he broke out in a sweat just watching Poorvi and Ba being lowered into the gap between the wall and the floor. Sure, there were iron railings to hang on to, but that was really all. For once in the past few hours, his physical response had nothing to do with Poorvi. He started to walk past.

"Uh, you're going to miss your turn." Poorvi pointed at the stone.

"I'm good. Ba said I didn't have to."

"But you've never been here before," she insisted. So she was listening to him.

"Well, yeah. But—" he glanced warily at the hole that led to the Blarney Stone "—I'm good."

"You're kidding, right?" Poorvi smirked at him, but stepped closer to him, studying him. Her smirk disappeared and was replaced with concern. "It's a really…small space." Her mouth gaped open as she put it all together.

He stared at her. She must think he was weak. That's what Naveen had thought of Kavan's fear of small spaces in any case. Naveen was forever trying to get Kavan into small spaces, convinced that if he faced his fears, he would overcome them. All it did was make Kavan trust his brother less and less.

Poorvi turned back and he followed her gaze. Ba was waiting for them, but had seemingly engrossed herself in the scenery. She turned back to him and watched him a minute before she moved closer to him and spoke softly. She smelled of floral shampoo, which was incredible considering they'd been on a plane overnight, and truth be told, he enjoyed her proximity. "It is a small place, and it is high, but it's only for a second. However, I think you already have a pretty good gift of gab, so no harm skipping it." She gave him a one-armed shrug and a small smile. Poorvi took a few steps away from the opening, so they coud allow others to have their turn.

Kavan followed her as if he'd always followed her, before glancing over again, clearly apprehensive. "I lied… I was here once before. With my whole family." Rather when his family was whole. "I couldn't do it. Naveen, my older brother, teased me the rest of the trip. Made me feel…"

"Weak," she said. Something in her eyes related. Anger flashed through them, and then she focused on him again. "No offense, but your brother sounds like an asshole."

He chuckled, relief flooding over him. Yes. Naveen was an ass at times. He inhaled. "Maybe. But that asshole raised me."

She quirked a smile, unapologetic that she had insulted the person who raised him. "Hard to believe." She squeezed his arm through his coat. He wished he wasn't wearing the coat so he could feel her hand. "In any case, it's up to you. No judgment."

"Really? Because you can be pretty judgy." He grinned at her.

"True." She chuckled. "But not for this. You saw how I was with the turbulence," she said quietly, her eyes huge as she let him in just a little. It felt like a door opening, and he found himself leaning into that feeling.

Ba approached him, motioning for him to bend down so she could reach him. "You never know when a chance will come again," she whispered, looking him in the eye. Apparently she had been listening. He had the distinct feeling she was not just talking about kissing the Blarney Stone.

He looked at Poorvi over Ba's shoulder and she nodded and smiled.

He walked back over to the staff and sat down, his back to the gaping hole in the floor that he would be lowered into. His heart raced and he broke out in a sweat. Ba stood by him and nodded encouragement. Poorvi stood on his other side. He had assumed she would mock him, but the only thing coming from her was encouragement.

Fear of small spaces be damned, he was doing this. He grabbed the railings, closed his eyes, and allowed the staff to lower him the few inches. He kissed the stone and they pulled him up. He stood, feeling a bit lightheaded and nauseous. Ba squeezed his shoulder and whispered to him, "If you can do that, you can do anything." She winked and glanced at Poorvi before moving on.

Poorvi approached him, her brow furrowed. "You okay? You look like you might vomit."

He looked up at her. "I might." But God, please don't let him vomit in front of her. "Ba is very convincing."

She grinned. It nearly stopped his heart. "Which is why we are here to begin with." Poorvi rolled her eyes.

"I guess we're both just big softies at heart," he said.

"Speak for yourself," she said with a half smile, turning away from him. "Let's go if you're done. The sooner we finish her tour, the sooner we move on with our lives."

"Yes, ma'am," he said under his breath. She had let down her wall for a split second and let him see her fear, just so he would know that he wasn't alone. She wasted no time putting the wall back up, but that moment was more intriguing than he had imagined.

Chapter Nine

"Chalo. Cliffs of Moher is next." Ba plowed ahead to the car, leaving Poorvi behind with Kavan. When she looked at him, he seemed completely fine, lighter even, after his experience kissing the Blarney Stone. Maybe the stone's magic was more than simply doling out the gift of gab.

They'd bonded. Against everything she'd intended, yet they'd bonded over their fears. It was only a tiny moment, but still…

It wasn't as horrible as she might have thought it would be, showing vulnerability like that. Surprisingly she wasn't the least bit mortified at having revealed her fears. And it had seemed to help him.

The sky was still gray, and the chill was hanging around. Poorvi pulled her winter coat tighter, as did Ba, and they all seemed prepared.

"Really?" Kavan asked Ba. "Because it's cold there this time of year. And no guarantee on visibility."

"How cold?" Poorvi asked. Not that it mattered, Ba seemed determined.

"Cold. But more than that, the fog can be thick." Kavan said. "The Cliffs of Moher is where the Atlantic meets Europe. The Cliffs are millions of years old, and the views of the water and the land are like nothing you've ever seen, trust me." He grinned. "It's an incredible experience, walking over them, the water just directly below you, yeah?" He grinned and his face lit up, all irritation from two minutes ago replaced by his boyish grin and accompanying enthusiasm. "You'll not want fog, because you want to see the ocean come right up on those cliffs. There's nothing like it." He rested his gaze on her for a second longer than was necessary, but it was long enough to stir something in her.

Ba nodded as if giving her approval. "Can't miss it."

"How far is it?" Poorvi asked.

"About three to four hours to the cliffs, give or take." He glanced up. "Though it looks like rain." He checked the weather app on his phone. "But not for a bit."

"We need to eat," Ba said as she opened her large purse, pulling out a ziplock bag that held something wrapped in foil.

Poorvi met his glance and shot him a quick smile. The spicy flatbread was a staple to travel with in case one needed a snack. "Perfect," she said. "We'll just have tepla while I drive." The sooner they finished this tour the better. She might have liked seeing the castle and the stone, but she was here for a reason. And it wasn't sightseeing.

Kavan raised his eyebrows at them. "Tepla? We can have that any time. We're only twenty minutes from Cork downtown and the English Market. Let's get something there. The food is amazing."

"It's an extra stop that we do not need to make." She motioned to the tepla. "Besides, Ba didn't say anything about the English Market."

"We're like twenty minutes away from this amazing meal—"

"Which we do not need," Poorvi insisted. "It's not on the itinerary."

"None of this is planned, is it?" Kavan retorted, maybe a bit more insistent than was necessary for a trip he was being forced into.

Ba eyed him a minute and her expression was unreadable. She sat down in the car. "Chalo. Kavan baraber kayche."

Poorvi sighed and shook her head at Ba's instruction to do what Kavan wanted. "Nicely done. We'll never get to Dublin at this rate."

Poorvi tried to hide it, but she was sure her anxiety was clear in the sweat on her brow and the way she clutched both the gearshift and the steering wheel. He couldn't blame her. He hadn't even bothered to learn how to drive a manual car.

Poorvi put the car in gear and pulled out. City driving was different than highway driving. She was not thrilled with having to drive into the downtown area, especially when she still wasn't familiar with driving on the opposite side of the road.

At home she was fine. But here… "Watch that pedestrian!" Kavan warned, somehow without raising his voice. Poorvi slammed the brake and the car stalled.

"All good," he said. "Just start her up."

Poorvi did that and they proceeded, with only a rude hand gesture from the pedestrian.

"The English Market is just a block away." Kavan looked at Ba as Poorvi parked. "You good with walking, Ba?"

"I may be old, but I am not feeble," Ba retorted as she bounded from the car and started walking to the market.

The English Market was a large market filled with various stalls ranging from savory food to sweets to paintings to pubs and everything in between. Sights, sounds and aromas of varying intensity surrounded them.

Poorvi inhaled deeply and, despite all her many reservations, her stomach rumbled.

"Coffee and a sandwich," Kavan stated to the group. "The meats here are amazing, as are our Irish cheeses. And the bread." He made the chef's kiss.

"Yeah, well, let's get the food quickly and get moving." Poorvi said. She shivered slightly, but it wasn't particularly cold. Maybe in the fifties. She glanced at the overcast sky. Sun would be nice.

Ba shook her head, a smile coming across her face. "You're missing out on the experience. Look around. Forget Dublin for a few minutes."

Poorvi stood and watched her. She was exhausted from the flight and the driving, but apparently Ba was not going to give in until she experienced the market. Poorvi had no choice.

Poorvi inhaled and looked around. Stall after stall of food, crafts, sweet treats, coffee, tourist knickknacks went on and on. They walked a bit and all the different aromas hit her. People were having coffee, buying trinkets or simply doing their daily food shopping. Movement and sound were constant. An obvious tourist destination, various languages from around the world hit her ears, a few familiar words here and there. The excitement in the air was palpable.

Kavan led the way to a large sandwich stall with a long line. "Worth the wait," he said as he got in line.

Poorvi rolled her eyes.

The line moved quickly and soon enough they each had a sandwich and a drink. Poorvi grabbed her sandwich and water and began walking back to the car. She got a few steps before Kavan called out to her.

"Poorvi!"

A spark shot down her spine. Her name in his voice sounded more tantalizing than it should.

She turned to face him.

"Join us at the park." Water bottle in hand, he motioned in the opposite direction.

"I really just want to keep—"

"Twenty minutes. How long will it take to eat a sandwich?" He opened his arms. "You might even like the fresh air," Kavan said, raising his eyebrows.

It would be nice to sit in the park.

"Poorvi. Chalo apray saathay," Ba insisted.

Poorvi sighed and turned around, telling herself she was acquiescing because of Ba's insistence and not because Kavan's voice was as irresistible as her favorite chocolate ice cream. She ignored the smirk on Ba's face and followed them to a park across from the English Market.

The three of them sat down on a bench. Kavan attacked his sandwich with gusto, nearly moaning in delight. "It's as good as I remember."

Poorvi looked at him. "When were you here last?"

"Been a while." He shook his head while chewing. "Like twenty years. We came here after the Blarney Stone." He met her eyes.

"Your family was here." She nodded understanding.

"My mom had taken Naveen to go see something else, so my dad brought me here for a sandwich. We're both foodies." Sadness floated over him. "Or we were. It was the best part of that trip."

"Dads are great that way."

The sadness in his eyes made way for gratitude. "Yes, they are."

"Ba," she said. "What else do you have in your bag?" Poorvi raised her eyebrows, hopeful. If Ba was anything like her grandmother... Ba grinned and pulled out a couple packets of hot sauce. Score!

Poorvi gleefully opened one and added it to her sandwich. She offered the sauce to Kavan, who stared at her, his mouth full, in complete disbelief. He chewed and swallowed.

"What are you doing?" he asked as if she were defiling a sacred spot.

"Adding a bit of spice."

"It's fine as is, isn't it?" he insisted.

"But now it's desi-fied!" She waved her sandwich in front of him as if trying to tempt him and laughed. She took a bite. "Add spice, make it desi!"

"I know what desi-fied means." He laughed. "We used to..." He shook his head.

Ba was eating slowly and with purpose. She took small bites and chewed as if she were savoring every crumb. She seemed to have forgotten that Poorvi and Kavan were there as she took in her surroundings. But the look on her face was not one of wonder so much that it was of nostalgia.

Poorvi and Kavan finished, while Ba took her time.

"I saw a coffee shop across the street. I'll get us some coffees, yeah?" Kavan left.

She nodded and watched him go. Tall, medium build. His jeans fit him perfectly. Not bad to look at at all.

She turned to find Ba grinning at her. Ba bobbed her head in happiness.

Poorvi just rolled her eyes. "Fine. He's handsome," she acquiesced. Extremely handsome. "But that doesn't mean anything."

She was still enjoying her view when her phone buzzed for the millionth time. She tore her attention away from Kavan's walk and pulled it out. Thirty texts and three missed calls. All from Bobby, her boss.

"Ba. I need to make a call," she explained in Gujarati.

"Atcha." Ba nodded her head in understanding.

Poorvi stood a few feet away, but not so far that she couldn't still see Ba, and called Bobby.

"Where have you been?" Bobby started.

"Hello to you too," she said.

"You are supposed to be at the hotel preparing for your presentation," Bobby barked into the phone.

"I texted you. My flight was rerouted. We landed in Cork," she explained blandly. She truly resented having to answer to Bobby, but here she was, and she really had no choice.

"Cork? Where the hell is that?" he demanded.

"Not far." She kept her voice neutral and her answers short.

"Great. I'll see you soon."

"No."

"What does that mean?"

She watched Ba walk around in the small park. There was something...she just couldn't place it. "It means I'll be in Dublin by Friday."

"Friday?" Bobby sounded like he was going to have a heart attack. "Your job, my job, it's all on the line here. We need time to go over your presentation. Which is Saturday. Friday will be too late."

"I am aware of what exactly is on the line here, Bobby." She refused to call him Dr. Wright. Not while he had her job. "No need to remind me." If she presented well, the lab stood to get a grant that would keep them in work for the next four years. They could potentially even hire more staff. "And I am working on it."

"I certainly hope you are aware and that you are working toward that goal."

Anger and frustration boiled inside her. This was not first time that Bobby had insinuated that her priorities may not be with the lab. "What does that mean?"

"It means that you should know that sabotaging the lab sabotages you as well." He sounded so superior. "And it's Dr. Wright."

"Why would I sabotage the lab, Bobby?"

"People talk, Poorvi. You didn't get the job, maybe you want revenge."

"You have some imagination. I, unlike some others, *care* about my work. It's the only reason I'm still there. I'll be there and I'll present." She hung up. *And when she did save the lab, Bobby could kiss her ass.* He wouldn't fire her; he needed her more than she needed him, and he knew it. She took a few deep breaths as tears of anger burned her eyes. She had to let them fall, to release the mountain of feelings inside her. She didn't mind; she was way past caring if people saw her cry. If it made them uncomfortable, that was their problem. Poorvi sat down and let her tears of anger fall for a moment. She watched Ba through her tears.

Ba was looking at the trees, smelling the flowers, looking at the sky. She walked a bit and ran her hand along one of the benches. Much like someone who was *remembering* something. She looked—pensive. Poorvi could not explain why she cared, but she did. She could not just leave Ba with Kavan and run off to Dublin. She didn't want to.

Besides, Poorvi thought with a small smile, who would drive the car?

Her anger and frustration tamed for the moment, she wiped her eyes and drank water, letting Ba have her moment.

Kavan placed a call to Naveen while he waited for their coffees. The aroma of coffee, while pleasant, wasn't what he associated with this place. His father had brought along a thermos of chai on that trip. He and his father had enjoyed piping hot, sweet and spicy milky chai after their sandwich—just the two of them. That was how they "desified" their trip. He could almost smell the cardamom and clove. The coffee shop sold chai, but he didn't trust it. Coffee shop chai would never compare with the fresh chai his father made. It would never deliver the same memories he carried inside him. The ones he felt so intensely.

His brother had been blowing up his phone all day with calls and texts. Kavan had let it go because he had been focused on Poorvi.

Navigating Poorvi. That's all.

The fact that she was beautiful had no bearing. She was argumentative and seemed to have no room for spontaneity. But she had shown him kindness.

Not that he was excited about this detour either. But the only way out seemed to be through, so if they moved at a good pace, they would show Ba everything on her list and make it to Dublin by tomorrow night. Which left him plenty of time to find this P. K. Gupta and have the discussion he needed.

"It's about time," Naveen greeted him.

"Hello to you too, then," Kavan said, instantly on guard.

"I've been trying to contact you all day. I heard your flight landed in—"

"Cork."

"Great, so you should be in Dublin soon then."

"Uh…well, there's been a bit of a holdup." Kavan waited for Naveen to fire up. He was not disappointed. Naveen's next words were edged with heat.

"What do you mean? Have I not made myself clear how important it is that you get to P. K. Gupta before he presents that paper?"

"You have." Kavan sighed. "And I will be there. I just have a few things I'm taking care of." Kavan did not need to be around to navigate Poorvi. She was smart; she'd be fine. He could easily get a train to Dublin and be there in a couple hours. But he didn't want to. He was enjoying Ba's company and was intrigued by Poorvi. She was irritating and captivating all in one and he wasn't ready to leave her.

"What does that mean? Little bhai, what—"

"Sorry I've lost you." Kavan faked a poor connection. "Can't…hear…you…"

"Kavan…don't you hang up—" Naveen warned.

Kavan disconnected the call as he grabbed the coffees. He had a road trip to get back to. His brother could wait.

Chapter Ten

The driving was getting easier. Poorvi had driven them into and out of the city area with little to no incident. They were on the highway on the four-hour trek to the Cliffs of Moher. She was quite proud of the fact that she had grown more comfortable driving on the opposite side of the road.

She was even comfortable enough to sip her black coffee as she drove. Kavan had offered cream and sugar, but she liked to taste her coffee.

"Okay. Black coffee."

"Wow," she had said as he began to dress his coffee. "Having a bit of coffee with your cream and sugar?"

He narrowed his eyes at her. "There isn't a thing you don't feel the need to judge, is there?"

She stared at him a minute. "No."

Kavan and Ba were presently conversing in fairly rapid Gujarati about Ba's family. Poorvi could hear Kavan's Gujarati getting more fluid the more he spoke with Ba. The sky darkened, warning them of an impending storm. She inhaled and gripped the wheel a bit tighter.

"You okay?" Kavan snapped his head to her. It was as if he could sense her apprehension.

"I'm fine." How did he know she was suddenly nervous?

Kavan turned around in his seat and faced forward. "Looks like a storm."

"Mmm-hmm." She nodded.

"You're not liking storms, are you?" he asked her.

She side-eyed him. "No."

"And why would that be?" He was focused on her rather intently.

She shook her head. "I've just never liked them—since I was a kid."

"No childhood trauma or anything?"

"Nothing that led to a fear of storms." She chuckled.

"Same for the small spaces. I just don't like them," he said.

Poorvi glanced in the rearview mirror. Ba had fallen asleep in the back seat. They drove in silence for a few minutes. The only sound came from the rain hitting the top of the car. Considering she hated storms, the pattering of the rain was strangely comforting. Or was it that Kavan was sitting beside her?

"I was dating this psychiatrist who insisted that I must have had some childhood trauma that led to my fear of storms." She shook her head. "He would have had a field day with you. Fear of small spaces was a specialty of his."

"You dated a psychiatrist?" Kavan raised his eyebrows.

She shrugged. "Yes. Brooks."

"As in past tense?"

"As in he turned out to be a less than stellar human being."

"What happened?" Kavan's voice was calm and inviting, and she found herself wanting to tell him.

"Well, things went down at my work—bad things—and instead of standing up for me, or at the very least sticking by me, Brooks bailed." Just another betrayal in a long list of betrayals.

"Sounds like you made a near escape there."

She grinned. "Sounds about right." It was easy, talking to this man. "What about you? Any dating horrors? Or—" It suddenly occurred to her, though her stomach dropped at the thought. "Maybe you have someone right now?"

Kavan simply grinned and shook his head. "Nah."

"Really? I'd have thought you would be fighting off the women, being that handsome."

He smirked at her. "You think I'm handsome?"

"Uh…duh. Everyone thinks you're handsome." She played it off even as she flushed.

"You're not everyone," he said quietly.

Her heart thudded at the implication that her opinion weighed heavier. "You're avoiding the question," she said to avoid his statement.

Rain started falling heavily suddenly, and it was as if buckets of water were being thrown at the windshield. She slowed her speed as visibility decreased drastically.

He cleared his throat. "Well then, you would be correct. I don't have trouble getting a date. It's just they aren't usually interested in anything more than how I look." He peered out his window. "Not that it matters. Naveen feels the need to vet any serious girlfriend I might have, and they usually run screaming into the night after meeting him."

She dared a glance at him and was taken by the anger and frustration on his face. Before she could speak, he suddenly turned and glanced out the front window.

"Oh! That's our exit!" He pointed. It was the one exit that was on the right.

"Seriously?" she grumbled. He had given her no warning. Poorvi hit the gas and navigated the car quickly to the far left lane to take the exit. She made the exit but went too fast for the curve. The car skidded and veered off the road in the exact spot where there wasn't a guardrail. They were thrown forward, and then yanked back by their seat belts. The bags in the trunk thumped against one another. The car came to stop, half in and half out of a ditch.

"Ba!" Poorvi and Kavan exclaimed together, turning to the back of the car.

"I'm okay," she said, her voice shaky. "Not hurt." She looked around. "My phone?"

"Poorvi! Are you okay?" He was breathless, his concern genuine.

Poorvi looked around and saw that they were all fine. All still buckled in, even though the car was at an odd angle. The rain had let up some but was still coming down. "I'm fine. No thanks to you," she barked at him, all happy thoughts and warm feelings dissolved away.

"What? How is this my fault? You're driving."

Her mouth gaped open. "Are you saying that it's my fault we're in a ditch?"

"You're the driver."

Was he serious right now? "You were too busy chatting to do your job, which was navigating," Poorvi spat at him.

"I told you to take the exit."

"When we were on top of it."

"Array!" Ba raised her voice and they turned to her. "I can't find my phone." There was panic in her voice.

"We'll find it, Ba," Poorvi said. "It has to be in the car."

"I need my phone." The panic in Ba's voice was turning to fear. "I need my phone."

Everyone was attached to their phones, and panicked to some degree when they couldn't find it. But Ba was shaking. "Ba. It's just under a seat or something—"

Before Kavan could finish, Ba had bent over to look under the seat for her phone.

He turned to Poorvi, the question on his face. She shook her head. She had no idea why Ba's phone was all of a sudden so important.

"Ba. Nothing left the car," Poorvi said.

"We will find it. Don't bend like that, you might hurt—"

"I am perfectly fine," she snapped. "Just because I am old does not mean I will break." She glared at the two of them. "Instead of arguing, how about you get us out of here?"

"Okay." Poorvi turned back to the wheel. She started the car and tried to move forward. Nothing. Backward. Nothing. She shook her head at Kavan. "I think we're stuck. Sounds like spinning tires."

"Right." Kavan nodded at her and stepped out into the rain without a thought or his coat. Poorvi followed with an umbrella from her backpack. Kavan was soaked through by the time she reached him.

"You should have taken the umbrella. It's cold and rainy," she said. He really should have, because now his T-shirt was stuck to his very fine, very muscular chest. She could see every one of those finely formed muscles. Holy Bollywood rain scene. She did her best not to stare. "Now you're...wet." She forced her gaze to the car as if she were studying the angle.

"The front tire is stuck in the mud. We need a tow," Kavan said. She held the umbrella over him so he could call AA. "They won't be here for hours," he said after speaking with them. "A bunch of accidents are keeping them busy." He continued to study his phone. "But there's a pub only about half a kilometer away. I'll see if I can borrow a car to come get you and Ba."

"I can walk. You're soaked through and it's cold." She made an honest effort to not to look at how his T-shirt was clinging to the lean muscles of his chest and arms. She failed. Was there any part of him that wasn't gorgeous? Ah, yes. He was irritating.

"Exactly. I'm already wet. We can't leave Ba alone," he said, bending to see Ba in the car.

Made sense. "Okay." She looked at him. "Do you want the umbrella?" She couldn't keep the laughter from her voice.

He looked at her and a wide grin spread across his face as laughter escaped him. Poorvi stared at him a minute, before joining him in laughter. She hadn't been trying to be funny, it just came out. Like most things she said around him, she was just being herself. She couldn't remember the last time she had been this uninhibited around anyone besides Niki. She was freezing and she could see that he was, too. But they both laughed to the point of not being able to breathe. Together. Also something that Poorvi hadn't done in awhile.

Just then Ba cracked open her window. "It's great you think this is so funny, but I have to pee. And I still can't find my phone."

Poorvi and Kavan got hold of themselves and their laughter. Poorvi got back in the car; the bottom of her pants were soaked, but other than that she was dry. She watched Kavan jog toward the pub, but lost sight of him quickly.

Ba was silent, still patting the seats, a look of anguish on her face. Poorvi managed to climb into the back seat and bent down to look for Ba's phone. She finally found it, lodged between the seat and the door.

"I'll have to open your door to get it," Poorvi said.

"Don't let it get wet," Ba said, her eyes huge. "Please."

Poorvi nodded. "I'll do my best." She quickly opened the door a couple inches and grabbed the phone before it fell out or got rained on. She breathed relief. "I got it!" She held it up and Ba grabbed it from her.

Ba tapped it and put it to her ear. A smile came across her face as she nodded. "Perfect," she told Poorvi. "Still works."

"That's great," Poorvi said as she crawled back to sitting, but Ba's elation went beyond getting a phone back. "Was that your daughter?"

"Hmm? Yes. She left me a message." A small smirk appeared on her face. "Kavan didn't even think twice about getting out into the rain." Now that she had her phone back, Ba was back to matchmaking.

Poorvi grinned and nodded. "Yes. That was very kind of him."

"Dependable," Ba clarified. "And now he is bringing a car for you."

"He's bringing a car for you." Though the gesture was not lost on her. He was…unselfish…he cared about people. It was definitely…rare…and attractive.

"You were laughing with him," Ba accused. "In the rain." Her eyes lit up and she clasped her hands together. "Soooo Bollywood."

Poorvi simply shook her head at Ba as if she were ridiculous, but the grin on her face wouldn't go away.

"Ba." A subject change was necessary. "You looked a bit sad at that park in Cork. Is everything okay?"

Ba studied her a moment. "Nice try," she blurted out, breaking out into a smile. "But I can tell you're attracted to Kavan."

"Ba. He's a kind, thoughtful and handsome man. *Anyone* would be attracted to him. It means nothing," Poorvi explained. It was true. Just because a man was attractive and she was attracted to him did not mean that there was anything to it. Brooks was attractive and intelligent, and they had enjoyed each other's company. But when push came to shove... Brooks had bolted. "He is also very argumentative."

"Hanh." Ba grinned and bobbled her head. "He argues back at you. But you admit you are attracted to him."

A knock at her window startled her and she turned to find a soaking wet version of the man himself. Back with a car.

Chapter Eleven

Kavan had managed to borrow a car from the young bartender, Melissa, with little effort. He deposited Poorvi and Ba—and their bags, Ba had insisted—at the pub. A typical pub, the bar was wooden and took up one side of the space. On the other side were rustic wooden tables with mismatched chairs. The walls were covered with football pennants from teams and their supporters from all over Ireland and the world. The lighting was dim as there was no sun, but the owner had cranked the heat so they were warm and comfortable. Near the back was a small doorway that led back to the bed and breakfast part of the establishment.

Kavan checked his phone and found that AA would be more than a few hours.

"Might as well have a pint," he told Poorvi and Ba. "We'll be here for a bit."

Melissa, the young blonde bartender, approached them. "This is Melissa. It's her car I borrowed." He turned to her. "Thank you again." He handed her the key.

"Of course." She flushed a bit, bounced her ponytail. "Can I get you a pint, some food?"

"Um. I'm sure that we would all appreciate that."

"Of course." Melissa eyed him, a smirk on her face. "A place to freshen up?"

"If it's not too much trouble," he said with a smile as he dripped all over the pub.

"Not at all. Not for you." She tilted her head for him to follow. "Come on then." She turned to Poorvi. "My da will be by in a moment for your food order."

Poorvi wiggled her fingers at him as she raised one eyebrow. "Have a nice...whatever." She smirked.

He shook his head at her but followed Melissa through that small door in the back and then through a small maze of hallways. "This area is available if you'd like to be more comfortable." She nodded at a small sitting area that had a sofa, a plush chair, a few tables and a small bar. She continued walking and opened a door. "This room is empty for the night. You're welcome to warm up in the shower."

"Thank you." Kavan said.

Melissa lingered a moment, eyeing Kavan appreciatively. "You seem very familiar. Do I know you from somewhere?" She moved toward him.

Kavan swallowed. "I have that kind of face." He waited for her to leave so he could shower. She did not seem in a hurry to go. The room was moderately sized with a queen bed and a sofa. His phone buzzed again. AA was not going to make it today.

"Looks like I'll be needing to rent a room for the night." He looked at Melissa. "The tow won't be getting here until after midnight."

Melissa grinned and stepped closer to him. "This here is the only room I have. But my room has space for one, handsome." It was clear what her thought process was, and sadly it wasn't the first time he'd been propositioned like this. He had half a mind to tell her off, but they needed a place to stay.

"Perfect, I can send my grandmother to share with you, then. My wife and I can take this room," Kavan blurted out.

"Your wife?"

"Oh yes. My wife." Kavan smiled innocently.

"But you haven't a ring," Melissa observed.

"We…ah…couldn't afford them just yet. Only been married a few months. Taking my grandmother to see our fair country…yeah?"

Melissa stepped back and forced a smile. "Of course. Makes sense. Forgive me."

"Oh yeah." He waved it off. "Honest mistake. No ring and all."

"Well, then I'll leave you to the shower," Melissa said, all business once more.

Kavan nodded as she left. He grabbed some dry clothes from his bag and hit the shower. He was cold to the core, and the warm shower was welcome.

He changed and headed down to Poorvi and Ba. Poorvi looked like she was enjoying an Irish coffee, while Ba had hit the Guiness.

"We need to spend the night here. The tow won't arrive until later," Kavan told them.

He saw Melissa chatting with an older man, must be her da. She'd be over for his drink order any minute. "Play along with me. Just pretend we're married," he said to Poorvi in Gujarati.

Poorvi furrowed her brow. "*What?* No way."

"We need a room for the night and I told her—" he flickered his eyes in Melissa's direction "—that we were married."

"Not my problem that you lied," Poorvi groused.

"She...she asked me to share her room," Kavan spit out.

Whatever he expected from Poorvi, it certainly wasn't rage.

"She did what?" Poorvi hissed. "Just because you're incredibly attractive does not mean she can ask... I'm going to give her a piece of my mind." Poorvi started to stand.

"Please don't. It was literally the first thing I could think of to politely refuse her." Kavan put his hand on her thigh, and she turned to look at him. She was warm and she did not push his hand away. His breathing evened out and he relaxed.

"Well, it shouldn't." Poorvi narrowed her eyes as she shifted her gaze behind him. "She's coming over."

Kavan held Poorvi's hand on the table, and it was as if they'd always held hands. She glanced at their hands and shook her head.

"Not enough." She leaned toward him, looking him in the eye. "Just kiss me," she demanded.

"What?"

"Just. Kiss me." She widened her eyes and encouraged him with a nod.

She nodded again, her dark eyes hard with determination. He was close enough to feel her breath, to catch the flower and rain scent of her. His heart gave a thud and he leaned toward her and gently pecked her lips.

"That's a kiss?" She mocked him, her lips near his. "Maybe this is why you don't have a girlfriend." Her mouth was poised in a smirk when she moved her lips back to his. She pressed her mouth against his and relaxed into him. Her mouth, so sassy, was soft and welcoming. She tasted sweet from the coffee and whiskey and he melted into her.

Kissing Poorvi felt like the most natural, but simultaneously the most wonderful sensation. He was starting to lose himself when—

"Ahem."

They startled and looked up to see the owner standing before them, a frown on his face. "I understand you are newlyweds, but this is not that kind of establishment. I believe you have rented a room from us, I expect ya to use it."

"Yes, sir, of course," Kavan said, still dazed. "Mister?"

"Every one just calls me Mr. O," said the older man.

Poorvi nodded and mumbled something, her eyes still glassy, her lips still wet from the kiss.

Still a bit off kilter, Kavan tried to slide away from Poorvi, thinking distance might set him straight, but his elbow hit Ba's pint, knocking it over. Guinness spilled everywhere, causing a commotion. "I'm so sorry!"

The owner shook his head as he mopped up the mess. "Wasting perfectly good Guinness, you are. Must have been some kiss."

"Yes, sir," Kavan said, helping to clean things off, a flush coming over him. "It certainly was." He threw a furtive glance at Poorvi, who also had a flush about her, but she was decidedly not looking at him as she chugged the remainder of her Irish coffee.

"Well now, boyo. What'll you be havin'?" asked the older man once he'd mopped up the mess.

"I'll be drinking Guinness," Kavan said. "And the soup will be fine."

"I'll have the soup as well. And another." Clearing her throat, Poorvi held up her empty glass.

Melissa put some peanuts on the table, still eyeing Kavan. "You really do look familiar."

He pulled down his ball cap. He always traveled with multiple. Those ads Naveen had him do were all over social media. He hated being recognized even more than he hated doing them.

"Ah. No. Never been to these parts," Kavan said, as he

took Poorvi's hand. It was the second time he'd done that in last few minutes, but he found it grounding. And happily she did not seem to mind. "Can we not have the nuts, please? I'm allergic."

"Sure." Melissa removed the nuts and her father went to fetch their drinks and food. Poorvi released her hand from his.

He flicked his gaze to her, but she was engrossed in her cup. Of course she let go of his hand, there was no one near by they were putting on a show for. But the logic did not take away the empty feeling of not having her hand in his. "The car is stuck until at least midnight," Kavan informed them softly. "Melissa here was kind enough to allow us to rent the only room they have left, for the night. You both can share the bed and I'll take the sofa."

Melissa showed up with their beers. "Something else to eat, ma'am?" she asked Ba.

Ba shook her head. "Another Guinness to replace the one he spilled?"

"Yes, ma'am," Melissa said. She started clearing away the snacks. "So how did you all meet?"

Kavan's heart thudded in his chest, but he kept a smile on his face as Poorvi took his hand. Comfort flooded over him. "You know, the normal way." He chuckled.

Ba looked at Melissa and started telling her a story in Gujarati. Kavan was flabbergasted. He looked at Poorvi, that same smile still plastered on his face. She was also smiling, but her attention was on Ba. She translated for Melissa.

"Well. I'll tell you the truth. They met one year ago at the temple. They were immediately drawn to each other, but they weren't sure if their parents would approve. So they arranged vacations for their families—separately of course—and planned to 'accidently' meet at various locations. Hawaii, India, London, even here in Dublin." Ba was more animated than they had seen her thus far. "Until finally their families caught on. By then the families were close friends and were thrilled that the two of them wanted to be married. A wedding was planned and these two are together." Ba smiled at them with such genuine affection, Kavan was taken aback. But more importantly, Melissa was wide-eyed and smiling.

"That is just beautiful." She turned to them both. "I wish you both the best."

Poorvi nodded, but her attention was on Ba. Once Melissa left, Poorvi leaned into Ba. "That was a beautiful story."

Ba nodded.

"Is that how you and Dada met?" she asked.

Ba froze her gaze on Poorvi, her mouth pressed together. "You are very smart," she said quietly.

"As are you." Poorvi grinned.

Poorvi reached across and held Ba's hand. Kavan reached his hand out and laid it on Poorvi's.

He raised his pint to them both and sipped. "Thank you, Ba."

Poorvi raised her glass as well, to Ba and then to him. "Thanks for finding us a place to stay."

"It was the least I could do since I wasn't paying attention to the navigating." He shrugged one shoulder sheepishly.

Poorvi raised her mug to him. "No kidding." She laughed. Her phone was on the table and began to buzz. She looked at it and scowled. "I'm sorry, I need to take this." Poorvi stood and walked to the back of the pub.

Kavan watched her go, his gaze lingering a bit longer than necessary. He turned to find Ba looking at him with a huge smile on her face.

"She is beautiful," Ba said.

"Yes." But it didn't mean anything. Though if he was honest, he was still a bit dazed from that kiss.

"She's a good person," Ba added.

"She's irritating," Kavan responded, but without any real gusto.

"That doesn't mean she's not a good person," Ba said, finishing off her Guiness.

Poorvi did not return after twenty minutes had passed. And she was no longer at the back of the bar. Kavan went to find her. She was standing alone on the back porch, watching the rain.

Something about the way she stood tugged at his heart. "Poorvi?" he called out gently.

She startled. Her hands went to her face as if she were wiping away tears. "Yes. Sorry. I just—"

"Everything okay?"

"Um." She turned to face him, her eyes rimmed red. "Yes. Nothing for you to be concerned about."

"Poorvi…"

She put a hand up. "I said I was fine. You got us a room and tow for the car. Enough heroism for the day," she snapped at him.

Tears brimmed in her eyes, but she clearly did not want to share. Disappointment came over him. He had thought after the car and maybe even the kiss that maybe she was opening up to him. Clearly he had read too much.

"Right. Of course." He backtracked. "Just wanted to know if you wanted another drink. It's your turn to pay." He forced a grin for her, a poor attempt to lighten whatever upset her.

She blinked and inhaled, smiling as she moved toward him. "No, it's not, Ba stole your credit card. So yeah, I'll have another drink." She walked past him and back to the pub. "Maybe even two." She smirked at him, but there was gratitude in her watery eyes.

"What do you mean Ba stole my card?" He followed her back into the pub. Just then his phone rang with a call from his cousin and best friend, Anand. "Go ahead and order another round. I'll be there in a minute."

Poorvi furrowed her brow but continued.

"What's up?"

"Where are you?" Anand asked.

"I don't know. Near Cliffs of Moher."

"You're sightseeing?"

"It's complicated."

"Well, Naveen keeps calling me," Anand said. "He's getting on my last nerve. He thinks you're with me, avoiding the conference, and more to the point avoiding the conversation you need to have with P. K. Gupta. Which I know you are because you disagree with him, but you never stand up to him."

"I'm not avoiding. And I have told him that I disagree. That we should consider the research," Kavan explained.

"But you haven't put your foot down."

"It's not that easy. He's my big brother. I owe him—"

"You don't owe him your whole life, Kavan." Anand sighed. "Yes, he pulled you out of a tough time. But that's what family does. It does not make you beholden to them for the rest of your life." Anand chuckled. "In any case, I support you not getting to that conference until you absolutely have to. About time you had a couple days off. How'd you end up there?"

"I was—" how to explain Poorvi and Ba and the storm and the car "—detoured."

"Ah. You're hooking up." Anand snickered. "About time. I can't even remember your last girlfriend."

"Well it's been awhile, hasn't it?" Kavan always seemed

to end up with the women who were more interested in his money and name more than anything. The last one, Laura, had been no different. They'd been together almost a year, when he'd found her kissing someone else. He'd been hurt by the betrayal, but he'd been more hurt by Naveen's words when he told him about the breakup. *You're too nice, Kavan. People are going to take advantage of you. Nice is not working for you. Get a backbone or keep getting your heart broken.*

"But, no. I am not hooking up."

"Well, you should."

"Goodbye, Anand."

"I'm not picking up if Naveen calls again."

"Agreed."

He ended the call with his cousin, feeling lighter. He and Anand were born a day apart, and had been best friends since birth.

He glanced outside. The rain had let up. He went back to the pub, a pep in his step, thinking about sitting next to Poorvi again.

Chapter Twelve

It was close to midnight, a few pints and a ton of delicious food later, when AA texted Kavan that they would meet him in fifteen minutes. He excused himself to go to the rental car.

Poorvi and Ba made their way to the room. No sooner had Poorvi lain down and turned off the light than Ba started snoring. Poorvi gently nudged her. It stopped. Poorvi closed her eyes and settled in just as the snoring started again.

This was not going to work. Poorvi grabbed her pillow and an extra blanket and headed for the back of the pub to the cute little sitting room where she had seen a sofa. She quietly navigated the dark inn by moonlight and found the room with the sofa in the back. She located a small lamp and turned it on. The light revealed a bookshelf. She chose a book and settled into the sofa. She wasn't waiting for Kavan to return. Not at all. She simply needed a distraction from the call earlier that day.

Her mother had called to find out how the prep was going

for the conference. Poorvi had chosen that moment to be forthright and tell her mother exactly what she was doing. Mistake. Huge mistake.

"What do you mean you befriended an old lady and are taking her to see Ireland with some strange man you don't know?"

"When you say it like that, Mom, it sounds ridiculous."

"How else would I say it?"

"She's all alone. I can't just leave her."

"Beti. Your priority should be this meeting. After everything that happened at the lab, you need to redeem yourself. You need to prove yourself."

"Redeem? Mom. I did nothing wrong." She was fired up. How did you redeem yourself when you had done nothing wrong?

"Well then how did Dr. Wright get the Principal Investigator job?"

"Mom. Are you saying that you believe those…rumors?"

"Of course not but—"

"But what, Mom?"

"But you must have done something for those rumors to start. People don't just make things up," she insisted.

"Mom. I can't." Tears of frustration had built up again. "I can't keep having this conversation with you. I did nothing wrong. All I did was be a woman in a man's field. I would think you would understand that."

"I do understand that, but instead of making a stink about it, sometimes you have to roll with it."

"No. I will not." Shaking with rage, Poorvi had tapped her phone off and let the tears come. That was when Kavan had found her.

The book must have distracted her, or she was simply that exhausted, because as she was close to drifting off she felt a gentle tap on her shoulder. She heard Kavan's velvet voice saying her name.

"Poorvi?"

She turned to look up at him, slightly confused but comforted by his presence. Unbidden, the kiss that they had shared earlier came to mind and she flushed. It was supposed to be fake, but kissing Kavan had not felt real, it had felt amazing. She could not recall ever being kissed like that.

"What's going on?" He walked around and sat down next to her. He sat close enough that she could feel the heat from his body. She was immediately tempted to curl herself into that warmth and comfort, and was only able to do so by reminding herself that she had no real right to his comfort.

She closed the book. "Ba snores. She sounds like a chain saw." Poorvi grinned.

He chuckled. "Of course she does. The car is here, surprisingly no damage, so we're all set for the morning." He stood.

He was leaving? "You going to bed?" She didn't want to be alone with only her thoughts for company.

"Uh...well." He looked around. "Unless you want a drop of whiskey?"

"If you want." She shrugged like she didn't care.

He poured two whiskeys and brought them over, sitting down on the sofa. "I don't see any ice for you." He shrugged.

"This is perfect," she said. They clinked glasses and sipped. Rather he sipped, she chugged. The alcohol was warm on the way, slight burn, but she'd been drinking whiskey for years.

"Okaaaay." He raised his eyebrows and grabbed the bottle, pouring her another glass.

"Don't judge." She sipped this second glass.

"You judged my coffee." He smirked.

"You can't even taste the coffee if you put all that—"

"But that's how I like it." He raised his eyebrows at her.

She opened her mouth, then closed it. "Fine."

He sat back, grinning at her. Her eyes went directly to his mouth. She forced her gaze to his eyes. "I would never judge you."

She stared into her drink. "That call I got? My mom. Telling me I don't have my priorities straight."

"Ah." Kavan moved closer to her on the sofa and grinned. "Seeing the sites in Ireland with a strange man doesn't make your mum's priority list?" He quirked an eyebrow as he sipped. "Odd."

"No." His attempt at humor was sweet and she appreciated it, but the tears made another showing. "She blames me for losing my promotion."

"I take it she's wrong." Kavan nodded. He turned to face her, their legs just shy of touching.

She longed to move her leg that half an inch so she could be touching him. "Yes." She nearly whispered it as if not saying out loud didn't make it true.

"What happened?"

Poorvi stared at Kavan. He had the kindest eyes, and right now he was looking at her with no judgment, no expectation.

"If you say it, you might feel better," he said softly as he took another sip of his drink.

"Or I might feel worse." She wasn't a sharer. She didn't tell anyone her personal things—by definition, they were *personal*. Even her Ba used to tell her she was a closed book. She had been since birth, but then the few times she did open up, she had gotten hurt. "Trusted" friends had told her secrets in high school, resulting in whispering behind her back, as well as comments to her face.

But right now, in this moment, she felt safe. She wanted to share with Kavan. She needed to.

He gave her a small smile, one that went all the way to his eyes. "That is a risk. But trust me. I've been told I'm a good listener."

She narrowed her eyes at him. "Yeah? By who?"

He paused and chuckled. "My mom."

Poorvi stared at him. There was no reason to laugh. His mother had faith in him. It was more than what she could say about her own mother.

"That's good enough for me." She paused and took off her glasses. "Dr. Bobby Wright and I were coinvestigators in the lab. When Dr. Steven Wang, our principal investigator, decided to move to another state to be with his wife, his job was up for grabs."

She leaned in toward Kavan. "That job was mine." She pointed at herself and paused as the anger became a lump in her throat. "When I say I'm smarter and better equipped to handle that job in every way possible, understand that that is not professional ego. That is fact. Not my opinion. Fact."

Kavan nodded. "I don't doubt it."

"Right before the announcement, Steve brought me into his office. He said things..." She shook her head, pressed her tears down and sat straight up. "He said that his boss, Dr. James Hardy, claimed that I had approached him, offering...sex..." Even now it was close to impossible to say, the notion was so ridiculous. "If he would tell Steve to pick me as the next PI."

Kavan sat up straight at this news, his eyes narrowed and brow furrowed, like he was trying to understand, but not believing what had happened. Pretty much how she had felt at the time.

"Dr. Hardy had many times over the years asked me to dinner. I had coffee with him one time when I happened to run into him in the cafeteria and he invited me to join him." She looked at Kavan; she needed him to believe her. "I never once accepted his invitations. For precisely this reason." She shivered. "He had always given me a creepy sort of vibe."

"Did you fight back?"

"With what? I had no proof that he'd asked me out. All of our interactions were verbal. I never told anyone but Niki that he asked me out. I told Steve and Bobby that Dr. Hardy was the one who pursued me. Whether they believed me or not, I don't know." Her voice became high pitched with frustration, and the tears were harder to stop.

"This Dr. Hardy, he didn't call for your outright removal from the lab for these alleged happenings?" Kavan was focused on her, his anger clearly simmering beneath the need to understand the logic.

She shook her head. "No. In fact, he even said that he didn't want to 'destroy' me by having me fired, he simply didn't think I was PI material. Like he was doing me some kind of favor." Tears of anger burned and spilled out onto her cheeks. "So I did not get promoted. And 'somehow' the rumors got out. Now the whole lab knows what Dr. Hardy said."

"Why didn't you leave?" His voice was low, a growl almost.

She fired up. "Because I shouldn't have to! My work is in that lab. All of my findings…" She shook her head. "No, I won't leave."

There. She'd told somebody and she was close to sobbing from the anger and the injustice of it all. "My mom, she thinks I should have just gone on one date, and he would have left me alone. She thinks that I must have done *something* to have lost the promotion. But I didn't. And I know how men like him operate, anyway. It wouldn't have been just one date. And anything I did with him would've become blackmail material."

She looked at him expecting to see sympathy, or kindness, or god forbid, pity. Instead, there was fury in his eyes. His jaw was clenched, and his mouth was set, his hand was fisted around his drink, which he seemed to have forgotten about.

"I'm sorry men are such assholes."

"Me, too," she said, and let loose her sobs. She couldn't help it. It was too big. Her anger at her mom, her frustration with Bobby and Steve, the power Hardy wielded, everyone in the lab second-guessing her character. Right now, it was too much for her to hold all on her own.

She wasn't sure when it happened, but Kavan's arms wrapped around her, holding her close while she sobbed into his T-shirt. She melted into the comfort she so needed, that Kavan so willingly gave. She honestly could not remember ever being held this way. Cherished.

"Wait," Kavan's voice hardened again and he pulled back a bit to look at her. "The psychiatrist?"

Fresh tears of anger filled her eyes as she nodded. "As soon as I told him, he backed away from me. He actually asked me if it was true."

"Complete dosser," Kavan grumbled.

Kavan had barely known her twenty-four hours and he had accepted her version as truth. "I don't know what that means, but it sounds exactly what like Brooks was. A dosser."

Kavan let loose a small chuckle as he wiped her tears and whispered. "You're not alone. It's a promise, yeah?"

Chapter Thirteen

Kavan held her face an extra beat as he wiped away her tears. He never could understood men like Brooks. Anger bloomed in his chest at the thought of how he had hurt Poorvi.

He said nothing, because what could he say that would change what had happened to her?

She quieted and he reached in his pocket for his handkerchief and offered it to her. "It's clean, I promise," he said.

She took it and wiped her eyes. "Who carries these anymore?"

He grinned, grateful that it was a habit for him to simply put one in his pocket always. Honestly, it was a way to remember his father. But today, it came in handy. "My dad told me and my brother to always have one on us. You can never know when one's needed."

"Well, he was right," she said. "Thank you."

"I wish I could tell him." Kavan paused.

She smiled at him, her eyes still wet from crying, grabbed

her drink, and curled back up on the sofa facing him. Not in his arms, just next to him, her thigh touching his knee. His arms felt empty, but at least some part of her was touching him. "Tell me about him."

"What?"

"If you want. Tell me about your dad." She was looking at him, her full attention on him. She really wanted to know.

Kavan took a gulp of his whiskey. He didn't talk about his dad much. No one around him ever wanted to discuss him. Naveen would merely grunt when he brought up their dad. His mother just got wistful. He looked at Poorvi.

He had gotten used to not talking about his dad, but suddenly he was excited to tell her all about him. Share all the ways in which he was a great dad. "Well, he was the one who took me to the Blarney Stone and the English Market."

"I already know that." Her eyes lit up. She had taken off her glasses, and sitting so close to her, he could see her eyes properly now. They were big and dark, dark brown, almost black. The kind of eyes that you wanted to fall into. At least he did. She narrowed them at him, pointing a finger. "Something else."

Kavan just looked at her. "He used to coach my football—soccer—teams when I was very little, like five or six. Back when we lived in the States."

Poorvi smiled all the way to her eyes.

"Then after, no matter how well or poorly we played, he'd take us to an ice cream truck and get every one of us an ice cream treat. Naveen had asked him why he did that even if we played badly." Kavan shook his head. A mix of sadness and pride filled him. "And my da would say that soccer should be fun, and he wanted us to always remember that playing should be fun."

Poorvi was gazing at him, her eyes glassy. "He sounds like an amazing dad."

Kavan nodded, a sense of peace coming over him. "He really was." Silence sat between them, comfortable and quiet.

"What ice cream did you get? From the truck."

Kavan grinned wide. "Same thing. Every time." His eyes went distant. "Well, almost every time. Oreo ice cream sandwich."

Poorvi's eyes bugged out. "Me too! My hands-down favorite."

Kavan focused on her a minute. Her dark eyes sparkled, her smile was animated, she looked as happy as a little girl with an Oreo ice cream sandwich.

Huh. Something niggled in the back of his mind. Like a thread of memory he couldn't quite grasp.

"Tell me more about him," she said, sipping her drink.

"Well, he would have liked you."

"Why is that?" She was smiling.

"Because he loved a strong, feisty, irritating woman."

She laughed and it was a beautiful thing, the way her face lit up and her eyes crinkled. "I do my best," she said as she raised her glass. "So, your mom. She's feisty?"

He shook his head. "Not anymore," he said quietly. "She changed when he died."

Poorvi pursed her lips and nodded. "I hear you. My mom and dad are like this." She crossed her fingers. "I hate to think what would happen if…"

"Sounds like they're happy," he said.

She shrugged.

"And what do you think of that?"

"Of getting married?" She shrugged. "I have my work. My mom of course would love for me to be married, but she really doesn't nag me about it. Though it would be nice to share your life with someone. To have that companion in life." She turned and crossed her legs, facing him fully.

It meant her legs were no longer touching his and he felt it like a loss. "Not just anyone, though. The right person. You know what I mean?"

He nodded as he sipped his drink. "I do know."

"So, what happened when your dad died? How come Naveen raised you?" She leaned in toward him.

He drew his gaze over her. Was she really interested or just passing the time? He shrugged. He wanted to share with her. "My brother kind of took over when our dad died. He was eighteen. I was fifteen.

"Grief hit my mom hard. So Naveen was the one feeding us, making sure we got to school, all that. Then after some time, I was getting myself mixed up with the wrong crowd. It was Naveen who pulled me away from all that. He saved me." Kavan gulped his whiskey. "Of course, he's never let me forget it."

"Sorry. He probably feels like he doesn't want to lose you as well as your dad." Poorvi looked him in the eye.

Silence floated between them as he considered this possibility.

She grinned at him. "Your American accent comes out every so often."

He nodded. "I was born in the States, we moved here when I six or seven?" He shrugged. "In any case I fluctuate depending on who I'm talking to. The American is coming out because I'm sitting here with you."

She nodded. More silence, but Kavan did not feel the pressure to fill it as he usually did.

Kavan believed that relationships took time to build. So maybe it was the whiskey, or the storm or the way Poorvi's dark wavy hair framed her face. Or maybe it was because they were being honest with each other, but the idea of an instant connection with someone was so incredibly unbelievable, he never would have given it any credence if it weren't for how he felt right then.

"You know, I noticed you at the airport," he said softly.

"Yeah. You took my outlet," she taunted him, smiling.

"I got there first." He chuckled softly, taking in her sassy smile, tousled hair and red-rimmed eyes. "But before that. I saw you."

She met his gaze as she sipped her whiskey, narrowing her eyes at him. "So when you took my outlet, that was your way of hitting on me…?"

"No. I would say it was the biggest mistake I'd ever made, but here we are anyway."

She locked his eyes with his. They had been leaning toward each other as he spoke.

"Here we are," she said softly. Her gaze dipped to his mouth. He leaned toward her, eager to taste the whiskey on her lips, eager to kiss her again. Once had most definitely not been enough.

Her movement was minute, but she did move toward him. Their breath mingled in the small space between them.

It did not matter that twenty-four hours ago he hadn't even known that she existed. It didn't matter that twenty hours ago, he thought she was the most irritating woman on the planet. What mattered was the connection he felt to her. It was beyond any connection he'd ever felt before. The time was irrelevant. He leaned down to taste her.

Ka-boom! Thunder rolled and Poorvi jumped up and away from him. The moment was gone. Kavan was flustered, his heart rapidly pounding.

Flustered, she stood. "I should go to bed. Try to get some sleep." She did not make a move to go upstairs.

So close to what must be heaven. He nodded and stood as well. "Right. Long day tomorrow."

"Right." She turned to go. "You know, Ba's snoring is really bad. One more whiskey might help." She picked up her glass.

"Makes sense." Anything for her not to go. He moved to get the bottle. When he turned back, Poorvi was right behind him. Their bodies grazed each other.

"I noticed you, too. At the airport." She spoke softly, but her words were sure. "But then you stole my outlet."

"Not my finest moment."

She shook her head. "No. So make up for it now. Kiss me."

Kavan did not need to be asked twice. Bottle in one hand and empty glass in the other, he lowered his mouth to hers, intending to gently place his mouth on hers. But that was impossible. He'd had a taste a few hours ago, which meant that as soon as his lips touched hers, he wanted more. The bottle and glass slipped from his hands and landed with a crash.

He barely noticed the whiskey that had splashed on him. She did not move.

She kissed him back with want and need that matched his own. He brought one of his free hands to her face and the other to her waist as he nipped and tasted. She stood on her toes and deepened their kiss as he pulled her closer.

It was as if there had never been a time when he hadn't known her. She always been here with him; he simply hadn't realized it until she showed up.

"Oi!"

They jumped away from each other and found Mr. O in a nightshirt taking in the mess they'd made.

"What's goin' on here?"

"Oh, so sorry, Mr. O," Poorvi said. "We'll clean it up. Not sure what happened."

"Looks like you dropped a bottle of whiskey trying to

kiss each other." He scowled at them. "Newlyweds. Keep spilling things in m' pub."

"Yep. That's us. Newlyweds." Poorvi smiled at Mr. O.

"We'll pay for it, sir. Apologies," Kavan said, finally finding his voice.

"Yeah. Well, all right then. Wasn't the good stuff anyway." He turned to go. "Clean up, then carry on."

Poorvi looked at Kavan, amusement in her eyes, biting her bottom lip trying to hold back laughter. Kavan met her eyes, overcome with the thought that he would give anything to bite that lip.

Chapter Fourteen

Poorvi woke to the sun shining down on her face, warm and yellow. She didn't open her eyes, not wanting the dream to end. She dreamed that she'd had the sexiest make-out session with Kavan last night.

"Hanh."

She opened her eyes. She looked to where the sound had come from. Ba.

She sat bolt upright. "Ba." No Kavan. Had she really dreamed it? It had seemed so real. How much whiskey had she had? Had she slept here on the sofa?

Though if she *had* dreamed it, that was for the better. She really didn't need to be kissing random men she'd only just met. Too risky, no matter what.

Ba narrowed her eyes, then tilted her head at her. She felt like Ba knew what she had been thinking. What did it matter? Ba wasn't even her real grandmother.

"You slept down here?" Ba asked.

"You snore, Ba," Poorvi said matter-of-factly.

"Ah." Ba nodded. "Next time I will get my own room."

"Where is—"

"There's no next time, Ba," Kavan said from behind her. Poorvi turned to find Kavan standing there, looking downright delectable in a fresh long-sleeved, fitted green T-shirt and jeans, his wet hair sticking out from under his ball cap. He grazed his eyes over her, and her heart pounded in her chest.

It hadn't been a dream.

He seemed unable to make eye contact. Of course. Look at him, he probably made out with random women all the time. She didn't really believe that.

She quickly brushed aside the disappointment that started to build. Disappointment that she had felt something, and he had not. Disappointment that she allowed herself to consider that they might have some sort of... connection. She'd barely known him a day. What kind of feelings could they really have beyond simple lust?

"We're finishing your list and getting to Dublin tonight." He was still addressing Ba, as if Poorvi weren't even there.

"I'll just go grab a shower," she said, putting as much ice in her voice as she could muster. She brushed past him and to their room.

She had quite literally cried in his arms. And then told him all about work—what an idiot. Must have been the whiskey.

But he had shown no signs of wanting to be anywhere but with her.

Anger at her mother popped up as she recalled their conversation yesterday. She squelched it down. She could only deal with one thing at a time. Right now, her focus had to be getting to Dublin. Once she presented her paper, she could return to her lab, where she would simply focus on work. Rumors be damned.

Science. Numbers. Facts. All were dependable. People. Feelings. Kissing. Not dependable.

She finished her shower, then wrapped a towel around herself before stepping back into the room, just as the door opened and Kavan entered the room. He stopped when he saw her. For an instant she forgot she was only clad in a towel. The way he was looking at her—eyes darkened with desire, mouth slightly open like he wanted her not only then and there, but to be *his*.

"Hey! What the hell are you doing here?" she shouted, tightening the towel around her. It was simple lust in his eyes. She should stop making more of things than they actually were.

"I came to get my computer," Kavan said as he grabbed her computer.

"That's *my* computer," she barked as she squeezed her arms tight around her. He wouldn't even look at her.

He looked down at what he had grabbed and dropped it on the bed, glancing around the room, presumably for his computer. "Uh… About last night…"

"What about it?" She glared at him, daring him to say anything. A spark of hope shot through her at the idea that he might really want something with her.

"I'm sorry."

Her eyebrows shot up. That spark of hope extinguished immediately. Anything but that. "You're…sorry?"

"We had a lot of whiskey…"

Any hope she might have had, any wish that they had some kind of connection, withered away, leaving a trail of disappointment. Heat rose to her face as mortification took over her and she realized she was standing alone in a room wearing nothing but a towel with a man who would rather

NOT have kissed her last night. Talk about about missing the message.

She should have known better. Brooks had taught her that lesson the hard way, and she had still let her guard down. That kind of thing only happened in books. Not real life.

"Right. Too much alcohol," she confirmed.

"Mmm-hmm." He bobbed his head.

"Okay then." She was short with him.

"Okay then." He started to leave.

"Your computer is over there." She pointed with her chin.

"Right." He walked over and picked it up, took one more glance at her and left, bumping into the door on his way out.

She threw herself on the bed. Seriously? She was an idiot. At least she knew who he was now before she was even more invested. Before she caught real feelings and had to get over him.

The thing was, she might already be too late.

Chapter Fifteen

Kavan did not need his computer. He'd used that as an excuse to see Poorvi. To talk about the amazing kiss they'd shared last night. Well, really, to kiss her again. To tell her there was simply no way he could ever get enough of her. Seeing her in nothing but a towel caught him off guard, in the best possible way, except that it had rendered him speechless. So he had acted like a complete dork. He burned with embarrassment.

But it was probably just as well. Because clearly, the kiss had meant very little to her.

Just a drunken kiss.

Except that he had not been drunk. He hadn't really thought she was, either.

No matter. He should know better than to believe that real connections could be made in twenty-four hours.

He made his way to the kitchen and found Ba teaching Mr. O and Melanie how to make tepla. She had a few going and they smelled fabulous. He also caught a whiff of cardamom, cinnamon, clove.

"Ba. Did you make chai?" he asked.

She nodded toward a teapot. "I strained it into there."

Fantastic. He poured himself a mug of the milky chai and settled down at the bar with the round spicy thin flatbread Ba was rolling out with a rolling pin and then roasting with oil on a flat pan. He was adding sugar to his chai when Poorvi arrived, her dark hair still damp on her shoulders. He tried not to stare at how great she looked in jeans, a pink blouse and matching pink-framed glasses.

"Smells fabulous, Ba," she said, a wide smile on her face, her voice light and breezy, as if she hadn't a care in the world. She poured herself some chai and sat down a couple stools away not even acknowledging him. She added sugar to her chai as Ba placed a plate with tepla in front of her.

Ba shifted her gaze between them, while Poorvi made conversation with their hosts. Mr. O kept shooting him confused looks like he was trying to process what he had seen last night with what was going on right now.

If he figured it out, Kavan would have loved his insight.

"You've lived in Ireland all your life and you have never been to the Cliffs of Moher?" Ba asked as Kavan loaded their bags into the car.

"Poorvi. I need your bag," he called out, unsuccessful in his attempt to hide his irritation. The sun was out today, adding some much-appreciated warmth to the air, but all he felt was the chill from Poorvi as she stomped over to him with her bag.

"I'll do it." She stepped up next to him, her jaw set.

"I'm happy to load the car." He glared at her.

"Just because you're a man doesn't mean that you have to put my bag in the car," she snapped.

"It's not because I'm a man." He spoke slowly. "It's because you're doing all the driving. I'm just trying to pull my weight."

"Fine. Whatever." She left the bag and sat down in the driver's seat.

"Fine," he snapped back. Probably better that there was no connection between them.

"You didn't answer my question," Ba said once they got on the road.

"We didn't travel much when I was younger." He shot a glance at Poorvi. "And now I never seem to have the time."

"Make time," Ba said. "You don't know how much you have."

"That is very true, Ba," he said softly. "But we're busy."

"What are you busy with? What are your jobs?" Ba asked them.

"Oh, well, I'm an—" He spotted the sign for the next exit. "You're going to need to be in the far-left lane, the exit is coming up," Kavan told Poorvi.

"Thank you." Her voice was polite, formal even. Like they'd just met. Except when they had just met, she was definitely not this polite. Not to mention the phenomenal kissing session they'd shared just hours ago. He side-eyed her so she wouldn't see him looking. She was completely focused in front of her, as if he weren't even there.

"Did your family travel, beti?" Ba asked.

"We traveled some. But my mom and dad work a lot, so it was hard," she answered.

"So you both have the world left to see. How wonderful!" Ba clapped her hands together as if this were something fabulous they had in common.

"I suppose," Poorvi answered.

Silence prevailed for the next hour or so. They were getting close when Kavan felt a thunk on the outside of the car. He snapped his head to Poorvi. She snapped her head to him in the same instant.

"Not good," they said in unison.

"Pull over! Pull over!" he cried.

"Really? You think I should pull over? Brilliant," she snarked, but she pulled over within a few seconds. They both jumped out of the car.

"Ba, stay put." Again they were in unison.

They glared at each other.

Sure enough, they had a flat tire.

"I thought you said there was no damage to the car," Poorvi snapped at him.

"There wasn't," Kavan told her between gritted teeth.

"Then what the hell is this?" she yelled.

"How is this anywhere near my fault? Flat tires happen all the time. Maybe you hit a nail or something."

"Oh, so now it's my fault?" she groused at him.

"I'm not saying that. But I am tiring of you blaming every little bit on me, yeah?" he growled at her.

"So, you're clearly not taking responsibility," she threw at him.

He inhaled deeply and stared at her. "Sometimes things just happen and they're nobody's fault."

"That doesn't even make sense." But he caught the confusion in her eyes. She rolled up her sleeves and opened the trunk. "Where's the spare? Must be under...ah, here it is." She grunted as she slowly lifted the spare out. Kavan knew better than to interfere, so he rolled up his sleeves and pulled out the jack and the lug wrench. He placed the jack under the car and began cranking it.

"I can do that," she grumbled.

"I got it," he mumbled.

She picked up the lug wrench and started to unscrew the bolts. He was shocked she didn't fight with him to do it all herself. This must be her way of accepting help. Not that he needed to be learning anything new about her.

Once they were loose, he knelt beside her. He put his hands on the part of the tire that was closest to him, she put out her hands on the side closest to her. They looked at each other and nodded. Then they pulled. The tire popped off.

He stole a glance at her. Her face was fixed in a scowl and she was focused on the tire. They were both sweating in the sun.

He picked up the spare and lined it up with the nuts and Poorvi tightened the bolts with the wrench. They worked side by side, each anticipating the other's moves, saying very little. In short time, they were functional again.

He put the flat tire back in the car. The physical activity had syphoned off some of his earlier angst with her. "We make a good team," he said, leaning against the car. He wiped his hands on a towel.

"I could have done that by myself," she said.

"I have no doubt. But you didn't have to," he said pleasantly. The more pleasant he was, the more irritated she seemed to get. He liked that.

"I didn't need help." She was firm.

He shrugged. "Maybe so, but we changed that tire together, like a team. There's no shame in that." He had enjoyed that moment of them being in sync.

Poorvi narrowed her eyes at him and huffed back into the car.

He inhaled and sat down in the passenger seat.

Chapter Sixteen

Poorvi was silent the rest of the journey. She was still worked up about their kiss and the fact that Kavan seemed to think it was okay to accept help. Against her natural tendencies, she was starting to see his point.

Not to mention that they had worked in tandem, and that had felt good. To know that he was going to work with her as a partner to change out that tire.

They arrived at the Cliffs of Moher without further incident. Poorvi pulled into the lot and calmly parked the car. The three of them exited the car without a word. The air was cool and misty, but the sun offered some warmth. People were milling about, or walking toward the trail that ran along the edge of the cliffs.

Ba looked from one to the other. "You two are boring today. I'm going to see the cliffs on my own." With that Ba walked away, her handbag hooked on her arm.

Poorvi gaped at Ba as she watched her walk away. "Nicely done." She turned on Kavan.

"You're blaming this on me, too?" He had the audacity to appear shocked, but more amused than irritated.

"Well, yes. *You* are clearly the extrovert here. Why didn't you talk to her?" Poorvi shook her head at him in disappointment. Wasn't that the point of extroverted people? To talk so introverts didn't have to?

"Why didn't you? Just because you're the introvert doesn't mean you can't make small talk with a sweet old lady," he shot back. "It's good to exercise those small talk muscles."

She stared at him. He did not back down from her—ever. Annoyance built in her throat. She hadn't made small talk with Ba because she had been preoccupied thinking about him.

Not to mention that he was clearly fighting a grin that indicated he knew that. While he was winning that battle, he could not hide the clear amusement in his eyes. Which was actually more irksome.

"Let's just go see the cliffs," she snapped. "We need to find a garage as well. Because the spare is not meant for long distances."

"Fine." Kavan extended his arm out. "After you."

"How polite," she sneered.

"I am, yes. As a matter of fact."

She rolled her eyes and led the way up the short hill to the edge of the cliffs where people were gathered. She approached an open spot and stopped. The sun was still out and had burned away the fog, so the view was clear. She had seen pictures and wondered what all the hubbub was. The cliffs just dropped into the ocean, the water smashed against the sides, relentlessly, patiently wearing down the rock. Smaller structures dotted the ocean, poking up from the water like giant triangles. She had never seen anything so frighteningly beautiful. She took in the sound of the water crashing into the cliffs, over and over, insistent in its effort to take down stone and earth. This was an experience without equal. The sheer persistence was inspiring.

Her irritation melted away. Kavan was standing behind her, silent and steady. His chest a mere inch from her back. She felt his body relax as hers did. She had the urge to lean back into that strong chest, to feel the comfort of his arms around her. She fought it.

"It's hard. Me asking for help," she said softly, her irritation with Kavan gone. She took off her glasses as they were getting sprayed with mist.

He said nothing so she turned to look at him. He was staring out at the cliffs, a small smile on his face. He was calm, a look of reverence on his face. "I know."

"I just never know—"

"When someone who seems like they're helping you is really trying to hurt you," Kavan finished her sentence, his eyes never leaving the sight before them.

"Yes," she answered, tears of gratitude building behind her eyes at having been seen. No one had ever understood her like that before.

He looked down at her. "I will never do that."

Poorvi's heart pounded in her chest, but more than that, a feeling of peace came over her that she hadn't ever experienced. She believed him, completely. She nodded and turned back to face the mighty ocean.

"My dad used to talk about this place all the time." He spoke softly so only she could hear. It was intimate and familiar, like he didn't talk this way with anyone else. "Among other beautiful places in the world—many of them in India." He sounded a bit sad. "His father—my grandfather—had taken them everywhere. All over India, Ireland, the States." He waved a hand to indicate there were more places. "But it had been the cliffs that stuck with my dad." He sighed. "We never made it here, Naveen and I. Not with him, anyway."

She took his hand in hers. The movement was instinctual. No thought involved. Even though the action was to comfort him, it was a risk she was taking, and her stomach filled with butterflies the instant she did it. She had no reason for concern however, because he immediately threaded his fingers through hers. "I'm sorry."

He nodded without looking at her. "Let's walk."

They walked the perimeter of the cliffs, gravel crunching beneath their shoes as they quietly enjoyed the magnificent view from different angles, never tiring of the sounds of the ocean. This silence between them was companionable, not fraught with the tension from the car. Poorvi thoroughly enjoyed the physical touch of threading her fingers with his. His hand was warm and strong, with a few rough spots. He didn't try to remove his hand from hers, either. They walked with their joined hands between them, arms entwined, leaning toward each other. They paused every so often to appreciate a certain angle or view.

Kavan stopped where they could see the cliffs and water crashing behind them. "We should take a picture," he said.

"We aren't really traveling together," she said.

"Except that we are," he said softly. "Come on. One selfie. What could it hurt?"

She shook her head at him and made a show of rolling her eyes. "Fiiiine. If it'll make you happy."

He beamed at her. "It really will." He removed his hat, held out the phone and glanced at her. "Closer."

She moved closer to him and looked up at the phone.

"You're going to have to move closer so we can get the waves," he insisted.

She inhaled and moved yet closer. There was almost no distance now between his body and hers. If it weren't for their coats, their bodies would be touching. She put the thought out of her head. No matter that they were getting along right now, she didn't want to expect more if it wasn't available to her.

He clicked and they looked at it together. Not bad.

"Nice," he said.

A group of middle-aged women passed them by, but then one of them did a double take and came back.

"You look familiar," she said to Kavan, eyes narrowed. "Can't place it, but I feel like I've seen your face before."

He quickly replaced his ball cap, pulling it low over his head. "I just have one of those faces, I suppose."

"Would you mind taking a picture of us?" another asked, smiling and quite literally batting her eyelashes. Poorvi rolled her eyes, even as a hint of jealousy hit her heart.

"Of course." Kavan took the woman's phone and took their photo with the cliffs in the back.

"We can take one of you two." A different woman offered. "For your kindness."

"Um. Sure." Kavan handed her his phone and stood next to Poorvi.

She turned to look at him and found him watching her from underneath his hat. She wasn't sure what he saw, but he was smiling, and she didn't think anyone had ever looked at her quite that way. Her heart gave a solid thud so loud she was sure he had heard it. She smiled at him and then turned to face the woman.

"There you go. Beautiful." She kept clicking. "Always lovely to see a young couple in love, yeah?"

Poorvi's jaw dropped and her eyes flashed as she flushed. "Oh we're not in—I mean we're not a couple—we just met yesterday." She stepped away from him, clamping her lips together.

The woman handed Kavan's phone back.

"Well, that don't mean a thing, does it now? What matters is the connection. And you two have it. Anyone with eyes can see it," the first woman said.

"Well, thank you," Kavan said, indicating his phone. "Enjoy your day." One of the women lingered a bit, looking at Kavan as if trying to place him.

Kavan put his hand at the small of Poorvi's back and gently steered her in the opposite direction of the women. Even through her coat, Poorvi had to admit she did not mind his hand there at all, his strength guiding her away from an uncomfortable situation. Kavan's phone buzzed a few times. He just kept sending it to voice mail.

"Is that your brother?"

He nodded.

"You're not answering."

"He's trying to get me to Dublin faster." He paused and looked at her, his hand still comfortably on her. "To be honest, I'm no longer in a huge hurry to get there. I need to be there by Friday. And I will be." He fixed his gaze on her. Something passed between them. Something intense and hot.

"What happens on Friday?" Poorvi tried to break the spell. It worked.

"Oh uh—I'm meeting—a colleague."

"Ah, there you are." Ba approached them, slightly out of breath. "Let's go to Doolin for lunch and a drink."

Kavan returned his hand to his pocket. Poorvi felt a chill. "Sure. I could eat."

Poorvi drove them the few minutes into Doolin, a small town next to the Cliffs of Moher. The Aran Islands (next on the list) was accessible via ferry from Doolin as well.

She felt his eyes on her while she drove. She didn't hate it.

"Left! Left! Left!" he called out loudly. He'd been pay-ing more attention to her than to her driving.

"I got it," she called back. "I'm good."

"No. You were not! These roads are narrow, you have to stay left," he insisted.

"You're not the one driving!" she snapped. "The 'road' is only wide enough for one car!"

"There's a garage." Kavan pointed. "Just down from that pub."

She nodded and pulled into the garage. Kavan got out and turned back to her. "Mind if I do the talking?"

Poorvi rolled her eyes but nodded. While Kavan spoke with the young mechanic, Poorvi took in the small ga-rage. Clearly it was privately owned—there seemed to be only the one bay, though car parts seemed scattered ev-erywhere, but what did she know? She didn't know much beyond changing tires.

The mechanic was a young petite blonde woman, her hair back in a braid. She wore a jumpsuit that bore her business logo. *Marlene's Garage.*

She listened to Kavan and nodded. She squinted at the car, and then looked at the tires.

"I don't stock these, normally. But I can get you one in a couple hours, if that suits you," she told them.

"Seriously?" Poorvi looked excited. "I thought for sure we were going to have to spend the night here."

"Not unless you'll be wanting to. Doolin's a great little town. Lots of good music, good food and Guiness."

"We're on a bit of a schedule," he answered quickly. "A few hours is perfect. We'll just be going to the islands, then." He nodded at her and walked out.

"Well, at least there's a pub." Ba started walking to-ward it.

Poorvi met his eyes and they both chuckled as they followed her. He could use a drink.

The three of them found themselves in a crowded pub. They seated themselves at the bar. Ba and Kavan ordered a Guinness, but Poorvi had fallen for Irish coffee. They clinked glasses and drank.

Ba put her Guinness down and smiled at the bartender. "I was here, fifty-three years ago, on my honeymoon," Ba told him.

Kavan snapped his head toward Ba at the same time as Poorvi. They made eye contact with wide eyes.

Ba had just spoken in English.

Really good English.

"In this very bar, with my new husband. I had never had a Guinness, and he got me my first one." Ba grinned at the bartender. "To this day, I only drink Guinness in Ireland."

The bartender chuckled. "Anywhere else, it's not really Guinness now, is it?"

"No, sir, it's not," Ba agreed.

Kavan was still speechless. She could speak English this whole time?

"Um, Ba—you speak English?" Poorvi asked.

Ba widened her eyes as if now just realizing what she had revealed. Then she grinned. "What of it?"

"We thought you were—" Kavan started.

"Old. Feeble?"

"Um. Well… No…" Poorvi started.

"No. We thought you did not speak English," Kavan told her.

"You let us believe it," Poorvi added.

Ba opened her mouth as if she were going to argue, but she shut her mouth. "Yes. I did let you believe it." She went back to her beer.

"Ba!" they both cried in unison.

"What?" she asked, annoyed, as if they were the ones hiding a secret.

"Why did you let us think you didn't speak English?" Kavan asked gently.

"Because both of you need help with your Gujarati," Ba shot back, but she didn't look at them.

"Ba," Poorvi said softly. "You've been to *all* these places before, haven't you, not just the cliffs?"

Ba looked at them both and nodded, sadness coming over her. She went back to speaking in Gujarati. She was obviously more comfortable doing so. "My husband died just over one year ago." She sighed. "I miss him terribly. He and I used to bicker the way you two do." She chuckled. "But I would not have had it any other way. That man was rock-solid and he drove me crazy, but I loved him with everything I had." Ba paused, tears in her eyes. Poorvi reached out and put her hand on Ba's.

"You needed someone to bring you here." Kavan sighed.

Ba nodded at him.

Poorvi furrowed her brow. "But why not ask your daughter, Devi?"

Ba waved a dismissive hand. "My children keep telling me to 'move on,' 'Dad is gone,' 'go on with your life.' How can I go on with my life when my life's partner is gone? I don't want to move on." Ba raised her voice and had gathered a bit of an audience. She lowered it now. "I don't want to forget him." She looked at them, apprehension in her eyes. "Sometimes…sometimes… I forget how his voice sounded." She widened her eyes, true fear mingled with the guilt that she might let that happen.

"Your phone—" Poorvi said.

"You have his voice on there," Kavan finished.

Ba nodded. "We made a pact to grow old and die together. I am not ready to die—I have grandchildren I love—

but he is supposed to be here with me." She pounded a fist on the bar. "He left me here before he was supposed to and sometimes…" She pressed her lips together as if she were afraid to finish that thought.

"Sometimes you get really angry at him for leaving you here." Kavan completed her sentence.

She nodded. "Isn't that terrible?"

Kavan shook his head. "I used to get mad at my father for dying and leaving my mum and me and Naveen. Our family has never been the same. We were all angry in our own way." He paused. "Maybe we still are." He remembered what Poorvi had said about Naveen being controlling because he was afraid to lose another person. "I think it's normal to be angry for a bit, when someone you love leaves us too soon, yeah?"

"All we had dreamed about after our children were married was spoiling our grandchildren until our children got mad at us." Teary laughter as she shook her head. "Now I have to do that all on my own. But worst of all. I have no one to bicker with anymore."

Tears filled her eyes. Kavan moved on instinct and wrapped his arms around her. Poorvi did the same. "We can bicker with you, Ba," she said.

They were rewarded with a cackle from Ba. She and Kavan pulled away from the older woman. "You two are amateurs. You'll get better after you've been together for a while."

Poorvi gaped at her. "We're not together."

Kavan's heart sank again. That was a quick answer.

"Well, you weren't yesterday. But now you've spent some time together." Ba wiped her eyes and cackled. "Are you sure?"

Kavan glanced at Poorvi. "Yes."

"You're both wrong." Ba shook her head.

"Ba!" they both said in unison.

She rolled her eyes. "You know, Dada and I did not meet at the temple. We met at Clerys' clock."

"You didn't." Kavan broke out into a smile.

"We did." Ba nodded.

"What's Clerys' clock?" Poorvi looked from Ba to Kavan.

"It's outside Clerys department store in Dublin. People arrange to meet under Clerys' clock for various things. It's an icon. There's a newer building next to it, Clery's Quarter, that has a bar and restaurant," Kavan explained. "We—you should check it out when you get there." He turned back to Ba. "Go on, tell us."

"Well, my friend had set me up with her boyfriend's friend. My parents, of course, back then, knew nothing of this. She had arranged for me and this young man to meet under Clerys' clock." Ba chuckled. "Well, ten, then fifteen minutes, then twenty minutes passes and the young man had not yet arrived." She closed her eyes a moment. "We did not have cell phones, see? There was this very handsome man who was also waiting for someone who he said was also late. He was very smooth and charming and we started chatting, as you do. We waited over thirty minutes for these two and neither person came! He had tickets for a movie, and asked if I would like to join him." Ba shrugged. "I was ready to join him when the man I was supposed to meet arrived. He was a mess. Out of breath from running, hair tousled." Ba shook her head.

"What happened?" Kavan asked.

"It seemed he had been held up with a last-minute assignment at his job. But I did not believe him." She chuckled. "He became rather cross with me and asked why he would lie."

"I did not have an answer, so he asked for another chance." She sighed. "Something about him—" she shook her head "—I don't know. But something about him, made me give him another chance. I let him take me to dinner, and by the end of that meal, I knew I had made the right choice."

Poorvi was looking at Ba with pure joy on her face. "You gave him another chance—" she snapped her fingers "—just like that?"

"Like I said, something about him…but it was the best risk I ever took." Ba finished her beer and stood. "Time for the Aran Islands."

Chapter Seventeen

They called an Uber to take them to the dock. It was much too early in the season to go to all three of the Aran Islands, so they were going to settle with going to the closest one. Ba seemed disappointed but didn't argue.

"Ba." Poorvi approached the older woman as they waited for the ferry. "Tell me what you love about the Aran Islands."

"Oh, they are rugged and beautiful. The one we are going to has castle remains and nice pubs. The views are very beautiful." Ba paused and looked out at the ocean. "Take the carriage for a quick tour, or just walk to the castle remains—you can't go wrong."

Poorvi squeezed Ba's hand. The older woman's hand was soft but strong when she squeezed back. "Will do. Thanks."

The ferry was large, with a viewing deck as well as an underdeck. Poorvi, Kavan and Ba stood on the viewing deck. No actual decision was made, they all just ended up there, taking in the view of the islands as well as the ocean. No one minded that the wind was cold.

They were on the ferry for about ten minutes when Poorvi grabbed Kavan's arm. She was pale and sweaty. Her eyes were huge. "Motion." She shook her head.

She was going to be sick. Ba pulled out a motion sickness bag that she must have gotten from the plane and handed it to him.

He raised an eyebrow at her. She shrugged. "You never know when you will need it." She nodded at Poorvi.

"You have something for your hair?" he asked Poorvi as he handed her the bag. She held out her wrist, and he took the hair tie and tied her hair back into a messy bun. She looked awful but somehow did not vomit.

Then it hit him. The turbulence. Motion sickness. "Why didn't you say anything?"

"I was hoping it wouldn't happen," Poorvi said. "I made it through the turbulence. I thought I could make it through this." She held up the bag. "I'm going to hold on to this."

They disembarked from the ferry with Kavan holding Poorvi's hand. This was beginning to feel natural to him, but he wasn't sure if that was a good thing or not. She didn't seem to mind holding his hand, but then she also yelled at him a lot. From the dock, the castle ruins were easily visible atop of a large hill, surrounded by green grass.

No sooner did their feet touch ground than Ba waved them off. "I will be back in time to catch the boat back to Doolin," she said. "I have things… I need to do."

Kavan waited with Poorvi on a small bench until she was okay to walk. He took her hand again and they trekked up the steep walkway to the castle ruins. The path wound around plots of land. They passed a beached shipwreck that was hundreds of years old. Once they reached the castle ruins, they were able to explore the parts of the castle that still remained. Kavan enjoyed every minute of finally being able to see the country he grew up in, and it was that much more precious because Poorvi never let go of his hand and they chatted like they'd known each other for years.

They sat next to each other for a bit on the grass in front of the castle. Their legs touched and the added warmth was welcome in the cold wind. The electric zing he felt was a bonus. They could see much of the island and the ocean around it. The view was breathtaking.

"Thank you," Poorvi said softly.

"For what?" Kavan was thoroughly enjoying the view of the ocean, but he gladly turned away from it to look at Poorvi. Her hair was tousled in the wind and she still appeared a bit pale, but her eyes were alert and her smile was beautiful.

"For the boat." She scrunched up her nose. "My hair and the bag."

He shrugged it off. "I also owe you some thanks, not to mention, an apology," he said to her.

"I'm sure you do," she said, smiling. "But what specifically are you talking about?"

"The bathroom on the plane. Thanks for opening the door—" He looked away.

"You don't like small spaces," she said quickly.

He shook his head. "You were trying to help."

"You were embarrassed."

He nodded. "Come on. There's another pub near the dock. I'll buy you a Guinness." He stood and took her hand. "Or a soda."

Chapter Eighteen

Kavan ordered them both another round. They'd been in the pub for a while; Poorvi'd had some soda to settle her stomach, but now she was ready for whiskey. And Ba would not be back for a while.

"Good call," she said as she raised her Irish coffee to him. "More whiskey is needed after our revelation this afternoon." She grinned. They were sitting side by side on a bench at a rustic wood table in the corner with a view of the ocean from a window across from them. The pub was slow at the moment; the bartender was cleaning glasses. They weren't touching, but the space between them was definitely charged. "I'd like to be Ba when I grow up. She's amazing."

Kavan tapped his pint to her glass. "I'll drink to that." He drank deeply and stared ahead for a moment. "Why do you think people wait until they're older to do what they want?"

Poorvi shrugged. "Older people know that time runs out and they want to do what they want to do."

Kavan took a gulp of his Guinness and then stared at the glass. "You know why I don't drive manual?"

"Too lazy to learn." She grinned. "You have a driver. You have a fear of shifters." She bumped her shoulder to his, and he thrilled at the intimacy of that gesture. Maybe she was done yelling at him. "I have a ton of them. I can go on."

He chuckled. "No, but thanks for that." He paused. "My dad's car was a manual. Naveen tried to teach me."

She raised her eyebrows and widened her eyes in mock surprise.

"My dad had taught Naveen," Kavan said. "He'd promised to teach me, but something always got in the way. And then he was gone.

"I was fifteen and I wanted to learn." He looked at her and she was focused on him, her eyes watching him intensely. "Naveen had learned in one day—or so he said. I was having a hard time coordinating the gas and the clutch and the shifter. Needless to say, Naveen's patience ran thin." Kavan paused, tears of anger and frustration burning at the back of his eyes. "We argued. I told him that Mom was in charge and he had to teach me until I learned."

Kavan turned to Poorvi. "The truth was that Mom was not in charge at that time. She barely got out of bed. Naveen had taken over. Bought groceries, cooked food, went to school—you name it." Kavan looked at his fingers. "I don't think he ever really grieved, you know?"

He paused and then Poorvi's hand was on his. "It's hard. And you were just kids. Both of you."

Kavan cleared his throat. "I tried the clutch and gas a few more times but kept stalling the car, grinding the gears. Naveen had about all he could take, I suppose. He yelled at me that I would never learn and that he had to go to work. So he left. And he took Dad's car." Kavan's voice cracked. "He told me I could just drive Mom's car, and he never bothered trying to teach me again.

"Truth is, I actually never bothered to ask." A tear escaped his eye and he wiped it away, the humiliation as fresh right now as it had been in that moment.

He looked out the window at the ocean, Poorvi's hand in his, grounding him. "I watched him drive my dad's car every day. It was a clear reminder that I had disappointed not only Naveen but my father as well." He had never voiced those words out loud. He almost did not want to look at Poorvi. To see the disappointment in her face.

"You know. You might think your brother is the hard-ass, but isn't it possible that he's just afraid of what would happen if he couldn't control everything? Maybe someone else would die," Poorvi said.

"That's what you got from that story?" Kavan turned to her, agitation coming off him in waves.

"No, that's what I got from the way you talk about him." Poorvi put down her drink and looked him in the eye. "I'm not saying it's okay for him to treat you that way, it's not." She squeezed his hand, and his irritation melted away. "He could learn a thing or two from you, about kindness and doing what needs to be done, without hurting anyone in the process."

Kavan scoffed. "Yeah, right. He'll not be learning anything from me, not ever. He'd have to admit there was something he didn't know now, wouldn't he?" Kavan looked at her, frustration in his eyes. "And that, he will never do."

Ba walked in the pub door an hour later. The last ferry back to Doolin was coming up. They got on and within minutes, Poorvi felt nauseous again. Honestly, she was all done with boats.

"Whiskey was not a great idea," she managed, as she

sat on the bench with her head in her hands. Kavan rested his hand on her back and made small soothing circles.

Her stomach was in knots and exhaustion had set in. The drive to Dublin was a solid three hours.

They took an Uber to the mechanic who thankfully had put a new tire on the car for them.

"Thank you," Kavan said as she handed him the keys.

"Anytime." The mechanic smiled at him.

Kavan started to hand Poorvi the keys. She tilted her head at him. "How drunk are you?"

"Not at all."

"Good." She nodded at the keys. "Keep them. You'll need them to drive."

"What the— Poorvi?" His eyes nearly bugged out his head, but a small grin had started forming on his mouth.

"Get in the car. You're a grown-ass man. This is as good a time as any to learn to drive a stick shift." She grinned at him. "Besides. Consider this me asking for help. My stomach is a mess." He broke out into what can only be described as a little-boy grin, he was so excited.

"Seriously?"

"You must be joking!" Ba exclaimed.

"I am not joking, Ba. He'll be great," she said to Ba. She sat down in the car. "Let's go, Kavan."

Chapter Nineteen

Kavan had learned to step back and let Naveen run things.

He stepped back when he went to uni. He stepped back when choosing his specialty. He stepped back when Naveen wanted to open the clinic. He let Naveen schedule photo shoots for him and use his image to sell surgery.

Maybe…maybe he did not have to step back. Maybe he could do what he wanted.

He got in the car.

"Okay, first…" Poorvi went into what Kavan could only call "teacher mode." He kind of liked it, authoritative, but kind. "The right is the gas pedal, and the far left is the clutch. The brake is the one in the middle. Every time you shift gears—" she put her hand on the gearshift "—press the clutch all the way, and ease on the gas. The key is the balance between the gas and clutch."

Sounded easy enough.

"It sounds simple, but it can take a bit to get used to," Poorvi said.

He nodded at her. It clearly hadn't been that easy when Naveen had tried to teach him.

"Start the car."

He did.

"Ease off the clutch and give some gas." She sounded confident, not at all wary.

He did as she said. The car lurched, he slammed the brake and the car stalled.

"Hai Ram!" Ba had pulled out her prayer beads again.

"Ba? Seriously? We're in a parking lot." Poorvi smiled.

"Ignore her," she said gently. "Maybe not so much gas."

He nodded and started over. And he stalled the car again. This time grating the gears. He stiffened for a reprimand. All he heard was Ba's murmuring of prayers. Instead, Poorvi laid her hand on his over the gearshift. "Take your time. It's a finesse thing."

He nodded.

She grinned. "Try again."

He did and this time, the car rolled some feet before stalling out again. He let out a breath.

"You're making progress. There's a learning curve here, as there is in most things." She sipped some water. "Try again."

It took some time, but finally Kavan was on the road, driving.

"Now just shift up."

He did.

"Again."

He did.

"Again."

He did. He was driving a stick-shift car! If Naveen could see him now! He would say it was about time and probably insinuate that Poorvi was some kind of miracle worker. If his dad could see him, he would say that he knew Kavan could do it all along.

"Great." Poorvi beamed at him, her smile broad. "That's fabulous! I've never taught anyone that. You're my first pupil."

"You are not my first teacher for this, but you are the most successful." And the most beautiful. He kept those words to himself. Poorvi had made it clear how she felt about last night. But he didn't want the angst of that to interfere with his moment now. "Thank you."

"Don't thank me yet, now you have to drive."

"Where to?" He would take her anywhere she wanted to go.

"Let's just drive around Doolin for practice. Then we'll head for Dublin," Poorvi said.

Kavan drove them around Doolin, which was a quaint if not touristy small town. She didn't know much about Ireland, but the green hills that went on forever seemed to be plucked from a movie.

She left her hand on his because not touching him was not acceptable. She told herself it was so she could cue him in to which gear he needed to be in, but it was really so she could just have an excuse. He was rubbing small circles on her hand with his thumb, and she let herself fall into the intimacy.

They were enjoying their little trek around Doolin when Bobby called. She had already let one call go to voice mail. He would just keep blowing up her phone if she didn't answer. But she was not about to have this call with an audience. "Hey, I need to take this. It's my boss." She pressed her lips together. "Do you mind pulling over?"

Kavan threw her a furtive look and proceeded to stall the car. "Oh shoot. Sorry."

"It's fine. Just start her up and then pull over up there."

The countryside was a lush green with no other cars at the moment, and the ocean could be seen from here.

Kavan did exactly that.

"Perfect." She beamed at him. "I'll be right back." She got out of the car and called Bobby.

"Are you in Dublin yet?" His clipped voice grated her ears.

He really needed some basic phone manners. "'Hey, Poorvi. How are you? Good? Okay, great to hear. By the way, when are you getting to Dublin?' That's how you talk on the phone, Bobby."

"Dr. Wright," he said, and she knew he had gritted his teeth.

"Whatever."

"I have the ability to fire you," Bobby threatened.

"True. But you won't."

"Why? Why wouldn't I? You've been nothing but a thorn in my side since I got this job."

"Two reasons. One. Only I can present this paper properly, and the lab needs the grant. And two. I'm smarter than you and you know it." She paused. "Why did you call?"

"I heard that the Shashane brothers are going to try to convince you not to present your findings."

"Who are the Shashane brothers?"

"They run Shashane Eye Clinic just outside of Dublin. They do more C-MORE than any other clinic," Bobby informed her. "At least in Ireland. Though their numbers are competitive in the States."

Huh. "Well. Whatever. Numbers don't lie. And the numbers are on my side. And I'm not telling them to stop forever—just until we get more data."

"Just giving you a heads-up to expect some pushback from them," Bobby said.

"Fine." She blew air from her mouth. What could they

possibly do? They could try to talk her out of presenting, but that would never happen, so whatever. "I can't worry about all that."

"You're welcome," Bobby said into the phone.

"I didn't thank you," Poorvi retorted. The day she thanked Bobby Wright—well, she never would. He used to be her friend. But when she had needed him, when she could have used his support, he had kept his mouth shut.

"I'll be there by Friday, Bobby, to go over my presentation before I give it on Saturday." She heard him say "Dr. Wright" as she tapped off the phone.

She walked back to the car to find Kavan also on the phone. She opened the door, but started to back away to give him privacy. He motioned for her to sit down.

"I'll find him. Don't worry." He tapped off his phone.

"Everything okay?" she asked.

"Let's not talk about work," he said, beaming at her. "We have this gorgeous countryside and I just learned how to drive this thing." He grinned at her like a little boy, and it was the happiest thing she'd seen in a while.

"Let's do it. Let's see Doolin." She laughed.

Chapter Twenty

After about an hour of practice, Poorvi guided him to the highway toward Dublin. Ba was still praying in the back seat, but her outbursts to God were fewer and further between. Poorvi seemed a bit less green, and she was doing a fine job of navigating them in the general direction of Dublin.

"Ba. I'm going to need Devi's address," Poorvi called to the back.

"Give me your phone. I'll enter an address." Ba held out her hand.

Poorvi handed her phone back. They followed the new directions, but they were being taken off the highway and into the countryside.

"Ba," Kavan said. "This is the long way around. We aren't closer to Dublin. And the signs say that Dublin is still at least an hour away. Ba?"

"She's asleep," Poorvi said.

They took a few more turns; the navigation indicated

that they were close to the destination, but they were clearly not in Dublin. Kavan glanced at Poorvi, and she nodded her head. Ba had pulled another one over on them.

The sun was just setting when they drove up to the address. Kavan was about to wake Ba and verify the address when he took a final turn and a true Irish castle loomed before them. Stone walls and turrets, ivy growing up the side, lights in all the windows gave the castle a majestic feeling.

"I don't think this is where Devi lives," Kavan said to Poorvi.

"It's not," Ba said as she bounded of the car. "But this is where we stay tonight."

"Are you kidding, Ba? You weren't even really sleeping," Poorvi said as she got out as well. Kavan could tell that her heart wasn't in it. She was gazing up at the castle in awe.

"No. And I got three rooms." She ran a disappointed gaze over them. "Come on."

The valet came for the car and the bellman for the bags. Kavan eyed Ba. "You paid for this?"

She smirked. "I have some money. And I spend it how I like."

"I will pay you back for the rooms."

"Yes, Ba," Poorvi chimed in.

"You most certainly will not. I can spend my money on my children if I so choose," Ba scolded them.

"Ba—" Kavan began his protest, though he warmed at the idea that Ba considered him and Poorvi her children. A glance at the soft look on Poorvi's face confirmed that she felt the same way.

"Stop arguing with me and come see. The pictures were beautiful." Ba started toward the door, the bellman in tow. The inside was as magnificent as the exterior promised. High ceilings, regal decor, massive chandeliers. Kavan took it all in, but he found himself watching Poorvi as she slowly realized the awesome beauty and splendor of her surroundings.

"Ba. This is…too much!" She focused back on Ba. "We can't let you pay for all this."

Ba turned to her. "Of course you can." She came close to them. "It's beautiful, nah?"

They both nodded.

"Dada and I had dreamed of staying here." Ba drew her gaze over the paintings, the red-carpeted double staircase and all the trimmings. "But something was always more important." She sighed. "We never made it." She looked from him to Poorvi. "Don't waste time. Don't save the good things for later."

Ba moved to the check-in desk. Kavan caught Poorvi's eye. She shrugged. *Might as well.* He was still stuck on the fact that she had said "we" like the two of them were a team, like they were…together.

Ba checked them in and handed them each a key. "The restaurant here is gorgeous. Have a fabulous dinner. Enjoy. I will take my dinner in my room." She grinned at them. "Think of it as payment since I held you hostage for two days. I promise, tomorrow we will be in Dublin." She nodded at the bellman and headed for the elevator.

Kavan turned to Poorvi. "I could eat. Up for having dinner with me?"

She narrowed her eyes as if she were thinking about it. She looked all around them, her face literally glowing. "I could eat." She grinned at him. "You got any fancy clothes in that bag of yours?"

Poorvi wasn't sure what had come over her. Maybe it was this castle. Maybe it was Ba's confession. Niki had insisted she pack one dress that was fun, and she had acquiesced at the last minute. This seemed to be the perfect time to wear it.

Not that she was trying to impress anyone or anything.

The three of them had rooms next to each other. Each just as gorgeous as the next. She took a few pictures and sent them to her sister. She was in an actual castle! Her sister was going to be so jealous. The setting was quite romantic. She needed to put herself in check.

Maybe dinner with handsome and kind Kavan was not a wise choice. What was the point in entertaining anything with him, anyway? They irritated each other constantly and he lived in Ireland. She did not.

But the way he'd held her hand in the car… She sighed.

She pulled out the dress from her bag. A simple black above-the-knee fitted cocktail dress with bell sleeves and rhinestone edging. She was rethinking the dress and reaching into her bag for her jeans and a nice top when the phone rang. FaceTime call from Niki.

She inhaled and answered. "Hey!"

"Where are you?" Niki asked. "That room is gorgeous! Please tell me you will be making proper use of that room tonight?"

"If you mean sleeping, then yes."

"Didi! Come on! Do something fun—or at least do *someone* fun!"

Poorvi bit her bottom lip. "I have…sort of…met somebody."

Niki's squeal was nearly deafening. "That's perfect. Who is he? What does he look like? Are you sharing this room with him?"

"His name is Kavan. Very handsome. And no."

"You *like* him!" It was an accusation more than anything.

"I mean…he's nice." And thoughtful and patient, and damn let's not forget hot.

"Oh my God! You really like him! You never say anyone is nice."

"It's complicated."

"Why? You have this gorgeous room in a castle! Enjoy yourself for once," Niki said.

"I already kissed him."

Niki squealed. "Perfect! So what's the problem?"

"The next day he acted like it was a mistake."

"He acted like it was a mistake, or you acted like it was a mistake?" Niki quirked an eyebrow. That was the thing about Niki, she knew Poorvi inside out. There was no hiding anything from her.

"Him, I…think." How *had* that gone down?

"Go to dinner tonight and find out. You deserve to have a fun night out. All you do is work. This doesn't have to be serious. You're allowed to just have fun. Especially after everything that happened at the lab. And with that jerk Brooks."

Tears sprang to her eyes at the thought of the lab. The place she loved had become a minefield. She was afraid to interact with people, not knowing how it would be interpreted, worrying that something she said (or didn't say) would be used against her in the future. When she realized that people were believing the lies despite having known her for years, she became angry. Anger turned to frustration, turned to fear. Then when Brooks, who was supposed to be her *boyfriend* basically ghosted her, she shut down.

"Come on, Didi. You don't always have to be responsible. Just let loose. Everything will be okay. Have a one-night stand if you want. It's fine."

"I don't…let loose. I'm not even sure I know how."

"There's a first time for everything." Niki's hazel eyes

danced with amusement. "What's the worst that could happen?"

Poorvi stared at her sister. After everything in the lab, along with Brooks's behaviour, if she put herself out there with Kavan and he didn't... She tried to mask her face. She failed.

Niki looked at her, her brow furrowed, and in the next instant, her mouth gaped open. "Didi." Her voice was gentle now. "You *really* like him—like you have *feelings.*"

Poorvi swallowed hard. "I don't know what I have." Or what he had, either. "It's been less than two days. It takes longer to have a *real* connection."

"Says who?" Niki smiled like Poorvi was a child. "All the more reason to find out. He could have feelings, he could not. It's better to find out, don't you think? Take the risk, either way, you'll be fine."

Niki was right. Life could not be lived only in the lab. "Okay, fine." She exaggerated an eye roll for Niki's benefit. "If you say so." Maybe one night of carefree fun was what she needed.

"I want a report tomorrow." Niki giggled.

"Bye, Niki." Poorvi tapped the phone off and hopped in the shower. Bobby was going to have a fit when she didn't show up tomorrow morning. Right now, she did not care. Her sister was right. Poorvi never did anything for herself. Tonight, she was going to have a lovely dinner with a handsome and kind man in a gorgeous castle. She would be at the meeting in time to present her paper. But tonight, she was going to enjoy herself.

Kavan did indeed have nice clothes in his bag. These conferences always had cocktail parties and usually one formal event. He pulled out black dress slacks and a pink button-down. He located an iron. Took a shower. Did something with his hair. He eyed his ball cap. Not tonight. Applied cologne. He was going on a date with Poorvi… huh, he didn't even have her last name. Didn't matter.

His phone buzzed somewhere. It was his mom's ring, so he looked for it. He had already ignored a couple calls from Naveen.

Kavan located his phone in his coat. FaceTime. Huh. "Mum."

"Hi, beta. Why is your brother constantly calling me?" She sighed heavily. She'd had it rough after their father died, but Veena Shashane had pulled herself together, gone to therapy and then gone back to school to become a therapist. She looked at least ten years younger than she was and she took care of herself. Right now, her hair was tied in a low bun, and she was in the kitchen, likely cooking for herself and a few friends.

"Maybe he misses you." Kavan chuckled to himself. Naveen would never allow himself to have such feelings. Everything he did was duty and obligation. He didn't doubt that his brother loved their mother. But missing her would likely not even occur to him.

His mother rolled her eyes. He'd been told more than once that he had his mother's eyes. She always said he had his father's everything else. "He is complaining that you are not doing what he asked."

Kavan sighed. "He wants me to convince another doctor not to present findings from a study that might make patients wary about having C-MORE done."

"You disagree?"

"I do."

"So, tell him, beta." She was stirring something.

"You know how that goes, Mum."

She sighed and put down her spoon, focusing her attention on him. "You're all dressed up. I thought you weren't in Dublin yet."

"I'm not, Mum."

"Where are you?"

"Just a couple hours away."

She narrowed her eyes at him. "You're acting strange. And the room behind you looks like—"

He sighed and stepped aside.

Her eyes widened and she gasped. "The inside of a castle." She focused her attention on him. "Kavan Shashane. You tell me what is going on."

He flushed and sighed. "I might have met someone."

"And you're going to propose at that castle!" She clasped her hands together in joy.

He furrowed his brow. "What? No, Mum. You haven't even met her—"

"I get to meet her?" She looked around her kitchen. "I will have to make something spectacular to impress her. How about dahi vada? Mine are very good. And I have been practicing jalebi—"

"Mum. Mum. No." Kavan inhaled. "What I'm meaning is that I would never propose before introducing her to you, yeah? But I'm not proposing to anyone. It's just dinner."

"You're having dinner with a woman?" His mother was as excited about the dinner as she had been about his potential proposal.

He sighed. "In a way."

"In a way? What does that mean? You either are or are not having dinner."

"I am having dinner with her, but I don't really know how she feels about it, do I?" He paused. "About me."

His mother smiled. "Is she smart?"

"Very."

"Tell me about her." His mother sighed like he was the exasperating one.

"I met her at the airport."

"You've known her two days?" Her voice went from excited to cautious.

"Yes."

"She likes you?"

He laughed. "I really have no idea. She argues with everything I say and I find her to be quite irritating at times, you see?"

His mother chuckled. "She keeps you on your toes."

"Yes, but she's also sweet and kind and accepting." His thoughts drifted to his driving lessons today. "She taught me how to drive a manual shift car."

"Well, it is about time."

"I know, but Naveen wouldn't teach me—"

"No. I mean it's about time you found someone you really liked. You deserve to be happy, beta." She grinned.

"Mom—don't get your hopes up. I don't even know what this is. We're just having dinner—"

"Does she know who you are?"

"No. She's American. She doesn't know who the Shashanes are." Thank God.

"Perfect. Then you know she really likes you. And not the money or the name."

"Mum." He started to protest, but she wasn't wrong. More than once he had been taken in by a woman who was only interested in the Shashane name or money.

"Beta, I haven't seen that smile on your face in a very long time. You work so hard all the time. There is more to life than just work."

"I know, Mum."

"Have a wonderful evening. I can't wait to meet her!"

"Mum!" But she had ended the call.

Chapter Twenty-One

Poorvi squeezed herself into the fitted dress, put on some lipstick and eyeliner, and took the time to blow out her hair. She started to don a brand new chic black pair of glasses, but then she put them down. She slipped on her heels and knocked on Kavan's door.

Butterflies fluttered around in her stomach as she waited for him to open the door. Ridiculous. This was Kavan, whom she'd spent the last two days sparring with. Kavan, whose kiss had melted her.

He didn't answer. He must be waiting in the restaurant. She walked down the hallway in her fitted cocktail dress and high heels and started down the first set of stairs. She saw him at the bottom of the stairs, his hands in his pockets, facing away from her, leaning against the railing.

He had on black dress pants and a light pink collared shirt that hugged his broad shoulders and grazed the muscles in his arms. He had left the ball cap behind, and he paced away from the steps. As she watched, he nearly bumped into a bellman, seemingly surprised that the bell-man was there to begin with.

A smile came to her face. She started down the steps, her gaze fixed on him. As if he could feel her eyes on him, he turned toward her. She knew the instant he saw her be-cause his eyes lit up, then his lips parted and stretched until his cheeks flushed and created the dimples she'd only seen once. As if his eyes had a direct link to the cells in her body, a thrill shot through her and she smiled back, stop-ping on the step before the bottom, now eye level with him.

"Wow," he said softly, a small smirk on his lips. "I thought you were going to dress up."

She shook her head, unable to stop smiling. "What?"

"That dress is hideous." He raised his eyebrows in mock disgust and wrinkled his nose as he slowly and deliber-ately passed his gaze over her, heating every inch of her. "But on you, this dress is transformed."

Poorvi's insides were turning to mush, and he hadn't even touched her yet. She rolled her eyes. "Let me guess. You can't believe how amazing I look in this dress."

He shook his head. "No. I can absolutely believe how beautiful you are in that dress. Because you are beautiful in everything." Heat simmered in his eyes as he dropped his gaze to her mouth.

Her heart pounded in anticipation of feeling his lips on hers again, of melting into him and forgetting the world. She leaned toward him.

"Hey!" a woman shouted near them. "It's him."

Kavan pulled back and turned around. He reached for his cap as if to pull it over his head, but it wasn't there.

"It's you, right? From those ads." She scrunched up her face. "I can't remember the ad, but I wouldn't forget that face." Her friends had come closer.

"I'm sorry. I believe you have me mistaken for some-one else," Kavan said softly, but he kept his head ducked as if hiding.

"No. I would never forget your face." She grinned.

"Well, sorry." He took Poorvi's hand and tried to walk away. "We have dinner plans."

"Wait. Can't we have a selfie?" The woman started to follow them.

"No." Poorvi turned toward the woman. "My husband and I are trying celebrate our wedding anniversary, we would like some privacy," she snapped. "He said you were mistaken, so you were mistaken." Poorvi drew herself up to her full five foot two—five foot five in the heels—and stared the woman in the eye, daring her to contradict Kavan again.

"Oh! I'm sorry. Uh…happy anniversary," the woman said, awkwardly forcing a smile and retreating.

"Thank you," Poorvi said kindly. Kavan tugged on her hand, and she turned to him and smiled as they walked to the restaurant. He settled his hand on the small of her back and leaned toward her ear.

"How long have we been married?" He chuckled.

"Not nearly long enough," she said.

Kavan sat down across from Poorvi as the sommelier poured them each a glass of wine. He raised his glass to her. "To quick thinking."

She laughed and clinked his glass. "Anytime. Anything to help a friend."

His sipped his wine and put the glass down. "Is that what we are? Friends?"

She shrugged. "Aren't we?"

"Well, yes. We are friends. But is that all we are?"

"I mean don't diminish friendship here like 'that's all we are.'" She waved her hands a bit, obviously trying not to answer him.

"Poorvi."

She put her hands down. "I don't know."

"You don't know?" He felt like a stone had fallen into his stomach.

"I mean can't we just have fun?" She looked him in the eye, like this was the most logical thing.

He stared at her. She just wanted to have fun. His heart thudded in his chest. Sure, he could absolutely have fun with her. Why not? They could have an amazing evening, and possibly even a fantastic night together. One night… that would be incredible. One night…that would quite possibly ruin him.

Kavan wanted more, much more, but he was starting to realize that he would be willing to take any part of Poorvi that she was willing to give. He did his best to mask the disappointment that bloomed like an ache in his heart.

"Not to mention, are you some kind of celebrity?" she asked.

"Celebrity? Why would you think that?"

"People recognize you. Like everywhere we go." She shook her head like he was dense.

"Oh, that's because I do ads for our family business." He shrugged.

"What's the family business?"

He waved a hand. He did not want to talk about Shashane Eye right now. And he certainly did not want to talk about the pictures Naveen had taken. "You really just want to have fun?"

She stared at him. "Yes. That's all I can do right now."

He nodded. Okay. He could do this. They could just have fun. He downed his wine, and the sommelier quickly refilled his glass as well as Poorvi's. "Then let's not talk about anything else. Fun it is."

* * *

They finished that bottle and then the next while they enjoyed a fabulous coursed-out meal. Poorvi ate her share and a decent portion of his as he had lost his appetite, despite the talent of the chef. Clearly "just having fun" with Poorvi was not sitting as easily as he thought it might.

The wine, however, was going down quite smoothly. It made it easier for him imagine Poorvi as simply someone he had met at the airport. As someone he had developed a *friendship* with, as opposed to someone who made his heart rate exceed normal and his palms sweat. Or someone he wanted to kiss senseless. The memory of her in a towel popped into his head and he envisioned untying it and letting it fall.

"Kavan?"

Kavan extinguished that image and looked at Poorvi. She was standing. "I think it's time to turn in. Long day tomorrow."

"Right." He stood. Of course. Tomorrow, they would be in Dublin.

They walked side by side, comfortable in their silence. They reached Poorvi's door first. His was right next door. With an adjoining door, he recalled. She stopped and turned to him. "Thank you for a fabulous evening."

"Anything for my wife on our anniversary." He chuckled.

"What would you do for your wife on an anniversary?" she asked. "Like your real wife. If you got married."

"Oh, uh, that would depend on my wife."

"What do you mean?"

"Well, does she like dinners out like this? Or would she rather order a pizza and stay in and watch a movie? Does she want to hike? Or maybe charter a boat?" He opened his mouth and stopped himself. *Or just stay in bed all day.* "You get the idea."

"Anything."

He nodded. "Anything that makes her happy."

She nodded as if she approved of his answer and light flooded inside him knowing he had made *her* happy. They were close enough that their bodies grazed each other. He inhaled the scent of flowers in the rain from her. Surely her lips would taste like the wine they'd been drinking. If he kissed her right now, he wouldn't stop. He could kiss her now, and he would have tonight. He leaned down, his mouth hovering millimeters from hers.

"Kavan." She whispered his name, her voice thick with desire and need. For him.

Just for tonight. *Just for fun.*

Tomorrow, everything would go back to where it was right now. She would go her own way, and he, his. She was happy being *friends.*

No.

With nothing less than sheer willpower and the need to protect his own heart, he pulled back and stepped toward his door. "Good night, then."

She looked confused and she shook her head. "Yes. Good night."

His door clicked shut and she stood in the hallway feeling like an idiot.

What the hell just happened?

She had been sure he wanted to kiss her. That he had been ready to spend the night with her. She certainly had been ready.

Had she read it wrong? Taking it slow, as friends, seemed to be the wisest way to go. She had been simply trying to follow Niki's advice to have fun. He had agreed. She opened her door just as Niki called. She answered.

"Why are you answering?" Niki chided.

"You called."

"I was hoping you would be otherwise preoccupied."

"Well, I am not. But I have had quite a bit of wine. So I'm going to bed."

"Did you at least have a good time?"

Poorvi grinned. "I did. We talked nonstop and joked and laughed—I don't even know where the time went."

"You should see your face. You sooo like this guy."

Poorvi shrugged. "Well, I must have read it wrong. Because he is not interested in anything more." Or even just one night.

"Well. All right." Niki yawned. "Bedtime."

"Good night, sis," Poorvi said as she disconnected. She stared at the door that divided their rooms. That first kiss must have been a mistake.

Chapter Twenty-Two

Poorvi woke the next morning with a grand headache. She ordered breakfast to her room so she could lie in bed a few extra minutes. It certainly wasn't because she vaguely remembered putting the moves on Kavan and him turning her down. She was a strong, modern woman—it was his loss if he didn't take what was offered. Right?

She flopped on the bed. Her head hammered and her stomach felt queasy. She was mortified. She had put her herself out there to him and he had turned her down. She glanced at the tray of food. She inhaled and sat up. Enough of that. She would simply act like she was fine with the fact that he hadn't wanted to have sex. All she had wanted was one night anyway, so *whatever*.

She was forcing down some toast and eggs when there was a loud knock at her door. Her ridiculous heart did a flip, hoping it was Kavan. But a second later, Ba walked into her room.

"Jai Shree Krishna, Ba." The greeting just fell out of her like it had whenever she had seen her own grandmother. It was still an ache she had from time to time, missing her grandmother. Like when she smelled jasmine hair oil or delicious fried masala puri.

Ba didn't miss a beat. "Jai Shree Krishna, beti." She looked around, taking in the bed and Poorvi's open bag, the dress from last night laid neatly over the chair. "Where is he?"

"Who?" Poorvi furrowed her brow and stuffed some muffin in her mouth, even though she knew exactly which "he" Ba was referring to.

"Kavan. Who else?" Ba looked at her with impatience.

"He has his own room." Poorvi worked to add irritation in her voice so her disappointment would not show through.

Ba stared at her, eyebrows almost lost, she raised them so high. "Really?"

"Really."

"I thought you both had dinner last night." Ba was now piercing her with narrow eyes and walking closer. "Together."

"We did."

Ba stopped short. "That's it?"

"That's it."

Ba stared at her a moment. Then she shook her head at her and started speaking in rapid Gujarati to God, the gist of which was: *What was she supposed to do with these children? They cannot even see what is in front of them!* She ranted like this for a moment. Then throwing Poorvi one last glare, she left. Poorvi ran for the door that divided her room from Kavan's and listened while Ba knocked on Kavan's door.

Kavan greeted Ba with a Jai Shree Krishna as well. Poorvi smiled. Huh. Then she stopped smiling. She needed to not find more things about him that she liked. Ba proceeded to rant at him for a few minutes about not seeing what was right in front of him.

After which there was silence.

"Come both of you. We have the Holi party at Devi's today."

"Yes, Ba," she heard him say.

"Poorvi?" Ba called.

She poked her head out the door. "Coming, Ba." She looked over and saw Kavan in his doorway. He glanced at her. And instead of the warm smile she had become accustomed to, he pressed his lips together and gave her a curt nod as a greeting.

She stared at him, not responding. Then she went back into her room without saying a word. What was his problem? *He* had turned *her* down last night. Fine. He just made it easier for her to ignore him. She hopped in the shower, then donned jeans and her blue blouse with her blue glasses. She barely looked at the dress as she packed it up. Better to just give it to Niki. She'd get more use out of it.

Poorvi strutted right out to the car to find Kavan already leaning against it.

He was scrolling his phone, sunglasses on, completely oblivious to her.

She approached. "You have the keys?"

He glanced at her over his glasses, his mouth set. "You didn't have breakfast." His voice was low and slow. He smelled amazing, like soap and rain.

"I had it sent to my room," she said as blandly as possible. Now that she was near him and could see and smell and hear him, a vise seemed to clamp over her heart. Also, her stomach was still unhappy with her alcohol choices from the night before, and her breakfast choices from this morning.

He just watched her over his sunglasses.

"Keys?" she asked, this time putting her hand out.

"I have them."

"So, open the trunk," she said, annoyed. What was he looking at?

Kavan stepped back and opened the trunk. She placed her bag in and walked around to the driver's seat.

"What are you doing?" he asked. She seemed annoyed, though he had no idea why. *She was the one who only wanted to be friends. Only wanted to have fun.*

"I'm driving," she said, as if it were obvious.

"No. I am." He corrected her as he walked over to the driver's seat. She was adorable in those blue glasses. Those might be his favorite. They were the same ones she'd had on in the airport when he first saw her. A lifetime ago, but only two days.

"Aren't you hungover?" he asked, trying to keep his voice neutral, like he didn't care one way or the other.

"I'm fine," she snapped, clearly irritated about something. He glanced at her, and she suddenly went pale. Poorvi bent over and vomited on the ground next to his feet.

"Yep." He grabbed her hair just in time, twisting it around his hand to keep it out of her way. With his other hand, he rubbed her back. "Get it out. You'll feel better."

He stood there like that until she finished. "Hold up." He went in and got her some water. She took the glass from him and simply looked up at him, clearly embarrassed.

"Drink this." He was more curt than he needed to be, but it was the only way to keep his feelings in check. Feelings that made him want to sweep her up and kiss her senseless, take her up to his room and undress her slowly so he could simply worship her.

"Thank you."

He just nodded. The sooner they parted ways, the better for him. He had paced the door between their rooms second-guessing his choices half the night. The other half he spent dreaming about her. Even right now, his instinct was to hold her until she felt better.

All thoughts of Dublin and finding P. K. Gupta had fallen from him. All he cared about right now was the fact that in a matter of hours, he would never see her again. Two days with her and his heart was going to break, and he'd only kissed her twice.

She took the water and sipped.

"You sleep in the back," he said. "I'll drive."

"Whatever." She wouldn't even look at him. She stood and went to the back seat. Ba sat in the front and shot him a glare as she handed him Devi's address.

He looked back at Poorvi. "You okay back there?"

"Fine," she said, but the edge was gone from her voice.

"Dublin, then."

She nodded. "Dublin." She leaned her head back and closed her eyes.

He put the car in gear and got on the road.

Chapter Twenty-Three

The sun had come out and was warming the air around them by the time they arrived at Devi's house.

Poorvi stepped out of the car and her mouth dropped open. Devi lived in a mini castle. At least her house was big enough, and the structure looked like a castle. Stone walls with a small turret and large wooden doors, and iron accents.

"Ba! This is gorgeous. Your daughter lives here?" Poorvi walked around with her head tilted up.

Ba nodded. "Come. There is much to do before the party."

"Oh. No. Ba, we have to go—" Kavan started looking at Poorvi.

Poorvi nodded. Sitting with him alone in the car was going to be uncomfortable, but she'd manage. Bobby might be angry she wasn't there this morning, but if she didn't show at all? "He's right. I'm already late for—"

"No." Ba was firm. "You both stay. This is Holi."

"Ba—" Kavan started.

"No!" she said. "This is the celebration of color and spring." She paused and narrowed her eyes at them. "Of love." She threw her arm out and pointed to the front door.

"You better listen to her. She's stubborn." A woman's voice chimed in, and they all turned to it.

"Devi!" Ba turned away from them and opened her arms. Her daughter rushed to hug her. Devi's long hair was in a ponytail, and she was about Poorvi's height. Her smile was the same as her mother's. Two small children trailed behind Devi and flung their arms around their grandmother.

"Where is Yash?" Ba asked, looking around.

"He has gone to get the colored powder for the Holi party." Devi answered. "Who are these people, Ma?" Devi narrowed her eyes at her mother. "You said you were with a tour group."

Ba shrugged. "Is that what I said?"

"Ma!" Devi's eyes widened. "Is this how you 'toured' Ireland?" She covered her face with her hands. "Oh my goodness." She looked at Poorvi and Kavan. "I'm so sorry. She told me she joined a bus tour… I should have known. I should have just come out to Cork and picked her up. She insisted she was fine."

Kavan broke out in laughter. Poorvi could not help but to follow. "Ba!"

Ba shrugged.

"You must both stay for the party—we have a ton of food, the community comes out, and it's a lot of fun. I insist. It's the least I can do for…taking care of my mother." She shook her head at her mother. "I promise I'll let you leave in the morning and get back to your jobs." Peering at Kavan, Devi did a double take. "Have we met? You look familiar."

Kavan shook his head as if he had no idea what she was

talking about. Poorvi furrowed her brow. Why didn't he just say that he did ads for their family business?

Devi started walking toward the house. "I will not take no for an answer. My stubborn streak comes from her."

Kavan met Poorvi's eyes. She shrugged and nodded at the car. She was right. They really had no choice. Pretty much the story of the past couple days. Kavan sighed and got the bags from the trunk. Poorvi grabbed hers and Ba's.

"I can get all that," he told her.

She shrugged. "Not a problem," she said as she rolled both bags to follow Ba and Devi into the small castle. He needed to get away from Poorvi, but that was not going to happen.

He locked up the car and caught up with Poorvi, taking Ba's suitcase from her.

"I said I could get it," she hissed at him.

"I got it," he hissed back.

"Just because I'm a woman does not mean I can't get things like luggage."

"I never said it was because you're a woman. I'm just trying to help, to be nice."

"No one asked you to be 'nice.'"

"That's the point of it. No one has to ask."

They had raised their voices without realizing it and now they turned to find four pairs of eyes watching them. Devi had a smirk on her face and looked at her mother. She nodded at her mother. "Ah ha."

Ba nodded. "See?"

A look passed between mother and daughter.

"So, I have some staff here today. They can take your bags up." She nodded behind them. "Liam."

Kavan turned to see a young man behind them. Liam stepped up and took the bags from them and disappeared.

"Come, I have lunch ready. The festivities will start late afternoon," Devi said.

The children looked up at him. "You are very tall," the young girl said. She was maybe five years old.

"He's too tall," her brother stated as they craned their little necks to see him. "What does everything look like from up there?"

"I could pick you up and show you," Kavan said to the little boy.

Kavan glanced at Devi. "May I?"

She nodded.

The boy narrowed his eyes in doubt and Kavan was immediately reminded of Ba. "You don't even know my name."

"Right, I'm Kavan. What's your name?"

"Dharmesh. But everyone calls me Dharm." He continued to eye Kavan with suspicion.

"Oh my God. He looks just like Ba right now," Poorvi said softly. Kavan turned to her and they shared a glance. He quickly turned back to the child.

The little boy raised his arms and Kavan picked him up and put him on his shoulders. He had a vague memory of his dad doing the same. Dharm squealed with delight.

"This is awesome!" Dharm determined. His sister was clamoring for her turn. "I'm Mira," she told him as she lifted her arms to him. Kavan gently returned Dharm to the ground and picked up Mira, who squealed with pure delight.

The children continued bombarding him with questions as they ate the spectacular but simple spread of chutney sandwiches and mango that Devi had made for lunch.

Kavan turned to Poorvi. "How's that on your belly?" he asked softly.

"Fine. I'm fine." She softened a bit but was far from the woman he'd had dinner with last night.

He had to remind himself that they would not be more than friends.

"Thank you for lunch, Devi, but we must be going," he said, this time not bothering to look Poorvi's way.

"He's right. Besides, we don't really have clothes for Holi…"

"Nonsense. We have plenty of white clothes," Devi insisted. "Yash will return shortly with the colored powder—"

"Then we'll throw the powder on each other to celebrate spring." Mira's eyes widened. "Plus we made water balloons filled with colored water, too!"

"You can't go." Dharm joined in. "We have to throw colors on you!"

Devi laughed. "Her aim is deadly."

Ba pierced them with a look. "Are you going to disappoint small children, now?"

Poorvi glanced at him and shrugged, as she reached for her phone.

Kavan grinned at the kids. "I'm pretty good at this Holi thing."

They cackled with glee.

Chapter Twenty-Four

Poorvi donned the white salwar kameez Devi had lent her, and washed up in what looked like a shared Jack and Jill bathroom. The family was wonderful, the kids were adorable, but she was struggling with Kavan. At times supersweet, at times cold, she didn't know what was happening.

He had turned her down.

Right? So why was he so angry?

Music and the call of the dhol interrupted her thoughts and she found her way to the back to enjoy the festivities. Devi had set up the colored powder under a tent in her spacious backyard. Somehow the sun was their companion today, so it was perfect weather. Poorvi took out her white frames that transitioned into sunglasses in the sun.

She had texted Bobby that she would be at the conference by tomorrow and that there was really no need for them to go over her presentation, because she was going to say what she was going to say regardless of what his input was.

Then she muted him.

By the time Poorvi got to the tent, many of the neighboring families had arrived. She squinted in the sunlight. She had forgotten her glasses in the room. The children had armed themselves with water balloons and water shooters filled with colored water and were attacking people indiscriminately. Kavan was already covered with purple, blue and yellow powder. She watched as the children stalked him and then soaked him through with water.

His white kurta was soaked through and stuck to his skin. She should look away. But she did not. She was so distracted that she wasn't paying attention when the children and their friends sneaked up on her—Poorvi was balloon-bombed before she knew it. The water was cold and a shock to her body. She froze for a second.

The sound of Kavan's laughter got her moving. She grabbed fistfuls of colored powder and tossed it in the air above the children. The colors landed on them, dusting them with yellow, green and pink. She grabbed another fistful and threw it (as much as one can throw powder) in Kavan's direction, dusting him again in purple and green. She cackled and then attempted to run as Kavan came toward her, a fistful of powder in one hand. He was too fast, and the children had her surrounded. He approached and came close, tossing the powder in the air above her, dusting her in yellow and red. She had stopped as he came close. He made eye contact; his breath was coming hard.

"Poorvi." There was a glint in his eye. He lifted a fist as if to throw the color up again, but instead, he opened that hand and rubbed it on her cheek. "Gotcha!" He laughed and tried to step away as her hand came up.

He was too slow, and she placed both of her hands on his face. "Right back at you." She laughed.

They played until everyone was soaked through. Poorvi could not remember the last time she had laughed this hard or had this much fun.

Kavan hadn't played Holi since he was kid, maybe no older than Devi's son. He leaned against a table under the tent and attempted to remove as much of the powder as possible before entering the house for a shower.

Poorvi was standing two tables away, doing the same and talking to Devi. She was soaked as badly as he was. Watching her laugh and relax the past half hour was a highlight for him. He had been told more than once that any woman he wanted, would surely want him back. He had never really believed it and at the moment, it seemed as though the one woman he did want did not want him.

Someone started the dhol beat and then the band picked up the tempo. The children came to get him for some dancing. He saw Devi and Poorvi hit the makeshift dance floor as well.

He watched for a moment as Poorvi started dancing, slowly at first to match the beat and then faster as the tempo increased. They were doing the traditional folk dancing, garba, a kind of line dance in a circle. Almost every Gujarati kid grew up learning garba and Poorvi was no exception. For that matter, neither was he. He waited for her to come around in the circle and then joined in beside her.

Who would have thought that Kavan could dance like that? Poorvi switched up the garba step to yet another complicated pattern and Kavan kept up. The music sped up and Kavan changed the pattern of steps. Poorvi kept up. The two of them twirled and clapped and stepped until the last beat.

Out of breath, they both stopped when the music stopped. "Impressive," Poorvi told him.

He nodded as he caught his breath. "You, too."

"Well, Niki and I have always loved dancing." She shrugged.

"My dad was a huge fan. Always took us to Navaratri." He shrugged. "Naveen used to be really good. He doesn't go anymore."

"Maybe it's too painful."

Kavan looked her in the eye. "I understand that."

Before she could question him further, the music started again. "Come on. If we're first, we get to pick the step." He grabbed her hand and took her to the dance floor as a slow beat garba started. Ba joined them for the simple step. Poorvi was going to miss them both.

They danced and ate until the sun set. Then tired and dirty and full, the guests began to leave, and Poorvi headed to her room. Kavan had disappeared. He must still be playing with the children.

She found her way back to the beautiful room with the attached bathroom Devi had shown her earlier so she could change her clothes. She gathered her shampoo and a towel and entered the bathroom to find Kavan standing there with nothing but a towel around his waist. Like low on his waist. Very low. Her reaction was slower than it should have been.

"Ah! What are you doing in my bathroom?" She was harsher than she had meant to be.

"This is the bathroom attached to my room," he said and made no move to leave.

She nodded, unable to keep her eyes off of him. Kavan with his clothes stuck to his muscles was one thing, but Kavan in nothing but a towel was breathtaking. She was quite unable to speak. "It's attached to my room, too." She tried to snap, but her words came out sounding as dazed as she felt.

"You okay?" he asked, leaning against the counter, his gaze running the length of her body. She became aware that her clothes were sopping wet and stuck to her as well.

"Yes. Sure. Except for seeing you in a towel. Wow." What was she saying? Stop talking. She clamped her lips together. She should leave. Just turn around and walk out of the bathroom that currently held one extremely sweet and excessively attractive man in nothing but a towel smelling like…lemon soap.

She didn't move.

Kavan tensed and stood. "Don't."

"Don't what?" She had no idea what he was talking about, although her brain wasn't fully functioning with him standing there, half-naked.

"Don't act like you want something more from me when all you want is to be friends," he growled at her.

"Friends is good though, right?" What was she saying? She was not having any friend-like thoughts right now, nor was she having them last night.

"I do not want to be friends with you, Poorvi." He shook his head.

"What do you want?"

"The question is what do you want?" he said.

"I wanted you last night. You walked away." She pursed her lips, challenging him to deny it.

"I wanted you like you wouldn't believe." Kavan's voice became low, intimate and more irresistible.

"Then why…?"

"Because according to you, that would've been it. One night."

"Are you saying you want more?" her breath hitched on her words.

He looked at her, his jaw clenched, his eyes on fire. Everything he felt was right there on his face. She knew his answer before he said it.

"Yes." He moved toward her and turned facing her, so he had a hand on either side of her, caging her with his body. It was not unpleasant. With him so close, the scent of lemon soap intensified. Which conjured images of him using said soap on his body. Her body heated.

"I'm saying that I've never known anyone like you. You drive me crazy, but I can't get enough of you." He moved even closer. "I'm saying all I can think about is how amazing it felt to kiss you two nights ago. And how badly I wanted to kiss you last night." He paused. "I didn't want to stop there." He leaned down toward her neck and inhaled deeply. "Flowers. In the rain," he whispered. "Every. Time."

Poorvi's heart pounded in her chest. He was so close and the things he was saying were things she had wanted to hear. "You said kissing me was a drunken mistake."

"*You* said kissing me was a drunken mistake. I came back to the room that morning to kiss you again, to tell you—" He stopped and raked his gaze over her. Her body electrified by his gaze, she nearly held her breath waiting for him to reveal what he had wanted to tell her.

"To tell me what?"

He studied her face for a moment. She saw the instant he decided to tell her everything, to be vulnerable, his heart be damned. "To tell you that I was attracted to you. To tell you that I feel that connection between us. I know it seems impossible after such a short time…but I know what I feel."

She turned and caught his eye, his breath mingling with hers. "Why didn't you say any of that?"

He flushed and chuckled. "Because you were wearing nothing but a towel and you were shouting at me."

"Seriously? You're going with 'I couldn't control my words around a half-naked woman'?" She swallowed again. Damn, he was getting closer to her. She might just melt right there.

"I certainly was not able to control my words around a half-naked *you*." He leaned down to her ear. "You are deliciously tantalizing in nothing but a towel."

She glanced down past his taut, bare chest and stomach and bit her bottom lip. "Right back at you."

He pulled back an inch and grinned at her. "I know it's only been a few days." He met her eyes with his, his voice earnest and beseeching. "I *know* I don't want to be without you." He tilted his head so she had to look into his eyes. "I don't want there to be any doubt like after that first kiss."

She nodded. He was so very close. "I'm not foggy now." She took off her glasses and dropped them. She wanted nothing between her and Kavan.

When Poorvi's lips touched his ever so gently, Kavan thought he would lose his mind. He was desperate for her, and there was no hiding that now. The heat from her body was a beacon to his hands. He lifted her damp salwar over her head and untied the drawstring on the bottoms, letting them pool at her feet.

"I don't want to be friends with you," he growled.

"Who needs friends?" she whispered, her breath grazing his bare chest.

He grinned at her and placed his hand on her cheek. "Have you seen you?" His voice was low and intimate. He bent down, his eyes focused on her mouth. "Your mouth, for example, is exquisite." He gently touched his lips to hers. She gasped and he relished it.

"Your eyes." He continued in that same voice as he

kissed each of her closed lids. "I would gladly fall into." He trailed kisses down her cheek. "This dimple, right here—" he licked it with his tongue "—deepens when you're angry." She groaned and moved closer to him, her body pressed against his.

He continued down to her neck. An almost feral animal sound built in her throat, which he felt rather than heard. "If kissing your neck elicits those sounds, I never want to stop."

"Poorvi."

"Hmmm," she groaned under him.

"The towel."

Chapter Twenty-Five

Poorvi woke in Kavan's arms, their bodies tangled together in the most pleasant way. The scent of that lemon soap was everywhere, mostly because they'd ended up in the shower together at some point. The sun had not yet risen, but the partially open blinds told her that dawn was upon them. Her phone was blowing up.

So was Kavan's.

"Hey." She kissed his shoulder, then sat up. Hmm. It may have been the one spot on his body that her lips had not touched last night. "Your phone."

Kavan groaned and gently tugged her back to him. She did not resist. She settled back into his arms. There were good men out there. Kavan was one of them. She didn't know what was happening between them, but this most certainly was not a hookup. Not for either of them.

Her phone rang. She groaned and turned it over to see who it was. *Bobby.* Again. She sent it to voice mail. Before she even settled back, it rang again. Mom. This time she sat up and answered. Kavan's phone was ringing, too. He finally rolled over and away from her to get his phone.

"What's up, Mom?" she said.

"What the heck are you doing over there?" Her mother sounded accusatory.

"What do you mean?" How could she possibly know she'd just had sex?

"I mean. I saw that post." Now she was accusatory and irritated.

"What post?"

"Instagram. Facebook, you name it."

"I don't know what you're talking about. Hold on." She sat up properly and put her mom on speaker to open her Instagram account. Kavan had stepped away to the other side of the room to deal with whoever he was talking to. A glance at his face told her that his conversation was no more pleasant than hers.

Funny. He looked like he was opening an app on his phone, too.

She apparently had over ninety notifications for every platform. Odd. Her heart started hammering. Her texts from Bobby and Niki were fifty deep. Bobby's face popped up on her screen again, but she sent it to voice mail. Poorvi finally opened her Instagram and there it was.

A picture of her and Kavan at the Cliffs of Moher. They were looking at each other and the attraction was obvious. She swiped and saw the selfie they had taken. Swiped again and saw a picture of her wide-eyed and looking annoyed. It was when she had told the woman that they were not together. Behind her, Kavan was looking—devastated. She hadn't seen that.

These were all pictures from his phone. He must have posted them, but he didn't really seem the social media type.

"Yeah, Mom. I met a guy—" She stopped as she read the caption. "I told Niki, but I was going to tell you when…"

Her voice trailed off as the meaning of the caption hit—and so did reality.

@pkguptamd and @kshashane together at the @cliffsofmoher before the @ICO meeting where Dr. Gupta is set to present her paper on the hazards of C-MORE. @Shashaneeye is the leading performer of that procedure. Wonder what recommendations she will make now that her fling with @kshashane looks to be over? This on the heels of the rumors that Dr. Gupta lost the position of principal investigator because of an alleged affair with her boss's boss.

Maybe this is how Dr. Gupta softens the blow? Or maybe @kshashane is hoping that he can influence her recommendations?

"Mom, I gotta go." She tapped off the phone and turned to Kavan, glaring.

"You're last name is Shashane?" She hopped out of the bed, grabbing the sheets to cover her, suddenly aware of how naked she was.

"You're P. K. Gupta?" He grabbed his pants, pulling them up as he stood and faced her.

"It's you! You and your brother. You're the ones who are trying to get me to present only certain facts, so that you can still do C-MORE no matter how questionable. All this time…" She shook her head at him. "Was this your plan?" She found her underwear and attempted to put it on without dropping the sheet. She ended up sitting on the floor to do it. "Did you think sleeping with me would change my professional opnion? Do you have any idea how bad those pictures are for my job future—especially given everything that had already gone down? I *trusted* you!" She paused for breath. "And you gave him these pictures and he posted them—or he gave them to someone to post."

"I did not give any pictures to anyone and I certainly did not post anything," Kavan shouted back at her.

A light went on. She glared at him from the floor. "This is about money. If I make my recommendations in line with my numbers, you stand to lose money."

"No. I mean yes, that's true. I didn't know who you were! But that's not—"

"I'm supposed to believe that?" She found a pair of jeans and a T-shirt that seemed clean and tossed them on. "You could Google me—it's a little too convenient, isn't it? You've been lying to me this whole time." Once she dressed, she tossed the remainder of her clothes and toiletries into her bag.

"Poorvi. Listen. Please…it's not like—"

"Stop talking." She nearly screamed at him as she rolled her suitcase to the door and stopped. "You don't care about me." The words caught in her throat. She was so angry she could hardly breathe. Tears threatened, but she refused to cry in front of him. "There's no 'connection.' That was all bullshit." She inhaled back her tears of fury. "I opened up to you. I didn't want to, I was afraid, but I let you into my…heart."

Her voice cracked. The tears were going to fall; she could do nothing about it. "I'll give you this much, you had me. I believed you were falling for me. Though it seems unnecessary to have gone through all this since you already had the photos. But I guess you got a good lay out of it."

Kavan flinched as if she had slapped him; she registered pain in his eyes. Her rage boiled inside her, but she didn't care. "I told you all of it, how I had trusted my colleagues and they stayed silent, how I had leaned into Brooks and he ghosted me. I don't know how you did it, but—*bravo*—" she smirked at him "—you made me trust you, when I trust no one." She never should have let him into her heart, but it had been too hard to fight it. "This was the best you could do? Try to discredit my reputation by painting me as a 'woman scorned'? At least have the balls to do it intellectually. At least fight me on the same turf. This—" she raised her eyebrows "—this is low, desperate."

She left without another word.

Chapter Twenty-Six

Poorvi called an Uber and waited on Devi's porch swing, facing out toward the road. She squeezed her eyes against the memory of what they had shared the past three days and nights. Falling asleep next to him last night had felt like a new beginning.

What the hell did she know? She knew the lab. She knew numbers. She did not know men. Her history with them was proof.

She felt someone come and sit next to her. She knew it wasn't Kavan before she opened her eyes. She already knew how his body felt next to hers. And no lemon soap.

"Beti." The voice was soft and sweet and filled with love.

Ba.

She opened her eyes. Ba placed a comforting hand on top of Poorvi's and Poorvi was visited by a round of grief for her own grandmother. "I'm sorry I lied to you."

Poorvi shook her head. "Ba. It's strange but I get it. You

needed to do something, you went after it." She leaned over and hugged Ba. "I'm glad we met."

She saw her Uber approaching. She squeezed Ba's hand one more time and got up.

"Beti. Listen. I don't know what happened between you two, and maybe I'm just an old busybody, but you have both built a bond in just a few days. Imagine your bond if you stay together and work at it. Love isn't easy. Trusting people and being vulnerable is scary. But it is worth it."

"Would you do it again, knowing what you know now?" Poorvi side-eyed Ba.

"Without hesitation, beti."

Poorvi sighed and picked up her bag. "It's complicated, Ba."

Ba nodded. "I know. But just remember, just because we fight with men, does not mean we have to fight like men." She got a glint in her eye. "We are women."

Poorvi stared at Ba and shook her head. "Okay."

"Text me when you get there."

Poorvi had to chuckle.

Ba frowned. "I'm serious."

"Okay." Poorvi opened the door of the car. She felt eyes on her and found Kavan watching her from the door of the house. Her heart thudded in her chest. She froze for a moment. Then she got in the car and left.

He was in love with P. K. Gupta.

And that's what it was. He knew it when he woke up this morning with her in his arms. He knew it last night when she walked in on him in the bathroom. What he felt was more than a connection.

He loved her.

He had stood frozen for a moment while the bedroom door closed behind her. Then he grabbed a T-shirt and ran

after her while trying to put it on. But he couldn't find
the arms and it got stuck on his head. He paused in the
middle of the hallway, fixed the T-shirt and then continued his chase.

She could not have gone far. She'd probably called an
Uber. He headed for what he thought was the front of the
house and ended up in the back where the tent was being
taken down. He turned around and ran back inside. Kavan
entered the kitchen and, to his luck, found Dharm having
cereal with his sister.

"Hey, Dharm. I need your help." Kavan was out of
breath.

"It'll cost you." Dharm eyed him.

"What?" Where was the sweet kid from last night?

"You need something, I have it. It'll cost you," Dharm
repeated.

"Fine, whatever." Kavan was not going to argue with
an eight-year-old. "I need to find that auntie I was with
yesterday."

"Your girlfriend?"

"Well, she's not really... It's complicated."

"Do you like her?" Dharm sighed.

"Yes. Very much."

"Does she like you?"

"I think so, but she's gone mad at me, see. So I need to
find her before she leaves, yeah?"

Dharm hopped off his chair. "Basically, you want her
to be your girlfriend, yeah? And she's mad." He folded his
arms in front of him. "It'll cost you extra."

"Fine. Okay," Kavan said.

"She's probably on the front porch."

Kavan grinned. "Right. And which way is that?"

"What did you do?"

"What do you mean?"

"I mean what did you do to make her mad?"

"Well... I... I mean she thinks that I... Look, it's complicated, and if she leaves, I'm done. Help a guy out, eh? Which way is the porch?"

Dharm eyed him and then huffed. "All right then. Follow me."

Kavan sighed and followed the young boy, who did indeed lead him to the front porch.

Just in time to see Poorvi getting into her Uber. She turned and saw him standing there. Her expression was wounded, hurt. She thought she was a master at hiding her feelings, but he could read her. Right then, her face and body begged him to stay away, she clearly wanted nothing to do with him. So he had stood there, frozen, unable to move, while she turned away from him. He did not move, even when the car drove away, taking his heart and soul with it.

Ba saw him and walked over. She smacked him on the arm.

"Ow. Ba!" He rubbed his arm and furrowed his brow at her. "What was that for?"

"Why are you standing here, watching her leave?" Ba barked at him. "You love her, don't you?"

"Yes."

"Go get yourself together and go after her."

"No. Ba. It's over." He shook his head. "She deserves— I treated her no better than every other man in her life."

"You must try." This time Ba was not shouting or scolding him. He looked at her. Tears brimmed in her eyes. "There is never enough time with our loved ones. Go. People make mistakes. That's how we learn and grow. Apologize for whatever you have done. And *be* with her." A tear escaped Ba's eye.

"Ba, don't." He wiped the tear away. He much preferred being smacked on the arm.

"If you love her, you have to fight for her!" Ba was adamant. "That connection—it is rare. You may never find it again. What do you have to lose?"

She wasn't wrong. He would never get over her. He would never find anyone like her again. "You're right, Ba. I'll go fight." He knew exactly where Poorvi was going.

Chapter Twenty-Seven

The city was a bit of a shock after three days of small towns, cozy and simple B and Bs, castles and local pubs. Dublin hustled and bustled like any other city. But if she looked closely, she saw the corner pubs, the cozy bakeries and the Irish hospitality she had enjoyed for the past few days. True, she was just a tourist.

She hurriedly exited the Uber and was approached by a bellman.

"Help wit' your luggage, ma'am?"

"No thank you. It's just the one bag." She forced a smile.

He nodded and opened the door for her. "Check-in is just up the stairs and to your right."

"Thank you," she said, and made her way to check-in. The hotel was gorgeous; she had splurged to stay in the same hotel as the conference. She had just been handed her room key card when a familiar voice called to her.

"Poorvi! It's about time."

She turned to see Bobby hurrying toward her. "Where have you been?"

"On my way. I told you I was held up."

He looked around and stepped closer to her. "Come with me." She followed him toward the large conference room. "They changed the schedule. You present in an hour," he said as they walked. They arrived at the conference room, which was more of a ballroom. She peeked at the crowd. There were hundreds of ophthalmologists here. Bobby led her around the corner of the staging area to a small alcove.

"Listen." He lowered his voice. "We need this grant. What the heck are you doing, fraternizing with the enemy?"

"Fraternizing with? What do you...?"

"Don't play dumb with me. You hooked up with Kavan Shashane and now they're going to use that to discredit our work. Maybe think about who you sleep with," Bobby spat at her.

"You know what, the hell with you. You've never had my back. Not before you were promoted and certainly not since you were promoted."

"What does that mean?"

"That means that you knew that James Hardy had asked me out multiple times and you knew that I turned him down, multiple times. We were friends—at the very least we were coworkers—and not once did you stand by me when all the accusations came down." She fumed at him. "Now I have my colleagues believing that my research and my recommendations, which existed long before I ever laid eyes on Kavan Shashane, will be affected by a supposed 'broken relationship.'" She was fired up. "And by the way, let's be clear. That work is not 'ours,' it's *mine*."

Bobby glared at her. "You may lay claim to the work, but where would you be without the lab? You just get up there and say whatever you must. The Shashane Brothers are having a panel discussion in favor of C-MORE, immediately following your presentation. We can't have people believing them over you, we'll lose that grant. You have an hour."

Poorvi was tired of her work being put second to whatever her personal life was. She worked hard and she was the smartest person in that lab. She knew it and she did not need Bobby—or anyone else—to tell her that.

Her phone dinged. Text from Ba. Did you arrive?!

Crap. She forgot. Yes, Ba.

Now she needed a shower.

Chapter Twenty-Eight

Kavan showered quickly and put on his suit. He threw his things in a bag and said hasty goodbyes to his hosts. Dharm gave him a hug after Kavan paid him.

It was Ba who stopped him. She was shaking her head at him. He could feel her disappointment. "I'll fix it, Ba. I promise."

"Uh-huh." She pursed her lips, but she hugged him. "Text me when you get there."

"Ba."

"Text. Me."

"Okay," he assured her, and got back in the car. So focused was he on what he needed to do, he drove the manual car without a thought. Anand called.

"What's this Instagram post?"

"It's Naveen," Kavan growled. "He did it."

"Who's the woman?"

"It says right there."

"No, brother. I mean, *who is she*?"

"She's The One." Kavan said. "She's *the one* and I messed it up."

"So make it right."

"I don't know if I can ever make it totally right. But I'm absolutely having words with Naveen."

"About time. If she's the reason you're finally standing up to Naveen, I like her already," Anand said. "Good luck."

Luck? He didn't need luck. Naveen had pushed him too far this time.

Kavan drove up to the hotel and valeted the car. He entered the lobby and texted Ba. Then he texted Naveen that he was here. Almost immediately, Naveen texted back. Meet me in my room.

Kavan took the elevator up to Naveen's room. He didn't even need to prep what he was going to say. He had a sense of calm within him that he had never experienced. He barged into Naveen's room.

"How could you do this?" He held up his phone to Naveen.

"You're welcome." Naveen said, with the ultra calm of someone who was confident in his every action. "I did your job for you."

"Bull, Naveen. You can't just make things up about people and post it. How did you even get the pictures?"

"We share the same cloud," Naveen said coolly, like Kavan was an idiot. Maybe he was. "Are you 'with' her?"

"No." Not after this.

"Were you?"

"Yes."

"Then it's not made up." Naveen grinned at him.

"Naveen. It's wrong. You're using her personal life to discredit her work. That's slimy and unethical! No more, Naveen. I'm done." Kavan was firm. "I'm not your lap dog anymore, Bhai. I will not blindly do whatever you want, are you hearing me?"

"I saved you." Naveen narrowed his eyes, his tone going cold. It was an old tactic he had used many times. Kavan had always given in. Not today.

Kavan sighed and paced the room. "That you did, yeah." he said with more calm than he felt. "Just like a good brother should. And I will forever be grateful to you for that." He stopped pacing and fixed his own gaze on his brother and hardened his tone. "That doesn't mean you own me."

Naveen stood and faced him. "I guided you away from those blokes in high school, to university, then medical college—"

"All true." Kavan did not move away but stood firm. He had never stood up to Naveen like this before. Kavan had seen the possibility of true happiness with Poorvi. Not only had Naveen used him to hurt the woman he loved, he had destroyed that possibility Poorvi would never forgive him, but Kavan no longer had to be at Naveen's beck and call. "What you fail to acknowledge is that once I got there, I did the work. I got the grades and skills that were necessary to be where I am today," Kavan said.

"So now that you have everything, you're not needing your older brother, is that it? You got what you wanted and now you can do whatever you want? You can walk away?" Naveen glared at him.

"I'm not walking away, Naveen. I want to be my own person. Decide what I want to do. I've been trying to tell you for years that I want to add a research aspect to my clinical work and you literally wave me off as if I'm a child. I'm not a child." Kavan shook his head at him.

"Is that what this has been about all these years? That I would have to need you?" Kavan softened. He recalled

Poorvi's assessment of Naveen. *He's afraid of losing you.* "You're my brother, I will always need you. What I don't need is you running my life." Kavan walked away a few steps, then turned back around. "You took over after dad died. You were barely eighteen. That's hard on anybody. But you don't have to be that hard-ass, driven, success-at-any-cost person. You never needed to be and you don't now. It's time for you to let things go, Bhai."

"Where is all this coming from, all of a sudden?" Naveen shook his head at him. "Her?"

"It's not sudden, Naveen," Kavan said. "And yes. She opened my eyes to a lot of things…"

Naveen's eyes popped open. "You think you're in love with her." He snapped his fingers. "Of course."

"Bhai, I *am* in love with her, but that has nothing to do with you and me," Kavan tried to explain.

"Before you say anything you're going to regret, let me stop you right there, little brother. Before you stand by a woman who is about to destroy you. Her lab needs a grant for further research, to survive. So don't think for one bloody minute that she won't do whatever is necessary— include damage your reputation—to get it."

"She can do whatever she needs to do to survive. If that means discrediting us, then it's well deserved."

"You can't do that, Kavan. I'm your family." Naveen was fuming.

"Then act like it." Kavan stormed out of the room and went down to hear Poorvi's presentation.

Chapter Twenty-Nine

Poorvi showered and donned her black dress pants, crisp white shirt and black blazer. Her black dress from the other night was scrunched in a ball on one side of her suitcase from where she had tossed it into her bag. Was that just the night before last? Seemed like a lifetime ago that she and Kavan had had their "date." Her heart ached at the thought of it. Of how she had allowed herself to be part of a scandal once again. The post had not come from Kavan's account, but the pictures were from his phone. It didn't matter. The damage was done.

She started to don her red-framed glasses but thought twice and left them behind. It was time to stop hiding.

Poorvi waited in the wings while she was introduced, and Ba's words came back to her. *Just because we are fighting men, does not mean we have to fight like men. We are women.*

We are women.

She took the podium to a murmuring in the crowd.

"Good afternoon." She glanced around as everyone fell silent. The seats were all full and people were standing two deep in the back. People loved a good scandal, and doctors were people, too.

"This is an exceptional turnout for a paper on refractive surgery," she said without humor. Some of the crowd chuckled.

Poorvi waited for silence. Then she spoke with authority. "My research on C-MORE has been ongoing for the past three years, and I will show that further research is necessary before we can safely continue this procedure in a clinical setting. Please focus your attention on my first slide." Methodically, Poorvi walked them through her research and her findings along with how she reached her conclusions.

"Based on these side effects, and the long-term implications of the procedure, I *do* recommend a halt to the C-MORE procedure until we have further study that can guide us toward the most positive clinical outcome." She looked around. "I understand that the numbers simply indicate caution, but it is my professional opinion that C-MORE be halted for the near future. Thank you for your time. I will take questions now."

"Aren't you just coming down on C-MORE to hurt Kavan Shashane?" someone called out. "Everyone knows the Shashane Clinic does more C-MORE than anyone else."

"Well. Thank you for asking." She squinted into the crowd. "Who asked that? It's an excellent point that should be addressed."

A man in the front stood, a smirk on his face.

"I'm sure you're not the only one who requires an answer to this question, am I right, Doctor?" Poorvi was cordial to the point of being over-polite.

A round of applause was her answer. She nodded her head and scanned the room.

"My answer to you all is, shame on you. Shame on those of you who came here today looking for drama instead of knowledge. Shame on you for judging your fellow women colleagues, not on their intelligence or character, but on who they may or may not be sleeping with. This is 2023 and women make up 30 percent of the eye care specialists in the world. Shame on you."

A hush fell over the room.

She paused. "Now I am happy to take questions that pertain to my work."

"You did not answer the question," the doctor up front insisted.

"Nor will she." A woman stood and faced him. "Unless you, too would like to tell us how your relationships—such that they are—affect your professional decisions."

"All I'm saying is that we are all going to lose money based on her recommendations. And she's only saying that because Shashane dumped her," Dr. Lewis fumed.

"Jeez, Lewis, did you listen to the presentation? I'm sure even a graduate of whatever school you hail from can do the simple math. This research has been going on for years. Dr. Gupta has been making this recommendation for over a year. Shut up and sit down, Lewis."

Dr. Lewis blanched and sat down.

The woman, who Poorvi recognized as a pioneer in refractive surgery, Dr. Jahigan, looked at her and smiled. "Continue."

The remaining questions did indeed refer to her presentation, and Poorvi happily and easily answered them.

"That's all the time I have. Please enjoy the rest of the meeting."

Everyone applauded and then started leaving the room.

Bobby was waiting for her when she exited the podium. "I've already received emails from the board. The grant is as good as ours."

She stared at him.

"Thank you."

She continued to stare at him.

"You're right. I saw an opportunity and I said nothing," Bobby told her. "I'm sorry."

Poorvi nodded at him. "Let's see." She started to walk away.

Bobby caught up and walked beside her. "You're incredible. You handled that crowd better than I ever could have."

"You know why, *Dr. Wright*?" She glanced his way and raised an eyebrow.

Bobby appeared confused. "Why?"

"Because I am *excellent* at my job." Poorvi grinned.

Chapter Thirty

Kavan exited the room full of pride. Poorvi had been amazing. Lewis was begging for a punch in the mouth. But other than that, Kavan felt as good as he possibly could, despite knowing that he and Poorvi could have had something, and he messed it up. He made his way to the panel discussion Naveen had set up. A very large crowd had already formed in the room.

"Dr. Shashanc. Dr. Shashane, do you have anything to say regarding that post of you and Dr. Gupta?" people were asking as he approached the stage.

He took his seat on the panel which consisted of Naveen as well as two other colleagues who performed high numbers of C-MORE.

"Yes, as a matter of fact I do. Dr. Gupta and I ended up at the Cliffs of Moher with a close friend. Neither of us had ever been, so we took some photos. It's that simple. The caption was written to have you believe what the narrator wanted you to believe. It wasn't posted from my account,"

Kavan said. "I agree with Dr. Gupta's sentiment. Shame on you for making her personal life an issue."

"What about her recommendations?" another doctor asked.

"If you are referring to Dr. Gupta's recommendation that C-MORE not be performed until further research is complete, I have to say that I also agree with her on that."

Murmuring flooded through the crowd. He met Naveen's eyes, the anger in them real and deep. The message was clear. *What the hell, Kavan?*

"And that," Kavan said clearly, "is my professional opinion."

"You agree? But your clinic does C-MORE almost regularly."

"That is true," Kavan said calmly. "But I do not."

Surprised murmuring floated in the crowd. "What do you mean?" one of the doctors spoke up.

"I mean, I have followed the research on C-MORE for years. Not just Dr. Gupta's, although hers is the most extensive. And I have collected data from the C-MORE procedures done in our office as well. The research indicates that there are long-term effects that need further study. Read the studies yourselves, doctors. You'll see that Dr. Gupta's recommendations are sound. And should be followed, regardless of financial cost."

"How about you, Dr. Shashane?" They turned to Naveen. "You do the procedure."

It was the first time that Kavan had ever really gone against his brother. The first time he had been his own man. Naveen plastered a smile on his face and turned to his colleagues. "Well, I did until today." He chuckled. "Dr. Gupta makes some excellent points, as does my brother. At Shashane Eye, our focus is always what is best for the patient. In the case of C-MORE, it appears that it is best to discontinue the procedure until we have more information." Naveen nodded at him. Kavan had forced his hand.

It was about time.

Kavan was elated and heartbroken all in the moment.

He had Poorvi to thank for that. He looked out into the crowd and saw her in the back, leaning against the door, her arms folded across her chest. Her mouth pursed and brow furrowed. She'd heard everything. She met his gaze for a moment, and hope ran free through his body. He smiled at her. She pressed her lips together in a tight smile and dipped her chin at him. In the next instant, she turned and left.

He'd never felt so free yet so alone.

Chapter Thirty-One

Two weeks later

Poorvi collapsed onto her sofa, exhausted.

"You need to eat." Niki sighed and stood.

"I ate," Poorvi said, her eyes closed. The lab was extra busy now; they were hiring some staff and gathering data from clinicians all over the world. Her research had hit a nerve, and everyone wanted answers.

"Probably out of the vending machine," Niki said as she placed a plate of shaak and a rotli in front of her.

"It was hummus from the vending machine." Poorvi defended herself. But Niki's food smelled amazing. Poorvi had not bothered to learn how to cook, always finding something more interesting to do than mixing spices and kneading dough. But Niki had loved learning at their mother's side and as a result, Niki was an amazing cook. Just one of many reasons having your sister as a roommate was not at all a bad idea.

MONA SHROFF   393

"Oh…you had hummus? So you don't need rotli shaak."
Niki started to take the plate away.

"I didn't say that." Poorvi sat up and took the dish from
Niki. She scooped some of the potato and spinach with a
piece of the flatbread. "This is fabulous. Thank you. What
would I do without you?"

"Wither away into nothingness," Niki said, sitting down
and diving into her own plate.

Poorvi's phone dinged and she eyed it.

"You know it's him," Niki said.

"Whatever." Poorvi went back to her amazing meal,
though she no longer had an appetite for it.

The phone dinged again.

Kavan had been texting her since she got back. Not
every day, just…whenever. Things like he'd been to Clerys'
clock and thought of her and Ba. Or Ba had made him
tepla. Or he was babysitting Dharm and Mira. Random
things. She never responded. Every so often he would
throw in a "can we please talk?"

She grabbed the phone.

"What does he say now?"

She furrowed her brow. "It's not him. It's Ba." She ignored the disappointment that washed over her. She had
to ignore it. She should not be looking forward to Kavan's
texts. But she had to control herself from jumping at her
phone when it dinged.

"You could call him, you know," Niki said. "Nothing
wrong with having feelings."

"Now you sound like Ba." Poorvi grinned at her sister. "She texts me the same thing every other day. Besides, he…"

"He what? Fell in love with you?"

"I'm just scared, that's all."

"Fine." Niki raised her hands in surrender.

Poorvi's phone dinged again. Another text from Ba. She was coming stateside to see her son and wanted to see Poorvi. Well, that sounded fun.

Poorvi texted back. Sounds wonderful. When?

Ba: Tomorrow. Can you meet me here? She left an address. For lunch.

Poorvi: Can't wait to see you.

A bit of lightness filled Poorvi at the thought of meeting Ba. And it was only partly because she knew that Ba kept in touch with Kavan as well.

Chapter Thirty-Two

"Why haven't you even called Poorvi?" Ba was on a roll. Devi's house was not too far from his, so he stopped by to visit every few days. Naveen was still mad at him, but Kavan found that while he wasn't a fan of that, he was okay. He was still mad at Naveen as well.

Naveen did have a brotherly attachment to him that was generally expressed in being bossy and telling Kavan what to do, but he'd come up with something more palatable, soon enough.

The office wasn't suffering quite as much as Naveen had predicted. It turns out that patients like ethical doctors who will look out for them, so when Shashane Eye put out an official statement that they would be doing the tried-and-true refractive methods for a while, the patients responded well.

The bottom line moved but not too much, so Naveen's argument fell flat. Naveen had taken the photos from their shared cloud and turned them over to their social media person "to do something." For this Kavan still fumed. Naveen might have admitted it wasn't the best way to do business, but the reality was that Kavan was finding it difficult to forgive Naveen for hurting Poorvi in that way.

The panel discussion had gone viral. Kavan was looking into teaching and research positions. He wanted a break from the clinic.

"I've been busy. With work. Besides, I did text her. And she never responded," he said as he sipped Ba's excellent chai and ate a piece of her tepla.

Ba waved at him, her expression disappointed. "You're afraid."

It was true. He had texted her a few times when she had left. Things like "we need to talk." She never responded. He switched up the content of the texts to refer to things he was doing. Clerys' clock for example, or meeting Ba, etc. He hadn't even had a chance to explain about the post. She never responded, so it would have been easy to assume that she didn't care.

But with Poorvi, she would have responded if she didn't care so much. The fact that she did care was the reason she was so hurt and therefore the reason she was unable to answer. He just stared at the older woman.

He knew that because he loved her. What he didn't know was how to reach her.

"I thought you had changed," Ba said, shrugging. "I thought you were the kind of man who went after what he wanted." Ba glared at him. "You sold your half of Shashane Eye to Naveen. That was brave. Be more brave. Text her again."

"Fine." He sipped more chai. Ba stared at him. "What? Now?"

Ba didn't budge.

He inhaled. Fine. He pulled out his phone. His thumbs

hovered over the screen. Nothing came to him. How could it? What he was feeling could not be done over text. He stared at his phone.

Having chai with Ba.

Ba picked up his phone and looked at it. She rolled her eyes into the back of her head, like a teenager. He looked at Ba. "Where did you learn the eye roll, Ba?"

She grinned. "It is good, right?"

"It's great," Kavan deadpanned.

"Dharm taught me."

Of course he did.

She shook her head at him in disappointment. His heart was broken. He needed to repair it. There was only one thing for it. "No more texting, Ba."

Chapter Thirty-Three

"I'm meeting someone for lunch. I'll come by after," Poorvi said to Bobby. "About an hour or two."

"Two hours?" Bobby's eyes widened. "Do you know how much work—?"

"Bobby." She met his eyes and was firm. "I'm taking the time. The lab—and you—will be fine." She grabbed her backpack and left. She texted Ba. On my way.

Ba responded instantly. Okay I'm here.

Poorvi hurried downstairs and quickly walked the few blocks to the café where she was meeting Ba. Late March was being kind, allowing them this day of gorgeous spring weather. She scanned the area for little old ladies in saris and came up empty. She scanned again and froze. Ba was not there.

But there was no denying the ball cap and the movie-star shades. He was pacing next to an empty table and, in the few seconds she watched him, nearly bumped into two waitstaff.

The second motioned for Kavan to sit down. Poorvi had to press away her smile. He was wearing what she imagined him in whenever she thought about him—which was all the time—jeans and a long sleeve T-shirt. He rolled up his sleeves just as someone came up beside her.

Ba.

"Don't just stand here. Go," Ba said softly.

Poorvi could not believe her eyes. "Ba?"

"Just go. He came all this way." Ba nudged her. "Just say hi."

Her stomach filled with butterflies as she walked toward him. He was turned away from her, so he didn't see her approach. She came close and removed his hat as a greeting.

"Still hiding?" she asked as he turned to see who had accosted him. He ran his hand through his hair as he smiled at her. Still handsome as ever.

"Hi."

"Hi." She watched him watch her. "You're getting old ladies to do your dirty work are you, now?"

"Guilty. You didn't respond to my texts, so drastic measures were needed."

"Well, when someone doesn't respond, it usually means they don't want to interact with you." Poorvi explained.

He pursed his lips and nodded. "Not you." Kavan sighed and spoke softly. "If you didn't want to interact with me, you would have texted me to eff off on day one. You would have dusted your hands off and moved on. You didn't do that because you were hurt."

She stared at him, her heart thudding in her chest. He was right, of course. She sat down next to him, careful to leave some distance. She took off her glasses.

"So why are you here?"

He took off his sunglasses. The eyes that she had become so familiar with in such a short a time were bloodshot and…sad. And you didn't even need to be an ophthalmologist to see that. "I came for two reasons."

He nodded to where Ba was still standing behind her. Poorvi expected to hear Ba's footsteps behind her, instead she heard dress shoes hitting the concrete. As she turned, the owner of said dress shoes came into view.

Naveen Shashane. Not quite as tall as Kavan, but easily just as fit. He was quite handsome, but not in the movie star way that Kavan was. Naveen wore an expensive suit with expensive dress shoes and carried himself as if he were better than everyone around him.

"Hello," he said to her. It was obvious that this was not his idea. Yet here he was.

"Sit down, Bhai," Kavan said.

Naveen pressed his lips together as he looked at his brother. Poorvi was about to get up. She had no interest in what Naveen Shashane had to say. She glanced at him to tell him so when she saw something soft flit over Naveen's face as he looked at his brother. He really cared about Kavan. It was only that look that kept Poorvi in her seat.

"Baltimore isn't…" He looked around as he took a seat next to his brother, facing Poorvi.

"Isn't what?" Poorvi asked.

Naveen looked at her and forced a smile. "It isn't Dublin."

She glanced at Kavan. *What the hell was going on here?*

Kavan looked at his brother. "Naveen."

"Of course." He inhaled and looked at Poorvi. "I am here to tell you that it was I who took those pictures from our shared cloud and had them posted on social media."

Poorvi looked at Kavan. "Is this true?"

"If you were going to believe him, there was really no need for me fly over here now, was there?" He sighed. "Of course, it's true. Kavan is too *good.* He's not capable of such…manipulation. But you already know that." He nodded at her. "I told our social media person that I wanted to…make you look bad. And he did." Naveen gave a small shrug. "He's very good at his job, you see—in any case. It was me, not Kavan." He paused and glanced at Kavan before looking back at her. His next words were likely the most sincere she'd heard yet. "All of that explanation to say that I am truly sorry for hurting you."

"You are?" Poorvi could not believe her ears. She harumphed.

Naveen glanced at Kavan. "I see what you mean, brother. She's not trusting. She's skeptical." He grinned. "I like that. She would be good for you." He leaned toward Poorvi. "Kavan is too trusting, don't you think?"

She stared at Naveen. Unbelievable. But still, he had flown here to apologize in person. Not to mention, Naveen wasn't wrong. Kavan was very trusting. A smile played at her lips but she fought it. She wasn't ready to be friendly with Naveen Shashane.

"I would also like to add that I found it quite interesting that you did not out us publicly when you had the chance. I don't know if I was impressed or relieved." Naveen looked at her with what she could only discern was—respect. Huh.

Poorvi simply looked at him for a moment. "I appreciate what you have said."

Naveen went wide-eyed. "Is that all? Appreciate?" He chuckled. "Oh, she is a tough one, little brother." Naveen pushed his chair back and looked at Kavan with a question on his face. Kavan nodded and Naveen stood. "Dr. Gupta." He turned to her. "My brother has been an absolute mess since you left. He doesn't come to clinic, even on his new part-time schedule, and it is starting to…be upsetting…for our mother." He paused. "Very well then, I will go occupy myself until it is time for my flight." He nodded at Poorvi and squeezed his brother's shoulder as he left.

Poorvi stared at Kavan. "You stood up to your brother." She grinned at him, impressed and proud. "That's fabulous."

Kavan nodded at her.

"What was the second thing?"

He leaned toward her, not close enough to touch, but close enough that she caught his scent. "I wanted to give you a chance to yell at me." There was no smirk. No cocked eyebrow. Just his heart open for her to see, to do with what she wanted. "And I needed to see you."

"I'm not going to yell," Poorvi said. Naveen was right. Kavan was not capable of that sort of manipulation.

"I left Shashane Eye Clinic," he told her. "Rather, I sold my half and work there a couple times a week, and I'll leave when I figure out what I want to do."

This was huge. "What did Naveen say?"

Kavan shrugged like it didn't matter. "Naveen does not get to say anything about my life anymore. I'm considering my options. I have a few offers to teach, some offers to aid in clinical trials, that kind of thing. But mostly, I'm going to travel. I've started with Ireland. Trying to see all the things my father used to talk about. India is next up." He grinned and there was a peace about him that hadn't been there before.

"It must have been hard, breaking free of Naveen," she said.

"Not as hard as I would have thought. He's my brother, but it's way past time that I do my own thing." Kavan continued to watch her.

"You're in the States, traveling with Ba?" Sounded like fun.

"No. I just got off the plane. Ba is here to see her son. Naveen and I are going back in a few hours."

"You came all this way to apologize?" Who does that?

"Yes." Kavan looked at her in earnest. "There is just one more thing." He paused and looked her in the eye. "I was not making anything up in Ireland. I made Naveen come here and apologize in person because I was appalled at the way he treated the woman I love."

He paused and her heartbeat accelerated.

"I love you. I think I knew I loved you when I took your outlet." He chuckled. "But I definitely knew I loved you the last night we spent together. You can say all you want about how we don't know each other, it's too fast, whatever. It makes not one bit of difference to me. I know we have a connection. I know how I feel. I love bickering with you. I love laughing with you. I love being challenged by you." He paused and touched her hand. It was as if electricity coursed through her body. "I love loving you."

She heard him.

"I know you might be too angry to ever consider having me in your life, to consider trusting me again. But I do know you have feelings for me."

She stared at him, her heart racing, her palms sweaty. "You're pretty cocky to say that you know I have feelings for you."

"It's not cockiness." He chuckled. "Not really." He looked at her smiling. "You took off your glasses around me the last few times we were together. And today too." He nodded at her glasses on the table.

She shrugged. "So?" How could he possibly know?

"There's no prescription in them. You only wear them to put a barrier between you and the world. It helps you focus and assess." He said it as if it were obvious.

Her mouth gaped open.

He shrugged. "We were only in each other's company a short time, but I pay attention. You like your coffee hot and black, but you want your chai sweet and milky. You don't let people in very easily, but once they're in, they live in your heart," he said softly. "If your glasses are off, you're comfortable, and you don't need that barrier." He nodded at them again.

"They're off." He leaned toward her, and she caught the scent of lemon soap. Not fair. But she inhaled deeply anyway. He spoke softly near her ear, sending chills to that side of her body. "If you ever want to give us a chance, if you ever want to even try and see what we could be, I'll be waiting for you."

He stood, put on his cap, and walked out.

Chapter Thirty-Four

Kavan's phone dinged as he finished up his emails for the day. He grabbed his phone, hope running eternal through him. But it wasn't Poorvi. It was Ba.

Ba: Meet for dinner in Dublin? Clerys. Today is the day.

Kavan: Sure.

Ba: I'm bringing the family. Bring yours.

Kavan: Okay.

If Ba wanted to celebrate the day she met Dada at Clerys' clock, then that's what they would do.

"Naveen," Kavan called out in the empty clinic.

He heard footsteps and then Naveen was at his door. "Why shout? I'm two doors down. Just get up and walk."

Kavan just stared at him.

"What is it you want?"

"Dinner tonight with Ba at Clerys. Mom too."

"Are you serious?" Naveen looked at his phone. "I have calls to make."

"You have to eat," Kavan insisted. "You're coming. Calls can wait one hour."

"Fine." Naveen was less than thrilled, but he had been quite cooperative since they returned from the States two days ago. "Any word?"

Kavan turned back to his computer. "No." Two days. And nothing. At least she hadn't officially dismissed him. And she didn't seem the type to ghost. He called his mother. She was thrilled to join them.

He went home and changed from his suit into dress pants and a shirt. He bypassed the pink one he had worn on his date with Poorvi and chose a blue one instead.

Ba texted. Reservation at 7:30 sharp!

Ya. Okay.

Kavan and his family arrived at Clerys by 7:20 p.m. It was easy enough to spot Ba and her family once they entered the restaurant. Dharm came running over from their table by the front window. Ba loved a view. Devi and Yash were there with their daughter, Mira, and a woman he did not know. She seemed familiar.

Dharm hugged Kavan's legs, nearly knocking him over.

"Whoa. Hey, bud." Kavan hugged him back.

"Kavan Uncle, wait 'til you hear what we have been doing in school." Dharm was overexcited as usual. "Learning about eyes!"

"That sounds absolutely fascinating," Naveen said. "You must tell me more."

Dharm started to tell Naveen all that he knew about eyes as they walked over to the table. Before Kavan could sit down, Ba tugged on his sleeve.

"Come out with me." She jutted her chin toward the outside. "To see the clock."

"Of course." Kavan followed Ba as she made her way outside. The building was white with columns, and the clock protruded out about half the way up. Black with a green face and golden roman numerals, Clerys' clock was a distinctive meeting place for many people. Including many couples—like it had been for Ba and her husband.

"This is where we met." She grinned as they stood under it.

"That's fantastic, Ba." Kavan could see the joy on her face.

"But I lied. Today is not the day." Ba grinned.

"What do you mean?" Honestly, Ba was always full of surprises; he had just started to go with it.

"I mean today is not the day that Dada and I met. But today is your day." Ba's eyes brimmed with tears.

"My day?" Kavan was confused. "What—?"

"Hey, Kavan." Poorvi's voice floated from behind him. Or that's what he thought he heard. He stared at Ba.

"Did you hear that, Ba?" He didn't want to turn around if it was his mind playing tricks on him.

Ba raised her eyebrows and turned to go back inside. "Kavan?"

He turned and sure enough, Poorvi Karina Gupta was standing there, looking more beautiful than his memory could possibly do justice to. Of course, she had an eyebrow raised.

"Did you not hear me?" her eyes sparkled as she playfully chided him.

He broke out in a huge grin. "I heard you."

She sighed and shook her head at him. "You like your coffee *and* your chai sweet and milky. You're left-handed, but you eat with your right. You don't hide how you feel, and even if you get hurt, you still open yourself to people." She stepped closer to him. "I pay attention, too."

"So you do." His fingers ached with the need to touch her, but he waited. He moved closer to her. She couldn't have come all this way to turn him down.

"You said that you would be waiting," she said softly, taking a step toward him.

"I did." He nodded. "It's only been two days, but I did say I would wait, and I will."

She moved yet closer. He smelled flowers in the rain and— "Lemon soap."

She flushed and looked up at him. She was close enough to graze his body with hers. He ached with longing to touch her.

"I wasn't looking for a connection with anyone—especially not you. I didn't think I needed that. I was my own person." She stood straight and met his eyes.

"You are your own person, Poorvi." He agreed.

"But I felt it, too," she said softly. "I felt that...connection."

Kavan held his breath.

"I'm not easy," she blurted out.

"I know." He grazed her bare arm with his fingers; his heart thudded in his chest.

"I like to get my way," she said.

"I know." He trailed his touch to her upper arm.

"I love my work."

"As do I." He reached her shoulder.

"I'm nerdy."

"It's what I love most about you." He let his hand rest over her heart.

"Love?" He felt her heart thud in her chest. For him.

"I told you that two days ago. Love is a feeling, Poorvi Karina Gupta. And I love you." He nudged closer to her.

"I don't know about love," she said softly. "It scares me."

"That's okay. Just give us a chance." His leaned down so his mouth was millimeters from hers. He would certainly burst if he couldn't taste her soon. "You didn't come here smelling like lemon soap to break my heart, now did you?"

"No. I came here to tell you I had feelings for you." She cocked a smile. "The lemon soap is just a bonus."

"Feelings, huh?" He kissed her cheek, his lips just grazing her skin. She sighed into him.

She closed her eyes and made that soft humming sound he craved. "Mmm. A feeling like..."

"Like...what?" He pressed his lips gently on one eye then the other. She moaned and pressed closer to him.

"Like love." She lifted her chin and pressed her lips to his, tenderly. "I love you, Kavan Shashane. And I always will."

It was like coming home.

"I was hoping you would say that," he said on a low growl. He pulled her close and kissed her like she was his.

Epilogue

Twenty-seven years ago

The ice cream truck jingle had all the children at the playground dashing for their respective adults.

Around the perimeter of the playground, their adults stood with a collective sigh and reached for cash. The price of outdoor play in any city in America.

Poorvi's mother handed her money for both her and her sister. "You got that, Poorvi?" her mother asked.

"Poorvi's fine," her father said, laughing. "She's a big girl now."

Poorvi beamed at her father's praise. She was six years old now, after all. She took Niki's hand. "Come on. Let's go." Both girls ran hand in hand and joined the line at the ice cream truck. A couple boys were in front of them. The taller one was reading out the list to his brother.

"Ice cream sandwich. Ooh! Choco Taco! Oreo ice cream sandwich! How about that, Kavan?"

"Oreo! It's my favorite!" the smaller boy said.

"Ha! That's my favorite, too!" squealed Niki.

Kavan turned to Niki and high-fived her. He looked at Poorvi. "What's your favorite?"

"I don't have a favorite," Poorvi answered, not really looking at the boy.

"Everyone has a favorite," insisted Kavan.

"No, they don't." Poorvi was firm. She turned to him to make a face, but he was looking at her so wide-eyed, she simply pursed her lips.

"Well, they have a favorite they love from the truck," he insisted.

Poorvi rolled her eyes. "Not so."

The boy looked at the list and seemed to study it. "Rocket pop?"

Poorvi sighed. "No."

"King Cone?" He grinned.

"Nope."

They moved closer; it was the boys' turn next. A lot of kids were walking away with Oreo ice cream sandwiches.

The boy looked at Poorvi for minute. She tried to ignore him as she watched all the Oreo ice cream sandwiches go by.

The boy's jaw dropped. "Your favorite is Oreo ice cream sandwich, too."

Poorvi just shrugged her shoulders. It was, but she hadn't wanted to say, because sometimes they ran out, and she wanted Niki to have what she wanted.

The boys gave their order. "One Choco Taco and one Oreo ice cream sandwich," the older boy said. They took their ice creams and paid. The older one tucked into his Choco Taco with gusto. Kavan hung back while Poorvi ordered.

"Two Oreo ice cream sandwiches, please," she said.

"I'm sorry, sweetheart, we only have one left," the ice cream man said.

"Then I'll take that one, and I'll get..." She let her gaze wander over the pictures. The first one to catch her eye was the Choco Taco, and she pointed. "That one."

"All right." The man took her money and gave out the ice cream.

The boy named Kavan came up to her. "Actually, my favorite is that." He pointed to her Choco Taco.

"No, it's not. You said it was Oreo ice cream sandwich," Poorvi said.

"I didn't mean it. Really. Want to trade?"

"Really?" She looked at the foil-wrapped ice cream in his hand hopefully.

"Sure! It's win-win," Kavan said.

"Well, if you mean it," Poorvi said.

"I do."

Poorvi handed over her Choco Taco and took the Oreo cookie sandwich he passed to her, a smile coming to her face. "Thank you."

"You're welcome," Kavan said.

Poorvi and Niki ran back to their parents to enjoy their ice cream.

"You can't eat that," Naveen said to Kavan. "You're allergic to peanuts."

"I know." Kavan handed it to his brother. "You get two today."

"Why did you do that, then?" Naveen sounded irritated.

"She looked so sad. And now she looks happy." Kavan shrugged as he watched Poorvi from afar.

After they finished their ice creams, Poorvi went over to the boy called Kavan. "My parents say we have to go now. But we might be back tomorrow."

Kavan lit up. "Maybe we can play together tomorrow."
Poorvi grinned. "Maybe."
Kavan nodded. "I'll be waiting."

* * * * *

A Q&A with Mona Shroff

What or who inspired you to write?
I have always loved writing—since I won my first young author's contest when I was nine! I never did anything about it until my mid-forties. At that point I knew I had to try or I would never know what I was capable of.

What is your daily writing routine?
It varies at the moment. But I need coffee or bubbly water and my laptop. Usually I sit in my office, but occasionally, I love to sit on my sofa!

Who are your favorite authors?
I really have favorite books—especially now, because I have so many author friends whom I respect and rely on; they're all my faves! But I love reading Tif Marcelo, Sonali Dev, Nisha Sharma, Namrata Patel for just a start!

Where do your story ideas come from?

My ideas come from real life. I love finding out how people met each other, and I incorporate those meet-cutes. Or I'll wonder what would've happened if I ran from the mandap, and boom, story. Sometimes it's a trope I want to investigate, sometimes it's an issue.

Do you have a favorite travel destination?

I love the beach anywhere. But I have a soft spot for Germany since we lived there for a few years when my husband was in the army. I recently experienced Ireland—and WOW! New Orleans spoke to me as well. I could go on...

What is your most treasured possession?

Right now, my laptop—LOL!

What is your favorite movie?

In no particular order: *My Cousin Vinny*, *The Proposal*, *To All the Boys I've Loved Before*, *A League of Their Own*, *Sleepless in Seattle*.

How did you meet your current love?

My husband and I met when I took his best friend to my senior prom! And then we became best friends and then fell in love. Everyone is still friends, and we all love each other!

What characteristic do you most value in your friends?

Loyalty.

Will you share your favorite reader response?

My favorite responses are when a reader tells me how much they relate to my characters. Relating to characters makes a reader invested in the outcome, and the pages keep turning.